Laura Lee Guhrke

Catch a Falling HEIRESS

❧ An American Heiress in London ❧

Central Islip Public Library
33 Hawthorne Avenue
Central Islip, NY 11722

AVON

An Imprint of HarperCollinsPublishers

3 1800 00310 6818

This is a work of fiction. Names, characters, places, and incidents are products of the author's imagination or are used fictitiously and are not to be construed as real. Any resemblance to actual events, locales, organizations, or persons, living or dead, is entirely coincidental.

AVON BOOKS
An Imprint of HarperCollins*Publishers*
195 Broadway
New York, New York 10007

Copyright © 2015 by Laura Lee Guhrke
ISBN 978-0-06-233465-7
www.avonromance.com

All rights reserved. No part of this book may be used or reproduced in any manner whatsoever without written permission, except in the case of brief quotations embodied in critical articles and reviews. For information address Avon Books, an Imprint of HarperCollins Publishers.

First Avon Books mass market printing: February 2015

Avon Trademark Reg. U.S. Pat. Off. and in Other Countries, Marca Registrada, Hecho en U.S.A.
HarperCollins® is a registered trademark of HarperCollins Publishers.

Printed in the U.S.A.

10 9 8 7 6 5 4 3 2 1

If you purchased this book without a cover, you should be aware that this book is stolen property. It was reported as "unsold and destroyed" to the publisher, and neither the author nor the publisher has received any payment for this "stripped book."

"Hide, then."

Jack didn't move. "It's too late. They know you're not alone."

"Well, you can't just stand there! Do something!"

"If you insist." He took a deep breath, grasped her hands in his, and fell to one knee. "Linnet Holland," he said, his voice alarmingly loud, overriding her sound of shock, "will you marry me?"

"Stand up," she hissed. "For God's sake, stand up."

She tried to pull free of his grip, but it was futile, and she cast a frantic glance over her shoulder just in time to see her mother sail into the pagoda, with Mrs. Dewey on her heels. At the scene that met their eyes, the two women came to an abrupt halt just inside the door, and their shocked faces told Linnet she was in serious trouble.

Featherstone rose to his feet, and she turned on him, prepared to unleash a fresh flood of wrathful protest at his unconscionable conduct.

He gave her no opportunity. Letting go of her hands, he wrapped an arm around her waist and pulled her hard against him.

"What are you doing?" she demanded in a shocked whisper.

"Saving your reputation," he murmured, bent his head, and kissed her.

By Laura Lee Guhrke

CATCH A FALLING HEIRESS
HOW TO LOSE A DUKE IN TEN DAYS
WHEN THE MARQUESS MET HIS MATCH
TROUBLE AT THE WEDDING
SCANDAL OF THE YEAR
WEDDING OF THE SEASON
WITH SEDUCTION IN MIND
SECRET DESIRES OF A GENTLEMAN
THE WICKED WAYS OF A DUKE
AND THEN HE KISSED HER
SHE'S NO PRINCESS
THE MARRIAGE BED
HIS EVERY KISS
GUILTY PLEASURES

ATTENTION: ORGANIZATIONS AND CORPORATIONS
HarperCollins books may be purchased for educational, business, or sales promotional use. For information, please e-mail the Special Markets Department at SPsales@harpercollins.com.

*To the Avon Addicts, for being such loyal,
dedicated fans of romance fiction.
This one's for you, with my heartfelt thanks.*

Catch a Falling
HEIRESS

Prologue

London, 1889

Only something extraordinary would bring a gentleman to London in late summer. The heat was often unbearable, the air was always foul, and with the season over, the company was usually nonexistent. For the Earl of Featherstone, however, the news that his oldest friend, the Duke of Margrave, was home from Africa was extraordinary enough to make even London in August worthwhile.

Jack was happy to travel from his flat in Paris to his club in London for a reunion with Margrave and their three closest friends. He didn't know that jaunt across the Channel would lead him on a quest for justice that would destroy a villain, turn his life upside down, and hurl a beautiful woman into his arms. If he'd known all that, he wouldn't have been late.

As it was, by the time he entered the private dining room at White's, his friends had already arrived. "Sorry I'm late, gentlemen," he said as he closed the door behind him and glanced at the other four men seated around the table.

Lord Somerton was the first to speak. "Forgive us if we're not surprised," Denys said as he turned in his chair to look at Jack over one shoulder. "You're always late."

Jack waved that aside, for he had an ironclad excuse. "Cut my line a bit of slack, would you?" he said, giving Denys a none-too-gentle slap on the back and nodding to James, the Earl of Hayward, as he circled the table toward the guest of honor. "I had to come all the way from Paris, after all. I just got off the train from Dover twenty minutes ago."

The Duke of Margrave rose to greet him, and Jack sized up the appearance of his oldest friend in a quick glance. Stuart didn't look too bad, all things considered. "Mauled by a lion were you?" he asked, and stuck out his hand. "You'll do anything for a lark."

"Damn straight." The duke grinned as they shook hands. "Want a drink?"

"Of course. You don't think I came here for you, do you?" Accepting the whisky Stuart poured for him, Jack pulled out the empty chair beside his friend.

"So, gentlemen," he said, nodding to the other men at the table as he took his chair, "now that we've all welcomed the lion slayer home, what shall we do tonight? Dinner first, I assume? Then cards? Possibly a bit of slumming in the East End pubs? Or shall we find the prettiest dancing girls of London's music halls and cart them off the stage?"

The Marquess of Trubridge was the first to answer. "None of those for me," Nicholas said with a shake of his head. I'm a happily married man now."

No one expressed surprise that slumming in the East End and carting off dancing girls weren't Nick's cup of tea these days. His next statement, however, was a surprise and made the perfect excuse for a toast. "With," Nick added as he reached for his glass and raised it, "a baby on the way."

Congratulations were offered at once, and a toast was drunk to the marquess's first progeny. "Nick may be out of it," Jack said, as the bottle was passed and glasses refilled, "but what about the rest of you?"

He looked first at the man beside him. Stuart, after all, was just back from the wilds. He was sure to be up for a bit of carousing.

But like Nick, Stuart also shook his head in refusal. "My wife and I have reconciled."

Surprised silence greeted this bit of news, for Stuart and Edie had been estranged for years, almost since their wedding day. In the end, it was left to Jack to ask the obvious question. "And are you happy about it?"

"I am, actually, yes. And I'm happy to be home."

"Well, all right, then." It was Jack's turn to raise his glass. "Here's to the hunter, home from the hill."

That toast once again emptied the glasses, and as the bottle went round to refill them, Jack tried again. "Still, what are the rest of us supposed to do? Happily married fellows are such tedious company." He glanced at James and Denys. "Don't tell me either of you have become ensnared?"

"Not I," Denys replied at once. "Still quite the carefree bachelor."

"As am I," James added.

Jack was glad that at least some of his friends could still be counted upon. "Well, that relieves my mind. Later, we shall leave these two—" He paused, gesturing to Stuart and Nicholas. "And go off for a bit of fun, shall we?"

"You three can invade the brothels, taverns, and gaming clubs of London all you please some other time, but not tonight," Stuart said, putting an end to any notions of revelry. "I didn't bring all of you here so you could carouse about town. Besides, London in August is deadly dull, so you shan't be missing much."

"So why are we here?" Jack turned to the man beside him. "Other than to see your scars, hear all about the mauling, and be suitably impressed by how you fought off the lions?"

Stuart shook his head. "I don't want to talk about that."

"Stuff," Jack said in disbelief. "It's the perfect chance to brag, and you don't want to talk about it? Why not?" Leaning sideways, he took a peek under the table. "Lions didn't eat anything important, did they?"

"Jones is dead."

Stuart's words banished any further teasing, and Jack straightened in his chair, aghast. "Your valet is dead? What happened? Was that the lions, too?"

"Yes."

"Hell." Jack gave a sigh and raked a hand through

his hair. "And here I am being flippant about it. Sorry, Stuart."

Murmurs of sympathy were expressed all around, but the duke cut them off. "Let's talk of something else, shall we? Gentlemen, as wonderful as it is to see all of you, a reunion isn't why I've asked you here. I have something to discuss with you, and I want to do it before the bottle goes around again, for it's quite a serious business."

Stuart reached into a leather case beside his chair and pulled out a sheaf of papers, which he dropped in the center of the table. With his next words, any frivolous notions Jack might have had to enliven London in August went to the wall.

"I want to ruin a man," Stuart said, his gaze going around the table, lighting last upon Jack. "I want to humiliate him and destroy him. Thoroughly, completely, and without mercy."

Stunned silence followed this uncompromising pronouncement, for Stuart was in no way a vengeful sort of man. But Jack knew he would never ask them to engineer a man's destruction unless it was both necessary and just, and he gave his answer without hesitation. "Lawd," he drawled, tilting his chair back on two legs to give the man standing beside him an impudent grin, "this sounds just my sort of lark."

Denys gave a cough. "It goes without saying that the man in question deserves it, but can you tell us why?"

"The gist, yes," Stuart replied, "but not the details. And I assure you, it is a matter of honor. And justice."

"The courts can't touch him, I assume?" James asked.

"No. He's American," Stuart added, as his gaze again went around the table, again stopping with Jack. "A Knickerbocker, with a very rich, very powerful father."

Under Stuart's thoughtful gaze, Jack received the distinct impression that more would be asked of him in this quest than of the other men present, but either way, it didn't really matter. Stuart was his best friend in the world. And though it was clear whatever the other man had in mind would be a challenge, Stuart knew quite well that nothing spurred Jack on more than a challenge. "Pfft," he said, making short shrift of wealthy American fathers and their power.

With that sound, Stuart's shoulders relaxed, and he leaned forward to rest his palms on the table. "Gentlemen, I would do this alone, but I can't. I need your help." He paused and cast another glance around the table. "We are all Eton men."

They all knew what that meant, but it was Nicholas who put words to the steel-strong bonds of honor, duty, and friendship they'd forged as boys at school. "There's no more to be said. What do you want us to do?"

Stuart's plan was vague, for as he explained, he was waiting for more information from New York, but it seemed to involve stock shares, venture capital, and allowing the villain's own greed and avarice to be the cause of his destruction.

"Hoisting a bastard by his own petard," Jack murmured. "I was right. A lark of epic proportions. And who is this man?"

"His name . . ." Stuart paused and swallowed, as if answering even such a simple question was difficult for him. "His name is Frederick Van Hausen."

The loathing in those words was plain, but though the name seemed familiar to Jack, he couldn't place it. Nick did it for him.

"Van Hausen? Isn't that the American who ruined your wife's reputation before you met her?"

"Yes." Stuart's answer was a clipped, guttural sound.

"But . . ." Nick paused, looking bewildered, but whatever he saw in Stuart's face stifled any questions he might want to ask. He shook his head. "Never mind."

James wasn't so tactful. "You want to ruin him for making Edie damaged goods before you married her? But why should you care now?"

"That's not why I want his head," Stuart said at once. "I know him to be guilty of at least one horrific crime that cannot ever be brought home to him. I cannot reveal the details of that crime, for I am honor-bound to secrecy, but it may not be the only one he's committed. And there will probably be more in the future if he is not stopped."

"We may discover the details of these crimes for ourselves," Denys pointed out.

Stuart conceded that possibility with a nod. "You may, and if you do, you will fully comprehend the reasons for my reticence on the matter, and will appreciate the need for discretion as much as I do." He must have perceived the bewildered glances that went around the table, for he asked, "Does my refusal to give details influence your decision to help me, gentlemen?"

"Of course not," Jack said, giving James a pointed glance. "We trust you implicitly. Whatever your reason, there's no doubt it's a good one."

"Forgive my curiosity," James said at once. "If we do

learn the truth for ourselves, you may be assured of our discretion."

"Thank you." Stuart took another swallow of whisky. "Van Hausen is a New York investment banker. He's also heavily in debt, and there are rumors that he's not above dipping into the venture capital of his investors to pay private debts though he's always managed to repay the funds in time to avoid prosecution. If the four of you form a joint venture with his firm, he just might find the temptation to spend your capital elsewhere irresistible. If that happens, he'll have committed embezzlement, and if we can catch him at it, he could be indicted for the crime."

"Do you have a particular investment in mind to lure him?" Denys asked.

"I'm thinking gold mines in Africa, gentlemen. If you gained the location of these mines from me, then we were to have a very public falling-out, you could form the company with Van Hausen in New York as a way to get revenge on me. Van Hausen would swallow that sort of line." Stuart paused, tapping his fingers thoughtfully against the side of the glass in his hand. "Given his history with my wife, I suspect getting one up on me would be something he'd enjoy immensely."

"Such a thing would take time to arrange," Nick said.

"Yes. One of you will have to spend a great deal of time in New York, building a relationship with this man, becoming his friend, earning his trust. I'd do it myself, but, of course, Van Hausen would never trust me in a thousand years."

He looked again at Jack, and in their exchange of glances, understanding passed between them, understanding based on a lifetime of friendship, understanding that confirmed Jack's earlier guess about what would be asked specifically of him.

He took his cue without being asked. "This sounds like the perfect task for a Featherstone," he said jokingly, making light of his family's checkered history as deceivers and fortune-hunting scoundrels.

Despite the fact that Stuart seemed to have had him in mind for the primary role all along, his friend also seemed inclined to warn him of what he'd be getting into. "It'll be a long business, Jack. It could take a year, perhaps longer."

"All the more reason for me to be the one to take it on, then." Jack brought the legs of his chair to the floor with a decisive thud. "I'm the only one here with no family ties and no responsibilities."

"It won't be easy. You'll be spearheading a man's destruction when I can't give you the reason why."

Jack looked into the face of his best friend, a face he'd known since they were both four years old. "I don't need the reason. Your word is always good enough for me."

"Feigning friendship, gaining his trust, all the while knowing you're helping to destroy him . . . it'll be hell."

"Hell doesn't worry me, Stuart. Why should it?" He raised his glass and grinned. "Hell never worries the devil."

Chapter 1

Newport, Rhode Island, 1890

Ever since the Prince of Wales paid a visit to the United States back in 1860, the female half of New York society had been enamored of the British aristocracy. As American millionaires grumbled about the typical British gentleman's seemingly idle lifestyle and anathema for hard work, their wives devised matchmaking schemes and their daughters dreamed of being countesses and duchesses.

By the time the Earl of Featherstone arrived on their shores in the autumn of 1889, the transatlantic marriage was a commonplace thing, and though the earl insisted to all of New York society that the purpose of his visit was business, women both inside and outside the Knickerbocker set waved that pesky detail to the side. The earl was a single man with no money, and business was such a vague term.

But though Jack's insistence that he was not looking for a wife didn't stop the ladies from engaging in hopeful speculation, it did reassure the gentlemen of New York that he wasn't there merely to poach one of their daughters. As a result, Jack soon found that not only were the doors of New York's drawing rooms opened to him, so were the men's clubs.

Within a month of his arrival, he was being invited to every important social event and hearing all the gossip. Within two, he was dining at the Oak Room and playing cards at the House With The Bronze Door. Within three, he and Frederick Van Hausen were discussing investment possibilities at Delmonico's over *Lobster à la Newberg*, playing tennis at the New York Tennis Club, and golfing at the newly founded St. Andrews course.

Befriending Van Hausen while plotting his destruction could have been every bit as hellish for Jack as Stuart had feared, for the American seemed a charming fellow—witty, intelligent, and easy to like. But the two of them had only been discussing venture capital, stock shares, and African gold mines for a fortnight when Pinkerton agents uncovered a servant girl formerly in the man's employ named Molly Grigg, whose departure from his household was still cause for gossip among his other servants. Curious, Jack had interviewed the girl himself, a conversation that revealed just what sort of animal lurked beneath Van Hausen's charming veneer and made clear the secret Stuart had been keeping.

After the discovery of Molly Grigg, Pinkerton's men had found more girls just like her, and with each one he interviewed, Jack found hell a more comfortable place to be. That didn't make his task an easy one, however, for ruining a man, however depraved he might be, wasn't a thing to be done lightly. It was also a complicated business that required time, patience, and forethought. And to honor Stuart's wishes, the destruction of Van Hausen required that he fall into a pit of his own making.

Still, by mid-August, Van Hausen's pit was well and truly dug, and all that remained was the fall.

Knowing what was about to rain down upon the other man after months of work, Jack wished he could feel a sense of satisfaction, but as he studied Van Hausen from the other side of an opulent Newport ballroom, he thought of Molly Grigg and Stuart's duchess and all the others, and he reminded himself it was too early to declare victory. When Van Hausen was in prison, then, perhaps, he'd allow himself some degree of satisfaction that justice had been served. But until then, no.

"Do you think he knows?"

The question caused Jack to take his eyes off their quarry long enough to glance at Viscount Somerton, who stood beside him. "He knows, Denys," he said, and returned his attention to the man on the other side of the ballroom. Between the dancers who swirled across the floor, Jack noted the restless way Van Hausen paced back and forth and the uneasy glances he gave his surroundings. He thought of their last conversation, of how the other man had come to him only a few hours ago, trying to explain, begging him for help, asking him to intercede with the other investors. He'd taken great pleasure in refusing, but he felt too tense, too on edge to relive that moment of pleasure now. "Believe me, he knows."

Van Hausen paused in his pacing and pulled out his pocketwatch, and as if in confirmation of Jack's conclusion, his hand shook badly as he opened it to check the time.

"Sorry I'm late," another voice entered the conversation before Denys could reply, and both men glanced back to find the Earl of Hayward behind them.

"Pongo!" they greeted him in unison, and at the utterance of his hated childhood nickname, the earl muttered an oath.

"My name is James, you bastards," he corrected through clenched teeth. "Not Pongo. *James.*"

This reminder did not impress his friends in the least. They both gave unrepentant shrugs and returned their attention to the man across the room.

"Is he here?" James asked, rising on his toes to look over his friend's shoulder at the dance floor and the onlookers beyond.

"He is," Jack confirmed. "And he's as jumpy as a cat on hot bricks." He shrugged his tense shoulders. "He's not the only one. I feel rather that way myself."

"It's almost over," James reminded as he moved to stand on his other side. "But I'm surprised he's here. I didn't think he'd dare after getting the telegram from Nick."

That telegram was the culmination of the plan Stuart had first outlined a year ago, a plan that had gone pretty much as the duke had expected. Under Jack's careful manipulation, Van Hausen had formed East Africa Mines, accepting the funds of Jack, Denys, James, and several other investors to do so. Also as expected, he'd speculated with those funds elsewhere to recoup his other losses, and was now mired in more debts than he could ever repay. Now, Nick's telegram was demanding Van Hausen's presence at a meeting of the investors in East Africa Mines three days hence in New York, and at that meeting, Van Hausen would be required to repay the investors or face indictment for fraud and embezzlement. It was that telegram that had spurred Van Hausen's visit to Jack earlier that day.

"I don't think any of us expected his appearance tonight," Denys said. "Most of the investors in East Africa Mines are here. Who'd have thought he'd have the courage to face us in light of Nick's telegram?"

Jack shook his head. "It's not courage. He's trying to brazen things out."

"But to what end?" Denys wondered. "Given all the stalling he's done, and the rumors James and I have been circulating since we arrived in town, everyone here knows he's drowning. He can't repay us or anyone else he owes. He's trapped."

Almost as if he'd heard those words, Van Hausen looked up, seeing them across the room. At Jack's exaggerated bow of greeting, he responded with a defiant scowl.

"Your friendship appears to be at an end," Denys commented in some amusement.

"So it would seem," Jack agreed, and wished the lifting of that burden had brought relief. But instead, he felt only an increasing uneasiness, a feeling akin to the unnatural calm that often came before a thunderstorm.

"The man must be thick as a brick to display such hostility toward us," James said. "Especially you, Jack. He'd be better served trying to placate you, butter you up, or gain your sympathy. At the very least, he ought to be asking you to plead his case with the rest of us."

"He already tried all of those," Jack replied. "He even begged."

"Did he?" James gave a low whistle. "When was this?"

"This afternoon. He cornered me at the Yacht Club after the two of you had already left. He admitted he didn't have the funds, he asked me for help, and swore on his life he'd pay me back if I'd stake him with everyone else. He reminded me of our friendship during the past year and what good times we've had."

Denys smiled. "And what was your reply?"

Jack allowed himself a grim, answering smile. "I gave him the Duke of Margrave's warmest regards."

The other two men laughed, but when Denys noticed he wasn't laughing with them, his own amusement faded. "What's wrong, Jack?"

"I don't know." He shrugged his shoulders again, trying to loosen his tense muscles. "I know this moment had to come, and I thought I'd be glad, but I'm not."

"That's understandable. You've had to maintain a friendship with the man for months. It can't have been easy." Denys gave him a thoughtful look. "Any regrets?"

"About losing Van Hausen's friendship?" He made a sound of derision. "Hardly."

"Then what is it?"

Jack frowned, not quite knowing how to put into words the uneasiness he felt. "He knows now that I've been toying with him all these months," he said slowly, thinking it out as he spoke. "He knows East Africa Mines was a trap we set for him at Stuart's behest, and he knows he fell right into that trap. He knows he's been played for a fool. In addition, he's cornered and desperate. I'm rather afraid of what he might do."

"Don't worry," James said, grinning as he clapped him on the back. "We'll protect you."

"It's not myself I'm afraid for."

With those words, James's grin faded, and he and Denys both stirred, confirming that his apprehension was not wholly unfounded. None of them had spoken of Molly Grigg, or any of the other women discussed in Pinkerton's reports, not even among themselves, and neither of his friends knew he'd been to interview those women, but it was clear his friends suspected what he already knew—that Van Hausen had done far more to the duchess than ruin her reputation.

"We can't worry about that," Denys said after a moment. "He was bound to be pushed over the brink at some point. And even the tiniest frustration could set him off."

"I know, but before, I was with him often enough to keep a pretty close watch on his activities. I can't be absolutely certain, of course, but I don't think he's assaulted any other women since I've been here. But now—" Jack stopped and swallowed at the true fear that was eating at his guts.

"We have Pinkerton men watching him every minute of every day," James pointed out.

"Yes, and I even warned him of that this afternoon. But desperate men do desperate things. I'm worried."

"Still, what else can you do?" Denys asked. "It's not as if we can sleep outside his door."

"I know, I know." Jack sighed, rubbing a hand over his face. "I'll just be glad when this is finally over."

The other two nodded in agreement, and Jack returned his gaze to the man across the room, and when he saw Van Hausen pause and again pull out his pocket watch and glance at the door, he tensed, suddenly alert. "He keeps looking at his watch. We're at a ball. Why should he care so much what time it is?"

"Perhaps he's just rattled," Denys suggested. "As you said, he's cornered, he's without friends or resources, and he knows it. With luck, before the week is out, he'll be in jail. Checking his watch is probably just a mindless action borne of frayed nerves."

Jack did not reply, for his attention was fixed on the object of their conversation. Van Hausen had shoved his watch back into his waistcoat pocket and was circling the room. For a moment, Jack thought he was actually coming to speak with them, but he passed them by without a glance, making for the doors into the ballroom where he paused to greet a young woman who had just come in.

"Or," Jack murmured, watching him capture the girl's hands in his, "he's been waiting for someone."

The moment he looked at her, Jack could see why.

Her face, with its symmetrical shape and delicately molded nose and chin, was enough for any man to deem her pretty. Like most American girls, she had fine teeth, straight and white and curved in a dazzling smile. But those features were not what made Jack's breath catch in his throat.

God, what eyes, he thought, fully aware that he was staring, unable to look away. *What lovely, lovely eyes.*

Deep-set and fringed by thick brown lashes, they seemed almost too large for her delicate face, but it was their color that made them extraordinary. Even from a dozen feet away, he could discern it—a deep, vivid blue, the vibrant hue of cornflowers at twilight.

Her blond hair, piled high atop her head, accentuated her long, graceful neck and slim, straight shoulders. Untouched by the hot tongs so many girls employed, it gleamed beneath the crystal chandeliers, and he wondered suddenly what it would look like loose and falling around her shoulders.

"I think you're right, Jack," Denys said beside him. "He's been waiting for her."

Jack didn't answer, for his attention was riveted on the girl. A wide expanse of her creamy skin was visible above the neckline of her ball gown, a neckline low enough to raise eyebrows in sedate, stuffy Newport. His gaze slid down, and he noted a slender waist and shapely hips sheathed in blush pink silk, and he could well imagine that beneath those skirts was a pair of absolutely ripping legs.

But who was she? He lifted his gaze again to her face, a move that was of no help at all in identifying her. Although he'd spent almost a year ingratiating his way into the Knickerbocker set, he'd never seen this woman before. If he had, he'd remember.

"By Jove," James murmured, "what a pretty girl."

It was clear many men shared that opinion, for a quick glance around told Jack her arrival had not gone unnoticed by the other men in the ballroom. More important, Van Hausen was among her admirers, for he still had her hands firmly clasped in his.

Jack turned to his companions. "Who the devil is she?"

Both his friends shook their heads, but it was James who spoke. "You're the one who's been living here. Don't you know?"

He shot his friend an impatient glance. "Really, Pongo, if I knew that, I wouldn't have asked you."

"No need to be so testy." James returned his attention to the doorway. "Did you notice her eyes?"

"I think any man would notice her eyes," Denys put in with fervent appreciation, his gaze also straying back to the subject of the conversation.

"Will the two of you stop gaping at her long enough to consider the vital point?" Jack muttered, his concern growing. "We do not know this woman, but it's clear Van Hausen does."

He took another glance over her, and this time, he saw more than her stunning face and luscious shape. He saw affection in the way she smiled at Van Hausen, and the halfheartedness of her attempts to pull her hands away. He saw an expensive ball gown as well as strands of magnificent pink diamonds that looped her slender neck and glinted amid the delicate sprays of heliotrope in her hair. Whoever she was, it was clear she had money, and that was something Van Hausen desperately needed right now.

Desperate men, he reminded himself, do desperate things.

Realization came in a flash, and he knew not only that Van Hausen intended to evade the trap they'd set but also just how he intended to do it. Jack swore, a curse loud enough for his friends to hear.

"Jack?" Denys gave him a searching glance. "Have you recognized her? Do you know who she is?"

"No," he answered, still watching the girl. "But I damn well intend to find out."

Chapter 2

Having been away from home a full year, Linnet Holland expected to find that many things had changed during her absence. She did not, however, expect Frederick Van Hausen to be one of the transformations.

In appearance, he seemed the same Frederick she'd always known—blond hair, brown eyes, boyishly handsome face—but his manner was so different from that of the man she remembered that she almost felt as if she were talking to a different person.

"Linnet. Dearest, dearest Linnet," he said for perhaps the fourth time. "It's so wonderful to see you."

"And you." As agreeable as it was to be so warmly greeted, it also felt a bit awkward, for she was unaccustomed to such effusiveness from Frederick. They had attended some of the same picnics, parties, and balls over the years, but he was a decade older than she, and though she'd been wildly infatuated with him as a young girl, he'd never fueled her adolescent hopes. Indulgent fondness was as close as he'd ever come, and Linnet had long ago given up any romantic notions about him. Never would she have predicted that upon her return from Europe, he would gaze hungrily into her eyes and hold her hands in his.

"Mrs. Dewey assured me you would attend her ball tonight," he was saying, as she tried to adjust to this new, less restrained Frederick. "But since you've just arrived home, I wasn't sure you would come." His gloved fingers tightened around hers. "I'm so glad you did."

"Our ship from Liverpool docked yesterday, and we journeyed up from New York on the morning train. We haven't had a moment to catch our breath." She glanced around, noting there were other friends waiting to greet her, and she tried without success to pull her hands from his. "Frederick, you must let go of my hands," she said, laughing. "People are staring."

"Let them. I don't mind."

Her astonishment must have shown on her face, for he laughed and capitulated. "Oh, have it your way, Linnet, but I'm so glad to see you, and I don't care who knows it."

She frowned, still bewildered. "Frederick, have you been drinking?"

That elicited another laugh from him. "No, though the sight of you does make me feel a bit tipsy. But—" He stopped and cocked his head. "Listen to that."

"Listen to what? You mean the music?"

"Of course the music, silly girl. It's a waltz." He once again seized her hand. "Dance with me."

He started to pull her toward the dance floor, but stopped almost at once. "Oh, but you've probably promised this waltz to someone. One of the men clamoring behind me, I'm sure," he added with a glance over his shoulder. "As beautiful a woman as you've become, your dance card is bound to be filled well in advance."

"On the contrary." She lifted her hand to show him the blank card tied to her wrist. "Not a single name. I know it's a shock," she added with a deprecating laugh, "but pride impels me to remind you that we did just arrive. My dozens of suitors," she added lightly, "haven't had the chance to line up."

He didn't laugh with her. Instead, his eyes were warm and earnest as they stared into hers. "That means I'm the first in line for once." He gestured to the dance floor. "Shall we?"

He led her out, and soon they were swirling across the floor to the lilting melody. "How was Europe?" he asked.

"Wonderful, at the start. The Italian lakes were beautiful in the summertime. Winter was nice, too, since we were in Egypt for much of that. The pyramids are an amazing sight, to be sure. But a year is such a long time to be away, and by the time we did the London season, I was too homesick to appreciate it."

"Were you homesick, truly?"

"Oh, yes. I missed the picnics in Central Park, and the clambakes here at Newport, and all our friends. And sleeping in my own bed and having a real bathroom with hot water. And I missed our muffins."

"Muffins?" He laughed. "Linnet, you amaze me."

She laughed, too. "They have these things in England they call muffins, but they're not like ours. I so missed our muffins with the blueberries inside. When I described them to the maître d'hôtel at the Savoy in London, he suggested I have the tea cakes as a substitute. They weren't at all the same."

"I think some of your other friends were over for the London season. Did you see any of them?"

"I did." She made a face. "Too many of them, if you want the truth."

Frederick gave her a quizzical look. "You just said you'd been missing your friends. Weren't you happy to see some of them in London if you were homesick?"

"Of course. But they all behaved so differently there than they do here. They fawned all over the British gentlemen, acting as if those men are so superior to our gentlemen here, which just isn't true."

His hand squeezed hers. "My patriotic Yankee girl."

"I am. Laugh at me if you want to."

"I'm not laughing. I agree with you. How could I not?" he added, still smiling. "I am an American gentleman myself, and I can't see that these British fellows are in any way superior to me. Take those three, for example. The ones with Mrs. Dewey."

He nodded toward a place near the doorway, and as they waltzed by, she spied the trio of men talking with their hostess. It was only the briefest glimpse, but she was sure she'd never seen them before. "British, are they?" she asked.

"Oh, yes." His long upper lip curled a bit with obvious contempt. "And titled, as if that means anything here."

Linnet's mind went back to her second season out,

and Lord Conrath, the first man with a title she'd ever met, the only man in her life who'd ever made her heart race and her breath catch. Conrath—so debonair, so charming, so very broke.

She stumbled a little, and it took a moment to regain her footing. "Are these men staying in Newport?" she asked once they had resumed the dance.

"Unfortunately. They are spending the season here at The Tides. Why the Deweys invited them is beyond my comprehension."

She groaned. "You mustn't tell my mother about them. She got it into her head ages ago that I must marry a British lord. No one else will do."

It was Frederick's turn to miss a step. "Sorry about that," he said as he maneuvered them back into the rhythm of the waltz. "Your happiness ought to come first. Why is she so adamant?"

"She feels the New Money girls are getting the jump on our set by marrying titled men, and she's decided beating them at their own game is the way to stop it. She's obsessed with the idea of making me a countess or duchess or some such."

"You mustn't let her." The fierceness of his voice surprised her, but she also found it quite gratifying.

"And reward her for having such snobbish social ambitions?" she replied with a wink. "Never."

"Good." His eyes looked into hers. "I don't want to see one of them hurt you, Linnet. Not again."

Linnet felt a rush of affection, a feeling almost as strong as the crush she'd had on him when she was fourteen. "I'm not pining for Conrath. He was just after my money, and he left me feeling quite jaded about the idea of a transatlantic marriage. And if he hadn't made me so, London would have."

"Was your season there very bad?" he asked with an air of sympathy she warmed to at once.

"You've no idea. Impoverished peers were thick on the ground, all expressing admiration and affection, but the entire time, I couldn't help wondering how much affection they'd have for me without my dowry."

"These British lords expect everything to be handed to them on a silver platter, including an income."

He sounded quite bitter all of a sudden, and she couldn't help wondering what lay behind it. "I don't remember you feeling so strongly about the British men who come here trolling for heiresses."

"Yes, well . . ." He broke off and looked away, seeming uncomfortable. "You're far too sweet to fall prey to a man who just wants your money. Which is why," he said, looking at her again and bending his head closer to hers, "you can't go back to England and marry a title like all your friends are doing."

"I don't intend to, and now that we're home, I hope Mother will give up the whole idea at last. I don't want to live in another country. I want to live here. And besides, I could never respect a man who didn't earn his way."

"Yes." He paused, and a hint of worry crossed his face. "I've had to earn mine, that's for sure."

"And done a fine job of it, too," she assured him. "Your father thinks very highly of your abilities."

"Does he?" The question was wistful. "God knows, he's not an easy man to please."

"He adores you. It's obvious."

"Is it?" He must have noticed her concern, for he added, "I know he's hard on me because I'm the only son, and I've got to make good. Unlike the Brits, I don't think work is something to be ashamed of or that it's honorable to marry for money."

Linnet made a face. "Well, our American girls don't seem to mind handing the money over. You should have seen the ones in London, flinging themselves at every British peer in sight, practically begging those men to marry them and take their dowries. And the pushy mothers . . ." She paused for a sigh. "Mine was one of the worst, I'm afraid. She kept dropping hints about my enormous dowry and how healthy I am. It was mortifying."

"Well, don't let her get you anywhere near those three," he advised, glancing at the trio by the doors. "One of them will try to steal you away from me before the evening is over, but I don't intend to let that happen."

She was too surprised to think of a reply, for it just wasn't like Frederick to be so forward. Quite the opposite, in fact. When he was younger, his reputation had been tainted by an unfortunate incident with a New Money girl who, it was said, had tried to trap him into marriage. Since then, he'd become all the more assiduously proper in his conduct toward the females in his company, including her.

"Why, Frederick," she said, laughing a little, "I didn't know you'd ever even noticed me."

"I noticed," he said. "How could I not? You're the loveliest girl in our set. But you're so young, my dear."

"Young?" she echoed, choosing to focus on that rather than the compliment. Flattery always made her uncomfortable, for she didn't quite trust it. "I'm twenty-one now, I'll have you know. According to my mother, I'm on the brink of spinsterhood."

"Yes, little Linnet's all grown-up," he teased. "Not the schoolgirl who used to moon over me. You did," he added before she could protest. "But you've got your revenge, for I'm the one who's mooning over you nowadays."

Her astonishment must have shown on her face, for he went on, "I know my feelings seem sudden to you, but that's because you've been away. What I feel has been deepening every day of your absence. The past year has opened my eyes, Linnet, and my heart."

She had long ago accepted Frederick as a family friend and nothing more, and to know that she had come to mean more to him was such a welcome surprise after the artificial courtship she'd been subjected to in London that she couldn't think what to say.

He smiled. "The picnics and clambakes weren't the same without you, and I missed you so. I vowed that when you came back, I would tell you how I felt at once, before I could lose my nerve. I love you. I didn't realize how much until you went away." His hand tightened around hers, and his fingers pressed the small of her back, bringing her closer. "Now, hearing how set your mother is on marrying you to one of those British fellows, I know I must speak boldly."

"Frederick," she admonished with a glance around, "you mustn't be so forward."

"I couldn't endure it if you went away again. I want you with me, now and always. Of course you want a marriage based on love, and you couldn't love me, not yet, not as I've come to love you. Still, I—" He broke off with an aggravated sigh. "Damn, the waltz is ending, and there's so much more I want to say, but that would require privacy, and we've no chance to be alone tonight. Unless—"

He paused again and glanced around. "Meet me," he said, with a sudden, fervent urgency. "Half an hour from now, in the Chinese pagoda. You know where it is?"

"The pagoda? Of course, but Frederick, I can't—"

"I swear to you, Linnet, my intentions are honorable, in case you doubt it. I want to ask you a question, one I've been practicing in preparation for your return, one your mother would not approve, given her plans." He looked into her eyes, his own gaze unwavering. "I think you can guess what that question is."

His hand slid away from her waist, and a stunned Linnet came to her senses, realizing the waltz had come to an end. She allowed him to lead her back to her place, where he kissed her hand, silently mouthed the words, "Half an hour," and turned to greet her parents with a naturalness no man ought to display after asking for a clandestine meeting.

She couldn't go, of course. Even as that thought passed through her mind, Linnet glanced at the watch ring on her right hand and noted the time. It was almost half past eleven.

Rendezvous at midnight. It sounded so romantic, she thought as she turned to other friends who were waiting to greet her, like something out of a novel. But she couldn't meet a man, even one she'd known all her life, alone at night, for it could put her reputation in jeopardy. And yet, his purpose was honorable, his feelings clear, his question obvious. She wavered. If she did go, what would her answer to his question be?

Marry Frederick? She'd never considered the possibility, not for years, but she considered it now as she smiled and nodded and renewed acquaintance with friends. She'd been infatuated with him as a girl, but that didn't really count for much now. Besides, every girl she knew had been infatuated with Frederick at one time or another. And why not?

He was handsome, charming, a true sportsman. He owned racehorses that ran at Saratoga and yachts that he sailed with expert skill. He was a successful investment banker, and he came from one of New York's oldest, finest families.

Marry Frederick?

She tried to envision it, and when she did, an agreeable future stretched before her—a modest but comfortable brownstone west of the park to start, and a small cottage here. As Frederick became even more successful, they might move to a larger home closer to their parents on Madison Avenue. Like many other couples they knew, they would winter in New York, take a brief trip to Paris in the spring, then come here for the summer. She would have all the picnics and clambakes and Newport summers she could want with a man she knew and understood, a man who came from the same world she did and wanted the same things she did, a man who cared for her, not her money, a man of whom she was genuinely fond.

Fond.

She grimaced a bit at the word, remembering several

of the men in London who had described their feelings for her in such a way. Her affection for Frederick went deeper than that, of course, for she'd known him all her life. And was romantic passion any better a guarantee of happiness than the affection she felt for Frederick? She thought of Conrath, and she decided it was not.

"Linnet?" Her mother's voice, low but urgent, called to her, and she came out of her reverie with a start. She glanced around and realized the object of her thoughts had disappeared.

"What happened to Frederick?" she asked, as her mother bustled over to her side. "He was talking to you a moment ago."

"Frederick?" Helen Holland's round face creased into a bewildered frown, showing that although that particular man might be dominating Linnet's thoughts, her parent's mind was on something else altogether. "He's wandered off somewhere," she added, waving a hand toward the French doors onto the terrace. "Never mind Frederick. We've something much more important to discuss." She pulled her daughter slightly away from the group of her friends. "Linnet, there are three British peers here tonight."

Linnet groaned. "Oh, Mother, not again."

Helen, of course, ignored this admonishment. "To think, after doing London with no success, you have another chance. Look over there." When Linnet didn't move, Helen gave an impatient sigh, put an arm around her shoulders, and turned her toward the three men Frederick had already pointed out to her, and she could only thank heaven that at this moment none of them were looking in her direction. "Don't stare, of course," her mother murmured in her ear, "but aren't they handsome?"

"For goodness' sake!" Without bothering to consider the question, Linnet shrugged to dislodge her mother's arm from around her shoulders, then turned to face her. "I don't want to marry a British lord. How many times must I say it?"

Helen's face creased again, this time with disapproval. "That is a most unladylike tone," she said with injured dignity. "The gentlemen are standing a dozen feet away at most, and if they heard you speaking to me this way, they might decide you would not suit as a peeress and dismiss you from consideration."

"If so, then I hope they would also believe I mean what I say and set their sights elsewhere."

"And if they do, where will you be?" Helen lifted a hand to indicate the assemblage around them. "You want to marry one of our own, but you've known these men all your life, and love hasn't bloomed for you with any of them. Will it ever? You're twenty-one, Linnet, and time is going by. Most of your friends are already married. Another year, maybe two, and you'll be an old maid. Is that what you want?"

Linnet lowered her head, pressing one gloved hand to her forehead. She'd hoped that in coming home, this topic would be laid to rest, at least for a while, but now she realized her mother's relentless campaign to marry her off would never stop, not until she'd walked down the aisle and said her vows.

"Now, about these three gentlemen," Helen resumed, mistaking Linnet's silence for acquiescence, "they are staying here at The Tides, so Mrs. Dewey was able to tell me all about them. The blond one is quite good-looking, don't you think?"

Linnet didn't bother to lift her head. Her mother didn't notice.

"He's the Earl of Hayward," Helen chirped on, "son of the Marquess of Wetherford. Still, I'm not sure he'll do for you."

Linnet didn't ask why, but, of course, she didn't have to.

"He's shorter than you, and it's never good for a man to be shorter than his wife. A pity, for he has the highest rank. Still," Helen added, her voice brightening, "the other two are taller, and every bit as good-looking. The brown-haired one is Viscount Somerton, the only son of Earl Conyers, but the black-haired one seems the most promising prospect. He's been in New York for some time, and Mrs. Dewey thinks he's here to find a wife."

"They always are," Linnet murmured without bothering to glance at the object of this discussion. "You needn't act as if it's such a revelation."

"Yes, but he asked Mrs. Dewey about you while you were dancing and seemed very interested. He is the Earl of Featherstone, and—"

Linnet lifted her head, frowning as the name stirred to life long-forgotten gossip. "Wasn't Featherstone the peer who married Belinda Hamilton of Cleveland? I thought he died."

"That was Charles Featherstone, and yes, he died. This is his brother, John—or Jack, as his friends call him. He inherited the title when his brother passed away."

Belinda Hamilton's marriage to the previous Earl of Featherstone was a lesson to any American girl with a sense of self-preservation, and might provide Linnet with the perfect way to yet again counter her mother's insistence she marry a peer.

Her attention captured at last, Linnet turned her head, following her mother's gaze, lighting at once on the man in the center of the group, a man now staring back at her, a man whose hair was as black as a raven's wing and whose heart, she could only conclude, was equally so.

Everything about him spoke of a rakehell. His body, tall and powerfully built, seemed designed for wild sport and reckless pursuits. His hair, thick and unruly, lacked the discipline of pomade, hinting at a similarly undisciplined character. His face was handsome enough, she supposed, but its lean planes and sharp, chiseled features gave the impression to Linnet's mind of a predatory hawk. His eyes, black and impenetrable, looked back at her without blinking—the hawk assessing possible prey.

Linnet, however, was no naïve, hapless little mouse to be plucked up for her fat dowry. Faced with such an unscrupulous stare, she lifted one eyebrow in response. Perfected during her days at finishing school, it was a pointed indication to a rude man that he was being rude, and its usual result was to send the man in question scurrying off in abashed dismay.

Not this man. Instead of looking away, he looked down, and those bold eyes roved with unnerving thoroughness over her person, from head to toe and back, pausing for far too long at the neckline of her gown, reminding her how low it was cut.

For no reason at all, she blushed, heat spreading outward from where his gaze lingered at her breasts to all the other parts of her body—down her legs and along her arms, up her neck and into her face. Her toes curled in her satin slippers, and without thinking, she lifted one gloved hand to her chest to shield herself from his ill-mannered observation.

His thick black lashes lifted. As his eyes met hers again, their corners creased with amusement, and one corner of his mouth curved up in a faint smile.

Furious, Linnet tore her gaze away, and as she did, she caught sight of a footman carrying a tray filled with glasses. Feeling in desperate need of a drink, she plucked one of the glasses from his tray as he passed, and ignoring her mother's disapproving stare, she downed half the cream sherry it contained in one swallow. She felt ready to address the point at issue.

"It's obvious the present Earl of Featherstone is no improvement over the previous one. Charles Featherstone married Belinda Hamilton for her money and everyone knows it. If the gossip is to be believed, he treated her badly after their marriage and made her miserable."

"Well, of course Belinda Hamilton was miserable in her marriage," Helen agreed without batting an eye. "She was very New Money, dear, and completely unprepared to be the wife of an earl."

"And yet, Belinda Hamilton married again two years ago," Linnet couldn't resist pointing out. "She wed the Marquess of Trubridge. If I recall all the lessons of the British peerage you've stuffed into my head, Trubridge is the only son of the Duke of Landsdowne, so she'll be a duchess one day."

"Her first marriage prepared her for her second, and that is preparation you don't need. You could step into the role of peeress without a qualm. I've seen to that."

"Yes, ever since Conrath, it's been nothing but English governesses and lessons upon lessons in British politics, British estates, British customs. I've wanted none of it."

"So, because of a broken heart over one peer, you've decided to never consider the possibility of another. Instead, you would limit yourself to this." Helen waved a hand disdainfully toward their surroundings. "This narrow, confined life."

"I want what I have, and I don't see what's so confined or narrow about it."

"But that's just it, my darling, I wish I could make you see." Helen looked at her, and a strange passion came into her face. "If you marry one of our Knickerbocker men, you would become *me*. You would live my life, a life where you run the house, and that is all. Where your husband shuts you out of anything important or meaningful, and society approves it. Where even philanthropic work is regarded as unseemly, and your greatest concern becomes giving a more exclusive ball than Mrs. Astor!"

Linnet stared at her mother, shocked by this impassioned speech. "Mother, aren't . . ." She hesitated, uncertain she wanted to ask. She'd never seen her mother as anything but cheerful, happy, and determined, soldiering on, as it were. The idea that Helen might be discontented had never occurred to her. "Aren't you happy with Daddy? With our life?"

The passion in Helen's face vanished, leaving nothing but the complacent certainty Linnet was used to, but she wasn't sure whether to be relieved by that or not. "Linnet, I love your father. I love our home, and I love you. My life is one that suits my temperament and my limited abilities. Don't argue," she added, as Linnet opened her mouth to protest this sort of self-disparagement. "I'm not a clever woman, and I've never been one to light up a room. But you, my beautiful, golden daughter, you can be so much more than I could ever be."

Linnet's eyes stung, and she blinked. "I don't like it when you talk this way about yourself."

Helen ignored her, of course. "When we came to know Conrath, I began to realize there were wider possibilities for you than our narrow, insular circle. I'd hoped our trip abroad would open your eyes. There could be such an exciting world out there for you if you married a peer. An English estate is a far more challenging thing to run than a New York brownstone. An English peeress has so much more freedom and power than I will ever have. Her circle of friends would not be horrified if she traveled the world, excavated ruins, wrote novels, or became a great political hostess. The English peeress can be part of a glittering, cosmopolitan world. Look to Jennie Jerome's example of what life could hold for you, if you don't believe me."

Linnet stared helplessly into her mother's wistful face. "But what if what you want for me is not what I want for myself? I don't think I'd want to live in a glittering, cosmopolitan world, or be a great political hostess. I'm an ordinary Yankee girl, and I can't imagine being anything else."

"Only because you've never thought about it."

"I don't have to think about it. I like my life as it is, and I want to marry someone who wants the same things I do."

"I'm not giving up." Helen's green eyes took on a determined, ambitious gleam Linnet knew all too well. "If you're not married by February, we're going back to London for another season. Maybe some of the British gentlemen who admired you so much when we were there would seem more attractive to you with a second look. The Duke of Carrington, for example, or Lord Danville, or perhaps Sir Roger Oliphant. Or some new gentleman perhaps. Meanwhile . . ." She gave another nod to the three British men nearby. "There are possibilities right here in Newport."

"Mother, you are impossible." Exasperated by her mother's singular talent for ruining any tender moment between them, Linnet turned her attention to the ballroom floor and strove to find a change of subject that wouldn't lead to another fight.

"Oh, look," she said, "there's Davis MacKay dancing with Cicely Morton. I wonder if he's at last worked up the nerve to ask for her hand? In her last letter to me, he hadn't."

But she was not destined to escape her mother's machinations so easily. "Never mind Cicely Morton," Helen whispered. "Featherstone is still watching you."

"Is he?" Uninterested, she rose on her toes, trying to see over the people in front of her to better watch the dancers.

"Yes, indeed. It's clear you've piqued his interest."

"Oh, I'm sure," she muttered without glancing in

that direction. "I suspect what he admires most is my pocketbook."

"I do hate seeing such cynicism from you, and based on what? You condemn Featherstone and every other peer because of one bad experience."

"I am not doing any such thing. I'm forming a logical conclusion based on facts. Everyone knows the previous Lord Featherstone was a ne'er-do-well who spent Belinda Hamilton's entire dowry before he died, so the present Lord Featherstone must be in desperate need of cash. I've no doubt he's in America to embark on the same nefarious course his brother pursued, but as we have discussed so many times, I have no intention of rewarding a fortune hunter with my dowry."

She cast a baleful glance at the subject of their conversation. "Heavens," she muttered as she returned her attention to the dance floor. "If he intends to pursue an American heiress, he ought to at least be somewhat discreet about it. Why, I might be a pastry in a shop window the way he stares at me. It's rude."

"Of course he's staring at you. Men stare at you everywhere you go. It's obvious Featherstone appreciates what a beauty you are and what an excellent countess you would make."

Having already had her romantic illusions shattered by just such a man two seasons ago, and having just departed England and its impoverished nobility in happy relief, Linnet could not imagine a worse fate than being married to that dark, hawklike reprobate across the room. Besides, she wanted to live here and enjoy the sort of the life she'd always had with a man she knew and understood, a man she could be certain cared for her, not her money. A man like Frederick.

She wasn't in love with him as she'd been as a girl, but when she thought of the warmth in his eyes and the way he'd pulled her close, she knew she could fall for him again if she let it happen. And she knew now that he loved her. He could give her everything she wanted in life.

With that thought, any doubts she had about a rendezvous with him vanished. She would meet him in the pagoda, and she would accept his proposal. Daddy would agree to the match, of course, for unlike her mother, her father was no more eager to hand over hard-earned American cash to some British ne'er-do-well than she was. He'd made that clear ever since Conrath.

Once her father's permission was obtained, she and Frederick would announce their engagement straightaway, perhaps even right here at this ball. That would put an end at last to her mother's relentless campaign.

Linnet took another glance at her watch ring. It was five minutes to midnight. If she intended to go through with this, she didn't have much time. She swallowed the last of her sherry, set the glass on a nearby table, and turned to her mother. "I fear I must withdraw for a few minutes."

Those words and the meaningful glance she gave her parent were met with immediate understanding. "I'll accompany you, dear."

"That's not necessary." She heard the sharpness in her voice, and she took care to temper her next words. "I'm twenty-one, Mother," she said, forcing a laugh. "I think I can manage a trip to the necessary by myself. Besides," she added before her mother could argue, "if this Lord Featherstone is interested in making my acquaintance, you should remain here and obtain an introduction through Mrs. Dewey so that you can present me to him when I return, don't you think?"

Helen beamed at her so happily that Linnet almost felt a twinge of guilt at her deception, but as her parent trundled off to find Mrs. Dewey, Lord Featherstone's dark face caught her attention and banished any guilt about what she was doing.

The man was still watching her, and she turned her back, hoping soon the news of her engagement would stop this embarrassing scrutiny and wipe that cocksure smile off his face.

To meet Frederick, she would have to take a circuitous route, for The Tides, Mr. and Mrs. Prescott Dewey's Newport house, was an enormous, sprawling structure. A pity she couldn't exit through one of the French doors that opened onto the terrace, for that would have provided a direct route to the Chinese pagoda, but people were milling about on the terrace, and someone might see her slipping down to the gardens. Besides, she was supposed to be headed for the necessary.

She exited through the main doors, crossed the ballroom's antechamber, and turned down the corridor that led to the ladies' withdrawing room and adjoining bath. The corridor was empty, and with a quick glance over her shoulder to be sure no one was following, she sped past the withdrawing room, ducked down another hallway, traversed several more, and was at last able to exit the house by a little-used side door.

The electric lights that shone through the windows enabled Linnet to see as she made her way around the north wing, and as she started along the winding path that led down to the sea, the moon was bright enough to guide her to a little plateau tucked beneath the cliffs. There, just above the high-water mark, stood the pagoda, a dainty structure of lacquer red with a green tile roof. It was Mrs. Dewey's favorite place to entertain in the afternoon, for the cliffs shielded her guests from the sun, and a wall of windows looked out over the boats the men of Newport loved to sail along the coast. It was the perfect place for a midnight rendezvous, for no one ever came here at night.

She turned the bronze dragon-head handle of the door, and as it swung noiselessly open, she saw Frederick standing at the other end of the long Oriental table, illuminated by the light of an oil lamp he must have brought from the house. He turned as she closed the door, and in the soft light, his boyish face took on an expression of pleasure and relief at the sight of her.

"Linnet." He held out his hands, and she crossed the room to take them. Through the fabric of their gloves, his fingers felt warm and reassuring as they clasped hers. "You came."

"Did you think I wouldn't?"

He gave her a disarming smile. "I wasn't sure. It's not as if you wear your heart on your sleeve, my dear."

"Neither do you. At least . . ." She paused, feeling shy all of a sudden. "You never have before."

"I know. Even I don't understand what's come over me. All I know is that when I saw you come in tonight, I couldn't wait another hour to tell you how much I love and adore you. I want to spend my life caring for you and making you happy. Linnet . . ."

He paused, and though she'd known proposing marriage was his intent, she still felt a thrill as he sank to one knee.

"Linnet, dearest Linnet, will you . . ." He paused again, but though the silence was agonizing, she relished it. This wasn't the only offer of marriage she'd received since Conrath, but it was the first one since then that she wanted to accept.

But the proposal never came. Instead, another male voice spoke, one that was deeply shocked and unmistakably British.

"Oh, I say!"

Even before she turned, Linnet could make a fair guess to whom that drawling, well-bred voice belonged, and when she looked over her shoulder, she found her awful suspicion confirmed by the sight of Lord Featherstone standing in the doorway, his hand still on the handle of the door.

"I'm so sorry." His dark eyes widened in a pretense of innocence, but his knowing smile made short shrift of both his innocent air and his apology. "Have I interrupted an enchanted moment?"

Chapter 3

"You!" Chagrined and dismayed, Linnet stared into the amused dark eyes of the man in the doorway. "What are you doing here?"

"It's such a beautiful night, I decided to take a walk." Lord Featherstone's gaze moved to Frederick as the other man rose from his knees. "And a good thing I did, too. Otherwise, who knows what might have happened?"

"Walk, my eye," she muttered. "You followed me."

"I did," he answered without looking at her, "though it wasn't really necessary to do so. I've been staying at The Tides long enough to know this is the ideal place to choose if a man wishes to compromise a lady."

"That's enough." Frederick took a step forward. "This is a private conversation. Leave at once."

Lord Featherstone propped one shoulder against the

door frame. "I don't believe I will," he said, folding his arms across his wide chest.

"Oh, this is ridiculous," Linnet burst out. "I am not being compromised."

"Granted," he went on in blithe indifference to her denial, "I'm not all that familiar with the nuances of American etiquette, but I've been in your country long enough to know that the rules are pretty much the same here as they are on my side of the pond. No gentleman with honorable intentions would ask a young lady to meet him in this clandestine fashion."

"I said, that's enough!" Frederick shouted, and Linnet glanced at him in some surprise as he moved to stand beside her. She'd never known Frederick to be so out of temper. Still, given the circumstances, he certainly had cause. It was clear Featherstone was needling him on purpose and taking great delight in doing so.

"What, did I touch a nerve?" the earl asked, smiling. "Or do you intend to claim that luring a young lady out for a midnight assignation is an honorable course?"

Frederick's lips pressed tight together. His nostrils flared, and his fists clenched at his sides. But when he spoke, his voice was calmer. "You're sailing very close to the wind, Featherstone."

"On the contrary, I believe it's you who's sailing close to the wind these days, old chap. Tuesday is, what, three days away?"

The flush in Frederick's cheeks paled to chalky white at those words, and Linnet knew there was more at stake here than notions of honor.

"What does he mean?" she asked, looking from

Frederick to Lord Featherstone and back again. "Frederick, what is happening on Tuesday?"

She watched as the man beside her worked to keep his control. His fists opened, and his shoulders relaxed, and when he turned to her, his face had regained its color and bore its usual expression of good-natured forbearance. "I have no idea what he's talking about, dearest."

"No?" Featherstone shrugged. "Given that you arranged this little rendezvous with Miss Holland, I thought certain you'd already been informed about Tuesday. My mistake."

With those light, careless words, Linnet's temper flared. She didn't know what he was talking about, but she didn't care. Accepting a marriage proposal was one of the most important moments of a girl's life, and for her, that moment was being ruined by this ill-mannered stranger. "You speak of the conduct of gentlemen," she said, "but as Frederick pointed out, this is a private conversation. Any gentleman who intruded upon such a circumstance would leave the moment he was asked to do so."

"Perhaps," he conceded at once. "But despite my title, I fear I have never been much of a gentleman. As a man, however . . ." He paused, returning his attention to Frederick. "As a man, I would never dream of using a woman to gain my own ends."

"You bastard." Frederick once again started forward, and Linnet put a hand on his arm to stop him. "No, don't," she pleaded. "He's just needling you. Ignore him."

Frederick drew a deep breath. "You're right, of

course," he said, and turned toward her. "Why let him ruin things? After all," he added, once again grasping her hands in his, "we're almost there. I've already told you my mind, and I believe I know yours as well—"

"Presumes to know your mind, does he?" Featherstone interjected with amusement. "How long before he tells you what thoughts need to be in it?"

Linnet kept her attention on the man before her. "Go on, Frederick," she urged. "We'll just pretend he isn't here."

He nodded. "I realize this all must seem a bit sudden to you, but—"

"A bit?" the earl echoed. "I should say so. He's being so impetuous, isn't he? And it's so unlike him. Perhaps before you give him an answer, Miss Holland, you should ask him why he's in such a hurry."

Even as she tried to tell herself not to listen to the interfering, impudent man in the doorway, Linnet felt a tiny glimmer of uncertainty. This behavior *was* uncharacteristic of Frederick. And what had Featherstone meant about Tuesday?

"Though perhaps you don't want to know his reasons," the earl went on. "American girls are so romantic about marriage, inclined to rush in headlong, thinking it's all about love, when sometimes, it's really about—"

"Shut your mouth!" Frederick let go of her hands, turned, and started toward the earl.

"And if I don't?" Featherstone unfolded his arms, straightened away from the door frame, and took a step forward as the other man approached him. "What will you do?"

Frederick stopped, still a few feet away, and Linnet heard him take a deep, steadying breath. "As much as I'd like to take you down a notch or two, it would be unthinkable to brawl in front of a lady."

"My, such chivalry." Featherstone laughed, a low, deep laugh of unmistakable mockery. "Or perhaps it's just cowardice."

This taunt proved too much even for Frederick to bear. With a roar of outrage, he took the last few steps and struck out with his fist, but the earl ducked, evading the blow. In the same instant, his own fist came up, catching Frederick hard under the chin, sending him stumbling backward. Two more lightning strikes, one straight beneath his ribs and the other hard to the jaw, and Frederick hit the wall behind him. He sank to the floor beside a lavish Oriental screen.

"Oh, no." Linnet hurried forward as he slumped sideways to the ground. "Frederick, are you all right?"

He didn't answer, and when she knelt beside him, he didn't stir. When she touched his shoulder, he didn't open his eyes.

The tap of footsteps had her looking up as Featherstone circled around the end of the long dining table. "He's unconscious."

The earl didn't spare more than the briefest glance at the unmoving figure on the floor. "He'll be all right."

"You knocked him out!"

"So I did." Featherstone tugged at his cuffs and straightened his white bow tie. "A most gratifying experience."

Anger washed over her in a hot flood, and she rose, facing him beside Frederick's prone body. "You did this on purpose for some despicable reason of your own. This wasn't about protecting a woman's honor at all. I just provided the excuse for you to make him lose his temper so you could strike him."

Featherstone didn't deny it. "Well, he's such an ass, he makes the temptation irresistible. And it's so easy to provoke him, too, rather like taking candy from a baby."

"But far more immoral."

Something hard glittered behind the amusement in those dark eyes. "I am not the immoral party in this situation, Miss Holland, trust me."

"Trust you?" Linnet raked an icy glance over him, making no effort to hide her disdain. "I would sooner trust a snake."

"Poor choice of words given the circumstances, I admit." He flashed her a grin that only slightly softened the hardness of his gaze. "But nonetheless, let me assure you that Frederick Van Hausen is not worthy of your defense. Or your hand in marriage, for that matter."

"That was not for you to decide."

"I beg to differ."

"Why?" she demanded in baffled fury. "Why would you do this? You don't even know me."

"No." He paused, and his grin vanished as he glanced with obvious contempt at the unconscious man on the floor. "But I know him."

"Because of a few short weeks' acquaintance in Newport?"

"It's a longer acquaintanceship than that, Miss Holland. I first met Mr. Van Hausen almost a year ago."

At that new information, Linnet felt another glimmer of uneasiness, but she pushed it aside. "And I've known Frederick my entire life. I would say I am a far better judge of his character than you are."

"Since you are actually considering marrying him, I doubt it."

"Indeed? And just what deficiencies in his character enable you to determine that he is unworthy to marry a woman you don't even know?"

Featherstone did not reply at once, and when at last he spoke, his answer was no answer at all. "I am afraid I cannot say."

"You cannot say?" she echoed, and gave a laugh of utter disbelief, not just at his words, but also at how this whole evening was turning out. "You interrupted another man's proposal of marriage, baited him, humiliated him, and struck him unconscious. In the process, you also humiliated me and ruined what could have been one of the most beautiful moments of my life. And you cannot even say why?"

"No. With regret, I cannot."

Linnet wanted to tell him what he could do with his regret, but much to her aggravation, she couldn't think of a reply scathing enough for the situation, so she forced herself to don an air of dignified composure she was far from feeling. "Frederick may need medical attention. I believe I saw Dr. Madison in the ballroom. I shall fetch him."

"And when he asks how Van Hausen came to be

in this state, and how you know of it, what will you say? Shall you tell him about your midnight rendezvous?"

There was a nuance of concern beneath the careless voice and offhand question that caused Linnet to stop in surprise halfway to the door. She turned to give him a searching glance over her shoulder, but his lean impassive face gave nothing away, and she wondered if she'd been mistaken, for she couldn't imagine why this man would be concerned by gossip about her and Frederick. "A doctor knows how to be discreet, I would say," she said at last, still watching him.

"You can't be sure of that, though, can you? What if word gets out?"

She hated being the subject of gossip, but she could see no way to prevent it. "It doesn't matter anyway," she pointed out, "since I shall be accepting Frederick's proposal at the first opportunity."

"I was afraid you'd say that," he said with a sigh. "Miss Holland, marrying him would be the worst mistake you could make."

"And yet you cannot explain why that is so."

He didn't reply, and she once again started toward the door, but she'd taken just one step when an unmistakable voice called to her through the doorway.

"Linnet? Linnet, where are you?"

"Oh, God," she gasped, appalled, and halted again, glancing back toward the man across the room. "That's my mother."

Before Featherstone could respond, another feminine voice also called her name, and Linnet knew her already-ruined evening had just become a disaster. "Mrs. Dewey, too? Oh, my Lord, that woman is the most notorious gossip in our set."

"I thought you didn't care about gossip." As he spoke, Featherstone reached for the painted Oriental screen against the wall. "That it didn't matter."

"It doesn't, not about me and Frederick. You, however, are a different story." She watched in puzzlement as the earl arranged the screen in front of Frederick's prone body. "What are you doing with that screen?"

"Hiding the evidence," he said enigmatically, but instead of ducking behind the screen with Frederick as she would have expected, he stepped back to study his handiwork. Seeming satisfied, he gave a nod and started toward her. "But if possible, I think it's best they don't see any of us down here."

Linnet couldn't argue with that point, and she turned to resume her departure, but she'd barely made it to the doorway before her mother's voice came again.

"Linnet? What are you doing down in the pagoda, young lady?"

Linnet jumped back out of sight at once and cannoned into Lord Featherstone. His hands came up to clasp her arms and steady her, and she felt a jolt of panic. Shrugging free, she whirled around. "You can't leave," she told him, keeping her voice low. "They've seen me, and if we both go out, they'll see you as well. You have to stay here. I'll go out alone and distract them, and you can slip away."

"Linnet?" her mother called. "Who are you talking to? Who's with you?"

"They're too close for slipping away," Featherstone muttered with a glance at the door. "No escape now, I fear."

"Linnet Katherine Holland, I am coming down there at once." Helen's voice, growing louder, made it clear she was already acting on that threat. "At once, do you hear me?"

"Go out one of the windows," she ordered Featherstone in a desperate whisper.

"There's no time."

"Hide, then." She pointed to the screen. "Quick."

The impossible man still didn't move. "It's too late. They know you're not alone."

"Well, you can't just stand there. Do something."

"If you insist." He took a deep breath, grasped her hands in his, and fell to one knee. "Linnet Holland," he said, his voice alarmingly loud, overriding her sound of shock, "will you marry me?"

"Stand up," she hissed. "For God's sake, stand up."

She tried to pull free of his grip, but it was futile, and she cast a frantic glance over her shoulder just in time to see her mother sail into the pagoda, with Mrs. Dewey on her heels. At the scene that met their eyes, the two women came to an abrupt halt just inside the door, and their shocked faces told Linnet she was in serious trouble.

Featherstone rose, and she turned on him, prepared to unleash a fresh flood of wrathful protest at his unconscionable conduct.

He gave her no opportunity. Letting go of her hands, he wrapped an arm around her waist, curled his free hand at the back of her neck, and pulled her hard against him.

"What are you doing?" she demanded in a shocked whisper.

"Saving your reputation," he murmured, bent his head, and kissed her.

Chapter 4

Jack was always agreeable to kissing beautiful women. Marrying any of them, however, was a notion he'd never wasted time contemplating. Matrimony was an expensive business, and everyone knew he hadn't a bean. Not that his dismal finances had ever mattered anyway since he'd never met a woman he could envision spending a lifetime with.

But now, with his lips on those of a woman he'd known less than fifteen minutes and his marriage proposal to her still hanging in the air, all Jack's previous notions about matrimony went straight out the window. With her velvety lips beneath his and her lithe body pressed against him, Jack felt as if the earth were caving under his feet and his body had been lit on fire. Suddenly, giving all his kisses to just one woman for the rest of his life seemed more like delight than deprivation.

Everything about her overwhelmed his senses. The taste of her mouth—warm and soft, with hints of sherry. The scent of her hair—delicate and luscious from the heliotrope. The shape of her—slim and lithe, with perfect curves that seemed to brand him on the spot. His own desire—pounding through his body, making his head spin and his heart thud in his chest.

Somewhere in the vague recesses of his mind, he knew what he was doing was terribly wrong—compromising an innocent girl and all that—but with his arms wrapped around her and his mouth on hers, he couldn't seem to conjure up a scrap of conscience about it, even with her mother standing right there. The fire in him was deepening and spreading, and he was falling, sinking with her into some dark, sweet oblivion where there were no regrets, no consequences—

"What in heaven's name is this?"

The shocked voice of Mrs. Dewey intruded, but even that wasn't enough to bring him back to reality. No, what pulled him from the brink, what forced him to appreciate just what he'd done, was the girl. He felt her body go rigid in his hold and her palms press against his chest, and he was forced to take his cue. When he pulled back, he noted with some chagrin the flush of maidenly outrage in her cheeks, but when her hands slid away and she took a step back, he perceived her intent and caught her wrist before she could act on it.

He might deserve a hard slap across the face, and if this were any other situation, he'd let her give him his comeuppance, but in this case, he couldn't allow it. Slapping him right now would ruin everything, not just for him, but also for her, for if he failed to stop her from marrying Van Hausen, her life would be ruined in ways she couldn't begin to fathom.

"Mrs. Dewey," he reminded in a whisper. "Biggest gossip in Newport."

This caution seemed to make no impression. Her stunning eyes narrowed, her full pink lips parted. "Mother," she said over her shoulder without taking her gaze from his, "this man—"

"Is a cad," he interrupted. Keeping firm hold of her by entwining their fingers, he moved to stand beside her and turned his attention to the ladies in the doorway. "I know these things ought to be done in the proper way," he added, offering his most disarming smile, "but I had to declare my intentions to Linnet before speaking with her father."

"Linnet Holland, as I live and breathe." It was clear Mrs. Dewey was scandalized, but beneath her shock there was unmistakable relish. "It's no wonder my husband said you were walking down to the pagoda in a furtive manner. Why, you were preparing to engage in a tryst."

The girl made a sound of protest at this accusation of her impropriety, but Jack squeezed her hand hard and came to her defense before she could do it herself. "I must protest, Mrs. Dewey. You speak as if something improper is in progress, when the truth is quite the contrary. My fiancée has done nothing to earn your reproach, I assure you."

"Fiancée?" As expected, Mrs. Dewey pounced on the word at once. "Why, Lord Featherstone, I wasn't even aware you and Linnet knew each other."

The girl jerked, managing to free her hand from his. "We don't. I—"

"It's been a whirlwind courtship," he cut her off again. She couldn't appreciate the true reason for his actions, but for the love of God, didn't she see that at this point, an engagement to him was the only way to save her from scandal?

"I appreciate that you often know everything about everyone in society, Mrs. Dewey, on both sides of the pond. But you must forgive me for keeping mum. I feared just speaking of Linnet might have done more to reveal my deeper feelings than I would have liked, and I'm not the sort of man inclined to wear my heart on my sleeve. Until I'd spoken to her, I could not think of revealing my feelings for her to anyone else."

Before his hostess could ask any more questions and impel him to more blatant lies on the topic, Mrs. Holland entered the conversation, playing up to him far better than her daughter was doing. "Why, Linnet, you sly girl, you never said a word, not even to me, your own mother. I am shocked. But at least I now understand why you refused every other suitor in London." She turned to her friend as her daughter spluttered incoherent protests. "Abigail, would you mind giving me a moment alone with my daughter, and her . . . umm . . . fiancé?"

"Of course, of course." Though her disappointment at not being able to remain was obvious, Jack hoped Mrs. Dewey would console herself by spreading the gossip of an honorable engagement rather than a midnight tryst, and spread it as fast as possible, preferably before Van Hausen woke up.

"No, wait," Miss Holland protested as their hostess

moved to leave. "You must understand. This isn't what it seems."

The older woman gave her a pitying smile. "It never is, my dear." With that, she departed, closing the door behind her.

The girl turned to her parent with a groan. "Oh, Mother, why on earth did you send her away before I had the chance to explain? You know she'll go back to the ball and tell everyone."

"Well, you'll be the subject of gossip, but that's what happens when you choose this sort of time and place to accept a young man's proposal of marriage. Which I believe—" She paused long enough to open the door and verify that Mrs. Dewey was not standing on the other side with one ear to the keyhole, then she closed it and returned her attention to Jack. "Which I believe," she resumed, "he was in the midst of offering when he was interrupted by my arrival?"

"I had, yes," he answered at once, for there was no way to prevaricate, even if he wanted to. "I realize it was very wrong of me to conduct things in such a clandestine fashion. My excuse—and it is a poor one, I admit—is that I was carried away by the depth of my feelings."

Beside him, the girl gave a derisive snort, but though the mother glanced at the daughter for a moment, she seemed willing to accept this version of events even if she suspected the whole thing to be a hum. After all, what other choice was there? "I trust you are willing to meet with her father and conduct the remainder of your suit in the proper manner?"

He didn't hesitate. "Of course."

"This is ridiculous," the girl burst out. "This man has no feelings for me. He doesn't even know me, and I don't know him. I didn't meet him out here. Why should I?"

"And yet, here you are," her mother pointed out, "caught with him in a secret assignation, allowing him the opportunity to propose—"

"That is not what happened."

A soft moan behind him caused Jack to cast an uneasy glance over his shoulder. "Perhaps, we should return to the house," he suggested in a louder voice, hoping to cover any more of Van Hausen's inconvenient groaning. "There, we can adjourn to the library for a fuller discussion of the situation?"

Flattening his palm against the base of Miss Holland's spine, he attempted to usher her toward the door, but he should have known her cooperation would not be forthcoming since nothing about this young woman was proving to be easy.

"I'm not going anywhere with you." Turning, she ducked past him and ran to the painted wooden screen. "This is who I came out here to meet, Mother," she went on as she shoved the screen aside to reveal Van Hausen's prone body.

"Frederick?" Mrs. Holland sounded appalled, a fact in which Jack took great satisfaction, despite the rather dire circumstances. The mother, if not the daughter, had some degree of taste and judgment. "Good heavens, you were conducting a midnight rendezvous with Frederick Van Hausen?"

As if hearing his name, the other man stirred, causing the girl to kneel beside him with a sound of relief.

"Frederick?" She shook his shoulder. "Oh, Frederick, do wake up. My mother's here, and you have to explain."

Van Hausen moved to sit up, but the moment he did, his eyes crossed and rolled back in his head, and Jack couldn't help grinning as the American gave a groan, slumped back to the floorboards, and once again passed out.

"Dear me." Mrs. Holland studied him with distaste. "Is he drunk?"

"Of course not." The girl jumped to her feet and strode forward to face her parent. "He was in the midst of proposing to me when that man—" She paused to jab a finger in Jack's direction. "Interrupted us, picked a fight, and struck poor Frederick unconscious."

"Frederick Van Hausen was proposing to you?" Mrs. Holland sounded even more appalled than before. "But I saw you kissing Lord Featherstone."

"I did not kiss him. He kissed me."

"I think," Jack murmured, leaning closer to her, "your mother would deem that a distinction without a difference, my darling."

She turned to give him a scowl at the endearment before returning her attention to her parent. "What you and Mrs. Dewey saw won't matter, even if she tells everyone in Newport about it, because I shall be marrying Frederick. My reputation will not suffer any lasting damage if our engagement is announced right away. Everyone will think it's just a misunderstanding."

Her mother didn't seem impressed by that. "Mrs. Dewey will never think what she saw was a misunderstanding. As for Frederick, he is unconscious, and you are not at liberty to speak for him. And even if his intentions were honorable, it doesn't matter. I wouldn't dream of allowing you to marry him."

"What?" The girl's cheeks, flushed from the warm night and the heat of the moment, went pale. "Are you saying that because he isn't a British peer? Even after I've told you what happened, you would still—"

"Nationality and titles have little to do with it now," her mother cut in. "I cannot allow you to marry Frederick Van Hausen when you have already been seen committing improprieties with another man, and the witness to this is one of Newport's biggest scandalmongers. Don't be absurd, Linnet."

Jack let out a sigh of profound relief, but the girl's next words told him he wasn't out of the weeds quite yet.

"But, Mother, what's the alternative? You can't expect me to marry this man. He's a complete stranger to me."

"Not such a stranger," Mrs. Holland reminded. "Not after what Abigail and I witnessed here."

"I already explained that."

"And I'm explaining to you, my dear daughter, that how this came about isn't as important as the fact that it did. There is only one thing that can be done." Mrs. Holland waved a gloved hand in Jack's direction. "It was Lord Featherstone who damaged your reputation, and it is his responsibility to repair it."

The girl gave a huff of exasperation. "You're insisting on this because it fits with your plans. We both know you want me to marry a peer, but as we have discussed many times before, I don't share your ambitions for my life. And I've got Daddy on my side. Unlike you, he has always wanted me to marry an American."

Jack tensed. If the girl's father ended up taking Van Hausen's part, all was lost. But Mrs. Holland didn't seem worried. "You think your father would approve of Frederick?" she asked.

"Of course. Why wouldn't he?"

"Why, indeed. Let's find out, shall we? He needs to be told at once what has occurred, for I shudder to think what he'll say if he hears the news of your conduct from someone outside the family. So why don't you go and tell him what's happened, hmm, while I have a talk with this young man?"

The girl hesitated, passing her tongue over her lips. Her apprehension was understandable. After all, no girl would want to face her father with the news that her reputation had just been compromised. Jack decided it was a good time for another display of chivalry. "With all due respect," he said, "I ought to be the one to explain. It's my office."

"Not a chance," the girl cut in before the mother could reply. "This is all your fault, yes, but I have no intention of allowing you to sugarcoat the story to press your suit. I'll be the one to tell my father what a despicable cad you are!"

She strode past him and started for the door, but she'd done no more than open it and cross the threshold before her mother spoke, causing her to stop and turn in the doorway.

"Linnet? Be sure to tell your father how determined you are to marry Frederick. When I come, I shall be interested to hear his views on that score. Very, very interested."

Van Hausen, it seemed, cut no ice with either of the

girl's parents, a fact that brightened Jack's spirits a bit. Without the approval of the girl's father, Van Hausen would never be able to borrow against his expectations as her future husband and escape his fate.

Miss Holland, he noticed, was frowning, and it was clear her mother's words puzzled her. "But what objection could Daddy have to Frederick?"

"We can discuss that later. Go. We shall join you and your father in the library shortly, and this matter will be decided."

"Whatever Daddy's own opinion, he'll understand I have to marry someone, and he won't look more favorably on this man than he would Frederick. Daddy," she added with a baleful glance at Jack, "doesn't like fortune hunters any more than I do."

With that, she marched out of the pagoda and closed the door behind her, leaving him alone with her mother.

Given a choice of which parent to deal with first, Jack supposed Mrs. Holland was the better bargain. After all, they'd at least been introduced. In addition, their few minutes of conversation in the ballroom had made it clear she had a high regard for men with titles, and though his title might be a bit tarnished, he did have one.

"How dare you?" she demanded, her voice and manner seething with outrage. "How dare you compromise my daughter? You will explain yourself at once, Lord Featherstone, or I will have my husband shoot you like a rabid dog."

He grimaced. Mrs. Holland's high regard for titled men clearly wasn't going to be of any help to him right now.

EPHRAIM CORNELIUS HOLLAND might have been born into wealth and privilege, but he was no weakling, a fact Linnet was reminded of a few moments after she began her account of the evening's events.

"Frederick Van Hausen has asked you to marry him?" he roared, the booming echo of his voice making his daughter wince. "Without my permission?"

Linnet glanced at the door of Prescott Dewey's library. Reassured that she had indeed closed it after pulling her father in here for this consultation, she attempted to placate her outraged parent.

"I know he should have come to you first," she began, but she got no further.

"Indeed, he should have," her father bellowed, his silver-gray brows knitting together to emphasize his disapproval, as if his raised voice wasn't enough to make the point. "Not that it matters, I suppose."

With those words, Linnet let out her breath with a sigh of relief. Not that she'd been worried, precisely, but the way her evening had been going gave her cause for some amount of concern, and the manner in which this engagement was coming about was less than exemplary. "I realize that bringing it to you as a *fait accompli* isn't the best way of going about it. No doubt you wish to speak to Frederick as soon as possible, but just now he's rather . . ." She paused for a little cough. "Ahem . . . indisposed. But later, the two of you can discuss the details, and—"

"You misunderstand me, Lin," her father cut in. "There will be no engagement between you and Van Hausen. I can't allow it."

"What?" Linnet blinked, her relief dissolving. Her mother had been right, then. "But why?" she asked, more confounded than ever. "Mother's opposed, and of course, I know why. But you, Daddy? Why should you be opposed?"

"He's not good enough for you."

"Not good enough?" That was so absurd, Linnet almost laughed, but her father's expression told her this was no laughing matter. "But Frederick is no different from us. I've known him all my life. His family is even older than ours, and almost as wealthy. And besides, I thought you liked Frederick."

"I do like him. Can't deny it. But he's still not the man for you, Lin. I can't give my consent."

Linnet stared, still not able to quite believe what she was hearing. Daddy wanted her to marry an American. He'd supported her position on this ever since Lord Conrath. "But I don't understand this at all. What possible objection could you have—"

"I said no, and that's the end of it."

In most situations, this sort of uncompromising refusal wouldn't worry her. Given enough time and enough persistence and tact on her part, she could get around her father's objections to just about anything. But in this case, she didn't have time. Mrs. Dewey would never keep silent about what she'd witnessed. The odious woman was probably whispering all the lurid details to various friends in the ballroom at this very moment. By tomorrow afternoon, everyone in Newport would know about it. Any delay in her engagement to Frederick would fuel the gossip about Featherstone and further endanger her reputation.

"But Daddy, you don't understand," she choked out, feeling a hint of panic. "I must marry."

He smiled and took her hand in both of his. "Now don't you go worrying about your future, Lin. Your mother's still got her head set on you marrying some Englishman with a title, but we've managed to nix that plan so far, haven't we?"

Linnet was pretty certain her mother's plan was anything but nixed, thanks to a certain British earl, but when her father winked at her, she couldn't help a little smile in return. "Poor Mother. If she knew how we've plotted against her in that regard. But she won't give up. Not until I'm married."

"I agree, but the man you wed won't be Frederick Van Hausen." He gave her hand a squeeze. "I want someone far better than that for you, someone who's good enough to marry you, someone who's good enough to be allied with our family."

She frowned, feeling a sudden uneasiness that had nothing to do with her father's refusal of Frederick and everything to do with his odd choice of words. She gave a little laugh. "Oh, Daddy, you talk as if you already have someone in mind."

Her father laughed, too. "I never can put anything over on you, Lin," he said, patting her hand. "Not for long."

Linnet froze, the implications of her father's words striking her with a force that left her unable to move or even react. Her uneasiness deepened into dread. It seemed like an eternity before she could bring herself to ask the vital question. "Who are you thinking of, Daddy?" she whispered.

"Davis MacKay."

"But . . . but . . ." She paused, for the notion was so

absurd, she couldn't even credit it, much less refute it. "But that's impossible," she managed at last. "I can't marry Davis."

"He's a good man, Lin." Ephraim's voice was pleasant, agreeable, and yet, that very quality seemed to worsen the horrible, sick feeling in her stomach. "With a good character. He'll make you a fine husband."

"But I don't love Davis, and he doesn't love me."

"Once the two of you are married, love will follow. No reason to think otherwise."

"I can give you a very important reason." She pulled her hand out of her father's grip. "He's already in love with Cicely Morton."

Her father shrugged as if that were of no consequence. "You turn your charms on him for a while, and he'll forget the Morton girl ever existed."

"I doubt that. He's been in love with Cicely since we were all playing in sandboxes. He's always intended to marry her. And from the letters Cicely's sent me and the way they looked together earlier this evening, their feelings for each other haven't changed in the year I've been away."

Her father's expression hardened into implacable lines. "Davis," Ephraim said, "will do as he's told."

Her stomach twisted with dread and something deeper, something she'd never felt near her father before, something a lot like fear. "Told?" she echoed, her voice just above a whisper. "Told by whom, Daddy?"

The ruthlessness faded, then vanished, leaving the face of the benevolent father she recognized, but to Linnet, it was too late. The affection in his expression seemed unreal to her now, like a mask. Her mind flashed back over the past year, to all the ways he'd helped her evade her mother's plans, particularly during her recent London season, to all the times he'd professed to understand that of course she wanted a husband who loved her and wasn't after her money, and she realized all his support and assistance had not been for the sake of her happiness but to further some secret ambition of his own. She'd always known her father was ruthless—he couldn't have turned their respectable family fortune into a vast empire of almost obscene wealth if he didn't possess that quality—but in her entire life, Linnet had never seen his ruthless ambitions directed at her.

He smiled. "I meant that Davis will appreciate the advantages of an alliance between our families, once his father and I have discussed it with him."

"Once you've bullied him, you mean," she corrected with asperity, in no mind to sacrifice her happiness—or Davis's either—for the sake of alliance. "Does Mother know this?" she demanded, remembering again Helen's complacent reaction to her earlier threat to take matters to her father. "Does she know Davis MacKay is whom you want me to marry?"

"Of course she knows."

"But she doesn't agree with your choice." Even as she spoke, Linnet felt as if she were grasping at straws.

Her father bristled. "It doesn't matter whether she agrees or not. We had a deal."

"A deal?" Linnet echoed, her voice rising, her dismay giving way to a renewed sense of outrage. "What sort of deal?"

"Your mother wanted the trip to Europe and she wanted to wind things up in London so you could do their season. I don't understand why, but even after that snake Conrath, she thinks a British husband would be better for your future, so I agreed to let you have a season there. The deal was that if you met some British lord and fell in love with him, I'd pay over the dowry and not kick up a fuss."

"While you did everything you could to discourage the possibility. Pretending to be on my side, but all the while, making your own plans for me to come home and marry Davis, without any consideration of his feelings or mine. Oh, Daddy." Her voice cracked on the last two words, and if she wasn't already spitting mad at the realization she'd been played between her parents like a pawn, she might have burst into tears.

Her father shifted his weight, looking for the first time a little guilty, but he brushed it off with a shrug of his shoulders. "Don't make me out to be some sort of domestic tyrant. Ever since the Conrath business, you've said you didn't want a British lord. You said you wanted to marry an American and keep living here in America."

"Which doesn't mean you should be choosing my husband for me," she cried, stunned by how little regard either of her parents seemed to have for her feelings. "Just because Davis MacKay is acceptable to you does not mean he's acceptable to me. He isn't. He's in love with one of my best friends, who also happens to be in love with him, and I wouldn't dream of tearing them apart. You can put aside any notion of Davis as a son-in-law right now, Daddy. I won't marry him."

"Don't take that defiant tone with me, young lady. I am thinking of your future."

With those words, Linnet was reminded of the brutal fact that as of right now, both her future and her reputation hung by a thread. This was not a good time to be ruled by anger. She needed her father's help, and she wouldn't get it by outright defiance. A lifetime of experience had taught her that.

Linnet took a deep breath and tamped down the chaotic mix of anger and hurt swirling inside her. "Why is Davis MacKay the best choice for my future?" she asked, working to keep her voice calm and reasonable. "Why him and not some other man in our set? Why . . ." She paused, stepping onto the thin ice. "Why Davis rather than Frederick?"

"Frederick's an investment banker, and his father's in shipping. Neither of those do anything to help Holland Oil. The MacKays, though, are fully invested in coal, now that Franklin MacKay bought out Kentucky Jubilee Coal. An alliance between our families would enable Franklin and I to control over half the fuel supplies from the Atlantic seaboard to the Midwest."

"I see," she murmured, her voice faint even to her own ears, her mind stunned by her father's mercenary logic. "To you, my marriage is just another business deal."

"We'd corner the market," Ephraim went on, so enthused by his own plans that he either hadn't heard or he'd chosen to ignore her comment. "Everyone, Albert Van Hausen included, would have to dance to our tune. The money to be made is enormous. Think of it, Linnet. Your children will inherit an empire."

Linnet didn't care about empires, and she doubted Davis did either. After all, he was intelligent enough to have grasped the advantages marriage to someone like her would bring him, and it hadn't seemed to dim his love for the poor, but wholly respectable Cicely one bit. Once he heard what had happened to Linnet this evening, Davis would seize on Lord Featherstone's supposed claim on her affections as the perfect excuse to evade the alliance their fathers had concocted. And she guessed his father wouldn't retain much enthusiasm for the match either, once the scandal hit the papers.

No, though Ephraim didn't know it, his candidate for her hand would soon be out of the picture. But Linnet knew she didn't have the luxury of waiting for the problem to play itself out on the front page of *Town Topics*. She had to become engaged to Frederick now, tonight, before news of the episode with Featherstone could spread. If that happened, she'd either have to marry the blackguard or face ruin. No, everyone had to be made to see as soon as possible that she had been innocent, Frederick had been honorable, and Lord Featherstone had been the one to behave inappropriately.

"Daddy, something's happened tonight that you don't know about, something I'm afraid throws a wrench into your plans."

With those words, Ephraim's entrepreneurial enthusiasm dimmed somewhat. He frowned. "What do you mean?"

She didn't answer. Instead, she stared at him, swamped by a sudden feeling of helplessness. How could a girl look into her father's face and tell him she was facing shame and ruin?

"Lin?" He took her by the shoulders, his frown deepening, his blue eyes so like hers scanning her face. "What haven't you told me?"

Linnet swallowed hard, mustered her courage, and started at the beginning. By the time she'd reached the part about being alone with Frederick in the pagoda, he had let go of her and was pacing the library. By the time she told of Featherstone's unexpected arrival, he was biting his thumbnail, and by the time she got to the impending approach of her mother and Mrs. Dewey, she knew his shrewd, businesslike brain was appreciating the possible consequences and coming up with stories to offer the papers. But Featherstone's marriage proposal must not have figured in Ephraim's chesslike calculations, for news of it stopped him in his tracks.

"But I thought you said you don't even know this man."

"I don't. I'd seen him in the ballroom, that was all. Mother pointed him out to me, but I never spoke to him. And when I went down to the pagoda, I never dreamed—"

"My God, Lin." Her father sighed and raked a hand through his silver hair. "My God, do you know what you've done?"

"I didn't do anything," she flared. "Why does everyone always blame the woman in circumstances like these?"

"Maybe because the woman in question put herself in these circumstances by sneaking off to meet with a cad."

Those words, coming from the man she'd always adored, felt like a slap across the face, but Linnet strove to maintain her dignity. "Frederick is not the cad in this. His intentions were honorable."

"Honorable?" her father echoed in disbelief. "That's not what I'd call it."

"He was there to propose marriage."

"This Lord Featherstone had the same intention, apparently. Would you call him honorable, too?"

"Of course not."

"Then what's the difference?"

"Featherstone didn't just propose. He—" She stopped and gave a grimace. "It's worse than that, I'm afraid."

"Tell me the rest. There is nothing you tell me," he added when she hesitated, "that could be worse than what I'm imagining."

"He kissed me."

"Kissed you?" Ephraim roared, and Linnet cast another alarmed glance at the closed door.

"Sssh. Daddy, keep your voice down. Things are bad enough already. If someone overhears—"

"I'll kill him," her father muttered between clenched teeth. "I'll kill that British, fortune-hunting son of a bitch."

Linnet might have been warmed by that show of paternal outrage but for the suspicion that his anger wasn't solely on her behalf. "Killing Featherstone won't save my reputation. Mrs. Dewey heard his proposal and saw what he did. No doubt she's telling everyone in the ballroom all about it right now. The one thing that will stop the scandal is an announcement of my engagement, followed as soon as possible by my wedding."

"You're right, of course." Her father stepped around her. "Which means there's no time to lose."

"Where are you going?" Linnet turned, watching as he strode toward the door. "What do you intend to do?"

"I'm going to find Franklin MacKay and tell him what's happened before he hears it from someone else. You and Davis will have to become engaged right away."

"What?" Linnet started across the room after him. "But I've already told you I can't marry Davis."

"You don't have a choice. As you said, you have to marry someone."

Desperate, she tried again to dissuade her father from his course. "Franklin MacKay won't agree to let Davis marry me. Not now. Mr. MacKay has a puritanical sense of respectability."

"We'll soon find out." Her father paused, hand on the doorknob, and when he looked at her, his smile was grim. "Let's hope the appeal of profits overcomes his scruples."

"But I want to marry Frederick."

Her father didn't argue the point, but his eyes glittered with all the ruthlessness she'd seen earlier. "Maybe you do," he countered, "but after this, what makes you think Frederick will still want to marry you?"

The question took her by surprise. "What do you mean? Of course he wants to marry me. He proposed, didn't he?"

"So you tell me, but that was before you became open to scandal. After what happened with Featherstone, you seem quite sure Davis won't have you. What makes you think Frederick will?"

"Because he was *there*. He knows—" She stopped, appreciating her father's point even before he voiced it.

"He knows nothing," Ephraim said. "From what you've told me, he was unconscious."

"Well, yes, but even so, that doesn't matter. All I have to do is tell him . . . tell him what . . ." Her voice trailed off into silence as doubts crept in. Until this moment, it hadn't occurred to her that Frederick might change his mind, that he would cease to want her because of what Featherstone had done. She tried to rally. "Frederick won't desert me because of this. He cares for me."

"Maybe so," her father acknowledged as he paused by the door. "But in light of Featherstone's actions, I doubt Albert Van Hausen will take Frederick's sentiments into consideration. At least Franklin Mackay knows there's a lucrative business deal in the offing if his son marries you. Van Hausen has no such incentive, and without his father's approval, I doubt Frederick will marry you."

"Why not?"

Her father opened the door. "Because he hasn't got the guts. Frederick is a noodle-spined jackass."

With that brutal and most unfair assessment, her father walked out the door, leaving Linnet alone with all the doubts he'd just planted in her head.

Chapter 5

Of all the nights of her life, this one had to rank as the absolute worst, Linnet decided as she stared at the closed door of the library.

It had started out so beautifully, too. She sank down onto one of Prescott Dewey's big leather armchairs in a pouf of pink silk, remembering in amazement how she'd felt sailing into the ballroom less than two hours ago—relieved that her months in the grinding London marriage market were over, hopeful that her mother's shameless matchmaking was at an end, aware that with her twenty-first birthday a month ago, she could not be forced into anything by her mother. She'd been happy to be home again among all her old friends and confident that her destiny would be in her own hands. And what a nice surprise it had been to find Frederick, his face so comfortingly familiar, his eyes gazing at her with such gratifying adoration. Her future had seemed full of promise, as bright as the morning sun on the waters of Easton Bay.

And now? Linnet fell back in her chair with a sigh. Now her romantic evening was in tatters, her heretofore pristine reputation was teetering on the brink of ruin, and any illusions she'd ever had that she was in control of her own destiny had been trampled into dust. How, she wondered in bewilderment, had everything gone so wrong?

It was that man. She straightened in her chair as the memory of Lord Featherstone hiding Frederick's unconscious body came into her mind. He'd known, she realized, just what he was doing. He'd seen his opportunity, the calculating bastard, and he'd taken full advantage of it, hiding Frederick from view so that the women wouldn't see him, then compromising her on purpose, shouting his proposal so it would be heard by her mother, then . . . and then . . . Linnet's rage blazed as she remembered that insufferable smile on his face just before he'd kissed her in front of her mother and Mrs. Dewey, sealing her fate and lining his own pocketbook.

Linnet ground her teeth, her lips burning from that kiss. His actions had been unconscionable, his intentions corrupt, and his motives so obvious a child wouldn't be deceived. Her mother, however, wasn't going to care two bits about any of that.

Helen's ambitions knew no bounds, and though Linnet had managed to stay strong in the face of her mother's relentless campaign, she knew her strength had been due in part to the bolstering support and reassurance of her father. Ephraim, she'd thought, was on her side. But now, she knew her father's support was nothing but an illusion.

At that reminder, Linnet's anger receded, giving way to bleak despair, as well as something sharper and even more painful—the stab of betrayal. All this time, she'd thought Ephraim to be her ally, that unlike her mother, he loved her more than his own ambition.

Pain squeezed her chest, pushing upward, erupting in a sob. *Oh, Daddy,* she thought, lifting a gloved hand to her mouth, *how could you?*

She closed her eyes and pressed her hand hard against her mouth, trying to stifle the sobs that seemed bent on coming out. *Damn it,* she thought, as a tear squeezed out between her closed lids and rolled down her cheek, crying wasn't going to help. She had to *think.*

Linnet fought back the tears of desolation and panic, striving to don some of her father's cool, mercenary business sense. After a moment, she pulled out her handkerchief, blotted her face, and took stock of things. It was clear she would be marrying someone, and to her mind, Frederick was the only possible choice.

What makes you think Frederick will want to marry you?

Her father's question, though cruel, was also valid. Like it or not, she would be tainted now, and there were many men who would cry off in such a circumstance. Was Frederick that sort of man? Would Frederick desert her once the story came out?

She turned the question over in her mind, and as she did, she realized that though she'd known Frederick her entire life, had at one time been in love with him and had almost agreed to marry him, she did not know him well enough to answer the question with any degree of certainty.

He cared what people thought of him. She was certain of that. In particular, he had a high degree of respect for his father's opinion, and Albert Van Hausen would never approve of her marriage to his son once the knowledge of Featherstone's kissing her became public knowledge. What if her father was right that Frederick was a bit weak? What if he caved to his own father's opinion and left her high and dry?

The door opened, diverting her from the appalling direction of her thoughts, and when she saw Frederick's blond head emerge through the doorway, she gave a cry of relief.

"Oh, thank heavens it's you." She jumped to her feet. "I thought it might be my mother with Lord Featherstone. Are you all right?"

He nodded as he came in and closed the door behind him. "What about you?"

She sighed. "I'm well enough, all things considered. How did you know where to find me?"

"I didn't. I've been looking everywhere. When I returned to the ballroom, I heard almost at once what Featherstone had done. The despicable swine. When I see him again—"

Linnet's cry of dismay interrupted him. "You know? You've . . ." She paused and swallowed hard. "You've heard, then?"

He sighed. "I'm afraid so. I wasn't in the ballroom ten seconds before Dotty Ridgeway rushed over and told me all about it."

"Dotty?" The idea that one of her own friends had so

eagerly imparted sordid gossip about her sent Linnet's spirits sinking even lower. "My, my," she murmured, squaring her shoulders and trying to force out a laugh. "Bad news travels fast, doesn't it?"

"It doesn't matter," Frederick cried and grasped her arms. "Not to me."

The bleakness around Linnet's heart lifted a little. "Really?"

He stared at her as if incredulous she'd even ask. "How could you think it would?"

"My father said—" She stopped and shook her head. "Never mind. It doesn't matter. I just thought that when you heard about what happened, that you might . . ." She paused and swallowed hard. "That you might change your mind about the whole thing."

"Why? Because Featherstone's a cad and an opportunistic fortune hunter?"

Linnet's spirits were rising higher with each word, but she tempered the feeling. She still didn't have a formal proposal of marriage from him, and given how her evening had gone so far, she didn't want to take anything for granted. "If you did feel differently about me now because of what he did, I would understand."

"Don't be a ninny. As things are, I'm tempted to force Featherstone to stand a second round of fisticuffs. If I did, the outcome of our fight would be very different, I promise you. But I doubt I'll have the chance. When I came out of the pagoda, I saw him with your mother in the garden. They were looking thick as thieves."

"Planning the wedding and discussing the dowry, I have no doubt," she countered with a grimace.

"I didn't stop to eavesdrop, but if what Dotty told me

is accurate, everyone thinks you're engaged to him, and given what he did, you'll be expected to marry him. I couldn't stand it, Linnet!" he cried, his voice rising with gratifying intensity. "If you married him instead of me, I'd—" He broke off, swallowed, and said, "The point is, your reputation is in serious jeopardy."

"Yes." She felt her throat clogging up, and she had to force out her next words. "I'm damaged goods now."

"No, you're not. Damn Featherstone to hell. And damn Mrs. Dewey's malicious tongue. I'm sorry," he added at once. "I didn't mean to swear."

"I think swearing is called for." She tried to smile, but it was a wobbly effort. "I've sworn a bit myself during the past hour."

"Everything's going to be all right. There's no avoiding a scandal, I'm afraid, but does that matter? I mean, you'll end up all right as long as we go forward with our own plans. I think we should be married as soon as possible."

A sigh of relief escaped her, but she had to be sure he was sure. "Within a week, what Featherstone did will be in all the gossip columns. If I don't marry him, I'll be branded a shameless wanton, and if I marry you, you'll be declared a laughingstock for wanting me."

"Nonsense. We'll just tell the truth. We had agreed to become engaged, and Featherstone intervened, assaulting me and making unspeakable advances toward you. You've done nothing wrong. And let people say what they like. I shan't care."

For those words alone, she wanted to fling her arms around his neck and kiss him, but there was still one obstacle in their path, and remembering that restrained her. "Frederick, even if . . . even if you do want to marry me, my father won't hear of it."

"You spoke with him about this?" Frederick's brows drew together in a frown. "You asked for his consent? Damn it, Linnet, why?"

"I had no choice. I had to tell him the truth of what happened tonight before he heard some sordid reiteration of the story from someone else. It never occurred to me he would refuse his permission."

"Did he give a reason? Did he speak against me?"

"No, of course he didn't. It's just that he's got someone else in mind for me to marry."

Frederick's frown deepened into a scowl. "Who?" he demanded, his voice tense and sharp.

"Davis MacKay. My father is off with Franklin Mackay right now, trying to persuade him to agree to the match."

He gave her a hard, searching stare. "And would you rather marry Davis than marry me?"

"Heavens, no."

His brow cleared, and he shrugged, seeming once again his usual carefree self. "Then we've got nothing to worry about."

She made a choked sound that was half laugh, half sob. "No? Then why do I have this sick feeling in the pit of my stomach? I don't want to marry Davis. And I'd rather spit nails than marry Featherstone. And Daddy won't let me marry you. Given all that, I don't see what I can do. There's no answer."

"Stop panicking," he ordered, once again putting his hands on her arms to give her a little shake. "Your mother can't make you marry Featherstone, and your father can't make you marry Davis. You're twenty-one. You don't need permission from either of them to marry me. We can elope."

"Elope?" She stared at him, dumbfounded, for as strong-minded as she could be, such a course had never occurred to her. "You want me to run away with you?"

"Why not?"

She considered. "Well, my father could disinherit me, for one thing."

"He won't. He adores you too much for that." He laughed. "And even if he did, why should it matter? Are you afraid I can't support you?"

She couldn't help laughing with him at that absurd idea. "Of course not, but I thought it only fair to warn you that he'll be furious and he might cut me off. Daddy can be . . ." She paused and swallowed hard. "He can be ruthless. Your father might cut you off, too, since my reputation will be ruined."

"I don't care about his money, or my father's either, if it comes to it." He kissed her nose. "I have plenty of my own, you know. I'll have more than enough to support us."

"An elopement between us will inflame the gossip all the more."

"Or it will make everyone realize the truth. Once we're married, we'll be able to tell the true story of what happened, and this whole mess will blow over."

"And everything in our garden will be lovely? That's a nice thought, Frederick, but I'm afraid it's a case of wishful thinking. People will talk about this for years."

"Even if they do, it still doesn't matter. If there's a

scandal to face, we'll face it together as husband and wife."

With those words, Linnet knew her reputation would be saved. She'd be marrying a man who wanted her, not her money, and her relief was so great, she felt her knees giving way. "Oh, Frederick," she cried, clutching at the lapels of his dinner jacket to stay on her feet. "Daddy told me you wouldn't want me once you knew what had happened."

"And you believed him? My darling, if you're going to marry me, you might give my character a little credit." He glanced at the door. "We don't have much time. Since your father's off with Mr. MacKay, and your mother's probably still with Featherstone, this is our chance. We'll slip away through a side door, take my carriage, and be gone before anyone knows we're missing."

"Leave right now? You mean this minute?"

"We have to be away now, for we won't have another chance. After tonight, your parents will watch over you like hawks."

"But look at us. We're not dressed for travel. We've no clothes, no proper shoes, not even toothbrushes. I'm in a ball gown and dancing slippers, for goodness' sake. We have to at least take time to change—"

"I told you, there is no time," he interrupted, his voice carrying a strident urgency she'd never heard before. "If we take my carriage, we'll put the top up and no one will see you. We can be in Providence by first light, and I'll put you in a hotel, purchase a change of clothes for both of us, and we'll find a justice of the peace. We'll be married by the afternoon and return in the evening as man and wife, and no one will be able to do anything about it."

Linnet bit her lip, seized by sudden doubt, though she had no idea why. She'd intended to accept Frederick's proposal anyway, and her only other choices were unthinkable. "It's just that this is happening so fast," she murmured.

"I know, darling. I know. But we don't have the luxury of taking more time. Well?" he urged when she didn't reply. "Shall we do this crazy thing then?"

Linnet didn't answer at once. She wasn't worried about her mother—she could deal with Helen well enough. But Ephraim did not like to be thwarted, and he could make things very difficult for Frederick. Still, if Frederick wasn't afraid of her father, why should she be? What could her father do about it after the fact? She thought of the plans he'd made, plans he'd been careful to conceal from her all these months, and she capitulated with a reckless laugh. "Elopement it is, then," she said. "Let's go."

He took her by the hand, and they started out of the room, but they weren't even halfway to the door before it opened, and her mother walked in, Lord Featherstone right behind her. The sight of Linnet hand in hand with Frederick brought both of them to an abrupt stop just inside the door.

"Featherstone!" Frederick cried, as he and Linnet came to a halt.

"I'm the proverbial bad penny, I'm afraid," the earl said with infuriating good cheer as he moved into the room with Helen. "I just keep turning up."

"Frederick Van Hausen, what are you doing here?"

Helen demanded. "And why are you holding my daughter's hand?"

Linnet felt Frederick's fingers tighten around hers, a gesture she might have found reassuring, except that another figure appeared in the doorway, and beneath her father's steely blue gaze, any sense of reassurance faded. Frederick might have been right that together they could face all the consequences of becoming man and wife, but she'd hoped to avoid those consequences at least until the wedding had taken place.

She wasn't to be that lucky, it seemed. Her gaze slid from her father to the tall, dark-haired devil just in front of him, and she realized that with Lord Featherstone anywhere in the vicinity, good luck might continue to be in very short supply.

Chapter 6

At the sight of Miss Holland hand in hand with Van Hausen, Jack wondered if a second round of fisticuffs would be necessary. But when another voice spoke behind him, he realized that if fisticuffs were required, he might be deprived of the pleasure.

"Remove your hand at once."

Jack glanced over his shoulder as a tall man with steel gray hair, a determined jaw, and eyes of the same brilliant blue as the girl's came up beside him. Ephraim Holland, he knew at once, and he noted the older man's clenched fists and powerful physique with a grin. If it came to giving Van Hausen a good thrashing, he'd be happy to step aside to allow an outraged father to do the honors. It seemed quite fitting, in fact.

"I said, remove your hand," Holland ordered through clenched teeth, "or I will do it for you."

Either Van Hausen had more courage than Jack had given him credit for, or he was desperate enough to take his chances, for he didn't move to comply with the older man's demand. "It's permissible for engaged couples to hold hands," he said instead. And Linnet and I intend to marry."

"Over my dead body," Jack muttered.

Holland didn't seem much more amenable to the idea of Van Hausen marrying the girl than he was. The man started forward as if to carry out his threat, but his wife put a hand on his arm. "Ephraim, don't," she pleaded. "Surely, we can discuss this without physical violence."

Holland paused, taking a deep breath. "I've already refused Linnet my consent to marry you, but I'm happy to repeat it. I will not allow you to marry her, not under any circumstances whatsoever."

This unequivocal statement did not cause Van Hausen to back down. "We don't need your consent. Besides, you must know by now what's happened tonight and what's being said in the ballroom." His hand tightened around the girl's. "Linnet's reputation is in jeopardy."

Jack decided he'd better speak up before this reminder of the precarious state of Miss Holland's reputation could force her father to reconsider his refusal. "Are you sure you know what you're doing, old chap?" he asked with a pretense of concern. "After all, without her father's consent, how will you ever obtain a loan?"

"You bastard." Van Hausen spat out the words like a bad taste in his mouth. "You interfering British bastard."

"You watch your language, young man," Ephraim

ordered, and turned to Jack. "As for you, who in Sam Hill are you?"

"My apologies, Mr. Holland, that there hasn't been time or opportunity for formal introductions," he said, and bowed. "I am Lord Featherstone."

"Featherstone?" Holland roared, causing Jack to grimace. "So you're the one responsible for my daughter's name being dragged through the mud. By God, I ought to horsewhip you."

"Indeed, you should," he agreed at once, "but might I suggest you postpone it to a later time? You have, I fear, a more immediate problem before you."

His gaze slid to the couple across the room and, much to his relief, the reminder seemed to change Holland's mind about taking out his paternal fury on Jack. "I suppose that's true," he conceded, his eyes narrowing. "For the moment anyway."

Glad of the reprieve, Jack went on, "Van Hausen is desperate for money, you see, and that's why he attempted to become engaged to your daughter earlier this evening. Once an engagement was declared, he could borrow against his expectations as your future son-in-law."

"That's ridiculous," Van Hausen scoffed, but there was a hint of fear in his voice. "I don't need to borrow money. And even if I did, I could get it from my father."

"Could you?" Jack countered. "Your father disowned you a year ago, refusing to pay any more of your debts. And who could blame him? He's paid for your mistakes so many times already."

"What?" Miss Holland's soft gasp of astonishment made it clear she'd been unaware of this. "Frederick, that's not true. It can't be true." When the man beside her didn't answer, she turned on Jack. "How do you even know something like that? How?"

He met her resentful gaze with a level one of his own. "I've had Pinkerton men investigating him for over a year."

"You can't be swallowing any of this," Van Hausen blustered. "It's absurd."

"It does sound that way," Mr. Holland put in. "Frederick has his own money, Lord Featherstone. Why, when I left last September, his father had just sunk a huge sum into his investment-banking firm."

"Yes," Jack agreed at once, "to cover his losses and keep his company solvent. When he handed over the money, Albert Van Hausen told his son that was the last time he'd cover any of his losses, and from that point on, Frederick would have to manage on his own. But he hasn't been able to, because he's a terrible investment banker. His company has been bleeding money, and he's had to borrow from other bankers, friends, even moneylenders to stay afloat. He keeps trying to recoup his previous losses by funding investments of higher and higher risk, which has caused him to lose even more. Now he's in a very deep hole, without his father to bail him out. If you doubt me on this, go into the ballroom and make inquiries. Some of his former friends will be glad to confirm what I've said. He owes money everywhere."

"But how are Frederick's financial troubles any of your concern?" the girl demanded. "What have you to do with it?"

He gave her the same part of the story he'd given

her mother earlier in the garden. "The man you were about to marry, Miss Holland, owes me a great deal of money. Along with several other investors, we put an enormous sum of capital with his firm. He placed those funds in an investment he created called East Africa Mines. The understanding was that our funds would be held in trust pending engineering reports, and repaid to us if those reports showed no gold in the mines. That circumstance was realized two weeks ago, at which point we demanded our investment money be returned, and we gave him until this coming Tuesday to do so. He's been trying to raise the funds, but as I said, no one will grant him a loan. He's in so deep, not even the crooked moneylenders will touch him."

"Lies," Van Hausen said. "All lies."

Everyone ignored him.

"Having been out of the country, you were unaware of his financial troubles," Jack went on. "He knew that, and he knew he didn't have much time. An announcement tonight of your betrothal would enable him to borrow against his expectations straightaway, pay everyone off, and avoid ruin. Thanks to my interference, his plan to use you to save himself has failed."

Her face was composed but pale, and her eyes reminded him of frost-encrusted crocuses peeking out of a snowbank. "My father knows all about your interference, Lord Featherstone."

"I do, indeed," Holland put in. "And by now, so does everyone else in that ballroom. You have a lot to answer for, young man, but I intend to deal with one scoundrel at a time."

The older man returned his attention to Van Hausen.

"If what Featherstone says is true, it won't do you any good. In light of this, Linnet has too much sense to marry you, and even if you could get round her, you can't get round me. I continue to refuse my consent. Try borrowing against your expectations when I declare my refusal publicly."

Van Hausen lifted his chin, trying to maintain a shred of dignity, but in Jack's view, all he managed to do was look even more like a pompous ass. "Declare your refusal in all the papers. It doesn't matter. I want to marry Linnet because I love her. I just didn't realize it until she went away."

Jack almost laughed. Deuce take it, the fellow almost sounded sincere. He couldn't possibly be in love with the girl. And yet . . .

His gaze slid to Miss Holland.

She was jaw-dropping gorgeous. Any man, even a villain, could be enraptured by those eyes. Jack's gaze lowered a fraction. And that mouth, he knew full well, was luscious indeed. Jack supposed even a dog like Van Hausen could be smitten. But love?

He glanced at their joined hands. The memory of them walking toward the door as he and her mother came in entered his mind, and with that, any glimmer of doubt went to the wall.

"Love?" he scoffed, giving a laugh. "In a pig's eye. You were spiriting her off. You meant to elope with her."

Van Hausen gave a start, and Jack knew his guess had been right. He pushed his advantage. "Cutting things a bit close, aren't you? Tuesday isn't far off, remember."

"But what you say makes no sense," Holland put in before Van Hausen could reply. "If he elopes with my daughter, I'd never reward him with her dowry. He must know that."

"I don't want her dowry," Van Hausen cut in, but though his voice was calmer now, in his eyes, Jack still saw fear.

"How commendable," Jack replied, "but we both know there are ways to get money from her father other than a dowry."

"I don't know what you're talking about, and I don't need to listen to any more of your vicious lies, nor does my fiancée. Linnet, shall we go?"

"Linnet?" Mrs. Holland cried, but if she feared the girl would walk out with Van Hausen, that fear was allayed at once. Despite his pulling at her, the girl didn't move.

"What does he have in mind, then?" she asked Jack. "Since you seem to know so much, explain that."

"I would be happy to give you my theory, Miss Holland. I have no doubt that when he returned to the ballroom, he heard the gossip about us and realized his plan to borrow against his marital expectations had failed. But he also knew that if he could persuade you to elope with him at once, he could still gain his ends. He probably told you an elopement was the only way you could be together, given your father's refusal."

She flung her head back as if startled, and not for the first time, Jack thanked heaven Van Hausen was so predictable.

"Don't listen to him, Linnet," the other man urged

before she could reply. "He's the one who wants your dowry. Isn't that obvious?"

The girl lifted her free hand in a bewildered gesture, then let it fall. "This still doesn't make sense. If I eloped with Frederick, my father wouldn't give him anything, even if he is in debt. He'd demand Frederick make good. He might bring him into the company and give him a salary to support me, or assist him with investments, but he wouldn't pay the debts of his banking firm. He just wouldn't do it."

"Not even to keep his son-in-law out of prison?"

"Prison?" Miss Holland and her parents echoed the word in astonished unison.

"Yes, prison. The funds we gave him were to be held in trust, and instead, he used them to pay other debts and make other investments. That is embezzlement and fraud. If he doesn't repay us by Tuesday, we will press charges, and he'll be indicted by New York prosecutors for his crimes."

"That's enough." Van Hausen turned on him in a blaze of fury. "You shut your mouth."

"Or what?" Jack laughed. "You'll shut it for me? You tried that already tonight without much luck. Do you want another go? No," he murmured as the other man didn't move. "I thought not."

Van Hausen drew a breath, working to regain what was left of his temper and his dignity. "I won't listen to any more of this, and Linnet won't either." He turned to the girl. "Don't let them ruin things for us. Come with me, Linnet, now, while we still have the chance."

The girl did not comply with this plea. Instead, she studied him for a moment, then she slowly pulled her hand out of his grasp. When she took a step back, shaking her head, Jack felt a jolt of jubilation and relief so strong, he wanted to haul her into his arms and kiss her all over again.

"Damn it, Linnet," Van Hausen cried, "you don't believe any of this, do you? It's all lies."

"If that's so," she replied softly, "then we have no reason to rush off in the night, do we?"

"But if we don't go, now, tonight, your reputation will be destroyed. I can't let that happen."

"But you said you don't care about my reputation, so waiting a few days shouldn't matter much to you."

"It matters for your sake."

"What if I say I don't care? It seems to me," she added when he didn't reply, "that by Tuesday, the truth of your situation will be known, which ought to clear you of any wrongdoing." She paused, watching him. "Won't it?"

"I can't wait!" he shouted at her. "Don't you understand? Waiting will ruin me."

"I do understand." She gave a nod. "I understand that a man doesn't have to be British to be a fortune hunter."

"Damn it, Linnet, you're my last chance." Van Hausen's voice was shrill with panic. "If you don't marry me, I'll go to jail, and it will be your fault."

Her face turned cool and hard, like a face carved in marble. "If you go to jail, it's your own actions that will have put you there," she answered, and there was an edge to her voice that was reminiscent of her father. "Not mine."

Jack looked at Van Hausen, saw the purple flush of rage come up in his face and the curl of his hands into fists. When he took another step toward Miss Holland, Jack was ready for it. He moved, putting himself in front of the girl before the snarling words, "You bitch!" were even out of Van Hausen's mouth.

Jack wrapped a hand around the other man's throat and hurtled forward, using all his weight as he slammed the cur against the wall beside the door. His rage, held so long in check, surged up until he almost couldn't contain it.

"You will depart at once," Jack told him through clenched teeth, his hand tightening until the other man couldn't breathe. "Because if you don't, I will beat you to a bloody pulp. And I can assure you, I will take great pleasure in doing so."

He left off choking Van Hausen and reached for the doorknob with his right hand as he grabbed a handful of the other man's evening jacket with his left. He opened the door and shoved Van Hausen over the threshold, sending him stumbling down the corridor. He waited until the other man had vanished around the corner before he closed the door.

"Well, this is a fine kettle of fish," Mr. Holland muttered behind him.

Jack couldn't help agreeing with that. He took a deep breath and turned to face the man who it seemed was about to become his father-in-law. "Mr. Holland," he began, but he got no further before the older man interrupted.

"I ought to kill you."

"An understandable reaction," he agreed at once. "But it might be better for all concerned if you don't. We know what's already being said about your daughter, and I am the man responsible. Honor demands I marry her."

"I won't marry you," the girl cut in before her father could speak. "And the idea that you think I would proves you are out of your mind."

"There are many people who know me well enough to share your opinion of my sanity," he answered as he turned to face her. "Nonetheless, we must marry. No other choice is possible."

"I can think of plenty of choices." She folded her arms, glaring at him. "Homicide comes to mind."

"Linnet," her mother remonstrated, "that is no way for a lady to talk."

"I'm not a lady, Mother, and as we have discussed many times before, I have no intention of becoming one. Let's not forget that Lord Featherstone's oh-so-noble effort to marry me in order to restore my reputation wouldn't have been necessary had he not so conveniently ruined me in the first place."

"Conveniently?" Jack echoed. "I find nothing convenient in this situation, believe me."

"No?" Her dark blond brows lifted in disbelief. "You'd be the first British lord, then, who didn't find a fat American dowry convenient."

He stared at her as the implications of her words sank in. "You think I ruined you to gain your dowry?"

"Well, you didn't do it to regain your investment," she countered. "If that was all you wanted, you'd have let Frederick become engaged to me and borrow what he needed. Then you'd have gotten paid. But instead, you took me for yourself, a much more lucrative investment, I'd bet."

"I didn't do any of this for money."

"Let's not pretend your actions were born of any tender regard for me. You don't even know me."

"The man is desperate, Miss Holland. I could not be sure what he would do if he got you alone. He—" Jack stopped. He couldn't reveal Van Hausen's deeper sins without offering proof, and that would mean naming the women Van Hausen had raped, something he could never do. He couldn't even hint such a thing, without jeopardizing the duchess's secret. "The man is a cur and a cad," he said instead. "I stopped him from taking advantage of you the only way I could think of on the spur of the moment."

"By taking advantage of me yourself. How heroic of you."

"You'd have been disgraced either way once Mrs. Dewey arrived. The only question was who would be the one to commit the disgrace, me or Van Hausen. You'll have to forgive me if I decided I was a better option for you than a despicable swindler."

"Yes, that's the point, isn't it? *You* decided. I had no say in the decision."

"There wasn't time for a discussion of your preferences on the subject," he shot back, fully aware that she'd just put him on the defensive.

"But you needn't have interfered in the pagoda," she pointed out, shrewdly honing in on the weak spot of his actions. You could have gone to my father instead and told him of Frederick's true intentions. Daddy would have postponed any promise of a dowry, and Frederick's fraud would have been revealed without jeopardizing my reputation. But you didn't do that.

Instead, you followed me, got him out of the way, and stepped into his shoes. Why?"

He stared at her, helpless to explain the risks to her safety. With the arrival of Mrs. Dewey and her mother, proposing marriage had been the only honorable thing to do. As for kissing her, well, that had been an irresistible impulse of the moment. Fighting it would have been like fighting forces of gravity or tidal waves. And even now, despite that he'd tainted her good name, he couldn't find cause to regret that kiss, for it had been like nothing he'd ever felt in his life before. "I couldn't be sure what Van Hausen intended. I certainly didn't plan to step into his shoes, as you put it."

"No? I'm supposed to believe that you, the brother of a notorious fortune hunter, compromised me with no dishonorable intentions?"

God, he was tired of having his brother's reputation hung around his neck. "I am not a fortune hunter."

"No?" Her eyes met his, a dare in their cool blue depths. "Then refuse my dowry. Right here, right now."

By God, he'd have liked to. At this moment, there was nothing he'd have enjoyed more than throwing her oodles of American money in her perfect American teeth. But as tempting as it was, he couldn't do it. Marriage brought responsibilities he couldn't fulfill without money, and he had just enough of an income to support himself. Without a marriage settlement, how would he support her? How could he provide her with a decent home, take care of their children?

He stared at her, a girl accustomed to every luxury money could buy, and he hated that he could not take

Central Islip Public Library

33 Hawthorne Avenue

Central Islip, NY 11722

up her challenge. Even more, he hated his father and his brother, not just for deceiving women and taking their money, but also for spending that money into oblivion, bankrupting the estates, and leaving him with no way to prove he was any different from them. And as the silence lengthened, he could see Linnet Holland's opinion of him hardening, settling into certainty in those lovely eyes.

He opened his mouth, but before he could make the nauseating admission that he couldn't afford to support her without her dowry, her mother intervened.

"For heaven's sake, Linnet, there are more important issues at stake here than the marriage settlement. Don't argue," she added, as her daughter started to disagree. "You know it's true."

With that, Helen turned to her husband. "Ephraim, by now, everyone in that ballroom knows what Abigail Dewey saw. Lord Featherstone is right. They must marry."

"Of course that's what you'd say, Mother," the girl put in. "Marry your daughter off to a lord, any lord."

"Enough." Holland stepped between the two women to halt any further squabbling between them, then he returned his attention to Jack. "For the sake of argument, let's say you didn't compromise my daughter for money. You've still got some explaining to do before I could consider giving my consent."

"Consent?" the girl echoed, staring at her father. "You intend to reward this man's conduct by giving him what he wants? You expect me to marry him?"

She looked so appalled that Jack's temper flared. All in all, he wasn't such a bad chap. Broke or not, he was a damned sight better than Van Hausen. But before he could reiterate that point, she spoke again.

"Offer your consent if you like, Daddy," she said. "But you're as delusional as he is if you think I'd ever agree to marry him."

"Well, you have to marry someone," Holland shot back. "And it isn't going to be Davis Mackay."

Despite the precarious state of her reputation, Miss Holland didn't seem upset by the news that another possible suitor was out of the running. Her anger faded, and her lips tilted into a faint smile. "What a shame."

"Don't sass me, young lady. The reason the MacKays won't accept you is the stain on your good name, a stain that's spreading wider with every moment we stand here. If you don't marry Featherstone, by the time the week is out, I doubt I'll be able to find a decent man from here to Pittsburgh to take you."

The girl's tiny smile vanished, and color washed into her cheeks. But she lifted her chin a notch, staring her father down. "That is not my fault."

"Part of it is." Once again, her father turned to Jack. "Let's get this cleared up right now. Linnet has made some valid points. If you didn't do this for money, why did you interfere? Why didn't you just come to us afterward? Linnet could have broken her engagement with no loss of her reputation."

"I cannot tell you the reason for my interference in the pagoda, I'm sorry to say. It pertains to a secret I am honor-bound to keep."

"Oh, a secret," Miss Holland murmured with such deceptive sweetness Jack felt his temper fraying yet again. "Of course."

He set his jaw and decided to deal with her father, since there was no reasoning with her on the subject at this point. "My friends, Lord Somerton, Lord Hayward, and Lord Trubridge, can vouch for the truth of what I say. They are aware of what it is that keeps me silent, and they are bound by the same secret that holds my tongue."

"That's hardly an answer," Holland complained.

"It is the only answer I can give you, other than to say it is a matter of honor."

"Honor?" Mr. Holland gave a harsh laugh—of disbelief, Jack suspected, not amusement. "You Brits have funny notions of honor. My daughter is ruined, damn you. Do you feel no shame?"

Shame? Jack thought of the other women who had been ruined, ruined in ways more sordid than Miss Holland had been. He thought of the women who would have been ruined in the future had Van Hausen been allowed to continue. He thought of Stuart, and how wrecked he must have been to know the pain inflicted on his wife. He thought of what he would feel if one of those women had been his wife, or his sister, or his daughter.

Shame? No, he felt no shame. Not a jot.

He squared his shoulders. "I regret that your daughter was caught up in this, and as I explained to her mother earlier, I am prepared to do all I can to make it right. That is why I proposed to her, and why I did it in front of Mrs. Dewey in such flamboyant fashion. I knew it was too late for any other course of action, and it needed to be made clear that an illicit tryst was not your daughter's reason for being there. It was, perhaps, not the most-thought-out action a man could have taken in the circumstances, but the deed is done, and I intend to do all I can to restore your daughter's reputation and ensure her happiness. That I swear to you on my life."

Holland's face was grim. "I had far better plans for my daughter than the likes of you."

"I realize that, sir."

"For heaven's sake, is no one listening to me?" The girl stepped forward. "I won't marry him. The idea is unthinkable. I don't even know him, and I already can't stand him."

If she thought he'd back down because of that particular problem, she was right to say she didn't know him. "Then I shall have to use the period of our engagement to change your opinion of me," he said.

"There is no engagement. I didn't spend five months in England dodging fortune hunters just to have one thrust on me at my own doorstep. I will not marry you, Lord Featherstone. I absolutely refuse. In fact—" She paused, glancing up and down his person with unmistakable scorn. "I'd rather marry a toad."

With that, she walked around Jack and opened the door of the library to depart. But her mother's wail of dismay stopped her at the threshold.

"But Linnet, what about your reputation?"

"Hang my reputation!" she shouted just before the door slammed behind her.

He turned at once to her father. "Best go after her," he advised. "Van Hausen is in very dire straits now, and it would not be beyond him to attempt a kidnapping. Until he's in prison, don't allow your daughter to be alone anywhere. Guard her every single moment."

"My daughter had better come out of this all right, Featherstone," the American said, and his face displayed all the ruthless determination that had made him rich. "If she doesn't, I'll destroy you."

Jack didn't doubt that for a moment, and he was quite relieved when the other man departed, leaving him alone with the only member of the Holland family who was on his side.

But even his one ally seemed ready to desert him. "Now what?" she asked, her voice anguished. "You swore to me in the garden that what you did to stop Van Hausen wouldn't be allowed to ruin my girl."

"And it won't."

"You swore you'd do the honorable thing and marry her."

"And I will."

"But she won't have you." Mrs. Holland seemed on the verge of tears. "Not even to restore her reputation. You saved her from Frederick's schemes, but at what cost?"

The die had been cast the moment he'd kissed the girl. From that point on, there had been no choice but marriage for either of them. "I'll change her mind."

Her mother did not seem to share his optimism. "You don't know Linnet." She pulled out her handkerchief and dabbed at her eyes. "She's stubborn as a mule."

Despite the circumstances, he couldn't help smiling a little at those words. "I'm more stubborn, I assure you."

"I doubt it." Even through her tears, the look she gave him was wry. "I love my daughter, Lord Featherstone, but I'm not blind to her faults. When she says she'd rather face scandal and ruin than marry you, she means it. She won't listen to me, and her father would never force her." Mrs. Holland's plump white shoulders sagged with all her maternal disappointment. "Everything I wanted for her is impossible. All my hopes for her are destroyed. It's over."

Jack set his jaw. Only a cad ruined a girl and didn't marry her, and though he might be wild, cavalier, and a bit of a devil in many respects, he was not a cad. "It is not over," he vowed. "Not by a long chalk."

HER MOTHER CRIED the whole way home while her father sat in stony silence—a fitting finale, Linnet supposed, to the worst evening of her life. The anger and disappointment of her parents was palpable in the close confines of the carriage, and the only way she could bear it was by keeping her face near the open window and taking deep breaths of sea air.

Thankfully, the ride was a short one. Desperate to be alone so that she could decide how to salvage her future, she started at once up the stairs, but her father's voice stopped her before she'd reached the landing, making it clear that if he had his way, nothing about her future would be in her own hands.

"I won't see you ruined and shamed, Linnet. If you won't have Featherstone, I'll find someone else for you to marry, even if I have to use my entire fortune to buy him."

His voice was the benevolent one so dear and familiar, but she could not help hearing the hardness beneath. Had it always been there, and she'd just never allowed herself to notice?

Linnet didn't reply, for she knew she'd defied her parents enough for one evening. She continued up the elegant marble staircase without a word, and once she was in her room, once Foster had helped her undress and she was alone, her earlier anger and defiance gave way to deeper emotions and darker contemplations.

Frederick was an embezzler. She'd scoffed at the notion, and yet, with Featherstone's accusations hanging in the air, she'd looked into Frederick's eyes, and the scales had fallen from her own. His sudden outpouring of affection, his loyalty in the face of her disgrace, his indifference to her fortune—all lies. She'd known it at once, in that one look, and she wondered how she'd been so blind to his true character.

Suddenly, nothing about her life seemed real. It was as if she was lost in a nightmare. Linnet sank down before her dressing table and stared at the pale, unhappy face in the mirror before her. Even her own face seemed like that of a stranger.

Was this the girl who'd donned her prettiest ball gown a few hours ago with such anticipation? Who'd felt so glad to be home and so ready to decide her own future? That girl hadn't known that soon her world would be torn apart and her reputation besmirched because of one indecent kiss.

The memory of it flamed up again with sudden force: his arm a strong, imprisoning band around her waist, and his mouth, bold and hot, taking possession of hers. Her heart pounding in her chest like a mad thing, her body burning with a strange, tingling fire—borne of shame, she had no doubt, and fury, and utter mortification.

She leaned close to the mirror, touched her lips, and grimaced. They were puffy and swollen, and they still seemed to burn.

Having been kissed only once before, she had little experience on which to draw, but Conrath's kiss had been nothing like what Featherstone had done tonight.

Conrath's kiss had been sweet, tender, a proper press of lips upon her acceptance of his proposal. In his eyes, there had been the promise of more, but more had never come. Within days, discussions of the marriage settlement had begun, and Daddy had discovered just how many of Conrath's debts he'd have to pay and the enormous income he'd have to provide. He had stalled while detectives investigated, and when it was discovered she wasn't the first heiress to whom Conrath had paid his addresses, Daddy had balked, and Conrath had found himself another heiress, making it clear his heart had never been hers.

In London, she'd had a slew of suitors, but none of them had kissed her, for it was most improper for a man to kiss a woman to whom he was not affianced. It was clear that Featherstone, however, cared nothing for propriety. With one kiss, insulting in its domination, outrageous in its presumption, he had taken all choices for her future away from her.

Her image blurred before her eyes, and Linnet stood up with a sound of impatience, blinking hard, refusing to cry. She would not give in to either anger or self-pity. She was made of sterner stuff than that. She was a Holland.

With that reminder, she began to pace, nibbling on one thumbnail in a manner much like her father, working, as she'd seen him work so many times, to find a solution that did not involve marrying Featherstone. He might have been right about Frederick, but that didn't excuse his conduct, and it didn't reconcile her to the idea of spending her life with him.

But what other choice was there? Marry no one and watch her reputation be destroyed? Linnet pressed a palm to her forehead with a sound of despair. She didn't know if she could bear that, not here, not among all her friends and family.

All very well to adopt a defiant stand tonight, but what about a week from now, when tongues were wagging and mud was being slung at her? Could she hold her head up when she heard titters behind her back at church, or when she walked into a luncheon and the table fell silent? Or when invitations were no longer issued and doors were slammed in her face all over New England?

No, she had to marry someone, but who? Men of a social status equal to hers would never consider her now. And shamed as she was, she'd have no social influence, so a New Money man wouldn't have her either. Her father could buy her a husband—some middle-class lawyer or clerk, but she knew how that would pan out. Laying aside the fact that she would still be an object of scorn and pity to all who knew her, with no social sway, her husband would be beholden to her father. Daddy would choose someone who suited his ambitions, someone he'd groom to take over the Holland empire and be the son he'd never had, while she'd be petted, indulged, and set aside.

You would become me.

Linnet stopped pacing as her mother's words from the ball came back to her. Suddenly, she saw those words in a whole new light.

You would have the life I have, where you run the house, and that is all. Where your husband shuts you out of anything important or meaningful and society approves it.

She might have escaped that fate if she'd found a man here who loved her. But the possibility of that, of the life she'd yearned for and dreamed about during her many months away was lost to her now. But maybe she could make a different life.

There could be such an exciting world out there for you if you married a peer. An English estate is a far more challenging thing to run than a New York brownstone. An English peeress has so much more freedom and more power than I will ever have.

Linnet stared at the landscape of Easton Bay that hung on her bedroom wall, seeing past it to something else, to a glittering, cosmopolitan world.

How strange that a single event could wreck a girl's life, and yet at the same time, it could open up a whole new one for consideration. For the first time, she saw and understood what her mother had been trying to tell her, and with that vision and understanding came a faint but unmistakable stirring of hope.

She'd have to leave behind many things she loved. No more clambakes in Newport and picnics in Central Park and living in a cozy brownstone with a man she'd known all her life. But at least she wouldn't have to marry a man who'd forced himself into her path. And she didn't have to sit back while her father married her off to someone who'd be forever under his thumb.

She'd have to act quickly. A few weeks might be all the time she had to find someone. Because of that, she'd need help, a very particular kind of help. It was all very risky, too, for if it didn't happen and happen fast, she'd be ruined. On the other hand, she'd be in control of her own future, and after being bandied about by the machinations of others, that was worth any amount of risk.

Linnet squared her shoulders and looked at her reflection again, and this time, she was relieved to discover that she recognized the girl in the mirror.

Chapter 7

When Jack had followed Miss Holland to the pagoda, there hadn't been time to tell Denys and James his plans. Not that he'd ever had a plan, really, other than to stop Van Hausen. His friends learned what he'd done the same way everyone else had, by the gossip Mrs. Dewey spread through the ballroom.

Their reaction proved a combination of emotions: shock, though they admitted that by now they shouldn't be shocked by anything Jack did, amazement she'd turned him down, a response Jack found quite gratifying under the circumstances, and amusement at his admission that she would have preferred to wed a toad.

Jack, determined to change her mind, let his friends have their laugh as his expense. When he learned she had left Newport with her parents and gone to New

York, he decided to do the same. He appreciated giving her a bit of time and distance was a wise idea, and he had no intention of calling on her, or otherwise trying to force the issue, but he wanted to be on the spot in case Van Hausen tried anything.

Leaving James and Denys in Newport to discuss the situation with the Knickerbocker investors there and to keep watch over Van Hausen, Jack went to New York to meet with Nicholas and prepare for Tuesday's meeting.

All of them were sure Van Hausen would make a strong, last-ditch effort to avoid scandal and stay out of prison, but his method of escape, when it came, was one that none of them had anticipated.

"Dead?" Jack stared at Denys through the doorway of his suite at the Park Avenue Hotel, numb and disbelieving. "Van Hausen's dead?"

He glanced past Denys's shoulder to James, who stood behind the other man in the corridor, but even at James's confirming nod, Jack still wasn't quite able to take it in. "Are you sure?"

"Quite sure." Denys gestured to the half-opened door. "Shall you let us in? Or shall we discuss it in the corridor?"

"Sorry." Jack shook his head to clear his dazed senses and opened the door wide. "But this sort of news rather gives one a shock."

"I daresay," James said as he followed Denys into the suite. "Imagine how we feel after being questioned for two hours by the Newport police."

"Police?" Nicholas, in Jack's suite to assist with last-minute preparations for the shareholders meeting on the morrow, rose from his chair. "Was foul play involved?"

"No." Denys tossed his hat onto one end of the sofa opposite Nick and sat down at the other end. "It was suicide right enough."

James brushed Denys's hat aside, tossed his own on top of it, and sank down beside the other man on the sofa, then looked at Jack. "He put a gun in his mouth late this afternoon."

Jack's mind formed the picture, and though he savored that justice had been done, he couldn't help feeling there was something wrong about it, and he didn't understand that at all. That despicable violator of women was dead. What more did he want?

Arrest, trial, prison—those things would have caused Van Hausen to experience humiliation, disgrace, and vast personal pain—a bit, at least, of what he'd visited on his victims. Now, with a simple shot to the head, he had escaped all justice of mortal men, and though Jack believed in God, he found the idea of handing justice over to God profoundly unsatisfying. "Damn you, Van Hausen, for taking the easy way out," he muttered to himself, feeling a wave of resentment. "You coward."

"Jack?" Nicholas's voice intruded. "Did you say something?"

"No." Jack took deep breath and forced himself out of this strange reverie. Van Hausen's death, quick as it had been, was satisfaction enough. "Does anyone want a drink?"

"Yes," the other three said in unison.

Having given his valet, Maguire, the evening off, Jack poured four glasses of bourbon and brought them to the men gathered at the other end of the sitting room. His own drink in hand, he took the chair beside Nick and faced the two men on the sofa. "Why did the police question you two?"

It was Denys who answered. "They were curious to know how East Africa Mines was involved with his money troubles."

"The inquest is Thursday," James added, "but it's just a formality. One of us will have to attend and offer testimony regarding East Africa Mines."

"I'll do it," Nicholas offered. "The three of you have done yeoman's duty on this already, especially Jack. I'll stay, and the rest of you can go home."

Home? Jack looked up, nonplussed. Home for him was a cheap flat on Paris's left bank, living hard and fast among the bohemians. And he'd had a smashing good time doing that in the old days, when Nick had shared the flat with him, and Denys and James had often come to visit. Even Stuart had managed to make the long journey from Africa once a year for a few weeks of carousing. But Stuart and Edie had reconciled, Nick was married and running a brewery with Denys, and James was starting to talk about finding a wife. Paris wasn't what it used to be.

He took a swallow of bourbon and glanced at the two men opposite. "Did you send word to Stuart?"

Both Denys and James shook their heads, but it was James who spoke. "We thought, since you've been his first lieutenant on this mission, you ought to be the one to do it."

Jack nodded. "I'll write him tomorrow." He paused, glancing at his companions. "Any regrets, gentlemen?"

"None," Nicholas said at once, a reply that was followed by equally definitive answers from the other two.

"It's over then." With those words, Jack felt strangely bereft. For a year, he'd had just one purpose, and now he had none. The realization brought a hint of panic.

He'd always been a carefree sort, ready for any amount of adventure but not one to be pinned down. He'd never spent much time planning his future or brooding about his past. No, he'd always lived very much in the present. So why did Van Hausen's death bring this feeling of emptiness? Why did the idea of returning to Paris and his former life leave him utterly cold?

Because, he realized in astonishment, he'd changed. Whether because of this mission, or just the passage of time, he wasn't the same fun-loving chap he used to be, and he had no desire to go back to his Paris days. But what else was there? With Van Hausen dead, he felt as if he'd been cut adrift, and the future that loomed ahead seemed without purpose.

But that, he reminded himself, wasn't quite true. He had a new task ahead of him: not the ruin of a man, but the redemption of a woman's honor. And with that woman, he'd be building a new life.

"You don't have to attend the inquest, Nick," he said. "I'll do it."

"But you've done so much already," his friend objected.

"I can't return to England yet anyway. There's Miss Holland to consider."

Nicholas gave him a blank look. "Who is Miss Holland?"

Denys answered before Jack had a chance. "Jack's fiancée. That is," he added, overriding Nick's sound of astonishment and giving Jack a questioning glance, "if he still means to go through with it?"

"I do." Jack took a swallow of bourbon. "Does she know Van Hausen's dead?"

Denys and James both shrugged, but it was Denys who spoke. "The news wasn't in the evening papers. Too late in the day, I expect. When the police finished questioning us, we caught the last train and came straight here. Someone might have telephoned her, I suppose, but it wasn't one of us."

"Wait," Nicholas interjected, holding up his hand. "Jack is engaged? Our Jack?" He glanced around. "This has to be a joke."

"If so, the joke's on Jack," Denys told him. "Miss Holland isn't his fiancée, not yet. But she is a beautiful woman of excellent taste who refused his proposal and called him a toad."

At Nick's chortle of laughter, Jack felt impelled to set the matter straight. "That's not what she said. What she said was that she'd rather marry a toad."

James grinned. "Either way, her emphatic refusal and her opinion of you will make winning her over quite a challenge."

"There's nothing I like better," he replied, displaying an air of bravado he didn't feel in the least. After all, a man had to put up a good show in front of his friends. "Besides," he added with dignity, "in the fable, the toad was a handsome prince all along. He just had to make the girl see it."

Of course, in the Grimm story, the toad's magical

transformation had taken place after he'd slept in the girl's bed, an occurrence that in Jack's case seemed an even dimmer prospect than it had for the frog. Thankfully, his friends did not point that out.

THOUGH JACK HAD compared his courtship of Miss Holland to a fairy tale, he was reminded on the following day that courtship in real life wasn't quite so simple.

"She's left town?" He stared at Ephraim Holland across the other man's study in astonishment. He'd steeled himself for her grief, her condemnation, or the possibility that she'd refuse to see him, but the idea that she'd flee had never entered his mind. Granted, he knew little about the girl he intended to wed, but he did know she was no coward. "But she only just arrived."

"I'm not sure how her departure concerns you, Lord Featherstone." Holland resumed his seat behind a massive mahogany desk and beckoned Jack forward to take one of the leather chairs opposite him. "If you've come to impart the news of Van Hausen's death, we've already been told. Suicide, I understand?" At Jack's nod, he added, "I can't say I'm surprised."

Jack studied the other man's face, noting the shrewd eyes and cynical mouth, and he suspected there wasn't much that surprised Ephraim Holland. "I felt I ought to be the one to tell your family of his death. I didn't realize you already knew."

"We were at breakfast this morning when Prescott Dewey telephoned to give us the news."

"I hope . . ." He paused and took a deep breath. "I hope your daughter was not too overcome by grief?"

"She was shocked, of course. But grieved? No, I wouldn't say so. Given the circumstances, she could hardly be expected to grieve."

"It would not be reasonable," Jack agreed. "But women's hearts are seldom reasonable. Might I ask where she has gone?"

"She and her mother departed for England this morning."

"England?" Jack jerked upright in his chair, dismayed. "With her reputation in jeopardy and no engagement between us announced? What is she thinking?"

"May I remind you there is no engagement? She refused you."

"You are mistaken if you think one refusal would deter me."

Holland tilted his head, giving Jack an assessing look. "Most men would not be so punctilious. At this point, they would deem honor satisfied. They'd shrug off any further sense of responsibility and go on their way."

"I don't know what another man would do, but I believe if I break something, it's my responsibility to repair it."

Something flickered in Holland's eyes. It might have been a hint of respect. He straightened in his chair. "Let's lay our cards on the table. I don't like you, Featherstone."

"Quite so. There's no reason why you should."

"My wife, however, has a better opinion of you than I. But then, she would. She has a soft spot for men with titles."

Jack managed a smile. "I wish your wife had demonstrated her good opinion by telling me what was in the wind before she took Miss Holland to England."

"In defense of my wife, I believe she did write to you before they departed for the pier. I imagine the letter will be at your hotel by morning. Either way, in light of Linnet's refusal, her mother has rather given up on you."

"I see. You do realize the longer an announcement of our engagement is delayed, the greater the scandal will become."

"Yes. Mind you, marriage to a British peer is not what I'd choose for my daughter. I have never desired to support a useless institution like the British aristocracy with my hard-earned dollars. I would prefer my daughter marry an American."

"Yes, a certain Davis MacKay, I believe?"

"Davis, at least, is a young man who believes in hard work and self-determination, not the entitlement you British lords espouse. I've been asking about you, Featherstone, and it seems your family in particular has seen itself as quite entitled, at least when it comes to American money."

Jack wondered with a hint of despair if the profligacy and debauchery of other members of his family were going to haunt his entire life. "True. My brother married an American heiress, and spent her fortune into oblivion before he died. But Charles always was a rotter, even when we were boys. And our father was no better. He also married for money. And his father. Most of my ancestors have been inveterate gamblers, notorious skirt-chasers, and fortune-hunting cads. In examining my family tree, I fear we should have to go all the way back to the third earl before we could find a man of honor and integrity." He paused, meeting the other man's eyes across the desk. "Until now."

"That's an easy thing to say, but given your actions, not particularly creditable."

"I realize that, but it's no less true. As for feeling a sense of entitlement, I don't. I'm a second son, you see, and I was raised to understand that I wasn't entitled to a damn thing. The fact that I became the earl was an accident of fate. It was also a responsibility I had no ability to assume."

"Why? Because you'd rather carouse around Paris with dancing girls than do something useful?"

Jack gave a grim smile. "You have been asking about me. A title is only useful, sir, if a peer has the ability to run his estates and provide employment for the people of his village. I lack the capital to do that."

"And you peers think it's beneath you to earn a living."

"The truth is more brutal. Most of us simply aren't qualified to do anything. We have excellent educations—I'm an Eton and Cambridge man, myself. But our education teaches us nothing useful, certainly not anything so middle-class as earning a living. There's the army, but one has to buy a commission, and my father refused. There's also politics, if your family has influence and can put up the money for political campaigns. My family met neither of those criteria. Until I became the earl, the only money I ever had was doled out to me at the whim of my father, and after him, my brother, and both of them were far more inclined to spend their money on themselves than on me, which left me in a perpetual state of economic uncertainty, a circumstance both of them found quite entertaining, by the way."

"I see. And when you became the earl?"

"I discovered that despite my family's penchant for advantageous marriages, every shilling poured into the Featherstone coffers had been spent. I leased the houses to pay the interest on their mortgages, and land rents cover the expenses, with just enough left to give me a small income. Until I came to New York, I chose to live in Paris because it's less expensive than London and less dull. As for the dancing girls . . ." He paused and shrugged. "Can you fault a bachelor for that?"

"You've never thought to marry before now?"

"I may be a Featherstone, but I've never regarded marrying well as a profession," he said dryly. "And once a peer marries, he assumes a position in society that isn't required of him as a bachelor. It's hard to maintain that position and support a wife and children on seventy quid a month."

"Yet you had enough capital to invest with Van Hausen?"

"I borrowed it from a friend. Investments are one of the few possibilities for a man in my position, which is why I came to New York. But now I've lost even that capital."

"And yet, you could have allowed Linnet to become engaged to Van Hausen, and you would have at least gotten back your seed money. But you didn't do that." When Jack didn't reply, Holland gave a sigh and sat back in his chair. "It's clear you're of no mind to explain your motives there, so I'll come to the point."

Jack didn't know whether to be relieved or not.

"An alliance for my daughter with any man of our circle is off the table now. I offered to find an American husband for her outside our set, but she refused my help." He raised his hands and let them fall, the gesture of a man who, despite vast wealth, success, intelligence, and strong will, found his daughter ungovernable. "After going at it hammer and tongs, I agreed to cooperate with her plans. She intends to accede to her mother's ambitions at last and find a British peer to marry."

Jack had enough masculine pride to feel annoyed. "She already has one British peer waiting in the wings. How many does she need?"

Holland picked up a pen on his desk and began toying with it in his fingers, giving him a wry look. "I believe her main criterion is that the man in question be any peer but you."

"And you accept that?"

"What choice do I have? Would it be better to refuse the dowry and let her be ruined? Or should I lock her in the attic? I couldn't talk her out of this, and it would be a waste of breath trying to convince her mother to do so. Thankfully, Linnet has plenty of sense. She knows she'll need an ironclad marriage settlement and a man of decent character, so she intends to put herself in the hands of Lady Trubridge."

"My sister-in-law?" Jack stared at the other man in dismay. "Your daughter intends to hire her to be her matchmaker?"

"Why shouldn't she? Lady Trubridge, I'm told, is the most famous marriage broker in England. The woman has made quite a name for herself arranging these transatlantic marriages."

"Belinda doesn't arrange marriages of convenience."

"Since you are responsible for the situation, Linnet hopes Lady Trubridge will make an exception to that rule."

Jack rubbed a hand over his forehead. He'd have to cable Belinda at once and give her an inkling of what was in the wind before the girl arrived. He'd also have to persuade his sister-in-law to take his side, and given what a dismal husband his late brother had been, that could be tricky.

Holland interrupted these contemplations by tossing his pen onto his desk. "Linnet thinks you did this for money. You might persuade her to accept you if you refuse a personal settlement."

"And what would I do for an income? Be as dependent upon my wife as I was upon my brother?" He shook his head. "No. I don't like accepting a dowry, but in making my estates into homes for Linnet and our children, I'll lose my income from leasing the houses, and as small as it is, I must have an income of my own."

"If you intend to marry into a wealthy American family, Lord Featherstone, you need to think bigger."

He frowned. "I'm not sure what you mean."

"I mean, I'll stake you a sum of your own outside the formal marriage settlement." Holland leaned forward, clasping his hands on the desk top. "Say, half a million dollars?"

Jack stared at him, dumbfounded. "Why would you do that?"

"I'm a realistic man, and I know how to face facts, however repugnant they may be. Whatever your motives, Linnet has to marry because of you. It looks as if that man is going to be a Brit, you or some other. Given that you're the one who ruined her, marrying you is less likely to leave a permanent stain on her reputation. And you did protect her, albeit in an unsavory way, from Van Hausen's schemes."

"Yes, I'm quite a hero." Jack gave the other man a sardonic look. "Forgive me if I wait for the other shoe to drop."

Holland smiled. "I have some conditions."

"Of course you do. After all, nothing is free in this world."

"You and I are beginning to understand each other. My first requirement is that you invest the funds, not spend them."

"A reasonable request. I hope you have some investment suggestions to offer?"

"I do. I'm told you know the Duke of Margrave?"

Jack blinked, surprised and wary. "I do. Why do you ask?"

"Margrave is a famous man. He navigated part of the Congo. He discovered a species of butterfly. He's quite the explorer."

"Yes, Stuart's rather a legend. It's hard on his friends, for we can't hope to compare, but—"

"So the two of you are still friends?" Holland interrupted, causing Jack to grimace. "I heard you'd had a falling-out."

He shrugged. There was no point in lying about being on the outs with Stuart, not now. "We've reconciled."

"How convenient." Holland smiled. "Prior to her marriage, his duchess was Edie Jewell. If memory serves, after her liaison with Van Hausen became known, he refused to marry her, and that ruined her reputation. I begin to think your actions involving Van Hausen have something to do with Margrave's wife."

He gave the other man a noncommittal smile. "I cannot say. But what I can tell you is that I don't like being cheated out of what little money I have. Why this interest in Stuart?"

"He knows Africa. Miss Jewell's marriage portion was enormous, and from what I understand, Margrave invested it quite wisely—diamond mines, gold mines, coffee, railways, shale . . . and I'm told he's become even wealthier as a result. Africa's brimming with opportunities like that. I've wanted to invest funds there for quite some time, but I've never had the connections."

Jack began to see. "So you want to buy mine."

"Yes. I propose that you, Margrave, and I form an investment group, much as you did with Van Hausen, and that you use the sum I stake you as your share of the investment."

Jack felt a jolt of excitement at those words, but he quashed it. "Are you sure you want to do this? My venture with Van Hausen didn't go so well."

"By design, unless I miss my guess." Holland's shrewd eyes met his across the desk. "Given all his successful investments, it's amazing Margrave wasn't able to steer you and Van Hausen toward mines that actually had gold in them."

"Yes," Jack agreed, working to keep his features blandly neutral. "Quite amazing."

"Still, I'm willing to take the chance our investment group would prove more profitable than Van Hausen's."

Jack's lips twitched a bit at that. "It could," he conceded. "In doing this, we would share out thirds, I assume? If so, Stuart should have the 34 percent, and you and I 33. Since he possesses the information we'd need, he should have the controlling interest."

"I'm amenable to that. So you like my proposal?"

"Like it?" Jack laughed a little, feeling dazed. But as he began to consider what such a venture could mean, shock began giving way to hope. This could be a chance, the first chance he'd ever had, to truly make something of his life. "You've just offered me the opportunity to change the Featherstone family history. How could I not like it?"

"Before you get too excited, I have one other condition. We can't tell Linnet about it until after the wedding."

Jack's exhilaration faltered at that, and he frowned. "I don't see why not. What is there for her to object to?"

"For one thing, it makes the motives for your proposal of marriage no less questionable. But the main objection she'd have is to me. If she knows we're forming a company together, she'll never marry you."

"Why should it bother her? I would think she'd prefer that to giving me a personal settlement. Make the groom earn his way, that sort of thing."

"Oh, Linnet's got a bee in her bonnet about me just now. She won't like my interference. It'll be hard enough convincing her to wed you after what you've done, and if you tell her about our deal, it'll be impossible. She'll view it that we're aligning together against her."

He raked a hand through his hair. "So, you want me to lie."

"It's not a lie," Holland corrected him at once. "We'll form the company after the wedding, and I'll put the money in trust until then. We'll do the usual settlements you Brits seem to need—funds for your estates, a trust for the children, that sort of thing. All you have to do is make the grand gesture and refuse a personal settlement."

"My God, you're ruthless," Jack muttered, not knowing whether to admire the other man or despise him. "I can see why you're rich."

"I'm not rich because I'm ruthless. I'm rich because I know how to turn adversities into opportunities. This is a winning situation all around, and I think you know it as well as I do. Linnet's temper will cool down at some point, but we don't have time to wait for that. If she marries you, you can tell her all about it after the honeymoon. What do you say?"

Jack didn't answer at once. Holland might be able to form a palatable rationale in his own mind for moving his daughter around like a chess piece, but when it came to deceiving a girl, Jack was not quite so sanguine.

On the other hand, there was more at stake here than Linnet's pride. This was, first and foremost, about doing the honorable thing. But it had also just become something more, something that took his breath away. He had the chance to change a fate thrust upon him before he'd been born. He could control his own destiny. He could make a future for himself and for the future generations of his family. How could he turn that down?

He couldn't. Holland knew it, too, and as he looked at the smile playing around the other man's mouth, he appreciated just why Linnet would be opposed to her father's interference in her life. But Jack knew his course had been set the moment he'd kissed her, and he wasn't about to back down just because everything he wanted had just been tossed in his lap if he succeeded.

"You have a deal," he said. "Provided Stuart agrees, and with one other condition. I have no intention of waiting until after the wedding to tell her. I'll tell her when we negotiate the marriage settlement, after the engagement has been announced."

Holland bristled at that. "She doesn't have to know beforehand. Business matters aren't a woman's concern anyway."

"We do it my way, or I won't be talking to Stuart at all."

"Oh, very well. I know my daughter, and I think it's a mistake, but I'll leave it to you. If she balks at the last minute, and she's ruined as a result, not only will we not be forming a company, I'll kill you."

"I'll keep that in mind. Now, I must go." Jack rose to his feet. "I have to book passage on the next ship home."

Holland also stood up. "I'll be following you to England in about two weeks. If you've done your part and convinced Linnet to change her mind, you'll arrange a meeting with Margrave, and we'll make the final arrangements for this venture when we settle the dowry, and I'll put your funds in a private trust."

Jack nodded, hoping like hell those funds didn't turn out to be thirty pieces of silver.

LONDON IN EARLY September was less pleasant than London in the season. It was hotter, smellier, and seemed swathed in more coal soot than ever. And despite the fact that the official end of the season had occurred several weeks earlier, the streets of the city were as congested with traffic as ever.

Linnet leaned out the window of the hansom cab, but the carriages along the Strand were jammed as tightly as sardines in a tin can, and she drew back with a sigh.

"I knew we should have stayed at Thomas's," she murmured. "We could have walked to our appointment from there. As it is now, we're going to be late."

"Nonsense." Helen settled herself more firmly in her seat. "We've still plenty of time to reach the West End. Though I wish I was sure you know what you're doing. Featherstone is willing to do the right thing, and since he is the one who compromised you—"

"I am not marrying Lord Featherstone. We've gone round and round on this during the voyage over. How many times must we discuss it before you accept my decision?"

"A bird in the hand is always worth two in the bush."

Linnet decided that if her mother uttered that phrase one more time, she was going to smash her head through a window. "I can't see that it matters to you whom I marry as long as he's a peer."

"I'm delighted you are reconsidering a peer, Linnet. But," she added, her voice suddenly tart, "I can't be expected to feel delight at the reason behind it. And a peer in the family is by no means certain. It won't take long for word of what happened to spread to London. How that information will be received by the British gentlemen here, I have no idea."

"Which is why we are going to Lady Trubridge. If she can't find me a husband, I don't know who can. Her reputation for introducing American girls to British peers is well established. She's quite successful."

"Yes, but still . . ." Helen paused and sighed. "Going to a matchmaker? It's all very well for the New Money girls, I suppose. But for a Knickerbocker? It seems a bit demeaning."

"I find the practicality of a marriage broker the most agreeable aspect of the transatlantic marriage. A girl can have potential mates vetted by an unbiased third party and not allow herself to be carried away by romantic notions about British lords and living in castles. And Lady Trubridge can negotiate a marriage settlement that gives me control of the money."

Her mother groaned. "You sound like your father. As if we're talking of a Wall Street business deal, not a marriage."

"Marriage has become a business deal," she reminded her mother. "At least for me. It's not what I wanted, but it's what I've got. And though I have to marry in haste, I am doing my best to ensure I don't repent at leisure. Lady Trubridge can help me."

"Looking about for other candidates seems quite risky to me, but as your father and I agreed, it's your decision."

"Thank you."

"Either way," her mother went on, ignoring her daughter's inflection of sarcasm, "I put my foot down about staying at Thomas's while we're in town. If you're to be looking for a husband, the Savoy is much more suitable."

Linnet knew her mother was right about that. Just a year old, it was already known as the hotel where the wealthy Americans stayed, and in its lavish tearoom, Yankee heiresses showed themselves to perfect advantage for the viewing pleasure of interested peers, even though it was obvious to anyone with a brain that those peers were trolling for heiresses like anglers on a stream trolled for fat trout.

To Linnet's mind, it was all highly embarrassing, each girl like a display of goods arranged in a shop window, but she could hardly condemn the show. She herself was goods now, damaged ones at that, and she feared that even if she obtained Lady Trubridge's help, her search for a husband would soon force her to preen before available peers in much the same way.

She felt a wave of resentment toward the men who had sent her down this path though she knew her own disregard for propriety had played a part. If she hadn't met Frederick in the pagoda, none of this would have happened.

Frederick. Thinking of him now brought with it an odd detachment, as if she were thinking of a stranger. But then, in a sense, Frederick was a stranger. The man she thought she knew was nothing like the man she'd seen that night in the library at The Tides. The latter, she knew now, was the real Frederick.

The rapidity of his transformation from charming

to malevolent had been nothing less than stunning. She'd pondered it through many a sleepless night on the voyage here and during the five days they'd been in London, and she still couldn't quite believe she'd been so blind to his true character.

Suicide, Prescott Dewey had said, and though Linnet had been shocked and saddened by the news, she was well aware she'd had a lucky escape. And though she was prepared to acknowledge Featherstone had been the reason for that escape, she had little desire to thank him for the favor, much less marry him in Frederick's stead.

The carriage jerked to a halt, and Linnet again glanced out the window to discover they had arrived at their destination.

Sixteen Berkeley Street was a narrow three-story residence of whitewashed brick, with black iron railings, window boxes of geraniums, and a red front door. When Linnet pressed the electric bell, they waited only a few moments before the door was opened by a very proper butler, who upon learning their names, led them up a flight of stairs and along a hallway to a pretty drawing room of pale green brocade and flowered chintz.

After announcing them, the butler stepped aside to reveal a slender, dark-haired woman in blue silk, and as she came forward to greet them, Linnet couldn't help being surprised. Lady Trubridge did not look at all like a matchmaker, at least not the sort of matchmaker Linnet had envisioned as she'd composed her letter a few days ago asking for an appointment.

For one thing, the woman looked quite young. Not at

all matronly, she had a pretty, heart-shaped face and a slim figure that made her seem more like nineteen than just under thirty.

"Mrs. Holland, Miss Holland," she was saying, "how delightful to meet you both. And I'm sorry we didn't have the opportunity to meet when you were in town before, but I had only recently given birth to my son, and I preferred to spend most of my time with him in the country."

A pair of sky blue eyes glanced over her, and though Lady Trubridge's smile remained warm and amiable, Linnet felt a hint of nervousness, perhaps because the stakes of this meeting were so high, or perhaps because of the shrewdness of that glance, but either way, Linnet knew she was being carefully assessed.

"Lady Trubridge," she said, giving the appropriate curtsy. "Thank you for agreeing to come up from the country to meet with us. I hope my request has not caused you any inconvenience?"

"Not at all. I often jaunt up to town. Kent is only two hours by train." She laughed. "That statement betrays my nationality, I fear. To Americans like us, a two-hour train trip is nothing, but no Englishwoman would deem it a jaunt."

At the other woman's laugh, Linnet's nervousness eased somewhat. "Still, we would have come to you in Kent."

"No, no, as I said, I often come to town, especially when my husband is away. He's in America, as a matter of fact." She glanced past them to the doorway. "You may go, Jervis."

"Very good, my lady." The butler bowed and left the

drawing room, and Lady Trubridge returned her attention to her guests.

"Please, do sit down," she said, and indicated the green settee where she'd been sitting upon their arrival. When they had taken seats there, she moved to the chintz chair opposite. "Your letter intrigued me, Miss Holland, I must say."

To Linnet's recollection, it had been a mere request for an appointment. "I can't imagine what was so intriguing about it."

"For one thing, you wrote to me yourself. A girl doesn't often take these matters into her own hands. She usually leaves such arrangements in the hands of her mother."

"Had it been up to me, we would be in New York, planning the wedding," Helen said, but waved a hand at once, before Linnet could say anything. "My daughter has other ideas."

Lady Trubridge glanced from Linnet to her mother and back again. "Do tell me how I can be of assistance to you."

Linnet took a deep breath, steeling herself to pour out the whole sordid story. "I'm in terrible trouble, Lady Trubridge, and I believe you are the only person who can help me."

"I see." She paused, tilting her dark head to one side and subjecting Linnet once again to that perceptive study. When her gaze lowered and paused at her lap, Linnet realized what implication her own words had carried.

"Oh, no, not that kind of trouble," she said at once, mortified by the idea that was clearly running through the other woman's head. "It's not that at all."

"I'm relieved to hear it, my dear. That would have made everything so much more difficult."

"It's going to be difficult anyway," Linnet assured her, still hotly embarrassed. "Once you know the whole story."

"This is a situation that calls for tea, I think." Lady Trubridge rose, walked to the bell pull against the wall, and gave it a brisk tug, then returned to her chair, and a few moments later, the butler appeared. "A full tea, Jervis," she said. "It's early, I know. Can Mrs. Willoughby manage it?"

"Of course, my lady. I shall bring it straightaway."

"Thank you, Jervis." As the butler departed, she returned her attention to her guests. "I find that in difficult situations, tea and cake can be a great comfort."

Lady Trubridge talked of other topics, but Linnet, anxious to have things decided, was quite relieved when tea had been brought and the marchioness at last broached the subject Linnet wanted to discuss. "Now, tell me all about your trouble, and we shall put our heads together and decide what's best."

"There's only one thing that can be done, Lady Trubridge. I must find a husband, and the sooner the better."

The marchioness's dark brows drew together in puzzlement. "From what I heard of your season here, you did not seem all that eager to marry a British peer. You had multiple offers, I understand, but you accepted none. And while that fact is another reason your recent letter intrigued me, I must understand what has changed your mind. If you are not in a family way—"

"Lady Trubridge," Helen interrupted, "is it necessary to discuss such indelicacies? Can we not accept that my daughter has had a change of heart and leave it at that?"

"I'm afraid it's not that simple," the marchioness said, and beneath the apologetic tone, there was a determination that could not be ignored. "When I take a girl on, I require all the facts of her situation. I cannot be of assistance to her otherwise."

There was no point in prevaricating, and Linnet could not allow her mother to antagonize the other woman. "My reputation has been compromised," she said before Helen could reply.

"And the man won't do right by you?" Lady Trubridge seemed surprised, though Linnet couldn't see why she should be. Surely a matchmaker must be accustomed to situations of this kind.

"He offered," she said, "but I refuse to reward his shameful behavior with my hand in marriage."

"I see. And you have come to me because . . . ?"

"I am now forced to marry, but time dictates a marriage of material considerations. I am hoping you can help me with that."

"I do not assist with marriages of that sort."

There was distaste in her tone, and Linnet felt a pang of fear that she might have come all this way for nothing. "I hope that in my case you can overcome your scruples," she said, her voice shaking a little. "Because if you don't find me a husband, I will have no choice but to marry your brother-in-law."

The marchioness displayed no surprise at this news, and Linnet could only conclude his relations must be accustomed to his rakish tendencies. "Oh, my dear girl," she said with a sigh. "What sort of imbroglio has Jack gotten you into?"

Linnet proceeded to explain. She left nothing out, and though her face was flaming when she reached the part where Featherstone and hauled her into his arms and kissed her, she was quite bolstered by the outraged, "Oh!" Lady Trubridge uttered on her behalf at that point in her narrative.

When she finished, she waited, hoping her story had altered the matchmaker's stance on assisting with material marriages.

"This is quite shocking," Lady Trubridge said after a moment. "I knew something serious was in the wind when I received Jack's cable, but I had no idea it was as bad as this."

"He cabled you?" Linnet was dismayed. "What did he say?"

"A cable allows very little detail, of course, but he said you had been compromised, it was his fault, you were coming to see me, and I shouldn't marry you off before he explained."

"Explained?" Linnet echoed with indignation. "What is there to explain? He did what he did for money, of course."

Again, the marchioness frowned as if puzzled. "You think he compromised you on purpose?"

"He denied it, of course, but he also admitted he can't support a wife unless he has a dowry, so what other explanation can there be? He doesn't know me at all. We'd never even been introduced. I cannot believe one gaze across a ballroom floor caused a man to be so swept away that he would do such a thing."

"He wouldn't be the first man to be so captivated," her mother pointed out. "Your father declared his love for me two hours after we met."

"Mother, Lord Featherstone's actions were not motivated by love, I assure you."

Lady Trubridge smiled. "Those of us who know Jack are never sure what he's going to take it into his head to do. But compromising a girl—whether for romantic feeling or money—does not sound at all like him. By your account, this Van Hausen was quite a villain. Could Jack have been motivated by chivalry?"

"He tried to justify his action that way," Linnet said, "but he admitted chivalry wasn't his reason for doing it."

"But, my dear girl, what explanation did he offer you?"

"He didn't. When I demanded to know his true motives, he said, 'I cannot say.' He insisted it was a matter of honor. I ask you, how can honor be the reason for ruining a woman's reputation? The two concepts are completely contradictory."

"I agree. And even if you were to take him at his word, I see why you refused him. No woman wants a man forced on her by circumstance. And to not even offer you an apology afterward? It's appalling, my dear, and I shall do all I can to help you."

At those words, Linnet was overcome by a wave of relief and gratitude. Since Featherstone was her brother-in-law, Lady Trubridge could have sided with him in this, leaving Linnet no choice but to fend for herself. "Thank you," she choked.

"Still, your options now are limited." Lady Trubridge's expression was grave. "There's no question you must marry, and I might be able to steer a few worthy gentlemen your way, but the rumors of what happened in Newport will come here. Many gentlemen will hesitate to consider you as a wife."

"I know, which is why I have rather a different idea in mind." Linnet swallowed hard and tried to smile. "As you know, there were several gentlemen who wished to marry me when I was here before. I refused them, for I did not want to marry a peer and live in England. But now . . ." She paused, her pride stinging at the idea of going back to men she had already refused.

But Lady Trubridge was right. Her options were limited, and she forced herself to go on. "I know I'm considered damaged goods now, but I'd prefer not to marry a stranger. And if their feelings for me were genuine before, perhaps they would still consider me, even with the scandal attached to my name."

"You wish me to facilitate a rapprochement with these men?" When Linnet nodded, she went on, "I can try, but I must point out that Jack is your safest option. Honor dictates he do right by you, and it's clear he's willing. If he obtained a special license, you could be married at once, possibly before the scandal arrived here."

"Lady Trubridge, forgive me, but I cannot imagine marrying Lord Featherstone. I find him to be one of the rudest, most highhanded, arrogant—"

"Lord Featherstone," Jervis interrupted from the doorway, his deep voice announcing the earl's name like a gong of doom.

Linnet's gaze flew to the door, and at the sight of the scoundrel who strode into the room, she gave a groan of exasperation. For heaven's sake, she'd left her own country to escape that wretched man. Didn't he ever give up?

Chapter 8

With her brutally honest opinion of him hanging in the air, Jack knew that almost a fortnight of time and distance hadn't done much to help him. Linnet's ire seemed just as high and his chances of winning her just as dismal as they had been in Prescott Dewey's library.

Still, as he watched her rise from the settee with her mother, he noted her flushed cheeks, and given her stinging condemnation, he couldn't help taking a little satisfaction that he'd caught her out in the midst of it.

"And they say eavesdroppers never hear good of themselves," he murmured, smiling. "Good afternoon, Mrs. Holland, Miss Holland. What a pleasure to see you again." He bowed and turned to his sister-in-law. "Belinda."

"Jack." She took his hands in hers as he approached and accepted his kiss on the cheek. "Had I known in advance you were coming *this afternoon*," she added with a meaningful glance that underscored the last two words, "I'd have ordered more sandwiches."

Before her second marriage, Belinda had been inclined to put Jack into the same pigeonhole as his late brother, but though Nick had helped elevate him in her estimation during the past two years, Jack couldn't be sure which side she'd be on in this. When it came to protecting the young ladies who were her clients, Belinda was like a mother tiger guarding her cubs.

In addition, his sister-in-law was a stickler for the proprieties, and he'd feared that would work against him, so overhearing her remind Miss Holland of the sensibility of accepting him was quite a relief. In Belinda's eyes at least, he wasn't damned beyond all redemption.

"Sorry I didn't leave a card this morning in the approved fashion," he told her, "but I've just arrived. I'm staying at my club, and you're a mere two blocks away. It seemed an opportune time to call." He gave her a wink. "Although given what I've just been hearing about myself, perhaps not."

She gave him a wry look as she reached for the teapot. "Miss Holland," she said as she poured tea for him, "has been telling me the latest gossip from America. You've been shocking the Knickerbocker set all out of countenance, from what I hear."

"Ah, so she's put you *au courant* of our situation, then?"

The girl spoke before his sister-in-law could answer. "I've told her everything. Every appalling detail."

"Splendid," he said, adopting a manner of deliberate good humor. "I'm prepared to do the honorable thing, of course," he assured his sister-in-law as he accepted his tea, "but she has refused me. Given the circumstances, I'm not sure why—"

"Because I'm *sane*," Miss Holland muttered.

"—but there it is," he resumed, ignoring the interruption. "I, however, am not giving up based upon one rejection."

"And what a rejection it was," Belinda replied. "Miss Holland, it seems, would prefer to marry a toad."

Linnet made a choked sound of smothered laughter, but Jack ignored it and moved to stand by the fireplace with his tea. "Yes, well," he replied to Belinda as he cast a meaningful glance at Linnet, "she doesn't yet know what a prince I am."

Miss Holland's amusement vanished. "This is my life we're discussing," she reminded him, "not some fairy tale. And besides . . ." She paused, gave him a disdainful up-and-down glance, and looked away. "I see no princes here."

It was a dismissal, meant to flick him on the raw. It worked, too, by God, but he didn't show it. "Quite right of you to correct me, Miss Holland. I'm not a prince, merely an earl. And no, ours is not a children's fairy story, by any means."

"I agree." She didn't look at him, but instead, plucked at a speck of lint on her skirt. "Not a happy ending in sight."

So this was how she wanted to play it, trading barbs? Very well, he was game. "No fairy stories for us, Linnet. I fear we're engaged in a different sort of tale altogether." He paused as if to consider. "Something out of Shakespeare, perhaps?"

She smiled at him. "The idea of marrying you does seem rather like Shakespearean tragedy."

"Or comedy." His smile vanished, and he met the cool resentment behind her smile with a pointed stare. "*Taming of the Shrew* comes to mind."

Those gorgeous eyes narrowed, and he supposed he was now expected to scurry off like an abashed rabbit, but Jack didn't move. He didn't even blink. "Such a look," he murmured. "Do you practice that in front of a mirror?"

She made an exasperated sound between her teeth, but before she could answer, Belinda intervened.

"Perhaps it would be best," she said, her voice a trifle louder than its usual well-modulated tone, "if Mrs. Holland and I left the two of you to discuss your situation in private."

"That won't be necessary," Linnet assured her. "Lord Featherstone and I have nothing to discuss. It's all been said."

"I fear I must disagree." Belinda stood up, bringing Mrs. Holland to her feet as well. "It hasn't all been said," she added as she moved toward the door with the girl's mother in tow, "or Lord Featherstone wouldn't be here."

"You can't leave us," Linnet protested, rising to her feet, and Jack noted the apprehension in her voice with some satisfaction. "We're not engaged, so we require a chaperone."

"Don't worry, Miss Holland." Belinda paused by the door and gave Jack a meaningful glance that told him he'd best mind his propers. "This door shall remain open, and your mother and I will be right across the corridor."

Linnet watched them go, and some of her cool poise

seemed to disintegrate with their departure. When he began walking toward her, she took a quick look around as if seeking escape.

"What's wrong, Linnet?" he asked as he approached. "Are you afraid?"

Her chin shot up. "I'm not the least bit afraid of you. Alarmed, perhaps, since having you anywhere near tends to wreak havoc in my life. But I'm certainly not afraid."

"Good. Any havoc," he added gently as he halted in front of her, "was unintentional."

"Was it? I doubt Frederick would agree." Her lips pressed together, and she looked away. "You got your revenge, it seems."

"It wasn't revenge. It was . . . justice."

"Rather harsh justice." She looked at him. "Over the loss of an investment."

"You know I cannot explain."

"Explanations are pointless now, anyway. He's dead."

This close to her, he could see faint smudges under her eyes, blue-black traces beneath the surface of her fine, luminous skin. Her face seemed thinner than it had twelve days ago, her already-slender frame even more so, and he had to know one thing before he could proceed. As hard as it was, he forced himself to ask. "Do you grieve for him so much then?"

"He was a friend. At least," she added with a humorless laugh, "I thought he was." Her jaw quivered. "I was wrong."

He didn't know what to say. Hell, what could he say? She was collateral damage in a war she hadn't asked for. "Linnet—"

"I realize you think you did me some sort of favor." She turned to look at him again, and her face bore an expression of implacability. "But you'll pardon me if I don't feel all that grateful."

With that, she stepped around him, but he had no intention of letting her get away so easily, and he followed her as she made for the tea table by Belinda's chair. "I don't want your gratitude," he said, halting behind her.

"What do you want?" she asked as she set down her tea cup and saucer and reached for the teapot as if to pour herself a second cup.

"You already know the answer to that."

"I thought my refusal quite unambiguous, but since you seem a glutton for punishment, I'll say it again." Setting down the teapot, she turned to face him. "I will not marry you to save my reputation."

"So you'll save it by finding some other man to marry? Why not just marry me instead? Much less fuss."

She looked at him as if he were daft. "For heaven's sake, isn't it obvious by now why I don't want to marry you?"

He thought of Newport. "Not to me, Linnet. Not after that kiss."

She stiffened. "After you pawed me, you mean."

"Pawed?" he echoed, the accusation hitting him like a blow to the chest. "Is that how you describe the kiss we shared?" he asked, forcing the words out. "As being 'pawed'?"

Something flashed in her eyes, a glint of steel amid the cornflowers. "We didn't share a kiss. You took it. So, yes, I think pawed is an accurate description."

His mind went back to that moment in the pagoda: the heady, cherry-and-vanilla scent of heliotrope, the feel of her mouth, warm as the night and soft as velvet, the heat of her body burning him like fire, the desire overcoming him in a flood.

Never, not once, had it occurred to him that kiss had been extraordinary only to him. Terribly conceited of him, perhaps, but he'd taken for granted that the desire that kiss had evoked in him had sparked an answering arousal in her. But no, by her reckoning, he'd *pawed* her.

"My God," he said after a moment, shaking his head, laughing a little in disbelief as he looked away. "You know just where to stick the knife in a chap."

"Do you think I ought to care how *you* feel?" There was such raw emotion in her voice that it startled him, bringing his gaze back to her face.

Her head was flung back, her stance was proud, but in her eyes, he saw now that the silvery glint was from tears—tears of anger and also of pain.

"You humiliated me," she choked. "You—a perfect stranger—subjected me to your advances in front of my own mother. I had to face my father and tell him of my shame at your hands. You made me the subject of sordid gossip and ridicule among my friends—friends who, if I don't marry, will be obliged to shun me or face the censure of their own families. You say you had reasons for what you did, but beyond Frederick's lack of character and vague talk of justice, you can't tell me what those reasons are. What regard should I have for your feelings since you had no regard for mine?"

He stared at her with no reply to offer. He'd done

all the things of which she accused him, and he could never tell her the true reasons why. And though he was now trying to make things right, he was appreciating in spades that wasn't as simple as marrying the girl he'd compromised.

He rubbed a hand over his face and forced himself to say something. "You've put me in my place, Linnet, I must say."

She bit her lip. "I'm sorry to be cruel, but perhaps now you see why I cannot marry you, and you'll go away."

"I never intended to cause you humiliation or shame. If you believe nothing else, believe that."

"Even if I did believe it, does it matter? Do you regret what you did? If you could do it all again, would you stay your hand?"

He might soften her toward him if he said yes. "No."

She lifted her hands in exasperation and let them fall. "And you still think I could ever marry you? Why would I?"

"Because I'm not going anywhere until you do? Because I'll move heaven and earth to change your mind?"

She didn't seem impressed. "You're wasting your time. I'll just keep rejecting you."

"I'm a fool, I daresay, but I want you enough to endure the sting of multiple rejections."

"I can't think why you want me at all."

"Can't you?" His gaze slid down, then back up.

Hot color washed into her face, and she backed up a step. When he came forward, once again closing the distance, she bristled, lifting her chin. "All right then," she said. "If you want me so much, I'm sure you'd be willing to prove it."

"In what way?"

"Sign a marriage settlement ceding all control of the dowry to me."

This was the moment to make the grand gesture, declare he wanted her, not her money, and show he was above mere fortune-hunting, just as he and Holland had discussed. And yet, as he looked into her face, as he noted the challenge in her eyes and the little smile around her mouth—a smile that reminded him forcibly of her parent at this moment—he knew she was attempting to push him into a no-win situation. If he refused, she'd keep hammering him as a fortune hunter and use that as her excuse to keep refusing him. But if he agreed to her terms, the noble gesture wasn't going to gain him a thing. She'd savor his capitulation and refuse him anyway.

As much as he hated being thought a fortune hunter, he'd take that over behaving like a spineless fool. "That's not going to be acceptable, I'm afraid."

"Too bad, then. I guess you're out of the running."

"I doubt it, since I'm sure these terms won't be acceptable to any other peer who might be considering you, and given that you've been compromised—"

"By you!"

"Your negotiating position's not very strong. And every marriage settlement has certain requirements."

"Which your family no doubt knows by heart."

"Oh, yes," he agreed with cheer, "Featherstone men are very proficient at this game, so allow me to sum up what's involved. Paying off the mortgages of a peer's estates, if there are any, providing an annual sum for their maintenance, and putting an amount in trust for each of the children. It's also customary," he added before she could respond, "to specify an annual income for the husband's personal use. And as long as the amount is stipulated in the marriage settlement, I'm sure your father and I can agree on an acceptable amount."

She shook her head. "No, no. I meant what I said. Your income would be ceded to me, to give to you at my discretion."

"Or withhold at your whim? Do you think any peer would agree to that?"

"They don't have to." She smiled. "Just you."

"Ah, so I'm being singled out for this honor?"

"I won't reward your despicable actions with a definite income. If I marry you—which is about as likely as pigs flying, by the way—you'll get whatever income I decide to give you."

"I see. So if you deign to marry me, I'll have to beg, will I?" He shook his head, smiling. "Not bloody likely."

If she felt any disappointment that he'd taken away her chance to bring him to heel, she didn't show it. "Good, because even seeing you beg wouldn't be enough to change my mind about marrying you. And now that you've also demonstrated that your assurances about not being a fortune hunter are false, I hope we can end this conversation?"

She moved to step around him, but he blocked her, using his superior size to keep her wedged within the little triangle formed by the tea table, Belinda's chair, and him. "If I agreed to a provision like that,

I wouldn't be a man, I'd be a worm, and a worm could never win the heart of a woman like you. You are imperious, strong-willed, and—let's be frank—a bit spoiled. That's quite all right with me," he added, overriding her sound of outrage, "for weak, helpless women have never appealed to me. In truth, I admire your strength."

"Whenever a man says that, it seems like a compliment, but it's not. It's an insult."

He shrugged. "In this case, it's neither. It's a fact. If you push me, Linnet, I'll push back. You dare me, I'll take it up. Tell me to beg, I'll laugh and tell you to go to the devil."

Once again, she tried to go around him, and once again, he prevented her. "What I won't do," he went on, "is have my wife doling out an income or withholding it to suit her book. That's not a marriage, that's servitude."

"It is not servitude for a husband to allow his wife control of her own money!"

"Well, not to split hairs," he said with a look of mock apology, "but it's not your money, is it? It's your father's money. By giving you absolute control of my income, you would control me, and I would never put myself in the position of allowing you that sort of power. If I did, you'd never respect me, and our marriage wouldn't have a prayer."

"That's absurd."

"Is it?" he asked. "You are your father's daughter. A man you could walk over is a man you could never respect, and any marriage worth its salt has to have respect. And you know that yourself, which is why you're not serious about this provision. You just wanted to watch me knuckle under."

"I'm not the one walking over anyone or trying to force anyone," she shot back. "You are. You took me away from another man against my will and without my consent. I can't decide if you compromised me on purpose because you were after my fortune, or because you wanted to score off Frederick for some kind of revenge, but either way, you never took a moment to consider my feelings on the matter, and you never gave a thought as to how your actions would affect me and my life."

"Yes, I took you from him, and yes, I did it on purpose. As to how it would affect you, what I thought was that he was an immoral bastard who was about to take despicable advantage of you. But, I have to be honest and admit that chivalry wasn't my reason for doing it. But nor was I trying to get your money. Hell, I didn't even do it because I wanted you for myself. I didn't. The first time I looked at you, I knew I cut no ice with you. But then, I kissed you, and that kiss changed everything."

Her lips parted, but she didn't speak, and he took advantage of her silence. "That kiss," he said, closing the last bit of distance between them, "was electric."

She was staring at him in wide-eyed shock, probably because she thought him a complete cad and deranged to boot, and he might be about to make an ass of himself, but he'd started this little speech and was compelled to finish it. "It was like no kiss I've ever had in my life. It was like . . . being hit by a lightning bolt out of a clear blue sky. And I just can't believe—no matter what you say, no matter how many times you deny it—I just can't believe that you didn't feel it, too."

"I don't . . ." She paused, rosy color flooding her face. Her tongue darted out to lick her lips, and she looked away. "I don't know what you're talking about."

In that moment, any doubts Jack might have had about that kiss and his course were annihilated. She might be offended by the liberties he took and resent him like hell, she might deny it to him, and even deny it to herself, but despite all that, he knew she felt at least a glimmer of what he felt. Relief rose within him—relief and jubilance and pure, manly satisfaction.

"Liar," he said. "You know just what I'm talking about."

"No, I don't." She jerked, skittish all of a sudden, and bumped into the table beside her, rattling the tea things. The sound seemed to steady her nerves, for she lifted her chin and scowled at him. "You called me a shrew."

He grinned. He couldn't help it, for this shift to a new accusation was a ploy of pure desperation. "No, I likened our situation to the play, which as this conversation illustrates, is proving to be an appropriate analogy."

"Now that you mention it, you do have some striking similarities to Petruchio, mainly in the area of uncivilized behavior. I assume you intend to employ the same tactics in your courtship that he used in his?"

"Whatever works, Linnet Katherine."

The pointed use of her middle name earned him that look again, the one that was supposed to send him scurrying away. "Shall you bully me into saying the sun is the moon?" she demanded, folding her arms. "Shall you behave like a cretin, throw me over your shoulder in the midst of dinner, and cart me off to your castle?"

"As to the former, I find the idea of spending my life with a woman who agrees with everything I say to be the dullest prospect imaginable. As to the latter . . ." He paused, his gaze roaming over her face as he savored the delightful notion of hauling her off to Featherstone Gate and into the massive oak bedstead in the master chamber. "It's tempting, I admit. Once I've got you all to myself inside the castle walls, who knows what might happen? I could ravish you all I liked. You might even like it. We cretins do have a certain appeal."

Her eyes narrowed to absolute slits. "Or just vivid imaginations."

"Well, yes. That, too." He smiled, his gaze lighting on her lips. "Would you like to know what I'm imagining right now?"

He heard her breathing quicken. He saw the flush rise in her cheeks and sensed agitation in the way she shifted her weight from one foot to the other. "Knowing you, it's bound to be something vulgar."

Amid the resentment of those words, he caught something else—a breathless nuance that gave him hope. He leaned down, bending his head close to hers as if to impart a secret. "I'm imagining," he whispered, "all the ways you might like to be kissed."

She jerked, and he braced himself for the inevitable slap across the face, or perhaps a hard kick in the shins, but she did neither. Instead, she tilted her head back to meet his gaze, and the glimmer of silver was in her eyes again, but this time, it wasn't tears. It was the unmistakable glint of battle. "Imagining is all it is, Featherstone. You've already proved you're barbaric enough to take kisses from me, but I didn't enjoy the first one in the least, and there's no chance I'd ever enjoy another."

"That sounds a lot like a dare, Linnet." He tilted his head, smiling a little. "And I've already warned you what happens when you give me a dare."

"For heaven's sake, why would I ever want another kiss from you? Your first one was quite enough. It ruined my life, impelled me to matrimony, forced me to move to another country and look for a British husband—"

"Forced?" he scoffed. "Nonsense. I didn't force you to take the actions you took. You chose that course yourself."

She moved, reaching for the tea table as if to push it out of her way, but he wasn't about to let her, not with this accusation of force hanging in the air. He curled his fingers around the edge of the table and leaned on his palm, using his weight to keep her from pushing the table away. "Your father could have found—or should I say, bought?—you an American husband. Some bright young man with promise in one of his city offices who would have jumped at the chance to marry up into the powerful, wealthy Holland family. But you refused. And with the men of your Knickerbocker set no longer available to you—"

"And why?" She stopped pushing and glared at him. "You, that's why."

"You deemed British lords the only suitable matrimonial prospects you had left, despite your aversion to our lot. I didn't force you to that. You chose it. Why?"

She didn't answer, and he pressed on. "The logical

conclusion is that you couldn't tolerate the idea that otherwise you'd have to marry beneath you."

"What?" She bristled, hands balling into fists at her sides. "Are you saying I'm a *snob*?"

"I don't know. But I do know that you chose to come here of your own free will, and I want that fact acknowledged, because I won't have you throwing accusations of force in my teeth every time you want to gain the upper hand."

"And I won't be meek and silent while you insult me and try to control me."

"Any man who expects you to be meek or silent, my sweet, is delusional."

"You're the delusional one if you think I'll marry you."

"Better me than the cad you initially chose. And if you still can't see that, it's no wonder you need Belinda, because your own judgment in regard to men is sadly lacking."

She inhaled a sharp breath, telling him that shot might have hit the mark, but she had no time to fire off a reply.

"Well done, Jack," Belinda said from the doorway. "With such sweet words, what woman could resist you?"

Jack didn't take his gaze from the woman in front of him. "If I'm to be damned, I'll be damned as a lion, not as a lamb."

Linnet made a sound of exasperation and shoved her elbow into his ribs. He allowed himself to be pushed back, enabling her to step around him. "I hope you now understand why I could never marry this man, Lady

Trubridge," she said, as Belinda and her mother came into the room. "He's insufferable."

Mrs. Holland gestured to the pair by the tea table. "You see? This is what I have been dealing with."

Belinda looked at Jack, shaking her head with a sigh, but if he thought he was about to be raked over the coals, he was mistaken. "Miss Holland, I appreciate how insulted you must be by what Jack did. Any respectable young woman would be insulted. Jack knows it, too," she added, giving him a pointed glance, "and I'm sure he regrets his rash actions in Newport."

He didn't regret a thing. In fact, the more he thought about it, the less regret he was inclined to feel, but he decided to keep mum on that topic.

"And," Belinda went on, returning her attention to the girl, "I'm sure we can all agree that, in hindsight, this fellow Van Hausen was not a suitable match for you."

"Well, yes, but that doesn't mean I would consider accepting this man in his stead, a man who . . . who . . . did what he—" She broke off, her face going scarlet. "I don't like him. I don't even know him. Oh, it's impossible!"

"I appreciate you prefer not to marry a stranger. But—"

"Wait," Jack cut in, holding up a hand to stop Belinda as he turned to Linnet. "You're here to have Belinda introduce you to potential marriage partners. How can marrying a stranger not be what you have in mind?"

"I didn't come to Lady Trubridge for introductions. I met many gentlemen during my season here, and some of them were kind enough to express deep admiration for me."

"More than admiration," Belinda seemed pleased to

add. "Miss Holland was the toast of the season. She received six marriage proposals during the time she was here."

"Only five," Linnet corrected, and this pretense of modesty about her conquests made Jack feel quite nettled. "I have asked Lady Trubridge to consider these gentlemen, inform me which ones she feels are men of worth and good character, determine if any might still have an interest in me despite the damage you've done to my reputation, and approach them on my behalf."

This scheme had a chance of working, but he tried not to seem worried. "I see. And who are these commendable fellows?"

"The Duke of Carrington, for one," she began.

"Carrington?" The idea of this temperamental American beauty with stodgy old Carrington was beyond bearing. "You're twenty-one, and Carrington's fifty if he's a day. I'll wager he's older than your father. You can't be serious."

She smiled as if savoring how appalled he was. "I do not want to marry a complete stranger. I would prefer to marry someone who knows me, someone who has expressed at least some romantic regard for me."

There were times when the logic of the feminine mind truly surpassed the reasoning ability of mere males. To Jack, this was one of those times. "But you turned Carrington down. You turned all these men down. You're an intelligent girl, and you must have had sound reasons for refusing them. Why on earth should these men be more appealing to you now than they were before?"

She smiled. "Because they are not you."

He turned to Belinda, someone he had at least the

possibility of reasoning with. "None of those men are the man responsible for her damaged reputation. I am, and honor demands I be the one to make it right. The fact that I am willing to do so will give any other gentlemen—Carrington included—pause before considering Miss Holland as a possible wife. You know that."

"That is a factor, certainly." Belinda turned to Linnet. "Lord Featherstone will be expected to right his wrong. That you won't allow him to do so will be viewed as quite extraordinary."

"Which is just what her father and I tried to tell her," Mrs. Holland put in. "But she is just not listening to reason."

"The decision to marry someone is not always one of reason, Mrs. Holland," Belinda replied. "And Linnet is right to expect the man who wins her hand to be worthy of it. But that's just it. A selection of such worthy men, even among those who have admired Miss Holland in the past, may now be hard to come by."

"You mean, now that I've been sullied by him," Linnet put in, "no other worthy man will want me?"

"Linnet," her mother remonstrated at this blunt speaking, "don't be indelicate."

"It's not quite as bad as that," Belinda said. "But a girl with a tarnished reputation—however it came about—would not be a worthy gentleman's first choice to marry. These men will wonder what part you might have played in the events. They might also feel that vying for your hand given Jack's interest is not quite playing the game. Like it or not, Jack has an obligation to you that cannot just be brushed aside."

He felt keen relief at this show of support, and he flashed his sister-in-law a grin. "I'm glad you're on my side, Belinda."

She frowned at this impudence. "I never take sides. I am offering Miss Holland my perspective, and that is all."

"And I do appreciate that, Lady Trubridge," Linnet put in. "I do. But you can tell everyone I have discharged him from any obligation. And I realize the gentlemen who considered me before might feel differently about me now because of what's happened, but I can't help that. I can only hope I might be able to marry an honorable gentleman and salvage my reputation."

"Saving your reputation isn't another man's office," Jack said, feeling as if he were pounding his head into a wall. "It's mine."

"How many times must I refuse you before—" She broke off, lifting her hands in a gesture of frustration as she turned away. "I give up," she said, stalked to the settee, and resumed her seat. "It's like talking to a stone wall."

"Rather what I was thinking," he said, and walked back to his place by the mantel. "Although it's clear we disagree on which of us is the stone wall in question."

She glared at him, he glared back, but neither of them spoke, and it was Belinda who broke the silence with a cough.

"It seems we have an impasse." She glanced at him, then at Linnet and back again. "I'm not sure I see a way to breach it."

"There is no way," Linnet said at once.

Mrs. Holland sighed, shaking her head, but Jack wasn't sure if that was her opinion of the situation, a response to her daughter's intransigence, or her disappointment at his failure to fulfill the promise he'd made to her in Mrs. Dewey's garden.

To his mind, however, nothing had changed. And though Linnet might be able to provoke his temper more quickly than any woman he'd ever known, she also had the unerring ability to provoke his desire.

Ah, but that could work both ways. A torrid hint or two on his part a few moments ago had quickened her breathing, heated her cheeks, and impelled her to fling accusations of force in his face. He was sure she'd felt a stirring of attraction at that moment, perhaps even arousal, and he knew what he had to do was stoke her desire, feed it until it burned hot enough to overcome her resistance and her resentment. But building a fire like that in a woman couldn't be rushed. It required patience, strategy, and time.

Time.

"As a rule," Belinda said, breaking the silence, "I don't arrange marriages of convenience, but in this case, I feel I must do what I can to help. A pity the season is over, but—"

"There might be a way past the impasse," Jack interrupted, straightening away from the mantel. "A way to compromise."

All three women looked at him, but he knew which woman he needed to convince. He turned to his sister-in-law. "Belinda, as Miss Holland has said, she and I are strangers to each other. That seems to be one of her main objections to marrying me."

Linnet started to speak, but Belinda held up one hand to stop her. "What of it?"

"Invite us both to Kent. She and I can spend time together at Honeywood to become acquainted. A fortnight, perhaps?"

"Absolutely not," Linnet said before Belinda could respond. "I can't afford to waste time in this man's company when I already know I won't have him. My reputation is in tatters as it is, and any delay will just make things worse."

"A fortnight won't matter all that much," he argued. "The news will be in the scandal sheets here within days, and you won't be able to hush it up even if you're engaged to someone else by the end of the week. Well, Belinda?" He returned his attention to his sister-in-law. "What is your opinion of my plan?"

"You seem quite determined on this course, Jack." She gave him a searching glance, then she nodded. "Very well, you may have one week to make your case."

"Lady Trubridge, please—" Linnet began, but again, Belinda stifled her protest with a gesture.

"One moment, Miss Holland, if you will indulge me?" She looked again at Jack. "I will allow you to spend time with Miss Holland and give you the chance to win her over, but I have certain conditions to the arrangement."

"I daresay." He braced himself for all manner of courtship rules and proprieties. "What are these conditions?"

"This week will encompass a house party, and you will not be the only single man invited. I shall invite the gentlemen Miss Holland has in mind, as well as one or two other men I think might suit her—"

He interrupted with a groan. "You're joking."

"What's wrong, Lord Featherstone?" Linnet asked with deceptive sweetness. "Are you alarmed by a little competition?"

Jack knew he could not afford to underestimate her resentment. He would have preferred to overcome it, as well as fire her passion, by having her all to himself, but it wasn't meant to be, so he worked to don a care-free air. "Belinda can invite whomever she pleases. It doesn't alter my course."

"If these gentlemen ask me about Newport, I shall have to confirm what happened," Belinda said, "but I don't think we need mention the part Van Hausen played. That would only muddy the waters and could reflect unfavorably on Miss Holland."

Jack was relieved by that bit of news. Linnet, however, didn't seem as inclined toward the version of events he preferred to paint. "But if no one knows about Frederick, won't people think I went to the pagoda to meet Featherstone?"

"Not at all." Belinda spread her hands in a self-evident gesture. "Any girl might go out for a bit of air during a party. If she is intercepted by a man behaving in a boorish fashion . . ." She paused for a glance at Jack, then she returned her attention to Linnet. "It's hardly her fault. If asked, I will mention that you refused Jack's intemperate proposal and spurned his inappropriate advance." She paused, tapping her finger against her chin. "I might venture a guess that Jack was drunk. After all, what other explanation could there be for such conduct? You *were* drunk, weren't you, Jack?" she added smoothly without looking at him.

"Absolutely sodding," he lied, straight-faced, lost in admiration for the skill with which Belinda could form palatable stories from unpalatable facts.

"Good. You'll be forgiven, of course; the English have an incomprehensible tolerance for a gentleman's alcoholic excesses. When it's discovered I'm sponsoring Miss Holland, I'll be besieged by the society papers as well, so I might whisper a word or two to them about what happened. I'm sure that Linnet, if she is asked, will offer no more than a delicate blush and allow her mother and me to provide any explanations necessary."

Linnet nodded. "I understand, and there's no point in denying the story anyway. Not when the principal witness is one of Knickerbocker society's leading matrons."

"I'm glad we all agree. And I promise that in my version of events, it will be quite clear Jack is wholly to blame."

"I will accept full responsibility," he assured her.

"Damned straight, you will," Belinda countered at once. "This house party will have to commence straightaway—say, this Thursday? We've no time for subtlety, so I will arrange the social activities so that each man is assured of a certain amount of Miss Holland's time each day."

It was Linnet's turn to groan. "Do I really have to spend time with him? Every single day?"

"What's wrong, Linnet?" he asked. "I thought you weren't afraid of me."

"If she were afraid of you, Jack," Belinda cut in

before the girl could answer, "I wouldn't blame her, given your past conduct. However, each gentleman, even Jack, ought to be given a chance to prove himself, unfettered by the presence of other suitors. No man shall have a monopoly on your attentions."

"Oh, very well." Linnet sighed. "I suppose I've no choice but to put up with him, but if he does anything untoward—"

"I'm sure Jack will behave in a much more gentlemanlike fashion in Kent than he did in Newport."

Jack doubted behaving himself would achieve the desired result, but it wouldn't do to tell Belinda that. "I think I can be trusted to behave like a gentleman . . . when the situation warrants it."

A slight frown marred his sister-in-law's brow, showing his careful answer didn't quite satisfy her, but she didn't pursue it. Instead, she rose to her feet, indicating this meeting was at an end, and as he watched the other ladies stand, he decided he'd best take what advantage he could while he had the chance. "Since we'll all be having engagements with Miss Holland each day, I'd like to set my first one now, if that's all right. Tea on Thursday afternoon?"

Linnet made a sound of protest, but he spoke again before she could voice any actual objections. "The evenings should prove quite a donnybrook, Belinda. Are you up to keeping a slew of clamoring bachelors in line?"

"I shall invite some single ladies to balance the numbers. And Miss Holland is free to spend her evenings conversing with any man she chooses."

"Of course, and I'm sure I shall spend the majority

of my time glowering in a corner while she ignores me, but I shall use that as an opportunity to study my competition."

"Very wise of you," Belinda replied, "for that competition will be stiff. I intend to ensure that she is offered a choice between men of good character, men not interested in just her fortune but who would appreciate her for her own sake. Men who do not think less of her because of your actions. You'll have your work cut out to convince her you are more worthy than they."

He accepted that with a nod. "If I want her, I'll have to fight for her, is that it?"

He looked at Linnet, who smiled back at him, a melting, pasted-on smile that confirmed it wouldn't only be her other suitors with whom he'd have to do battle. Still, whatever it took, he was determined to win.

"A fight it is," he said, and bowed, smiling back at her. "And may the best man win."

Chapter 9

As Belinda showed the ladies out, Jack could see that artificial smile still lingering on Linnet's lips, and he vowed that the next time he kissed her, there'd be no accusation of pawing thrown in his face afterward. No, he'd have to be sure she wanted it as much as he did, that she'd welcome it when it came and need it so much she'd fling her arms around his neck, press that luscious body up against his, and kiss him right back.

Just now, that delicious scenario seemed rather akin to melting glaciers with matches or digging one's way to China. But there was no other course possible, not because honor was at stake, or even because for the first time in his life, he had a promising future ahead of him. No, he feared he was far more shallow than that. He was determined to succeed because he wasn't giving up on the most ripping kiss he'd ever had from the most challenging woman he'd ever met without one hell of a fight.

Still, Linnet had a strong sense of feminine pride, and he'd offended that, not an easy thing to make up for. He knew he had to arouse her curiosity before he could arouse her body. He had to engage her mind before he could engage her desire. Most of all, he had to build her anticipation. And he had to accomplish all that while keeping his own desire in check. That, he appreciated with some chagrin, was going to be the hardest part. Alone with her ten minutes, one or two erotic imaginings going through his head, and he'd found the desire to haul her back into his arms and kiss her again almost irresistible.

"Are you out of your mind?"

Belinda's urgent voice forced him out of these delicious contemplations. "Sorry," he said with a shake of his head as his sister-in-law reentered the drawing room. "What did you say?"

"I was questioning your sanity. I suppose I should know better than to do that by now, for I cannot even count the number of scrapes you've gotten into over the years, but this passes all bounds, Jack. Kissing a respectable young lady in front of her mother and Abigail Dewey, two of the pillars of Knickerbocker society? What in heaven's name were you thinking?"

He gave her a wry look. "I'm not sure thinking had much to do with it."

"I imagine not. But why did you do it?"

"Van Hausen had to be stopped. I stopped him."

"Yes, this Van Hausen fellow was a thorough-paced villain, from what I gather, but nonetheless—" She broke off, her blue eyes going wide and indicating to Jack that the fat might be in the fire. "Oh, my God. Frederick Van Hausen. I thought the name sounded familiar when Miss Holland mentioned him, but I couldn't place it until now. That's the man who ruined Edie's reputation years ago, then wouldn't marry her."

He pasted an expression of bewilderment on his face. "Who?"

"Edie. The Duchess of Margrave," she added when he continued to give her the pretense of an uncomprehending stare. "The wife of your best friend."

"Van Hausen ruined the Duchess of Margrave's reputation?" He hoped he sounded sufficiently ignorant of the topic, but from Belinda's face, he could tell it was pointless.

"As if you didn't know. Stop prevaricating, John James Featherstone. Does what you did have anything to do with his having compromised Edie? Was this some sort of . . . of revenge?"

He didn't have to think how to answer. Ever since he'd discovered Linnet was on her way to see Belinda, he'd been rehearsing the reply he'd have to give her in answer to this question. "I swear to you, Belinda, what I did to Van Hausen was not in retaliation for his ruin of the duchess's reputation."

Her reputation had nothing to do with it.

"Then why, Jack?"

He drew a deep breath, knowing he was going to be uttering the same tiresome phrase quite often from now on, but there was nothing to be done about that. "I cannot say."

"If saving the girl from the man's dishonorable intentions was your aim, there were ways other than dishonoring her yourself. I can think of several right off the top of my head."

"I daresay. It's too bad you weren't there to advise me at the time. As it was, I did the only thing I could think of."

"Miss Holland suspects that you compromised her on purpose, to marry her and gain her dowry. You do realize that?"

"Of course I do. She made no bones about telling me her opinion on that score. Do you think the same?"

"If I did," she countered with asperity, "I'd never invite you to a house party or allow you anywhere near a client of mine. In fact, you'd never darken my door again."

"I'm glad to know that you do not put me in the same classification as my brother, Belinda. Very glad, indeed."

"I know you well enough by now to discern the difference. But this girl doesn't know you at all, and she has every reason to suspect your motives. And refusing to turn down the money makes it appear . . ." Her voice trailed off, and she sighed, lifting her hands and letting them fall as she gave him a helpless look.

"Yes, I'm quite aware how it appears. But that does not negate the fact that Van Hausen had to be stopped. It was a matter of honor. I realize," he added at the lifting of her brows, "that a dishonorable act cannot be excused because it furthered an honorable purpose, but as I say, my brains took rather a holiday that night. Still, my intentions were honorable, if not the actions I took.

If you don't believe me, ask Nick. I expect he'll be arriving within a few days."

"Yes, yes, he cabled me that he'll be in Kent by Thursday evening. But what does Nick have to do with your actions? He told me," she added when Jack remained silent, "that he was going to New York to see you about an investment the two of you were involved in. And Miss Holland mentioned that you and Van Hausen were in some investment scheme. Are the two the same?"

"Yes. Nick lost a good deal of money, I'm afraid. We both did."

She waved that aside with an impatient gesture and thankfully didn't ask where he'd gotten the capital to invest. "But if all you wanted was to regain your investment—"

"It's complicated," he cut her off. "But you can read all about how he defrauded us in the papers. I'm sure the British press will be taking up the story any day now."

"I don't care about the stories printed in the papers. What I care about is the truth. Was Nick involved in your ruin of Miss Holland?"

"No. He knew nothing of that part."

"That part?" she echoed, and Jack knew he was once again in deep waters. "What parts did he know of?"

Jack gave her a look of apology. "I cannot say."

"You cannot say. You cannot say." She gave a sigh. "I'm beginning to appreciate why Miss Holland finds you so vexing."

"Nonetheless, save your breath to cool your porridge, Belinda, because I can offer you no more information."

"Then I shall be asking Nick for the details of his involvement in this affair and your actions, you may be sure."

He didn't point out the futility of that course. "Do what you must. By the way," he added, hoping to turn the conversation, "I want to thank you for supporting me earlier."

"Under the circumstances, I could hardly do otherwise. You ruined her, and the ideal solution is for you to marry her."

"She doesn't see it that way."

"You can't blame her for that."

"I don't, but when I found out she was on her way to you, I rather feared the worst. You're so staunchly proper, Belinda, and I know you've always rather disapproved of me."

"Yes, because you are a wild and undisciplined rogue, an opinion borne out by this most recent escapade."

He grimaced at the condemnation, but he was in no position to deny it.

"But then," she added before he could reply, "Nick was a rogue, too, in his day, and every bit as wild as you. And, of course, there's my own father, who's the worst of all your lot." She sighed. "I fear I've got a soft spot for rogues."

He grinned. "Does that mean you'll use your influence to steer Miss Holland in my direction?"

Belinda's answering look was rueful. "Somehow, I don't think Miss Holland is the sort of girl to be steered by anyone."

He laughed at that. "She does chart her own course, doesn't she?"

"Yes, and that rather worries me."

"Why should it?"

"A ship usually has one captain. I cannot envision either of you ceding the role and becoming first mate."

"Well, I shan't."

"Oh?" Belinda countered with spirit, folding her arms in a manner that rather reminded him of Linnet. "So she'll have to, is that it?"

"No need to ruffle up your suffragist feathers, Belinda. I'd like to think she and I will find a way to row our boat together."

"Only if the two of you can stop arguing long enough to agree which direction to go," Belinda countered dryly.

Jack could have replied that there were some very delicious ways to stop an argument, but he decided he'd best keep mum on that topic. Belinda was such a stickler for the proprieties.

ALL IN ALL, Linnet was both pleased and relieved by how her appointment with Lady Trubridge had turned out, despite Lord Featherstone's unexpected appearance on the scene.

When that man had walked into the marchioness's drawing room, the fact that he'd caught her in the midst of a most unflattering opinion of him hadn't caused him to turn a hair. But for her part, after her emphatic refusal to marry him, she thought he'd go away, plague some other unfortunate heiress, and leave her in peace. She hadn't expected him to come sailing through the door of his sister-in-law's drawing room in hot pursuit. And if attempting to right his earlier wrong was his intent, how was it necessary for him to insult her and infuriate her and commandeer her time for an engagement for tea without so much as a by-your-leave?

During the week that followed, Linnet had plenty of time to review the entire baffling episode, and though that didn't do much to alleviate her indignation or her bafflement, by the time she and her mother were on the train to Kent for the house party, she had come to understand there was a simple explanation for everything Jack Featherstone said and did.

The man was insane.

He was also obstinate, maddening, and—quite obviously—a very poor judge of character.

The logical conclusion is that you couldn't tolerate the idea that otherwise you'd have to marry beneath you.

Even now, those words made her mad enough to spit nails. She turned her attention to the view out the window, but she found it impossible to appreciate the pretty countryside, for in her mind's eye, the only view was Featherstone's dark eyes daring her to contradict his preposterous notions even as he'd given her no chance to do so. The result was that she'd been contradicting them in her mind ever since.

For one thing, she was not a snob. She didn't care two bits for titles, but other people did. And since a marriage of love was out the window thanks to him, marriage to a man with a title could at least give her a life with purpose, as her mother had pointed out. It took gall for Jack Featherstone to deem her a snob for trying to regain her footing after he'd been the one to pull the rug out from under her in the first place.

But then, gall was something that man had plenty of.

A bright young man with promise in one of his city offices who would have jumped at the chance to marry into the powerful, wealthy Holland family . . .

Linnet stirred in her seat and wished, not for the first time, that she'd been able to get a word in at that point. If she had, she'd have said that as far as husbands go, any man of any station, even a pimple-faced errand boy from the corner grocery, would be *vastly* superior to him. But she'd been too angry to think of a speech like that, not until it was too late. Why did the best answers to unfounded criticism always come to a person while stewing about the situation afterward?

Her consolation—if there was such a thing to be found in anything to do with that man—was that whatever reply she'd offered, however fitting or satisfying, probably wouldn't have made the least impression. In addition to his other faults, Jack also seemed to be deaf, at least to anything she had to say.

He, on the other hand, had managed to say plenty.

You are an imperious woman, strong-willed, and— let's be frank—a bit spoiled.

Imperious? She wasn't the one who interfered in other people's lives, rode roughshod over their wishes, and deemed it for their own good. That would be him.

Spoiled? She wasn't the one who thought money was just handed over to a husband as a matter of course. That distinction belonged to the fortune hunters, a breed of men she ought to be quite familiar with by now.

It's clear your own judgment in regard to men is sadly lacking.

Even now, those words had the power to sting, for as much as she hated to admit he could be right about anything, there was truth in at least that much of what he'd said. Her judgment regarding Frederick had been nonexistent. And Conrath hadn't been much of a testament to her ability to weed out fortune hunters. But it wasn't as if she was prepared to defy her own judgment to the extent that she'd fall into Jack's arms, even if her mother and Lady Trubridge thought marrying him was the safest course. Safe? Jack Featherstone was as safe as dynamite.

That kiss was electric.

Electric was one way of describing it. Linnet shifted the other way in her seat as the memory of that kiss came flooding back. His mouth on hers had been hot, shocking, the kiss almost painful in its intensity. She'd never felt anything like it in her life. Not even Conrath's kiss, as heady as it had seemed to her at the time, had evoked so many emotions within her at once.

When Jack had captured her mouth with his, she'd been overwhelmed with shock, outrage, and mortification, and yet, looking back now, she sensed that in the midst of that maelstrom, there had been something else, something vague and elusive she couldn't quite define. She tried to pin it down, but that wasn't easy, for she had so little experience on which to draw. Nonetheless, there had been something—

Oh, my God.

Linnet sat straight up in her seat, appalled, appreciating for the first time that amid the powerful negative emotions his kiss had evoked, there had also been a faint, answering thrill.

No, it wasn't possible. But even as she tried to deny it, she knew denial was useless. Her initial anger and shock had receded, mortification had been faced, consequences and ruin dealt with. Now, it was that tiny thrill that urged its way forward into her consciousness, showing her that shock and outrage and mortification were not the only things that had robbed her of breath and set her heart pounding and her body burning that night in Newport.

She transferred her gaze from the view outside to her fellow passengers in the first-class carriage, but even a change of view could not block Jack's intense black eyes and torrid words from her mind.

What I'm imagining is all the ways you might like to be kissed.

Just that, just the memory of what he'd said, and heat shimmered over her skin and tingled along her spine, the same heat she'd felt when she'd caught him staring at her in Mrs. Dewey's ballroom, the same heat that had become a raging blaze when his mouth had captured hers in the pagoda. Now, it seemed all the blasted man had to do was talk about kissing her to bring it all roaring back.

She didn't like it. She didn't want it. It was too intimate, too . . . too intense. It was something she'd never felt before, something much darker than the girlish thrills inspired by Conrath's tender kiss and feckless charm. And though it called to mind the thrill she'd felt in agreeing to meet Frederick in the pagoda, Jack's kiss evoked feelings much stronger than any inspired by Frederick's improper suggestions of rendezvous and elopement. Jack's kiss pulled up within her wild, primitive emotions she hadn't even known existed. *Why?* she wondered miserably. *Why him?*

She'd loved Conrath, or at least, she'd thought of it as love. She'd been fond, very fond of Frederick. Jack inspired nothing tender, sweet, or fond. She didn't even like the man, for goodness' sake. And why should she? That afternoon at Lady Trubridge's, he'd managed to insult her, tease her, embarrass her, infuriate her, and almost make love to her all in the space of ten minutes.

Did he think that was the way to court a woman? Make her feel so off-balance, so confused, so . . . so . . . stirred up?

Electric.

The strange, painful heat shimmering through Linnet's body coalesced, centering in her torso from her bosom to her thighs, and she shifted in her seat again, wriggling her hips, folding her arms, and crossing her legs tight.

"Linnet, for heaven's sake, what is wrong with you?" Helen looked up from her book, peering at her over the pair of reading spectacles perched on her nose. "You keep moving around in your seat like a schoolgirl." Her mother frowned, studying her. "And you look quite flushed, dear."

"Do I?" Linnet unfolded her arms, pressing her palms to her hot cheeks, working to regain her composure.

"Why, you're pink as a peony. Oh, I hope you've not come down with a fever." She began pulling off her glove, leaning forward as if she intended to verify her daughter's temperature.

"It's not fever," Linnet assured her, but even as she spoke, she grimaced, appreciating how much what she felt was like fever. But she could hardly confess to her mother the reason for her distress. "I'm not ill. It's just . . . it's just that it's so warm on this train."

"Well, open the window then. It won't do to become overheated. If you do, you might faint."

With those words, Linnet stood up. She let down the window, but she didn't sit back down. Instead, she remained on her feet, and she hoped the rushing air of the fine September afternoon would cool the heat inside her, because the idea of fainting due to that man was just too awful a notion to contemplate.

BY THE TIME they disembarked at Maidstone, the tiny village near Lord Trubridge's estate, Linnet had managed to push Jack Featherstone to the back of her mind and regain a measure of self-possession.

Lady Trubridge had sent a carriage to fetch them and their maids from the train station, and as the vehicle rolled along a lane carved between fields of golden hops and barley, she was better able to appreciate the beauty of the scenery than she had on the train.

The house, of ivy-covered brick, white plaster, dark half-timbering, and diamond-paned windows, seemed very English to Linnet's American eyes, reminding her of her purpose and her possible future. It wasn't a future she'd chosen, but she hoped to make it a happy one. As she stepped down from the carriage, she saw

Lady Trubridge waiting to greet them, a group of servants behind her, and she realized she might soon be standing by the steps of a house like this in some other part of England. As she studied the brick façade before her, she couldn't help wondering if that house, wherever it was, would ever feel like home.

"Mrs. Holland, Miss Holland, welcome to Honeywood."

At the sound of Lady Trubridge's voice, Linnet turned her attention from the house as her hostess gestured to the tall, gray-haired man in black who stood nearby.

"This is Forbisher, the butler," the marchioness told them, then moved on to the thin, almost gaunt woman beside him. "And this is Mrs. Tumblety, the housekeeper. If there is anything you desire during your stay that we have not provided, you have only to ask. The dressing gong is rung at half past six, and dinner is at eight."

She led her guests into the house and paused with them in the foyer. "Most of the other guests have already arrived, so I fear I must leave you straightaway and return to them. Forbisher will show you to your rooms, and Mrs. Tumblety will take your maids to their quarters. When you come down, you'll find most of us gathered on the south lawn for croquet and tennis. Tea will be served there shortly, but I believe you and your mother are taking tea with Jack?"

Linnet smiled. "That is what *he* decided."

Helen gave her a sharp glance, but if Lady Trubridge noticed her emphasis on the pronoun and the deceptive sweetness of her voice, she didn't show it. "Still, perhaps we can have a nice visit after dinner," she suggested, and nodded to Forbisher.

The butler stepped forward. "If you will follow me?" he said with a bow, and turned toward the carved-oak staircase as the housekeeper led the maids away. Helen fell in step with him, and Linnet started to follow, but Lady Trubridge stopped her.

"Miss Holland, before I rejoin the others, I wanted to make you aware of where things stand. Gossip is always slower to circulate at this time of year, but there is a bit of talk about what happened in Newport. No details have appeared in the press here yet, but I do have word that the American scandal sheets are now full of the story."

Linnet knew it wouldn't be long before the British scandal sheets were the same. "At least your guests won't be reading the story over breakfast." She tried to smile. "Not tomorrow morning, at least."

"They wouldn't anyway, my dear. I won't have scandal rags at the breakfast table. And speaking of my other guests, I have good news. Three of your former suitors consented to come. The Duke of Carrington is here, and Lord Tufton, and Sir Roger Oliphant. All three expressed the willingness to renew their acquaintance with you, despite your current situation. The other gentlemen who had proposed marriage to you or otherwise expressed their admiration during your season declined to come."

Linnet was not surprised. "I understand."

"They informed me that their plans for the coming week had already been made. Of course, we can't know for certain if that's so, but it might be. This party is such short notice."

"It makes my choice easier though, doesn't it?" She swallowed hard. "A process of elimination."

"You mustn't lose heart. Lord Hansborough is here also. You have not met him before, I understand?" At Linnet's shake of the head, she went on, "While I appreciate your preference for a man with whom you have some acquaintance, I do think Hansborough might be a possibility for you. He is a viscount with several estates, and he's quite a handsome man. He does have debts, but though he made it clear that he could not afford to marry a woman without money, I would not dismiss him as a mere fortune hunter. He is adamant that he could not marry without mutual attraction."

Linnet nodded. "And what is your opinion of his character?"

"Sound, I think. He keeps no mistress, and his debts don't stem from gambling, or anything of that kind. I have also invited several single gentlemen of the county for various events during the week, and one of them might take your fancy. So your choices are not quite as limited as they may seem. Now, when you come down, join us on the south lawn, and I will introduce you and take you around a bit before your tea with Jack. So hold your head up," she added, giving Linnet's arm an encouraging pat. "You have nothing to reproach yourself with."

Linnet knew that already, but the knowledge didn't make things easier an hour later when she prepared to join the other guests. She paused by the terrace, staring at the people mingling on the lawn, and her stomach twisted with sudden dread.

With the story in the American papers, her friends—if she had any left—were pitying her, and those who didn't like her were relishing her fall. By refusing the fate thrust upon her, she'd known she would be heading into an uncertain future, but until now, she hadn't appreciated how hard facing that uncertainty would be. These people knew, or soon would know, of her disgrace, and the man who'd caused it all was going to be hanging about the entire week, his presence a constant reminder of her shame.

Everyone around her, including Jack himself, had taken her acceptance of him for granted, and she'd had to fight hard for other options. Standing here now, Linnet was seized with sudden doubt about the course she'd chosen, and she wondered: Was it better to be strong-willed and take risks with one's future or play it safe and accept the inevitability of one's fate? Was it better to be imperious or to be a foregone conclusion?

"There you are." Her mother paused beside her. "I went to your room, but Foster said you'd already gone down."

"I couldn't sit in my room any longer," Linnet confessed. "I'm too nervous." She turned, running her hands down the skirt of her lilac-colored silk frock. "Do I look all right?"

Her mother pursed her lips, studying her with a critical and practiced eye. After a moment, she reached up, tweaking the arrangement of violet flowers and pink ribbons that decorated Linnet's wide-brimmed straw hat, then gave a nod. "You look pretty as a picture. Featherstone will be delighted, I'm sure."

Linnet strove to keep her expression neutral. "And why should I care if he's delighted or not?"

Helen stared at her as if she'd grown a second head. "Because tea with him is your first engagement of the house party. Which reminds me—" She broke off, reached into the pocket of her skirt, and pulled out a sheet of paper. "He sent a note to tell me he shall await us in the Gatehouse Garden. I've had no chance to find out where that is, but a footman is to fetch us at four o'clock." She refolded the note and put it in her pocket. "Gatehouse Garden. Doesn't that sound lovely?"

Linnet thought it might sound more lovely if he'd invited them to take tea instead of deciding that they would do so, but she didn't express her opinion aloud. Instead, she looked away, returning her attention to the group on the lawn. "I'm sure you will enjoy yourself, Mother. But I'm not going to tea with Lord Featherstone. I have other plans for my afternoon."

"Now, Linnet, is this how you're going to be? You got your way, didn't you? Featherstone isn't the only man you'll be able to consider, which is what you wanted. And Lady Trubridge has arranged things with the understanding that each man will spend time with you, including Featherstone. You can't avoid him, and I can't think why you'd wish to. It's not as if your suitors are lining up in droves the way they used to. What purpose can it serve to antagonize one of the few you have left?"

Linnet winced, wondering if all mothers had such an unerring instinct for finding their daughters' tender spots or if her own mother was somehow extraordinary in that regard. "Thank you, Mother," she said. "I know I can always rely on you to bolster my spirits when they start to flag. But I admit I am surprised by your continued support of Featherstone. The Duke of Carrington is here, and I'd have thought you'd be pushing me in his direction. A duke outranks an earl, and Carrington was your choice before, wasn't he?"

"There's no need to be so pert, miss. In order to deflate the scandal and rehabilitate your reputation, marrying Featherstone would serve you best, as I have pointed out on numerous occasions. And it's not as if I'm alone in my opinion. Lady Trubridge also pointed out that fact."

"What would serve me best is to make my own decisions about with whom to have tea and with whom to spend my life. And given his continued highhandedness, I am even less inclined than before to think of Lord Featherstone as that man. Now, I believe I shall join Lady Trubridge and her other guests."

"But what shall I tell Featherstone?" Helen asked, as Linnet started down to the lawn.

"Tell him . . ." She paused at the bottom of the terrace steps, considering. "Tell him I'm no man's foregone conclusion," she said at last. "If he wants to take tea with me, he can damn well ask me." With that, she took a deep breath and started across the lawn, her shoulders back and her head high.

IT WAS ALMOST time.

Tucking his watch back into the pocket of his waistcoat, Jack glanced skyward, considered the sun's descent, and pulled the blanket a bit closer to the crumbling stone wall nearby, just to be sure the ladies would have plenty of shade. He verified there was plenty of chipped ice nestled around the champagne and tucked beneath the plates of meat and salad, he rearranged the picnic hampers for the third time and plucked away a few stray leaves of ivy.

"Well, Noah?" he asked as he surveyed his handiwork. "What do you think? Is there anything we've forgotten?"

The footman bent to set a crystal dish of pickles and another of olives beside the blanket and straightened before he replied. "I don't believe so, sir. Not for the menu you've selected, at least. But . . ." He paused and frowned, eying the various dishes and condiments with doubt. "It's not like any proper tea I've ever served before. Why, you've not even got the tea, nor a teapot to put it in."

Jack laughed. Noah was right, of course. This wasn't anything like an English tea, but after considering Linnet's nationality and consulting her mother about her preferences in food and drink, he'd decided to forgo the typical English menu of cucumber sandwiches, scones, and Earl Grey. "But tea's an English habit, remember," he told Noah, "and our guests are American. Speaking of our guests . . ."

He paused, once again pulling out his pocket watch. "You'd best go and fetch them. It won't do for us to seem unpunctual."

"Very good, my lord." The footman bowed and departed through the arched opening of the ancient gatehouse while Jack settled himself on a corner of the blanket to wait.

He didn't expect to wait long, for the castle ruins he'd chosen for tea were at most a ten-minute walk from the house. But as the ten minutes came and went, and his guests did not appear, Jack remembered that little smile on her face in Belinda's drawing room and felt a glimmer of worry. When ten minutes became fifteen, he accepted that his worry was justified. When fifteen minutes became twenty, Noah at last reappeared, and worry became fact.

The footman held up a folded sheet of paper as he came through the gatehouse arch and approached the blanket. "Mrs. Holland asked me to give you this," he said, and held out the note.

Jack read it, folded it, and put it into the breast pocket of his tweed jacket. "Noah, go back to Mrs. Holland. Tell her I appreciate her efforts on my behalf and the information she has given me. Then you are free to return to your duties. In about two hours, you may come back to fetch the dishes and the picnic hampers."

"Yes, sir." Once again, the footman departed.

Jack sat there several minutes, staring at the repast he'd arranged as he considered what his next move should be. But he knew there was only one thing he could do in a situation like this, and it sure as hell wasn't meek acquiescence.

He took a deep breath and stood up. He left the gatehouse, descended the path that wound around the hill, and crossed the stretch of woods. Bypassing the south lawn, where guests were having tea, he headed to the Cottage Gardens. There, according to Mrs. Holland's note, he would find Linnet walking with Sir Roger Oliphant and his sister, Meagan.

He'd been to Honeywood often enough to know which parts of the Cottage Gardens were the prettiest at this time of year, and that knowledge enabled him to find his quarry and her companions without much trouble. She was strolling with them along a wide stretch of turf beside the herbaceous border, picking late roses and Michaelmas daisies, with a basket on her arm, Sir Roger beside her, and the sister following a discreet distance behind.

He cut across the turf, bisecting their path halfway along the border. He could tell that Linnet had discerned his approach, for she turned her back to him, pretending vast interest in the flowers.

"Miss Holland," he greeted, but when she continued to ignore him, he pasted on a polite smile and turned to the man by her side, whom he knew slightly from school days. "Sir Roger. This must be your sister?"

Roger made the appropriate introduction while Linnet continued to pick flowers from the border nearby with no regard for his presence whatsoever. "Beautiful afternoon, isn't it, Miss Holland," he said at last, using the voice he usually reserved for his deaf great-aunt. "Perfect for afternoon tea outdoors, don't you agree?"

"Actually, no." She plucked a purple daisy and straightened, turning toward him, but not quite meeting his gaze. "I preferred to take a stroll this afternoon."

"Indeed?" He moved closer, stepping between her and Sir Roger. "I understood you were to take tea."

She looked up, and as their gazes met, her nostrils flared slightly, reminding him of a fine but defiant Thoroughbred. "You were mistaken."

He wasn't surprised by her reply, but he decided to give her one more chance. "Is there no way to persuade you to tea?"

"No." She dropped the daisy into her basket. "Not today."

Jack knew damn well there'd never be such a day in the future either, not unless he took it. And from what he could remember of Roger's character from school days, the other man wouldn't stop him from doing so. "Very well," he said, "since persuasion is useless . . ."

He bent down, wrapped an arm around her legs, and straightened, lifting her off the ground and hefting her body over his shoulder, a move that sent her basket of flowers tumbling to the ground. "Brute force is my only choice."

Chapter 10

Considering everything Jack Feather-
stone had already done to wreck her life, Linnet wouldn't
have thought it possible to be even more furious with
him. But now, slung over his shoulder like a sack of po-
tatoes, she appreciated how wrong such a conclusion
would have been. This man was capable of taking her
outrage to new heights every time she saw him.

"Damn you, Featherstone!" she shouted, struggling
against this undignified position. "Let go of me."

A smothered sound in front of her that might have
been a giggle reminded Linnet that there were witnesses to this indignity, but then, every indignity Jack
committed upon her person seemed to be in front of
witnesses. With a lunatic like him out and about, a girl
wasn't safe *anywhere*.

She struggled, trying to roll off his shoulder or at
least get in a good kick with her toe, but he had both

arms wrapped so tight around her legs that either action proved impossible. The only thing her exertions accomplished was to work her hatpin free and send it, along with her bonnet and a slew of hairpins, tumbling to the grass.

She lifted her head, shaking back the locks of her once-elegant chignon, and found Sir Roger and his sister staring at her. Miss Oliphant must have been the one who'd found the situation amusing enough for a giggle, for her hand was pressed over her mouth. Roger, his eyes bulging and his mouth open, looked disturbingly like an oxygen-deprived fish.

"Well, don't just stand there," Linnet cried as Jack started carting her off across the grass. "For the love of heaven, Sir Roger, do something."

Sir Roger lifted a fist to his mouth and gave a cough. "I say, Featherstone," he began, in what Linnet could only think a most feeble tone of voice, "don't you think you ought—"

"No." With that uncompromising reply, Jack hefted Linnet a bit farther back on his shoulder, causing her to give a most unladylike grunt, and continued on, while Roger did nothing, absolutely nothing, to rescue her.

"Put me down, you . . . you . . . you . . ." Unable to find a scathing enough description, she balled her hands and pounded his back, but she might as well have been smashing her fists into a mountainside. "You *are* a cretin."

"Yes," he agreed without breaking stride. "I believe we established that fact the other day."

"I knew one day you'd haul me off to your castle against my will."

"Not my castle," he corrected. "That's in Northumberland, which would be rather a long walk from here. But I am taking you to a castle, and though it's not mine, it'll have to do."

Linnet felt a pang of alarm at those words. Do for what? Was he intending to ravish her inside the walls of some nearby ruin? Not that she knew what ravishment was, precisely, but whatever it entailed, she'd probably have to marry him afterward, and that would suit his book.

He wouldn't dare. Would he?

Linnet realized in dismay that she couldn't be quite sure about that.

You give me a dare, I'll take it up.

The memory of those words was sufficient to renew Linnet's struggles to free herself, but the result was that she ended up out of breath, while he—after carting her through a grove of trees, across a meadow, and halfway up a hill—was barely winded. She decided it was time to try a different tactic.

"All right," she said in as lofty a tone as she could manage, given that she was wearing a whalebone corset and his shoulder was lodged against her tummy like a rock, "you've made your point."

"Knowing you, I doubt it."

"You can put me down now."

He didn't pause. "I don't think so."

"For heaven's sake, you've brought me to the middle of nowhere. It's not as if I'd go running off alone. I do have some sense."

"That's a debatable point."

She punched him, hard, right between the shoulder

blades, but he didn't even flinch. "Damn it, Jack, I can't breathe."

Chivalry, of course, was a concept this man did not understand, so even that appeal wasn't enough to make him put her down. He pitched her forward a few inches to better enable her to breathe and kept on walking.

It wasn't until he'd reached the top of the grass-covered hill that he stopped. "Before I set you down," he said, "I am honor-bound to warn you—"

"Honor-bound?" she cut in, panting. "Is that supposed to be amusing?"

"I am honor-bound to warn you that I was among the fastest footballers at Cambridge. If you bolt, you won't get ten feet before I catch you. And if that happens, well . . ." His voice trailed away, leaving unmistakably sinister implications hanging in the air.

"I won't run," she promised at once. "As I told you before, I've got some sense. I know it would be useless."

"Good." He moved as if to free her at last, but any relief she might have felt was mitigated at once, because as he slid her off his shoulder, his hand cupped her bottom, and though she knew it was to ease her to the ground, she couldn't help a gasp of shock, not just because no man had ever dared to touch her there in her entire life, but also because even through the layers of her clothing, his palm felt blazing hot.

If he noticed her discomfiture at such intimate contact, he didn't show it. His hand slid away at once, his arms freed her, and he straightened. "Shall we?" he asked, gesturing to something behind her.

Shoving loose tresses of hair out of her face, she

turned and found the crumbling, ivy-covered wall of a medieval gatehouse in front of her. Through the arched doorway at its center, she could see the tumbledown walls of what had once been castle fortifications. In their midst, a blanket had been spread over the grass, and on it, cushions, picnic baskets, and napkin-covered plates of food had been arranged. An ice bucket containing a bottle of champagne reposed on a block of ancient stone nearby, its silver surface gleaming in the late-afternoon sun.

Linnet moved through the archway, and as she approached the blanket he'd laid out, she noted the china and crystal, and the care he'd taken with the arrangements, and she felt the sting of her conscience. When she paused at the edge of the blanket, he paused beside her, and she slid a sideways glance at him. His lean, handsome face was grave as he looked back at her, but she could read nothing in those dark, dark eyes.

"This is highly improper," she pointed out, desperate for something to say. "We have no chaperone."

Even as the words came out of her mouth, she appreciated that the lack of a chaperone was partly her own fault, and she hastened on, "You should have asked me to tea. Not commandeered me."

"Would you have come? Be honest," he said, as she started to answer. "Had I asked you directly, would you have said yes?"

"I don't know. I wasn't given the chance to decide."

He didn't reply, but he continued to watch her, waiting, and at last she gave a sigh. "Probably not," she conceded. "But that isn't the point."

"It is the point. Because . . ." He turned and bent

down to retrieve a cloth-covered basket. "If you hadn't come, you'd have missed these."

He pulled back the red-and-white-checked covering, and at the sight of what was inside, Linnet gave a cry of surprise. "Muffins?"

"So I'm told." He studied them, looking doubtful. "They seem more like tea cakes to me, but Mrs. Fraser assured me she followed the receipt in every detail."

"Receipt?" She was taken aback, and it took her a moment to understand the English nomenclature. "Oh, you mean *recipe*," she said, laughing a little. "But how on earth did an English cook have a recipe for blueberry muffins? Even the Savoy doesn't make them."

He shrugged, as if presenting her with a food that was as rare in England as hen's teeth was no great feat. "I cabled your cook in New York a few days ago, asking him to cable back the receipt, which he did. I couldn't obtain fresh blueberries, since we don't seem to grow them in England. Still, I managed to find a tin of them at a grocer's in London before I came down."

"You went shopping for blueberries so that we could have American muffins for tea?"

"Yes, well, blueberry muffins are a particular favorite food of yours. At least, that's what I was told."

Linnet stared at him, confounded. Cabling for her cook's recipe, shopping for the proper ingredients, arranging for Lady Trubridge's cook to prepare them—all because she liked them?

"I know your custom is to have them for breakfast," he went on before she could recover enough to reply. "But I thought they'd be all right for tea although it's not tea, not anymore. Your mother informed me you don't much care for the custom, so I changed the menu a bit and made this outing more like a picnic. You do like picnics, she told me."

"You—" She broke off, staring at the muffins, memories coming back to her, memories of Conrath and little gifts very much like this one. She swallowed, forcing herself to say something. "You went to a great deal of trouble."

"Yes," he said. "I did."

A nuance in his voice caused her to look up, and when she met his gaze, she was taken aback by what she saw. His eyes were so dark they appeared black, and yet, despite the seeming impenetrability of their color, they were not opaque.

She'd hurt him.

The discovery astonished her. She'd never have thought she had any power over his feelings. She'd have deemed him impervious to hurt—callous, even. But looking at him now, she knew she'd have been wrong to think that. Quite, quite wrong.

A strange tightness squeezed her chest and made it hard to breathe. "I didn't realize you would do . . . all this." She waved a hand to the picnic arrangements. "I assumed you'd just order tea and crumpets, or what have you, from the kitchens. I didn't think you'd take such pains—finding out my favorite foods, shopping for blueberries, consulting with cooks—" She stopped, took a deep breath, and met his gaze again. "I'm sorry I didn't come."

"Apology accepted," he said at once. "And I'm sorry I commandeered your time rather than asked for it."

She nodded, but when she reached out her hand to take a muffin, he pulled the basket back, out of her reach.

"These muffins are my way of holding out the olive branch," he told her. "From now on, I promise to invite you for outings and engagements rather than attempt to commandeer you. But in return, I'd like you to make a promise to me."

That made her smile a little. "And I suppose my promise should be to always say yes to these outings of yours?"

"No. You don't always have to say yes. All I want you to promise is to give me a second chance. The same chance you're giving the other chaps here."

"Lady Trubridge has already given you that. She invited you here."

"That's not what I mean, and you know it. I'm talking about a fair chance, Linnet. That means you'll have to put aside the preconceived ideas you've formed about me and about my character. Can you do that?"

She considered. "It won't be an easy thing for me," she confessed, and though acknowledging that he'd been right about certain facets of her character was a difficult admission to have to make, she made it. "I am somewhat . . . strong-willed, you see. Imperious, even. And maybe a little bit spoiled. At least, that's what I've been told."

She watched him smile, and she felt compelled to add, "But, just so you know, I am not a snob. It was most unfair of you to say so."

"Then it seems I, too, will have to put aside some preconceived ideas." He held out the basket again. "Truce?"

She considered. If they called a truce, she had no doubt he'd find a way to take advantage of it. Still . . . she looked down at the muffins, and her resolve crumbled.

"All right, it's a truce," she agreed, but she couldn't help giving him a wry look as she took a muffin and sat down on the blanket. "Why do I feel I'm making a deal with the devil?"

"Because you are," he answered as he sat down opposite her. "And I mean that in a literal sense."

He laughed at her bewildered expression, but he set the basket of muffins beside them and retrieved a pair of plates from the nearest picnic basket before he explained. "Devil," he said as he put one of the plates in front of her, "was my nickname at school."

She wrinkled up her nose at him. "How appropriate."

"You have no idea. I was always getting into scrapes and causing trouble. Breaking curfew. Setting off fire-crackers under the dean's window at midnight. Walking on the grass—which at Eton is one of the gravest sins imaginable. Hiding my tutor's chalk, kidnapping his dog. Dumping salt in the Eton Mess. That sort of thing."

She frowned, perplexed. "Eton Mess?"

"It's a dessert. Strawberries, crushed meringues, and cream. It's served on Prize-Giving Day in June, when all the parents come to visit."

She couldn't help laughing. "Salt?"

"Yes, well, my years at Eton are rather legendary. Never were the tutors happier to see a boy go than when I departed their hallowed halls. Cambridge wasn't any better. I was so wild there, I was very nearly sent down."

"Sent down? You mean expelled? Why?" she asked, as he nodded. "What did you do?"

He grinned. "Which time?"

She laughed. "You were in danger of expulsion more than once? For what? More pranks?"

"Well, yes, among other things."

"Gambling?" she guessed.

"No, I couldn't afford to gamble, for I hadn't the blunt. No, I spent what little money I had on other things."

"Drink?"

"Of course. Drink, women . . . but I could be heading into dangerous territory with this topic, so enough about me. What about you? Did you have a nickname as a child?"

She wanted to know more about the women, but she didn't want to display any curiosity on the subject, so she was forced to let it drop. "I did have a nickname, but I shan't tell it to you."

"Why not?" He eyed her with sympathy. "Was it very horrid?"

Linnet's mind flashed back to the merciless teasing of her childhood. "Very," she said, and gave a shrug as if it didn't matter. Gesturing to the plates and baskets all around them, she went on, "Are we going to eat this food, or are we going to let the ants have it all?"

"I say we eat it. The ants can starve. But do you not want to eat your muffin first?"

She smiled at the reminder. Returning her attention to the treat on her plate, she broke it apart and took a bite.

"Well," he asked. "Does it pass muster?"

"Umm-hmm," she murmured around a mouthful of

muffin, savoring the taste of her favorite treat as she chewed and swallowed. "It's delicious. Almost as good as the ones back home."

"Almost?" he echoed as if in disbelief, but she wasn't fooled. She could tell her pronouncement pleased him, for an unmistakable smile curved the corners of his mouth and creased the edges of his eyes. "Almost?"

"Well, something like this is never quite the same when some other cook makes it," she explained. "It's always a little different. But these are very close. And so much better than the ones the Savoy tried to make for me."

"Perhaps, but still . . ." He paused, and his smile took on a devilish curve that had no doubt been just as responsible for his nickname as his pranks had been. "If it's not as good as the ones back home, perhaps you shouldn't have any more."

He reached for her plate, but she snatched it back. "No, no," she protested, laughing as she turned away to keep her treat out of his reach. "Don't take my muffin."

He rose on his knees behind her, leaning closer. "But Linnet, I'd hate for your discerning palate to be compromised with inferior muffins. If it isn't good enough—"

"I never said that." She twisted, still laughing, shifting her plate from one hand to the other as his arms came up on either side of her to reach for it. "It's wonderful. Perfect. Every bit as good as our cook's, I swear."

"That's a relief. I should hate to think my peace offering tasted like sawdust." His arms fell to his sides, but he didn't move away. Instead, he bent down, leaning closer. "I'd be in dire straits then," he murmured, his breath stirring the loose tendril of hair at her cheek. "You might take back our truce."

She froze, paralyzed by a sudden jolt of nervousness, and she didn't know why. It was just a muffin, and he wasn't even touching her. "I won't take it back," she blurted out, her hands clenching tight around her plate.

"No?"

She shook her head, and much to her relief, he returned to his side of the blanket, enabling her to turn around.

"Good," he said, tilting his head as he looked at her. "Because if you did, it would grieve me enormously, Linnet."

His smile was gone, his expression grave as he looked at her, and she felt again that tight pinch in her chest, a pang of pain and pleasure mixed with a hefty dollop of insecurity. It wasn't something she was often inclined to feel, and she was impelled to look away, seeking a distraction.

"What have we here?" she asked, pulling the napkin back from one of the plates beside her. "Ham. How lovely."

Her voice sounded so arch and artificial, it made her wince, but if he noticed, he didn't tease her about it. "I suppose that's another hint that it's time to eat," he said and opened the picnic basket closest to him. "There's chicken and salad by you as well," he told her, nodding to the other plates on the grass by her hip as he began pulling bread, cheese, and little pots of butter and mustard out of the basket.

But if she thought he was done teasing her, she was mistaken. "I hope you realize," he said as he began tearing bread into pieces, "that these diversionary tactics of yours aren't going to work."

"Diversionary tactics?" She reached for a piece of the bread and a knife. "I don't know what you mean," she said as she spread some of the soft cheese onto her hunk of bread.

"There is a concept called *quid pro quo*," he explained. "And since I learned Latin at school, among many other useless things, I can tell you that it translates roughly as, 'something for something.'"

Maybe all his teasing was muddling her brain, for she didn't have a clue what he was talking about. Her bafflement must have shown on her face, for he went on, "I told you my nickname. So that means you have to tell me yours."

"I don't have to do anything just because you expect it," she reminded, but though he grinned at that, he continued to look at her, waiting.

She tried to ignore him. She pulled some ham and chicken onto her plate, reached for a fork, and went on eating, but his gaze remained fixed on her, and she gave up. "Oh, for heaven's sake," she cried, setting down her plate, "what does it matter what my nickname was?"

His grin widened. "Because it's so obvious you don't want to tell me. You've piqued my curiosity, and I shall pursue this topic with relentless zeal."

"Even so, your curiosity shall remain unsatisfied," she said primly, and gestured to the champagne. "Are you going to open that or let it grow warm?"

"I'm happy to open it, but you can't have any."

"Why not?" She straightened on the blanket, indignant. "Because I won't tell you my nickname?"

"I would never use champagne as leverage of that kind. No, no. It's just that I was told you prefer ginger ale, so I brought that for you instead."

"Told? By whom?" The moment the question was out of her mouth, she groaned. "My mother, I suppose?"

He nodded, pulling the bottle from the ice bucket. "After I learned tea was not a favorite beverage of yours, I decided to change our outing to a picnic," he explained as he opened the champagne. "When I inquired of your mother what wine you would prefer, she told me ginger ale would do for you quite nicely. A young lady, she informed me, does not drink wine until after six o'clock."

Linnet rolled her eyes and took a bite of ham. "As if the time of day has anything to do with it. My mother thinks it is inappropriate for an unmarried woman to drink anything at any time. She glares daggers at me whenever I defy her and do it anyway."

"Ah." The cork popped, and he reached for one of the flutes that sat on the rock behind him. "That's why she scowled at you with such ferocity when you were drinking sherry in Newport."

"Well, that was your fault," Linnet told him, taking the filled glass he held out to her. "She was pushing you at me, pointing out I still had a chance to marry a lord, going on and on about you to such a nauseating degree that I felt in desperate need of a drink. But," she added, struck by a sudden thought, "how did you know sherry was what I was drinking that night? There were trays of port going around the ballroom, too, as I recall."

He smiled a little as he filled a champagne flute for himself. "You weren't drinking port."

He spoke with such positive assurance she felt impelled to debate the point. "Tawny port and cream sherry look alike. You cannot know for certain which of the two I was drinking."

"But I can." He set the bottle back in the ice and returned his attention to her. "I know you were drinking sherry because I tasted it on your mouth."

"Oh." Heat flooded through her, so sudden and overpowering that she couldn't move, or even breathe. Her heart began to pound with painful force. This was the same sensation she'd felt when he'd stared at her so openly at Mrs. Dewey's ball, and how he'd looked at her that afternoon in Lady Trubridge's drawing room, and she supposed she ought to be used to it by now, but she wasn't. In fact, here alone with him in the middle of nowhere, it seemed more potent than ever. It was almost like . . . pleasure.

His lashes lowered as he looked at her lips, and she could only watch, immobile, fixed by his gaze like a butterfly on a pin, knowing he was remembering the sherry-laced taste of her kiss. The pleasure was unmistakable now, unfurling inside her like flowers opening in the sun.

His gaze moved lower, to where her heart was thudding in her chest, and the heat and tension inside her deepened and spread, radiating outward until she was tingling from head to toe, and she was sure she must be blushing all over. It became unbearable, and she tore her gaze away.

"Rabbit," she choked, desperate enough that confessing one of her worst childhood memories seemed an easy choice. Better that than to sit here silent with his intense, heated gaze on her and his mind imagining any number of naughty things. "My nickname as a girl was Rabbit."

"What?" He made a sound of derision, and she was relieved that he seemed distracted from her lips at last. "That's the most ill-fitting nickname I've heard in my life, for I can't imagine any woman less like a rabbit than you."

"Yes, well, timidity wasn't the reason." She took a gulp from her glass, and the sparkling wine burned her throat as she swallowed. "My teeth stuck out," she explained, striving to seem nonchalant about something that was, after all, a long time ago. "And my skin has always been quite pale, and my hair was very light when I was a little girl, almost white. So the other girls teased me and called me Rabbit. Luckily, my hair got darker as I got older, and my mother found a dentist to put a plate on my teeth and straighten them. But when I was ten, I fear I did look rather like a rabbit."

"Still, that is not a nickname," he said, sounding appalled. "It's a taunt, and that's a different thing altogether. And looks aside, I'd wager that even as a little girl, you had the soul of a lioness. That could be your new nickname." His smile returned, wry this time. "It suits, for you've certainly scratched me a time or two."

"Only when you've deserved it."

"Lioness it is, then. But I'm curious, why such reluctance to tell me the story?"

It was her turn for a wry smile. "Yes, well, now you know another one of my flaws. Vanity. I don't like being reminded of how plain I was as a child."

"Or you don't like the fact that it still hurts how much you were teased."

"It's silly, I know," she said with a shrug, trying to sound as if it didn't matter. "One should be over that sort of thing by the time one has grown up."

"Perhaps, but it's not an easy thing to do, especially for someone like you."

"Thank you for underscoring my point about my vanity," she said, making a face at him.

"You're not vain, Linnet. You're proud, and that's a whole different thing."

"I'm not sure that's better," she said jokingly, and took a swallow of champagne. "You know what they say about pride. It goes before a fall, doesn't it?"

She watched his lips press together, and she regretted her words at once. "I didn't mean to bring that up. It's bad enough that you think me a shrew. You mustn't think I'm some sort of . . . of nagging fishwife, too. What?" she demanded as his mouth began curving upward. "Why are you smiling?"

"Because I'm making headway."

She looked away with a toss of her head. "That's your vivid imagination at work."

"No, it's not." Setting aside his champagne, he moved closer, his hip brushing her knee as he stretched out his long legs beside her. "You are starting to care what I think, so I must be making headway."

She felt impelled to retreat to safer ground. "I only meant that I'm stuck with you all week, and I can't very well keep throwing what happened in your face and blaming you. At some point, for the sake of civility, if nothing else, I am forced to give you the benefit of the doubt."

"Though I always favor being given the benefit of the

doubt, I have to object to your phrasing. These accusations that I make you do things," he added with mock severity, "are quite unfair, Linnet, really."

"Says the man who picked me up and carted me off against my will."

"But you're not sorry I did it. Not now." He sat back, resting his weight on his elbows, looking far too pleased with himself. "I gave you blueberry muffins."

She tried to seem unimpressed, but she feared it was too late for that sort of pretense. "You bribed me."

"First force, then bribery. And now, I've even wheedled your childhood nickname out of you. I'm such an unscrupulous chap. But I've given you a new one, and Rabbit can be laid to rest forever."

"I'm not sure about Lioness, though." She considered. "Don't the female lions do all the hunting, while the males laze about in the sun all day?"

He laughed. "That does sound most unfair, doesn't it? Still, that's not how it is in England. Men do the hunting though ladies are allowed to join us on occasion if they ride well. And you might like hunting if you did it. Do you ride?"

"I do. And I did hunt, in Italy, last autumn."

"And did you like it?"

She smiled. "I did. It was boar hunting. Very exciting."

"Well, there you are, then. Lioness suits you down to the ground—even your hair's the right color, all tawny and golden."

Linnet gave him a wide-eyed stare as if he'd just said something amazing. "Why, Jack Featherstone, is that a compliment you've just given me?"

"Fishing for compliments, are you, Lioness? I don't see why." He sat up and began making himself a sandwich. "I daresay you've received quite a few of those in your life already. You don't need them from me."

"Yes, but from you, they would make such a nice change from the usual."

He shook his head. "No, I won't play. Far be it from me to feed that vanity you're so ashamed of. Besides, I've never been much good at flattery. You'd think I would be," he added with a laugh, "since I had the finest possible examples to emulate, but I'm not."

Linnet stopped eating, for there was a nuance in his demeanor—a shadow across his face and a bitter tinge to his voice—that belied his amusement. "What do you mean?" she asked when he didn't elaborate. "What examples?"

He was silent for a moment, eating his sandwich, but at last he said, "My brother Charles could gain any amount of feminine attention just by walking into a room."

"That's not such a terrible thing." Linnet wriggled on the blanket, uncomfortable. "Is it?"

He slanted her a knowing look. "Why, because you have the same gift when it comes to men?"

She shook her head, and yet even as she made that gesture, she couldn't really deny it, not beneath that perceptive gaze of his. "No . . . I mean, yes, sort of . . . but I'm not . . . it isn't . . ." She stopped, terribly embarrassed. "You may be right that I have a lot of pride," she burst out at last, "but that particular trait is not something I'm proud of."

"I realize that."

His voice was gentle, but she felt compelled to explain. "It's just that as a girl, I was plain as plain could be, and yes, some girls were mean and called me a rabbit. Now, because I was very, very fortunate, now I'm pretty, but I am not any different, not on the inside. Some men look at me and decide they want me, but they don't know me."

He nodded. "And when we met, you put me in that category, of course. Why wouldn't you?"

"Few men see past my face, or my money, or my powerful family. They don't—" She broke off, waving a hand beside her cheek, groping for words to explain. "They don't see me, *me*, Linnet. They see Ephraim Holland's daughter, or the Holland heiress, or the pretty blonde with the blue, blue eyes."

He smiled a little. "Well, in defense of my sex, it's pretty hard to get past your eyes, Linnet. They look at a chap and hit him square on. It's rather like being coshed with a cricket bat. I know that's how it felt when you first looked in my direction."

She bit her lip. "You're better with compliments than you think."

"That's not a compliment. That's just a fact, like the sun coming up in the east or a compass needle pointing north. But I know what you mean, and I can safely say that your speech proves beyond any doubt—not that any proof was needed—that although you may flummox every member of the opposite sex when you walk into a room, you are not the least bit like my brother. He was not only aware of his magnetic attraction, he enjoyed using it at every opportunity."

"He was a flirt, you mean?"

Jack shook his head. "It was far more potent than flirtation. Charles could ensnare a woman's heart with nothing more than a few minutes of conversation, and he could break it, too, without sparing a second for regret. That's not a talent I ever possessed."

Linnet looked at him, at his devil-may-care face and his dark, dark eyes, and she didn't believe him. She thought of his kiss and how he could recognize the taste of sherry on her mouth. "I daresay you've broken a few hearts in your life," she said faintly.

"But not on purpose. Not for amusement. Not just because I could. Winning a woman is work. At least, it ought to be. But for Charles?" He shook his head. "It was never work. It was easy as winking."

"No wonder he became a fortune hunter, then."

"Yes. A dubious profession, to be sure, but a lucrative one. My father was the same. Both of them married rich women for their money, and both of them proceeded to ignore their marriage vows to a legendary degree. I know you think I'm a fortune hunter, too, and though I could say time and again that I'm not, it wouldn't do a bit of good at easing your doubts. But I can at least say this: To my father and my brother, women were toys, amusing little things to be picked up and played with and put down again with never a thought. I've had my share of women, Linnet, I can't deny it, but I've never thought of a woman, any woman, as a toy. And as wild as I've been, as madcap as I can be, I've never committed a dishonorable act against a woman in my life." He paused, his eyes steady and unwavering as they looked into hers. "At least, not until Newport.

"I can't explain to you why I did it," he rushed on, as

if afraid she was going to ask, "and I shall never be able to do so. But what I can do, if you'll let me, is prove my character."

She swallowed hard. "I have to let you," she whispered. "We called a truce."

"So we did. And given our new spirit of cooperation and peace . . ." He paused and leaned closer. "I should very much like to kiss you again, Lioness."

She felt a jolt of apprehension and anticipation, and it took her a moment to remember which of those emotions ought to be dictating her actions. When he leaned even closer, she flattened her palm against his chest to keep him at bay. "Didn't you just say you wanted to prove your character to me?"

"Well, yes, but—" He broke off with a sigh and sat back. "Oh, very well. I suppose kissing you would be a bit hypocritical right after that little speech. I ought to have kissed you first, dash it. After softening you up with blueberry muffins, I had the perfect opportunity, too."

She objected with a scoffing sound. "That's an insufferable presumption on your part."

"Still, it's too late for regrets now, I suppose," he went on, blithely ignoring her protest, "and since the sun's going down, I'd best take you back to the house. Besides," he added as he stood up and reached out his free hand to help her to her feet, "I'm sure Sir Roger or his sister has already gone to Belinda with tales of my barbaric conduct. I've no doubt she's wearing out the carpet right now and cursing my name. Either that, or she's searching Nick's gun cabinets for a pistol with which to shoot me."

His glass was still in his hand, and as she watched him swirl the contents and down the last swallow, she reminded herself that it was his kiss that had plunged her entire life into chaos, but she couldn't help wondering if he had kissed her just now what champagne on his mouth would have tasted like.

Chapter 11

Jack's prediction that Belinda would pounce on him the moment they arrived back at the house proved unfounded. Nicholas had arrived home from America, and Jack guessed that might perhaps have diverted his sister-in-law's attention, for he was able to gain his room, have a bath and a shave, and change into evening clothes, all without having to face Belinda's wrath. But when Jack joined the other guests gathering in the drawing room for aperitifs before dinner, he soon discovered he was not to escape un-scathed.

Belinda cornered him before he'd even poured his port. "Sir Roger and his sister have left Honeywood," she murmured, halting beside where he stood at the liquor cabinet.

"Indeed?" He was not facing her straight on, for if he had been, she'd have seen the smile that tweaked his mouth at that news before he could hide it. As it was, he managed to pour his drink and savor the departure of one of his competitors without being caught out. "But they've just arrived."

"They departed on the evening train for London. He tried to pretend it was a matter of business, but I don't believe that for a moment."

"No?" Drink in hand, he strove to don an expression of mild curiosity as he turned toward her, but Belinda, with her razor-sharp perceptions, always saw through pretenses of that kind.

She studied his face for two seconds, then gave a nod, as if some suspicion lurking in her mind had now been confirmed. "You had something to do with his leaving, didn't you?"

She didn't know, he realized, and he thanked heaven that Sir Roger and his sister seemed to possess the rare quality of discretion. "My dear Belinda, I'm barely acquainted with Sir Roger. What have I to do with his business matters?"

"When I pressed him about staying, he said something curious. He said there was no point in remaining, for it had been made clear to him that any courtship of Miss Holland would require him to engage in conduct beneath the dignity of a gentleman, and he wanted no part of it. What does that mean?"

It meant Sir Roger didn't have the guts to step up and prevent a rival from throwing a woman over his shoulder and making off with her. But Jack couldn't enlighten Belinda on that point, and he chose his words with care. "Miss Holland had an engagement for tea with me, remember? Perhaps Sir Roger took umbrage to the fact. And if he has removed himself from consideration for her hand, I shall not mourn his departure."

If he thought his words would put an end to the discussion, he was mistaken. Belinda's blue eyes studied him even more intently than before. "What did you do, Jack?"

At that moment, a distraction arrived and saved him from having to admit any culpability, at least for now. "Nick," he said with heartfelt relief, looking past Belinda's shoulder to the blond-haired man coming across the drawing room to greet him. "Back from America, I see."

"Don't think you're off the hook," Belinda murmured, bringing his attention back to her as her husband paused beside them. "We'll talk more about this later."

"In trouble with my wife, are you?" Nicholas asked, as Belinda moved off to converse with other guests.

"I always seem to be in trouble with your wife. I am a Featherstone, after all." He moved aside to give Nicholas access to the liquor. "It's good to see you. How was the inquest?"

"Uneventful. A matter purely of routine. Nothing we need to be concerned with now. It's truly over."

"Good. You just arrived from Dover, I take it?"

"Actually, no. I landed at Liverpool a few days ago."

"Liverpool? But why not come through Dover? Much easier to reach Kent that way."

Drink in hand, Nick turned toward him. "Not if one decides to make a stop in Norfolk along the way."

"Ah." Jack took a sip of his port. "And how is Stuart?"

"Content with the outcome. Relieved it's over. Grateful to us all. But he's also a bit puzzled."

"Oh? What puzzles him?"

"He wondered why he learned of Van Hausen's suicide from the newspapers and not from us. I thought you intended to write to him?"

"I did write to him. I composed a letter that very night—" Jack broke off with a groan, slapping a palm to his forehead. "Hells bells, I forgot to post it. It's probably still in my dispatch case."

"Really, Jack." Nick shook his head with a sigh. "How could you forget a thing like that?"

"I've been rather pressed with other matters, in case you hadn't heard. Still, that's no excuse. He should have learned the news from me. I shall write tomorrow and express my apologies. I have to write to him anyway about another matter."

"Write if you like, but there's no need for apologies with Stuart, you know that. And I was able to elucidate any points the papers missed or got wrong. He does want to see you, though, and Denys and James as well, to express his gratitude."

Jack shook his head. "He owes me no such sentiments. I was glad to do it. We all were. I hope you assured him of that."

"I did. But he was adamant, and since Belinda's giving this house party already, I've invited all of them, and Edie, too, of course, to join us here afterward. They'll be arriving late next week."

Jack was pleased by this news, for it would give him time to discuss Holland's offer with Stuart in person without having to journey to Norfolk and perhaps abandon Linnet to the machinations of his rivals. "Excellent. I wish I'd had time to call on him when I returned, but as it was . . ." He paused, giving his friend a rueful look.

"Yes, you've been quite busy, I know. The American gossip rags are filled with stories of you and the girl. I daresay every scandal-ridden American is grateful you've succeeded in diverting the attentions of *Town Topics* from their troubles."

Jack grimaced. "Linnet's father is beside himself, I'm sure. And you must have been inundated with questions as well."

"Pressed at every turn, I'm afraid. The American reporters . . ." Nick paused, rolling his eyes. "They're even more relentless than ours."

"What story did you offer?"

"I said I was not privy to any details of your courtship of Miss Holland." Nick took a sip of port. "How's that proceeding, by the way?"

"I'll win her over," he said with far more assurance than he felt. "These other chaps haven't got a chance."

The words were barely out of his mouth before Linnet and her mother entered the drawing room, and the moment they did, several of the other single men present began to gravitate toward the doorway.

"Odd," Nick drawled beside him, watching men swarm Linnet like bees to honey. "Those other chaps don't seem to see the situation the same way you do."

THE TRUTH OF Nick's assessment was demonstrated to Jack with tiresome frequency during the course of the evening. The dinner gong sounded before he had the chance to speak to Linnet at all, and he was not, worse luck, seated anywhere close to her at the table. The distance was not so great that he couldn't see her, however. Across the table and five chairs down, she was well within his line of vision, and he found that fact something of a consolation, at least for the first few minutes.

Her hair, piled high atop her head, gleamed like molten gold, and the candlelight of the dining room lit her pale skin with a luminous glow. She seemed even more beautiful now than she had that afternoon, but any enjoyment he might have taken in the view evaporated once the meal began, for she turned her attention to Lord Hansborough, the man seated beside her, which meant that whenever Jack looked her way, his view was most often the nape of her neck and a bit of her profile.

The fact that she seemed to find Hansborough such a fascinating dinner companion did nothing to rouse Jack's spirits, especially since her penchant for fashionable Parisian evening frocks with daring, low-cut necklines had not gone unnoticed by the viscount. His gaze dropped to her bosom with aggravating frequency, a fact that made Jack want to snarl every time he saw it happen, and there wasn't a damn thing he could do about it.

After dinner, when the ladies had gone through, and the port was passed, he had the opportunity to take the measure of Hansborough, as well as his other rivals. He talked little, choosing instead to listen and observe. He was well aware that with Linnet, a man couldn't take anything for granted, of course, but after about ten minutes over the port, he was able to form several conclusions.

Carrington, despite being three decades older than Linnet, was still a handsome fellow and quite fit. But he was also every bit as dull as Jack remembered, and as he droned on and on about Cecil's obvious superiority to Gladstone as a prime minister, Jack concluded that it was the duke's inability to make interesting conversation that must have done for him with Linnet the first time around. Watching Carrington, he decided he'd have to put in a word with the fellow about her abject ignorance of the British political system, or something along that line. An hour or two of this, and she just might decide she didn't want to hear it for the rest of her life.

Jack turned his attention to Lord Tufton. Most British girls, he thought as he studied the marquess down the table, would consider Tufton quite an attractive fellow, but Linnet, thank heaven, was an American, and American girls placed a great deal more emphasis on white teeth and fresh breath than did their British counterparts. As he watched the cigar smoke swirl around Tufton's head, he rather hoped the marquess tried stealing a kiss from Linnet in the next day or two. That might be enough to do him in.

And then there was Hansborough. In the viscount, he knew he had a dangerous rival. Other than a predilection for gazing at Linnet's bosom more often than her face, Hansborough didn't seem to possess any weaknesses that might work to Jack's advantage. The other man was, unfortunately, handsome, urbane, and intelligent—all qualities that appealed to women. Still, it was early days yet, and every man had weaknesses.

"You're terribly quiet, Jack."

Hearing Nick say his name roused him from his contemplations, and he turned to his friend, but a cough from the doorway gave him no chance to respond.

All the men turned toward the entrance to the dining room, where a stout, middle-aged woman in black stood with a baby in her arms.

"Oh, I say," Hansborough murmured, sounding rather shocked by this domestic invasion into such a masculine enclave, and a quick glance around told Jack the other men were just as surprised. The only exception was Nick, who smiled at once at the sight of his son.

"Ah, Nanny Brown," he greeted her, standing up. "So Colin's awake, is he?"

"Yes, my lord. Begging your pardon, but you did say if he woke up, you wanted to see him straightaway."

"So I did. Forgive me, gentlemen," Nicholas added to the men at the table as he moved to the doorway and took his son from the nanny's arms. "But I've been away for several weeks, and since I returned, I've had no chance to see my son."

"What he really means, gentlemen," Jack said, pushing back his chair, "is that he's had no chance to show him off."

Most of the men laughed at that, but it didn't escape his notice as he stood up and circled the table that Hansborough wasn't laughing.

He paused behind Nick, studying the baby over his friend's shoulder. "Ah, now it's clear why he's so proud," he told the men around the table. "The boy's quite bonny. That fact is due to his mother, of course, as we can all attest."

"I'd object to that," Nick said amid another round of laughter. "But it's true. He's got my wife's dark hair and blue eyes." He paused to lift the baby in his hands, turning him so that the other men could have a look. "Which means he's ripping gorgeous, as you can see."

Being held up for display must not have agreed with Colin, for he let out a wail of protest, wriggled violently, and started to cry. Nicholas resumed cradling him at once, but the damage seemed to be done, for Colin would not be placated. His feet kicked, his fists flailed, and his wails grew louder.

"Really, Trubridge," Hansborough said, his voice loud enough to carry over the baby's crying, "can the nanny not take him away until we've at least had our port?"

There was distinct annoyance in the viscount's voice that caught Jack's attention even over Colin's lusty wails, and when he looked in that direction, there was no mistaking the viscount's pained expression.

Jack studied the other man's disapproving face for a moment, considering possibilities, then he looked at Colin again and decided he'd have to pull Nanny Brown aside sometime soon for a little chat.

"It's VITAL THAT Salisbury keep a conservative government in power, for if Gladstone's Liberals ever get back in, it will spell chaos. Do you see, Miss Holland?"

"Oh, yes," she murmured with perhaps too much fervor. "I do, indeed, Your Grace."

She raised a gloved hand to her mouth, hoping to hide the yawn that refused to be suppressed. She glanced past the duke as he continued on about former Prime Minister Gladstone, and at once she caught sight of Jack, who was watching her from the other side of the room with a grin on his face. She forced her yawn away, snatched her hand down, and returned her attention to the duke, pasting an expression of rapturous attention on her face.

Still, after two hours of listening to explanations on the inner workings of British politics, she was waning. When Carrington paused to take a sip of his port, she was quick to get a word in, hoping to turn the conversation. "Your British ways are very different from those of my country."

"Yes, yes, you've a republic over there. Very different form of government, indeed. It's no wonder the differences confuse you."

Thanks to her mother, Linnet had been blessed with a very through education, one well beyond the scope of most young ladies, one that had included not only French, German, and poetry, but also world politics, finance, economics, and an extensive study of all things British. She wasn't confused in the least, but she was well aware that most men liked to think their own intellect superior to that of any female, and they never liked to be proved wrong on that point. "I am so grateful for your explanations, Your Grace," she assured him. "You've clarified some points of the British parliamentary system that have baffled me in the past."

"I'm glad I've been able to enlighten you. Feather-stone had mentioned your lack of knowledge on the subject."

"Oh?" Linnet stiffened, but kept her smile in place. "Did he, indeed?"

"Yes. He mentioned over the port that you would probably find an explanation most useful."

"I see." She glanced across the room again, but she found that Jack was now immersed in conversation with a group of ladies, so her murderous glance at him was wasted. "Well," she said, returning her attention to the duke. "As I said, I'm most grateful. But now I fear I must circulate a bit. I do hope that's all right?"

Carrington, though he might not be the most exciting of men, was a perfect gentleman. "Of course," he said. "I mustn't keep you all to myself."

He bowed politely, and Linnet was able to move on. By now, her earlier nervousness had abated, for despite her fears, no one was looking at her as if she had a scarlet A emblazoned on her dress. She mingled about the room, conversing with other guests with much greater ease than she'd felt this afternoon on the lawn. But she also kept an eye on Jack as well, and when she was able to catch his eye again, she jerked her head toward the open French doors leading onto the terrace. He gave a slight nod of acknowledgment, and she made her way in that direction.

The night was fine, and the air felt cool and refreshing after the stuffy confines of the crowded drawing room. She crossed the terrace, but when she glanced over her shoulder, she could see Jack through the door-way still deep in conversation, and though she turned her back to him and stared out at the darkened gardens, that didn't distract her thoughts.

Really, she thought in exasperation, that man was the end all. Telling Carrington to school her in British politics as if she knew nothing about it. She knew why he'd done it, of course, and when he came out here, she intended to inform him of just how ineffective his mischievous joke had been.

But she knew it hadn't been quite as ineffective as she'd have liked to believe. Linnet sighed, slumping forward to lean against the stone railing in front of her. She knew she'd been too close-minded during her season in London, too determined to go home and marry an American, too stubborn in defying her mother to consider the gentlemen who had pursued her here in an objective fashion. But if she'd hoped a second look would make her decision an easy one, that hope was already dashed.

The duke had not impressed her as a very exciting man during her first visit, and Jack's little joke had served to remind her that the duke was no more exciting this time around.

Still, she thought, looking on the bright side, he also had some fine qualities. He was a handsome man, for one thing. And he was kind, so very kind. He'd treat her well. He'd assured Belinda he found the very strict terms of her marriage settlement perfectly agreeable. His only concerns were that the estates be well maintained and the children taken care of. And he had no doubt Featherstone was wholly to blame for what had occurred in Newport.

All of that ought to have reassured her, and yet now,

as she tried to envision spending the next twenty years or so with the duke, as she reminded herself of how much he had to offer her and how good it was of him to want her in spite of her disgrace, she felt anything but reassured.

She moved on to consider Lord Tufton. He was a pleasant man, every bit as amiable as he'd been during their few brief encounters in London, and like Carrington, he had no objection to the marriage settlement she wanted. But though the marquess would no doubt make some girl a fine husband, Linnet knew that girl would not be her. Perhaps it was shallow of her, but she found the cigar-smoking habit quite vile. A polite inquiry on the subject had confirmed for her that Tufton had abandoned his smoking habit before she met him in London and taken it up again once the season had ended.

He could perhaps be persuaded to give up tobacco a second time, but until he did, she could not even consider kissing him, and without kissing him, she couldn't agree to spend her life with him.

A few weeks ago, the question of a man's kissing ability would never have been a consideration of his suitability for marriage. Conrath hadn't kissed her until after she'd accepted his proposal, a fact that paralleled the experience of most girls of her acquaintance. On the other hand, a girl didn't usually have a devil like Jack Featherstone come striding into her life, bend her backward, and open his mouth over hers as if he owned her. And though Jack's kiss had offended her sense of propriety, aroused her anger—among other things—and ruined her reputation, she feared that it had also made a man's kissing ability one of her most crucial considerations for matrimony.

That meant Tufton was out of the question.

She shifted her thoughts to Hansborough. A handsome man, no doubt. Amusing, too, for he'd made her laugh more than once at dinner, and she did have a weakness for men who made her laugh. And he admired her, she could tell, although when she thought of how often his admiring gaze had lowered to her bosom, she knew certain of her qualities evoked more of his admiration than others. But that was to be expected; calling attention to that particular attribute was the entire reason a girl wore a low-cut gown in the first place. And he'd been quite gentlemanly about it, often reaching for his wineglass as the excuse to lower his gaze. Still, every time he had glanced at her chest, all she'd been able to think of was the way Jack had stared at her so openly in Mrs. Dewey's ballroom—a stare far less discreet. A few weeks ago, she'd found his open scrutiny appalling, and yet now, the pleasant, agreeable warmth of Hansborough's admiration seemed almost tame by comparison.

She made a sound through her teeth, her exasperation transferring from Jack to herself. That picnic had changed things. She wanted to hate Jack, she ought to hate him. His persistence was aggravating, his arrogance was astonishing, and his continual interference in her life—urging Carrington on being a perfect example—was downright infuriating. And yet, he'd given her blueberry muffins, one of her favorite things. Even as she'd reminded herself such gifts were trivial and could even be deceitful, she also knew their power to charm and captivate.

She reminded herself that he hadn't asked her to have tea. He'd decided that she would. Granted, he'd promised that wouldn't happen again, but it was clear he wasn't above using his superior strength to get his way.

She touched her fingertips to her mouth, remembering how his kiss had seared her lips and her senses. It had also taken all her choices from her, and she'd been wrestling to regain them ever since. If she married him, would he continue to ride roughshod over her wishes? How could she be sure he wouldn't? He said he wouldn't let her dominate him, but she had no reason to believe that he wouldn't dominate her. If they wed, he would have all the legal rights in that regard; the husband always did. What would happen to her plans, her desires, her wishes? Could she trust him to consider those?

The tap of footsteps on the stone behind her had Linnet glancing over her shoulder, and when she saw Jack approaching her, she felt even less inclined to good spirits. Turning away, she gazed out over the moonlit gardens as he paused beside her.

"Beautiful evening," he commented. "There's nothing like cool breezes and fresh air to reinvigorate a person."

She knew what he meant by that remark, and she shot him a glance of reproof. "His Grace is a very nice man."

"I never said he wasn't."

"He's also very thoughtful. And intelligent. And a perfect gentleman."

"Indeed. He's also quite a responsible landlord to his tenants, from what I understand."

Jack's bland way of agreeing with her about Carrington had the strange effect of depressing her spirits further. "If I married him, I'd be a duchess."

"Yes. And if you care about a man's rank, that would be an important consideration for you."

"Being a duchess would restore my tarnished reputation," she said, feeling a bit desperate. "And give me a strong social position. And Carrington's admiration for me is obvious."

"Very obvious, I should say. But—" He turned to look at her. "Do you think he would make you happy?"

Since that was the exact question in her own mind, Linnet found it particularly frustrating coming from someone else. "I don't think he would make me unhappy."

"A ringing endorsement," he murmured, making her wince.

"I happen to have a great interest in politics," she told him, feeling compelled to further justifications. "So this attempt to deter me from the duke by suggesting he discuss the subject with me won't succeed. Yes, I know you urged him to educate me on the subject."

"I'm as transparent as glass, it seems. Which makes it all the more stunning that Carrington wasn't able to see right through me."

"Because he's not as devious as you."

"Quite so," he agreed at once. "And I never doubted that you might have an interest in politics, Linnet. What I doubted was Carrington's ability to maintain your interest for a lifetime. I hoped yawning your way through a conversation with him would help you reach the same conclusion."

"It's been a long day," she said with dignity. "The train journey down, settling in, meeting everyone . . . it's been exhausting. Any girl might be excused a yawn now and again."

"Of course," he agreed gravely. "And once you've had a good night's sleep, Carrington's pontifications will become much more fascinating to you, I'm sure."

She scowled. "You are so damnably aggravating."

"But am I not right?"

"You're most aggravating when you're right."

"As aggravating as I am, at least I won't ever bore you, Lioness."

"Chaos is never boring," she countered. "But it's difficult to live with. If you want to convince me to marry you instead of Carrington, or any other man, you'll have to come up with a better reason than excitement."

"Will I?" He tilted his head, looking at her, and as his dark gaze roamed over her face, she felt a sudden jolt of nervousness. "I'm not sure about that, Linnet," he said after a moment. "There's a part of you that likes excitement, perhaps even craves it."

She opened her mouth to deny what he said, but he moved closer, and her pulses quickened in immediate response, making a denial seem quite hypocritical. "How do you make that out?" she said instead.

"Because if it were not so, you'd never have gone sneaking out to meet Frederick Van Hausen. You'd have insisted he propose to you in your mother's drawing room in the proper manner, and you'd have stayed in the ballroom."

"You talk as if I'm willing to throw propriety to the winds. I've had eight marriage proposals, I'll have you know, and Frederick's was the only one I went sneaking off to hear."

"Eight? I'm one, of course, and Van Hausen. And you had five in London—Carrington, Sir Roger, Tufton, and Hansborough," he said, counting on his fingers. "That's four in London and six altogether."

She shook her head. "Carrington and Sir Roger both proposed to me, yes. But I met Lord Hansborough for the first time today, and I met Lord Tufton only a few weeks before we departed for home. Three of the men who proposed to me in London could not come." She paused, looking out over the garden. "Prior engagements. At least . . ." She paused, leaning forward, pretending vast interest in the garden. "That's what they said."

"It could be true."

"It probably wasn't," she said, lifting her chin, trying to act as if the reasons didn't matter, reminding herself she still had choices. "The story about Newport has spread to England now, and I expect those men heard about it. I just hope once I marry, it'll all die down and be forgotten."

"It will. Scandals are hard to live down for those involved, but they're also a bit like trains. Another one always comes along. And what happened between us didn't happen here, so it will be easier for British society to forget about it. But to return to our discussion, your arithmetic seems faulty. I've counted seven proposals, so who proffered the eighth? I only ask," he added when she hesitated, "because I've got enough of your present suitors to defeat before I can win your hand. I should hate to think a former one might pop up and wreck my chances."

"No fear of that. He's married now." She turned. "It was Lord Conrath."

"Viscount Conrath?" Jack frowned with an effort of memory. "His wife is an American, isn't she?"

"Yes. Lizzie Hutchison. We both met him when he visited New York two years ago, but I'm the one he pursued first."

"And when you turned him down, he turned to Lizzie?"

"It wasn't quite like that. He proposed, I accepted. But then Daddy investigated him, found out how broke he was, and though he didn't refuse his permission, he put very strict restrictions on the dowry."

"Ah." There was such a wealth of meaning in the word, she winced. "And Conrath wasn't willing to live with that."

"No. He withdrew his proposal. Two weeks later, he was engaged to Lizzie. Her family is very New Money, you see, so her father wasn't as adverse as mine to handing over a pile of cash with no questions asked."

"A man who engaged himself to another girl a fortnight after jilting you wasn't worth having, Linnet."

"Oh, I know, and I'm not pining for Conrath."

"But you did pine for him?" He stirred, moved closer. "Were you in love with him?"

The blunt question took her back. "I don't . . ." She paused and swallowed hard. "I don't see how that's any of your business."

"Well, we're friends now. We have a truce. We've

broken bread. We told each other our childhood nick-
names. I even gave you a new one." He eased even
closer, and though he wasn't touching her, he was close
enough to remind her how carelessly he disregarded
propriety. "We have to share confidences now."

"I knew taking that muffin was a deal with the devil,"
she murmured, and moved back a step. Studying him,
she considered his question for a moment, then nodded.
"All right, I'll answer you, but first, you have to answer
a question of mine."

"Fair enough. I can't tell you anything more about
Van Hausen, but with that exception, I'll answer any
questions you ask." He spread his arms wide. "Fire
away."

She hadn't expected such thorough capitulation, and
it took her a moment to think of what to ask first. "Have
you ever been in love?"

"Yes. Her name was Lola."

He stopped, the provoking man.

"Really, Jack, you can't leave it at that. Where did
you meet her? And when? And what was she like?"

"I met her in Paris the summer I was twenty-five." A
slight smile curved his mouth as he spoke, and Linnet
felt a sudden, sharp stab of jealousy. It was so startling,
and so unexpected, she had to turn away so nothing of
it caught his perceptive attention.

"Paris?" she echoed, staring out into the darkness
beyond the terrace, striving to sound politely interested
and nothing more. "So she was a French girl, then?"

"No, she was American. But she wasn't a girl. No,
Lola was a woman through and through."

The way he said it made Linnet's hands clench around

the railing in front of her, but even as she reminded herself she had no right to be jealous, she wondered what being a "woman through and through" actually meant, and instead of dissipating, that horrid, stinging jealousy deepened and spread, and she cursed herself for ever agreeing to share confidences with him. It took her several moments to regain her composure enough to look at him again. "Was she an heiress? I might know her."

"Lola was no heiress. She was a dancer and chorus girl."

"A chorus girl?" Even as sheltered as she was, she knew men often kept company with such women, and though she'd been schooled all her life that women like that were of low moral character and nothing for a well-bred girl to be jealous of, Linnet proved herself quite impervious to the proper teachings of her girlhood. Even as she told herself she didn't want to know any more, she couldn't resist asking another question. "Was she your mistress?"

"God, no. I rarely had the blunt to keep a mistress." He paused, laughing a little. "She was Denys's mistress. Viscount Somerton."

"Your friend, Somerton? One of the men with you at Mrs. Dewey's ball? You fell in love with your friend's mistress?"

"It wasn't intentional," he said dryly. "And I wasn't the only one. Pongo was in love with her, too. And Nick. We were all in love with Lola at one time or another—well, I don't think Stuart ever was, but the rest of us were. Lola," he added, "was that kind of woman."

Linnet's jealousy receded a bit with this list of the

woman's conquests. "Who are Pongo, Nick, and Stuart?"

"My friends. The best friends a man could have. Pongo is the Earl of Hayward, who was also at the Newport ball. Pongo's a nickname, although don't ask me how he got it because I honestly don't remember. None of us do. Nick is Lord Trubridge—this was long before his marriage to Belinda, of course. Stuart is the Duke of Margrave."

She looked at him, skeptical. "Are you making this up?"

He held up his hand, palm toward her in a gesture of solemnity. "God's truth. Why would you think I made it up?"

"Isn't it obvious?" She laughed, bemused. "How can four men be in love with the same woman and still remain friends?"

"It did muddy the waters for a bit," he admitted, laughing with her. "Nick and Denys didn't speak for ages. And, of course, it didn't help when Pongo shot Nick although he was aiming for Denys. That was over a barmaid, but since it was in retaliation for Lola, it counts, rather. It's a long story," he added as if in apology.

"And what about you? Did you quarrel? Did you shoot anyone over this girl?"

"No, thank heaven. I stayed out of the fray, got drunk a great deal, and pined from afar. Denys gave her up after a time and returned to London, Lola went back to America, and we all recovered. Maybe not Denys. He might still be pining although if you asked him, he'd deny it."

"I envy you," she murmured. "I mean, I have friends,

of course, but a friendship that can withstand what you describe must be an extraordinary one."

"It is." He looked at her, and his eyes seemed darker than ever, like a night sky without any stars. "I'd do anything for my friends." Though his voice was low, he spoke with a strange intensity that made his declaration seem like a shout of defiance. "Anything."

It startled her, that intensity, and she swallowed hard. "That sounds so unequivocal. We're friends now, you said."

"Yes," he agreed. "We are."

That simple reply, soft and so sure, did strange things to her. Her tummy dipped, as if she'd just stepped off a cliff. His gaze bored into hers, making her nervous because she didn't know what he saw there. Her lips were dry, and she licked them, a movement that drew his attention at once. His thick, straight lashes lowered a fraction as his gaze moved to her mouth. She thought of the pagoda, of his arm bending her back, of his mouth taking hers and tasting sherry.

Oh, God. Her toes curled in her slippers. Her lips burned. She couldn't seem to breathe.

"I say, Featherstone," Hansborough's voice drawled from the doorway to the drawing room, and it was like a bucket of ice water being thrown over her heated skin. Linnet jerked, turning toward the doors as the viscount went on, "You can't keep Miss Holland to yourself for the entire evening."

"You're quite right," he called back, but though she wasn't looking at him, Linnet could still feel his riveting gaze on her as if he were touching her. "Fair play and all that."

He straightened away from the railing, but he didn't start back toward the house. "Speaking of fair play," he murmured, pausing beside her, "I've answered your questions. So that means tomorrow, it'll be your turn to answer mine."

Her heart slammed against her ribs with such force, it was hard to reply. "*Quid pro quo?*" she managed.

"Just so." He leaned close to her, smiling a little. "And then," he whispered in her ear, "it'll be my turn to be jealous."

Ignoring her sound of exasperation at how easily he'd seen through her, he walked away.

Chapter 12

Despite Hansborough's untimely interruption, Jack had no intention of letting his question to Linnet go unanswered, and the following day, he looked for an opportunity to corner her on the subject.

Belinda had promised to arrange things so that each of her suitors had time with her each day, but his turn didn't come until late afternoon, leaving him no choice but to cool his heels while she went for a morning ride with Carrington, sat beside Tufton at lunch, and played afternoon croquet with Hansborough. He wasn't sure Belinda hadn't arranged things this way on purpose, deeming the suspense of waiting all day to see her as no more than he deserved. But even if that had been her intent, Belinda was a woman of her word.

While all the others began gathering on the south lawn for tea, his sister-in-law took him aside, mentioned that Linnet and her mother had decided to cut flowers for the dinner table instead, and handed him a basket. He was happy to take his cue, and five minutes later, he was in the rose garden, basket in hand, ready to give his assistance to Linnet and her mother.

As he made his offer of help, he glanced at Helen and noticed that she was already moving a discreet distance away, making for the rose bed beyond. He knew Helen favored him above Linnet's other suitors, and though he didn't know if that was because it was best for the girl's reputation if he was the one to marry her, or because he'd saved her from Van Hausen's clutches, but either way, he intended to take full advantage of the opportunity he'd been given, and he moved to stand beside Linnet, who was bent over a boxwood-edged flower bed.

She paused to glance at him. "If you came out to help, I fear you'll be quite useless. You don't have a pair of shears."

He improvised at once. "I'm here to fetch and carry," he said, gesturing to the oblong basket over her arm filled with stems and the empty one he was carrying. She handed her basket over, then returned her attention to the flowers as she moved farther along the bed.

He fell in step beside her and decided it was best to be direct, for they didn't have much time before the dressing gong. "We never did finish our conversation from last night."

She paused and turned away to snip off a late rose. "Didn't we?"

"Don't be coy. You left me in suspense, and you know it."

"I'm sure you were awake all night as a result."

"No." He paused. "Not all night."

That made her smile a little. "Far be it from me to cause you to lose any sleep," she murmured. "Yes, I was very much in love with Conrath." She turned away again and resumed cutting flowers. "I believe that answers your question."

"Ah, but you didn't ask me just one question last night," he pointed out, moving to stand beside her. "You asked me twenty questions."

She turned her head to give him a dubious look. "You were counting them?"

"Of course I was. *Quid pro quo*. That means I have nineteen questions left."

She made a scoffing sound and cut three stems in quick succession. "So our conversations are to be games of twenty questions?"

Seduction was always a game, but he decided he'd better not point that out. "Why not?" he said instead. "Games are fun. And besides, I didn't set the number. You did. Last night. And I answered every question you asked, so now it's my turn. That's only fair."

"Yes, far be it from you to take an *unfair* advantage," she murmured, giving him a wry look as she placed her flowers in the basket. "All right, ask your questions, but you can be sure I shall count them."

"I'm sure your mother approved of Conrath, but I can't think your father did. He doesn't seem to hold men from my side of the pond in very high regard."

"Yes, well, Conrath is part of the reason why." She resumed walking, scanning the rose bed for blossoms to cut as she talked. "My mother is different. She got the notion that I ought to marry a man with a title because of Conrath. She realized soon after I met him that a peer would give me a wider world than a man in New York would do."

"She's right. Knickerbockers are a stodgy lot. In New York, society is very stifling, far more so than in London, or Paris."

"I know, and when all this happened with my reputation, I decided that since I had to marry, I would marry a peer. After all, even if you can't have a marriage based on love, you still have to base your marriage on something. Being the wife of a peer could provide a deeper purpose to my life than being the wife of a Knickerbocker. I could run charities, manage estates, be involved in my husband's political affairs or business matters—all things that would be looked down upon in New York."

"And do you want that kind of life?"

"I didn't always. I mean, I didn't think about it. Love, marriage, children . . . those are the inevitable things a woman's world centers around, and I've always wanted those things, but I never thought beyond them. My mother did. When I met Conrath, my mother soon discovered that in England, marriage is more of a partnership than it is back home. Conrath made her aware of what my life would be like in England when he and I were courting, and she felt a marriage like that would make me happier."

"And what did you think?"

"I didn't think much about that part of it, about what our marriage would be like, or how we would raise our children, or what we would do with our life together. I was very much in and of the moment. I was just—"

She broke off, but Jack knew what she'd been about to say, and he finished the sentence for her. "You were just a girl in love."

"Yes. A foolish one, as it turned out." She turned and resumed walking. "I trust your curiosity is now satisfied?"

"Not by a long way. Besides, I still have eighteen questions left."

"Oh, you do not. You've asked five already."

"No, I've asked two. Statements don't count."

She gave a huff of vexation. "Is this how you play all games? Making up rules as you go along?"

"Not at all. If we count statements as questions, my quota is even higher." He gave her a look of mock apology. "You talked a lot last night, Lioness."

She pressed a smile from her lips, but not before he saw it. "Oh, very well," she said. "Go on."

"When did you meet? Where?"

"It was in Newport, two years ago, at the yacht races. He came to New York that winter, he proposed in the spring, and I accepted." As if that dry summary was satisfactory, she turned away to resume her task.

He glanced behind them and found that her mother had wandered at least twenty yards away and was exhibiting great interest in the herbaceous border, her back to them. He took advantage of the fact at once, moving to stand in front of Linnet so that he could still keep an eye on her mother. "I want to know how he courted you."

"Why?" she asked, her voice light as she scanned the flowers. "Do you need pointers?"

"No, just information." He leaned in beside her,

edging his head beneath her wide-brimmed hat, moving in close enough to catch the fragrance of heliotrope on the afternoon breeze.

"So you can emulate him? Do you think that will move me to marry you?"

"My purpose is much more devious than that, I'm afraid, but if you want to know what it is, you'll have to wait until tomorrow. Today it's my turn to ask questions."

"Very well," she said, reaching to cup her hand over the top of a rose, "but you'll have to ask me an actual question. As you said, statements don't count."

"Why did you fall in love with Conrath?"

She stilled, then her shears snapped through the stem of the rose, and she shifted the cut flower to her left hand, then she cut another. "I'm not sure I know what you mean."

"Was it because he was charming, or serious, or intellectual, or because he made you laugh? What was it about him that you loved?"

She shot him a prim sideways glance from beneath the brim of her straw boater. "For one thing, he didn't ask me improper questions. He was always a perfect gentleman."

"Quite unlike me, then."

"Quite," she agreed with disheartening speed. "He asked me to marry him in the proper manner."

"I asked in the proper manner, too," he said with mock severity. "I even went down on one knee."

She gave him a sorrowful look, shaking her head. "The fact that you can even use the word 'proper' in speaking of what you did amazes me."

He grinned at that, mainly because in describing that night in Newport she sounded bemused, but not resentful, which gave him hope. "You can't tell me that you fell in love with Conrath because he was a perfect gentleman."

"Oh, but I did. He was the most elegant, urbane, charming man I had ever met." She put the handful of roses in the basket, but she didn't turn away to cut more. Instead, she stared past him into space, as if remembering. "If he looked at me, my heart would stop. If he spoke, I hung on every word. If he bent over my hand, the thrill lasted a week." She shook her head, laughing a little. "I was crazy in love with him, and yet he never did anything untoward."

"I don't believe it. I don't believe that a man could court you for nine months and never do anything untoward."

"Why? Because you wouldn't?"

He decided he'd better not answer that. "Still, you're telling me he never stepped outside the bounds. Never?"

"He did once," she admitted. "But only once."

"Oh, once. Well . . ." He attempted a bit of ho-hum and nodded sagely, earning himself a look of reproof for his impudence.

"It was at our home in New York. We were seated beside each other at dinner, and he took my hand in his under the table. Of course, neither of us was wearing gloves at the time. He held my fingers, and he . . . he caressed my palm with his fingers. It was so shocking, so . . . so intimate, I almost couldn't breathe."

Jack slid a glance over her and began imagining all

the shocking, intimate things he'd like to do to her. Hand-holding wasn't one of them, and he feared he was far more depraved than Conrath.

"I sat there," she went on, "with my bare hand in his, everyone around me making ordinary dinner conversation, Conrath included, while I was almost swooning at the table."

It occurred to him that if he ever met Conrath in the flesh, he'd have to stand the man a drink for having more fortitude than any other man living. Jack knew if he were forced to draw out the mating dance with Linnet for nine months without doing anything naughtier than holding her hand—once—under the table and caressing her palm, he'd never get that far. He'd have to hurl himself off a cliff.

Something of what he was thinking must have shown in his face, for she frowned a little. "What?"

"Nothing." He glanced past her, making sure Helen was still well out of earshot as he began figuring how he could use this information to his advantage. "And once you were engaged, was he still a perfect gentleman? Even when he kissed you?"

She cast a look back over her shoulder. "I can't tell you things like that," she whispered, looking at him again.

"Of course you can." He gave her a wicked smile. "We're friends now."

"Not close enough friends for such an intimate conversation as that."

"Oh, come now, Linnet," he said, laughing. "Don't tell me that the first time Conrath kissed you, you didn't go tearing back to your friends at the first opportunity and tell every last one of them all about his kissing ability, for I shan't believe it."

"Even if I did, that's not the same thing as telling you. And, anyway, I can't imagine why you want to know."

"Because I want to see how I stack up, of course." He tilted his head, still smiling a little. "How was his kiss different from mine?"

Her blush deepened, but when she spoke her voice was tart. "In every way possible."

"Can you be a bit more specific? Let's put it another way, then," he added when she didn't answer. "Why don't you tell me how you like to be kissed?"

"I can't tell you things like that. It wouldn't be decent."

"So you like indecent kisses, do you?" He grinned. "How naughty you are."

"Stop twisting my words to make fun. You know I meant it isn't decent to talk about kissing."

"You'd be amazed, my sweet innocent, at the number of things people do that aren't decent."

She made a huff and returned her attention to the roses, clipping three off in rapid succession. "How am I supposed to answer a question like that, anyway? It's not as if I go around conducting experiments on the subject. I've only been kissed twice in my life."

It took a moment for her words to sink in.

"Wait," he commanded, putting a hand on her arm, and when she turned, he stared into her stunning face in disbelief. "You mean to tell me that when I kissed you, it was just the second kiss you've ever had? Conrath kissed you once? Once?"

These questions seemed to touch on her feminine pride, for she jerked her chin and looked away. "He didn't have much time. We were engaged just one week before he broke it off. And I don't know why it's so astonishing. What?" she added, as he began to laugh. "I don't see why you're laughing."

"Disbelief," he answered. "This sort of knowledge defies rational explanation. All I can think is Conrath's a saint, all the men of New York have seriously deficient eyesight, and I've been a quite dissolute chap for the past two-thirds of my life."

"Why?" She turned her head to frown at him. "How many girls have you kissed, anyway?"

"More than two."

"How many?"

"Oh, I don't know. Fewer than a hundred." He paused, teasing her by pretending to consider. "I think."

"Heavens," she whispered, sounding quite shocked. "And I'd bet you weren't engaged to any of them."

He knew, of course, that most young ladies were innocent as lambs, but until now, he'd never thought much about just *how* innocent that was. Linnet excepted, he hadn't kissed an innocent young lady since he was seventeen. But now, looking at her, he realized just how far outside her experience that kiss in the pagoda had been. He wanted to tell her all the other kisses he'd had were nothing like hers, and though it was true, he feared that coming off his lips, a declaration like that would sound nauseatingly self-serving. Charles, he was sure, would have found a way to say it with aplomb. He, alas, was not so glib.

Still, as he looked into Linnet's shocked face, he

couldn't resist contemplating various ways to remedy this deficiency in her life experience. But given that her mother would be hovering nearby every time he was with her, any lessons of that sort weren't likely to happen unless she agreed to marry him, a prospect that was by no means a certainty. But there might be a way to whet her appetite and improve his odds.

"Linnet, when you see sense at last and agree to marry me, I can promise you that, unlike Conrath, I'll be kissing you at every possible opportunity. In the first week, I'll kiss you so many times, you'll lose count."

Her shock vanished, and she bristled. "First of all, I've no intention of agreeing to marry you. I've already turned you down twice. Second, even if I were to take leave of my sanity and accept you, you would not be kissing me at every opportunity. There are times and places for . . . for . . ." Her cheeks grew pinker. "For such things."

"Which places for which things?" He glanced past her, and found Helen had moved even farther away, her back still to them. He returned his attention to Linnet. "If we were engaged—no need to protest," he assured her as she opened her mouth. "We're speaking in hypothetical terms, so just play along for a moment. If we were engaged, where and when would I be able to kiss you?"

She stirred a little in agitation, and he felt his own body responding, desire rising inside him. Her lips parted, but she didn't answer, and he pushed his advantage while he had it. "Right now, for instance, if we were engaged, could I kiss you?"

"Here?" she squeaked, and cast a panicked glance around. "You couldn't. People would see us!"

"Then it would have to be a very chaste kiss." He dropped the baskets he was carrying to the ground, glanced past her to make doubly sure her mother wasn't watching, and reached up one hand to graze her cheekbone with his fingertip. "Right there, perhaps," he murmured.

She stiffened and turned her face away to cast a frantic glance over her shoulder. The move allowed him to slide his hand down to her slender neck, and when she looked at him again, he was able to cup her cheek and touch his thumb to the tip of her nose. "Or there."

He heard her breathing quicken. She shook her head a little, and the delicate wisps of hair beneath her hat brim tickled his fingers where they caressed her nape.

"Or . . ." He paused, pressing his thumb against her lower lip. It felt like velvet, and arousal thrummed through his body. "Right there. I'd have to be quick about that one, though. Even if we were engaged, long, deep mouth kissing has to be done behind the shelter of the rose arbor."

Her lip trembled, darkening to a deeper pink, a sign that his strategy was working. "You shouldn't say things like this to me," she whispered against his thumb, squeezing her eyes shut.

But she didn't draw back, she didn't move away. She quivered in his hold, and lust rolled in his body like thunder.

He knew he had to stop, for the effort of holding back, of not kissing her right now, was becoming intolerable. He drew back, letting his hand fall, and when she opened her eyes, he gave her an artless look. "What, this isn't the sort of conversation you had with Carrington when he took you for a ride this morning?"

"Heavens, no." She gave a wild little laugh, pressing her fingers to her flushed cheek, right where he'd caressed her a moment ago. "I can't imagine ever having a conversation like this with Carrington."

Encouraged by that information, he went on, "Tufton, then?"

The way she wrinkled up her nose and pursed her lips told him that he didn't have anything to worry about from that quarter, but then she spoke again and shredded any cocky notions Jack might have had that he'd moved into first place.

"Hansborough, though," she murmured, drumming her fingertips against her cheek, a speculative note in her voice that caught him up sharp. "He might be a different story."

Jack set his jaw. "Why?"

"Well, he's so good-looking."

"Good-looking?" Jack couldn't believe what he was hearing. "The man wears pomade in his hair."

"He's quite charming," she went on, ignoring Jack's criticism of his rival. "Witty, too. He's kissed a few girls in his life, I daresay." She lowered her hand and gave a shrug. "Any girl would be willing to have a conversation about kissing with Hansborough."

He felt his guts twist with dread, and his arousal gave way to something else, something dark and dangerous he'd never had cause to feel in his life before. "You can't have a conversation with Hansborough about kissing."

"I *can't*?" she echoed, emphasizing the word, reminding him of just how well she responded to autocratic commands. "Oh, really? Why not?"

"Because it would be impossible," he countered, aware that he sounded as belligerent as Androcles' lion. "He'd have to lift his gaze from your bosom long enough to pay attention to what you were saying, a feat far beyond him, I fear."

"Jack, are you—" She paused as a smile started to curve her mouth, but then she bit her lip to catch it back. "Jack, are you jealous of Hansborough?"

God, yes.

The idea that she could even contemplate kissing Hansborough or any other man but him made Jack feel absolutely violent. He wanted to smash his head into the garden wall or rip Hansborough's throat out. Never in his life had he felt like this, not about any other woman he'd ever known, and he realized why the kiss in Newport had about knocked him off his feet and why he'd been so dead set to win her ever since. From the moment his lips had touched hers, he belonged to her, body and soul. He knew that as surely as he knew his name.

He wanted her to know it, too. He wanted to haul her into his arms right here, right now, right in front of her mother, and show her why he was the only man in the world who ought to have the right to kiss her.

But past experience had already taught him doing such a thing wasn't going to win her over, so he could only stand there, staring into her eyes, motionless and mute, cursing himself for teasing her with her jealousy yesterday, and for pushing her to tell him about Conrath, and most of all, for ever starting this silly game in the first place.

He felt exposed, vulnerable, and in desperation, he bent to pick up the baskets he'd dropped earlier. But as he straightened, he knew he had to give her some sort of reply, preferably something offhand and clever that would put him back on safer ground. "Linnet, you know I can't tell you that," he said, working to keep his voice light and teasing when what he felt was dark and feral. "It's not your day to ask questions."

He managed a flirtatious smile before he turned away and started back to the house. Charles, he thought with chagrin, would have been quite proud of him for that.

HE WAS JEALOUS of Hansborough.

Linnet watched him go, too astonished to move. He'd said last night that today it would be his turn to be jealous, but she had deemed those light words an attempt to tease her and nothing more. In turning the tables today, she hadn't expected him to react with such force, and for a moment those usually impenetrable eyes of his had revealed something far more turbulent than teasing ought to evoke. Like their picnic, when she realized her failure to arrive had wounded him, she felt as if a curtain had just been drawn back, showing her the truth.

Or what she thought to be the truth, she amended at once. She'd been sure more than once that a man cared about her, only to discover how easily she'd been deceived. And right now, her wits felt thick as tar, all her senses were in tumult, and there was no way to be sure about anything.

She lifted her hand to her face, brushing her own

thumb over her lower lip where he'd caressed her moments before, just as stunned by that as she was by the discovery of his jealousy. After his intimate questions, provocative suggestions, and light caresses, her insides were still quivering.

He hadn't touched her since that night in Newport, but even the fact that he would be so bold as to touch her a second time right under her mother's nose wasn't what left her standing here as if rooted to the spot.

The fluttering agitation evoked by his words, the anticipation as he'd lifted his hand, and the pleasure that had fissured through her at his touch, and yes, the tension and excitement of knowing her mother was a mere twenty yards away—all that was a combination that left her breathless and giddy.

It was very similar to what she'd felt when Conrath had held her hand under the table.

The realization was like a dousing of cold water.

He'd done it on purpose. Right after she'd told him about Conrath holding her hand, he must have started plotting how he could do the same thing. And he'd succeeded, too, touching her face and her neck and her mouth until she was awash in sensation, and doing it all right under her mother's nose. That conniving, sneaky—

"Don't you want to walk back with Lord Featherstone?"

Her mother's voice interrupted her, and Linnet came out of her outraged contemplations with a start to find her parent standing beside her.

"No, I don't," she answered as she bent to reach for the two baskets of roses he'd left on the ground. "Trust me, Mother, being anywhere near that man right now is the last thing I want to do."

She ignored her mother's disappointed sigh as she walked away.

IF THAT AFTERNOON in the garden had given him any hope he was making progress in his courtship, the evening dashed it to smithereens. Linnet spent her entire evening glued to Hansborough's side like a limpet, and Jack had to watch the fellow lower his gaze to where it damn well didn't belong all through dinner and dessert. One thing he didn't have to do, however, was sit through the port while Hansborough smirked at him across the table.

"Pardon me, gentlemen," he said, rising, port glass in hand. "I'm going out for a breath of air. It's quite warm in here this evening."

He excused himself from the dining room, slipped out the nearest side door, and went outside. He walked along the house, taking deep breaths of the cool evening air, striving to clear his head and regain his control before he joined the ladies. Piano music floated to him as he came around the corner of the house, but as he started up the steps of the terrace, Linnet's voice floated to him over the soft melody of the sonata being played, and he kept walking, straight past the French doors and down the steps at the opposite end of the terrace. But he stopped at the bottom and closed his eyes, listening for her voice again.

He had to get hold of himself before the other men finished their port, for the idea of Hansborough having

Linnet's attentions all evening while he stood out here and did nothing about it was unthinkable.

God, he thought, once it hit a chap, jealousy was an odious thing. He didn't know why it was deemed the green-eyed monster, for to him, it was no serpent or dragon. It was a black, smothering wave.

It hadn't been all that difficult for him to ask Linnet about a man from her past, for he felt no jealousy over a memory. In fact, he'd dived into that pond expecting Conrath's seduction to be far more wicked than it had proved in reality. Hansborough, however, was here and now, and that was a whole different thing.

The viscount had the power to say and do the same things he was doing; there was nothing to stop him. And if Jack was any judge of character, the fellow knew his way about when it came to women. The idea that Linnet would contemplate even a discussion of kissing, much less engage in the act of it, with any man but him was unbearable, and yet, if it happened, he knew he could do little to stop it.

He downed his port in one draught, set the crystal goblet on the stone pedestal beside him, and took a few more steps along the side of the house, moving out of the light that spilled from the windows along the terrace and into the shadows beyond the steps.

This was only the second evening. He stopped walking again and raked his hands through his hair, wondering in desperation how he was going to endure four more nights of this without going insane or giving in to the same wild impulse he'd had in Newport to claim her for himself.

He could not allow either of those things to happen.

He had to tamp down this dark, smothering jealousy before it could have power over his actions. He closed his eyes, but when he did, an equally dark and powerful emotion stirred inside him, and here, alone in the darkened garden, he couldn't resist allowing it to take hold of him. He closed his eyes.

The image that came into his mind was of her as he'd first seen her in the ballroom at Newport, a golden beauty with lovely eyes who'd riveted the gazes of half the men in the room the moment she stepped through the door. He imagined her now as he'd imagined her then, seeing past the upswept hair, glittering jewels, and Worth gown. He imagined now what he'd imagined then, all that tawny hair down around her shoulders. In his imagination, he stripped away pink silk to expose exquisite breasts, shapely hips, and long, slim legs. Arousal stirred in him.

He tilted his head back, breathing in the remembered scent of heliotrope and tasting sherry on his tongue as he relived the extraordinary moment when his mouth had touched hers and everything in the world had changed for him. His arousal deepened into lust.

He thought of this afternoon, of how touching her cheek had stirred her desire. She was an innocent, he reminded himself, but here in the darkness of his imagination, that thought seemed to enhance his lust instead of suppressing it, spreading it through his body in a thick, hot wave. The passion in her was unmistakable; it lurked deep down, waiting for the right man to bring it out. He wanted to take her innocence, revel in that passion, and show her he was that man.

"I know what you did."

Saints preserve us.

Jack almost groaned aloud at the sound of Linnet's voice, low but unmistakable despite the music coming from the drawing room. His self-control was barely tethered as it was. Did she have to come out here and test it further?

He glanced at the line of tall boxwoods along the side of the house, and he cursed himself for not having the sense to hide among them before he started thinking lusty thoughts. "You shouldn't be out here," he said, not daring to turn around. "Not alone with me."

"I saw you pass by a few minutes ago, but I doubt anyone else did," she murmured, still keeping her voice low.

Desperate, he tried again. "You can't be sure of that."

"I've just come out for a stroll along the terrace, and you're down there in the dark where no one can see you."

"Thank God for that, at least," he muttered, and took a deep breath, working to tamp down lust as best he could. "Still, best if you go back in."

"I just came out to tell you I know what you were doing."

Walk away, he told himself. Walk away now. But even as he thought it, he knew he wasn't going to. Striving to seem as if he were under perfect control, he turned to face her.

She stood at the top of the steps, and the light behind her that spilled through the drawing room windows illuminated the golden locks of her hair like a halo and lent a faint glow to the edges of her white silk evening frock. She looked angelic, innocent, and somehow, that harkened to the devil inside him like no siren ever could.

He took another deep breath. "I shan't use one of my three remaining questions today to ask what you mean, but if you care to explain, I'm all ears."

"This afternoon in the rose garden, you did what Conrath did. I told you about his holding my hand, of how he . . . caressed it, and you turned right around and tried the same sort of thing. Don't deny it."

If he pursued this topic, he was risking annihilation, but then he reminded himself of the goal he'd set that afternoon in Belinda's drawing room. His purpose in all of this was to spark her arousal and light her on fire and make her want him as much as he wanted her. He couldn't light her on fire if he didn't strike any matches. "I won't deny it, but I do have to wonder if you know why I did it."

"It's obvious, isn't it? You wanted to make me feel . . . feel . . ." She paused and looked away, and though the light behind her and the darkness in front of her prevented him from seeing the blush in her cheeks, he knew it was there. He didn't see it, but he felt it—the first stir of desire in her. It called to him. He took a step forward.

"Aroused," he supplied. "I believe 'aroused' is the word you're looking for. Yes, I wanted to arouse you."

"So you admit it."

"Of course I admit it. I see no reason not to." He took another step, like a moth to flame. "Did it work?"

She stirred, glancing over her shoulder and back at him. "When you play twenty questions, do you always ask such inappropriate ones?"

"You came out here," he reminded her. "You brought up the topic. Besides, there's nothing wrong with desire, Linnet. It would be much more wrong if you didn't feel it."

She shook her head, looking away. "You asked me why I fell in love with Conrath. I'll tell you why."

She paused for a long moment before she looked at him again. "Once a girl makes her debut, she is allowed to accept gifts from suitors if they are suitable ones."

Jack frowned slightly at the seeming shift in the subject. "I'm sure you received heaps of them."

"Yes." It was a simple admission, said without vanity, an acceptance of fact. "Books of poetry bound in leather covers, boxes of expensive chocolates, and enormous bouquets with all the appropriate sentiments expressed by the flowers chosen. And yet—"

"And yet . . ." he prompted when she fell silent.

"None of the young men who gave me these gifts bothered to find out what I liked to read, or if I cared for chocolates, or which flowers were my favorites. Conrath was different. In our very first conversation, I mentioned how much I loved the sound of the sea. His first gift to me was a conch shell."

Jack began to understand where this was going, and it gave him a sinking feeling in his guts.

"All his gifts were like that," she went on before he could respond. "So simple, and yet, so thoughtful. They were meant to show me how much he cared for me, but it was all a lie because he didn't care. It was a fortune-hunter's trick. Blueberry muffins," she added, "would have been just his sort of present."

"And that's why you think I did it, as a trick?"

"I don't know."

"I did it to please you."

She nodded, not seeming surprised. She looked into his upturned face. "So did he," she said simply, and Jack felt as if he'd just been kicked in the teeth. He sucked in his breath.

"Every word he said, everything he did—the gifts, the attentions, caressing my hand to arouse me—all deliberate, all designed to please me, and disarm me, and move me to fall in love with him. He manipulated me. And I think you know just how he did it."

He knew. He'd known all his life. How could he not, having watched the same scenario play out for his father, then his brother, over and over? Conrath had nothing on either of them. But how could he convince her he wasn't like that? "Linnet—"

"He deceived me, and he broke my heart, but I got over him, and I forgave myself for being a fool. Any girl, I told myself, can make a mistake. But I was determined not to make the same mistake twice, which is why I was so resistant to any suitor over here. I felt sure they were all after my money and nothing more. That night in Newport, when I walked into the ball, I was so confident, so sure of myself and my judgment and what I wanted. But it was proved to me that night that my judgment about men is . . ." She paused and grimaced. "Flawed."

He cursed Conrath, and Van Hausen, and his brother and his father and every other fortune-hunting scoundrel to hell. "What you're saying is that you still think I'm a fortune hunter."

"No, what I'm saying is that I don't know you're *not* one."

He thought of her father, and the deal they'd made, and frustration rose up inside him, a dangerous addition to the desire already coursing through him. "You could say the same about all the other men here," he said, stabbing a finger at the drawing room. "You dismissed one or two of them for that very reason last spring."

"There's one enormous difference between them and you, and I've known it all along."

"What's that?"

She looked at him, but she didn't answer. In the silence, piano music and feminine laughter echoed from the drawing room, a sharp contrast to the frustration and arousal coursing through him.

It seemed an eternity before she spoke. "They don't make me feel the way you do."

Her words were like paraffin tossed onto flames. His desire flared, and he started forward, but then her words in Belinda's drawing room came back to him, reminding him that what he wanted so badly to do was the one thing he could not do. It took all he had, but he stopped. He drew a deep breath, leashed his lust, and used his last question of the day. "How do I make you feel, Linnet?"

"You know," she said, her voice almost indiscernible over the music. "What you said."

"Not good enough. I want you to say it."

"Aroused." Her tongue touched her lips. "You make me feel aroused."

Oh, God. The tension was becoming unbearable. He lowered his gaze along that splendid body and back up again, torturing himself, knowing that what he was about to do could backfire utterly. "I think that's something you'll have to prove."

She blinked. "What do you mean?"

"I'm aroused, too, Linnet. So aroused, I can barely think, I can barely breathe, and all I want in this world is to walk up those steps, haul you into my arms, and kiss you again. But I'll be damned before I'll give you cause to say I took your kiss against your will. So, that means you have two choices. The first choice is the proper one: Turn around, go back inside, and leave me alone."

Her chin lifted a notch. "And the second one?"

"You can come down those steps, Lioness, walk over here, and kiss me."

Chapter 13

Linnet's heart slammed against her ribs, a jolt of pure panic. "I can't do that," she gasped.

"Why not?"

She cast a glance over her shoulder, then looked at him again. "If anyone came out on the terrace, we'd be seen."

She watched in dismay as he backed up three paces, stepped between two of the enormous boxwood pillars that lined the wall of the house, and vanished from view.

She stared at the shadowy recess into which he had slipped, torn by the agony of a decision she shouldn't even be trying to make. The obvious thing to do, the one thing a well-bred girl could do in these circumstances, was go back inside.

Linnet didn't move.

He was the most provoking man, the most aggravating man she'd ever known. That kiss in the pagoda had seemed like the most shameful, ruinous thing that had ever happened to her, and yet, that wasn't what she felt right now. That kiss had stained her reputation and wrecked her life, but for no reason that made any sense whatsoever, she wondered what it would be like to risk ruin again, to go down those steps, slide in between those boxwoods, and walk into his arms so that he could kiss her again. How would it feel?

Her body responded at once, before her mind could even consider. Arousal stirred, opening inside her— vibrant and quivering with life. Slowly, she walked down the steps and moved toward the recess where he'd vanished from view. With one last glance over her shoulder, she followed him.

The sharp scent of the boxwood and the mellower one of bay rum filled her nostrils, but she could see nothing at first. The darkness was almost total. She was a scant three feet away from him, but all she could make out was the glimmer of white from his shirt and waistcoat. She blinked, and after a moment, her eyes adjusted, enabling her to discern his tall form leaning against the brick wall behind him, and when she blinked again, she saw his face. His expression was grave, his eyes like pitch.

She waited, standing in front of him, her insides shaking, and she had no idea what to do next.

"Well, go on," he said when she didn't move. "We don't have much time before someone comes out here looking for you." His voice sounded amiable, almost friendly, and yet, she knew that wasn't what he felt. She sensed the tension in him. It was palpable in the confined space and short distance between them. "Best if you kiss me quick."

Her heart seemed to stop for a second, then it began to hammer in her chest. She moved closer, then closer still, until their bodies were almost touching. The quivering inside her intensified as she rose on her toes and brought her mouth up to his. By the time she was a hairsbreadth away, her anticipation was so acute, it felt like pain.

She pressed her lips to his, and pleasure pierced her at once, pleasure so sweet, so acute and unexpected, she groaned against his mouth.

He stiffened, straightening away from the wall, and for a moment, she thought he was going to embrace her or push her away, but he did neither. Instead, with her lips barely touching his, he stilled again, and she realized he was waiting for her to do something more.

She didn't know quite what that something was, for this light brush of lips was where her experience with kissing ended, but she did know she wasn't ready to pull back, so she moved her mouth experimentally against his. It was a tentative, exploring caress, and as she did, the arousal within her grew hotter. Her hand came up to touch his cheek.

His response was immediate, as if her touch was just what he'd been waiting for. He slid an arm around her, and his fingertips pressed the base of her spine, urging her even closer. She did, and when her breasts brushed his chest, the pleasure spread through all her limbs, bringing a strange, boneless sensation that made her knees go weak.

Without conscious direction, her arms came up to

wrap around his neck. She wanted to be even closer, and he seemed to know it, for his arm tightened around her waist, and his other arm came around her shoulders, embracing her totally, just as he he'd done in Newport. Her head was spinning, her knees were weak, her body was on fire, just like in Newport. And yet, it all felt so different. Whether it was because this time she'd come willingly into his embrace, or because there were no witnesses, or because he was no longer a stranger to her, Linnet didn't know, but she felt no shock, no shame, and no outrage. All she felt was a deepening excitement, and a need for even more.

He tilted his head, and his mouth opened over hers. His tongue touched her closed lips as if he wanted her to part them, and when she did, she tasted port. She had no time to savor it, however, for his tongue entered her mouth, and she jerked, jolted by the sudden, electrifying shock. A man's tongue in her mouth? Never in her wildest dreams had she imagined that.

As if sensing her surprise, he eased back, but she pursued, duplicating his move, her tongue touching his. The move seemed to ignite something inside him, for his embrace tightened even more, lifting her almost off the ground, bringing her against him so fully that she could feel the hard length of his body everywhere he pressed against her. He seemed especially hard where his hips were pressed to hers, and the intimacy of it shocked her. She broke the kiss with a gasp, lowering her arms, flattening her palms against his shoulders.

He eased her to the ground at once and released her, his arms falling away and his body pulling back from hers to flatten against the wall behind him. She ought to have been relieved, for her body was in turmoil, her head spinning like a top, and her breathing hard and quick, but she didn't feel relieved by his withdrawal. Quite the opposite. She felt bereft. She felt frustrated. She felt . . . incomplete.

His breathing was every bit as ragged as hers, stirring the hair at her temple. The satin lapels of his dinner jacket felt slick against her palms as she slid her hands down from his shoulders. His chest was like a wall against her palms, and even as she recalled how easily he had carried her across a meadow and up a hill, she knew as she had not known yesterday, that he wasn't the only one with power.

It was a heady feeling.

After a few moments, she looked up, and in the darkened shadows, she watched a faint smile curve his mouth. "Damned if I'm not the luckiest chap in the world," he murmured, his voice a bit unsteady. "How many men get struck by lightning twice?"

She didn't have time to think of a response.

"Linnet?" Her mother's voice floated to where they stood between the boxwoods.

She felt Jack's hand tighten at her waist, and she watched him press a finger to his lips. She nodded in understanding, and he lowered his hand, leaned out to peek at the terrace nearby, then straightened again to look at her. "She's gone back in. Follow her, quick."

Linnet felt a jolt of panic, and her hand flew to her mouth. "I can't."

For some reason, his smile widened. "Don't worry," he said as he pulled her hand down and pressed a quick kiss to her lips. "You don't look debauched.

Good thing for both of us my valet shaved me just before dinner."

She had no idea what shaving had to do with it, and she couldn't seem to gather her dazed senses enough to figure it out. There wasn't time for contemplations on the subject anyway, for Jack was already shoving her out from between the boxwoods. She turned toward the terrace, took a deep breath, and went up the steps, her heart still pounding, her pulses still racing, her lips still tingling. Despite his reassurance, she felt debauched, and she had no idea how to hide what seemed so obvious.

But unless she became a very good actress in very short order, being found out was a distinct possibility, so Linnet squared her shoulders, notched up her chin, and pasted on the most serene expression she could manage.

"Ah, so you've changed your mind and come back in after all." Helen's voice was light, but Linnet knew those words were for the benefit of anyone who might have noted the length of her absence from the drawing room.

"I like standing out on the terrace," she replied, but she wasn't quite able to meet her mother's gaze as she sat down beside her on the settee. "It's a beautiful evening."

A glance around the drawing room told her the other ladies hadn't seemed to notice her return, and conversation didn't pause, but when her mother leaned close to her and spoke again, Linnet knew she wasn't off the hook just yet. "Just where were you, young lady?"

Linnet turned, giving her mother what she hoped

was a convincing enough expression of bewilderment as she prepared to tell the most blatant lie of her life. "I don't know what you mean. I was right below you."

"Were you, indeed?" Helen murmured.

Linnet felt a shimmer of guilt and looked away before her mother could see it. "Of course," she lied again, her guilt deepening as she reminded herself that she wasn't the only one affected by her ruined reputation. Her scandal reflected on her family, too.

"You shouldn't go off the terrace," Helen said after a moment.

Still, there was little Helen could do but accept her explanation. No one had seen her with Jack, no harm had been done, and though her pulses were still racing, and she still felt wild and wanton, Jack must have been right that there was no outward sign of what had just happened, for none of the women in the room were staring at her.

But that conclusion had just crossed her mind when her gaze paused at Lady Trubridge, and she felt a sudden jolt of apprehension. She didn't know quite why, for the marchioness wasn't even looking at her. She was talking with a group of ladies on the other side of the room. But then, as if she sensed Linnet's gaze, she turned her head, and her shrewd and thoughtful gaze rested on Linnet. Not a flicker of emotion showed on her face, but Linnet's apprehension deepened into fear.

Working to keep her expression as neutral as possible, she looked away, drew in a slow, deep, steadying breath, and reminded herself that not only her reputation, but her entire future was at stake.

This wasn't Newport. Tonight, she had not been the

innocent recipient of a man's advances. Instead, she had chosen his kiss, she had welcomed it, she had reveled in it. And it had been glorious. But it couldn't happen again, not unless she agreed to marry him. And two wild, wanton kisses or not, marrying Jack Featherstone was a choice Linnet just wasn't ready to make.

UNLIKE LINNET, WHO'D had to go straight back to the drawing room, Jack had the luxury of taking a bit of time before rejoining the men. A good thing, too, for lust was thrumming through his body, and despite several minutes lingering by the side door into the house, he found it damned difficult to douse the flame. As he reentered the dining room, he could only pray he'd managed to don the nonchalant air of a man who'd been out for an innocent little walk.

When he'd dared her to come down those steps and kiss him, he hadn't expected her to do it. He'd hoped she might, for Linnet wasn't any more inclined to back down from challenges than he was. But he'd also known what she was risking to take up a dare like the one he'd thrown down, so he'd stood in that shadowy recess, hardly willing to hope or even breathe. When she'd appeared in front of him, her gold hair and white dress glinting in the dim light, exhilaration and excitement had risen in him at once, like fireworks shooting skyward, and it had taken all the will he had to stand there and wait for her to close that last bit of distance. The wait had been agony.

When at last, she'd pressed her lips to his so sweetly, so innocently, he'd nearly gone to his knees, and the carnal sound of her moan against his mouth had been almost more than he could bear. But when she'd touched him, that had brought the lightning down, sending the lust he was working so hard to contain coursing through every cell and nerve of his body, and he'd been unable to hold back another second.

He might have ravished her then and there if she hadn't brought him back to earth. Appreciating that fact, however, didn't have quite the dampening effect it ought to have. Rather, it started his mind thinking of ravishment rather than self-control.

Jack's imagination wasn't allowed to go too far down that particular road, however, before Nick stood up, indicating it was time to rejoin the ladies, and he supposed he ought to be grateful for that. As he followed the others out of the dining room, he reminded himself of what was at stake. He had to keep his head, for if he didn't, Linnet would be the one to pay the price.

Fate, however, didn't seem willing to trust Linnet's welfare solely to Jack's willpower, for the moment they walked into the drawing room, he saw Belinda's gaze hone in on him, and he was reminded of an alert cat sitting outside a mousehole, ready to pounce. A moment later, when he saw her walk over to her husband, he suspected his absence from the dining room was the topic of their discussion, and when she started in his direction a moment later, he knew it for certain.

"Jack," she said as she passed him. "A word."

She made for an unoccupied part of the room, and he followed, glad that where she was leading him was where the liquor cabinet was located, for if she brought up the topic he feared she was about to bring up, he was going to need a second glass of port.

She denied his offer to pour her a sherry, and he reached for the port decanter instead, but he'd barely removed the crystal stopper before she spoke.

"Did you approach Miss Holland when she was alone on the terrace?"

He paused a second before answering. "Not exactly."

"She was out of the drawing room ten minutes, about the same amount of time you were out of the dining room. What happened?"

He could not allow Belinda to think any of this was Linnet's fault. "Nothing happened," he said, but he didn't look at her as he said it. Instead, he kept his attention on his task, but he could feel her gaze boring into him as he poured his port, and her next words told him that though Linnet might be cleared of any wrongdoing, he was not going to escape tonight's events unscathed.

"I've always known you were wild, Jack, wild, daring, and a bit of a hellion," she said, her voice low beside him. "But in all the years I've known you, I've never known you to lie to me."

Jack inhaled a sharp breath, feeling the pain of her words like a knife in his chest. "Are you saying I'm like Charles?" he asked, setting aside the decanter and forcing himself to look at her.

"If you're not, then don't lie to me. When Miss Holland was outside, did you speak to her?"

"Yes."

"Her mother went out on the terrace to fetch her, but

came back in without her. The girl wasn't on the terrace, was she? She was with you."

"It wasn't some sort of planned rendezvous, if that's what you're implying. I'd gone outside for a bit of fresh air, and so had she, and we just happened to . . . encounter each other."

"Jack!" She glanced around, then back at him. "You cannot detain a young woman when she's unaccompanied, especially at night, and I shouldn't even have to tell you that. What happened with Sir Roger? His sudden departure had something to do with you, didn't it?"

The abrupt shift in the subject was a bit of a relief. "I daresay it did."

"What happened?"

He told her, and she stared at him in horror. "You carried off a girl—an unmarried girl—over your shoulder in front of two witnesses?" she whispered. "And made her have a picnic with you alone in the countryside? Are you mad?"

He rubbed a hand over his forehead. "That's quite possible."

"Did you force your attentions on her as you did in Newport?"

He grimaced, but the question, though brutal, was a fair one. "No." He swallowed his port in one draught and looked into her eyes. "Neither yesterday, nor tonight."

"Well, we can be grateful for that, at least. And let us hope Sir Roger and his sister haven't told all their friends what they witnessed. As for you, this sort of behavior is beyond the pale. It must stop."

"You're right, of course. And I take full responsibility for everything that's happened."

"As you should. You are a man of the world. She is a young lady and far more innocent than you."

"I know, I know. It's just—" He paused, staring helplessly at his sister-in-law. "I want her, Belinda."

"Your lust," she said in withering accents, "is not relevant. We are not talking about a cancan dancer or an actress."

He shook his head, impatient. "No, I know. That's not what I mean. I mean, I really want her. This isn't just about doing the honorable thing. It's much more than that."

She studied his face for a moment. "I think you mean that. Which is all the more reason," she added before he could reply, "for you to treat her with the respect she deserves. You will conduct your courtship in an open, honorable fashion, or not at all."

He nodded, but he couldn't help a frustrated sigh. "I don't see how any man can conduct a courtship under these damnable circumstances," he muttered, running his finger around the inside of his collar in irritation. "It's maddening, having chaperones hovering about all the time. I ask you, how on earth can two people ever come to know each other well enough to decide if they want to wed when they can't even have a private conversation?"

For the first time since they'd begun this set-to, Belinda's expression softened. "People have been courting this way for centuries, Jack."

"I never thought I would be. I've never been very good at being good, I'm afraid."

"Then you'd better be a quick study, because unless and until she has agreed to marry you, you cannot be alone with her again. Is that understood?"

"Yes, of course. Belinda?" he added as she started to turn away. "I don't suppose you'd care to offer any advice?"

"If you were any other man, I'd advise you to just be yourself," she said dryly. "Given your crazy impulses, however, I'm rather afraid of offering that particular advice. All I can say is, keep your head, Jack."

He nodded, but as he watched her go, he wished she'd told him how on earth he was to keep his head when he felt as if he was losing his mind.

THE FOLLOWING DAY, the men had a very early breakfast and went shooting, returning just before the dressing gong. A full day away from Linnet gave Jack plenty of time to regain his equilibrium and put his priorities in order. He also managed to keep any wayward, lust-filled thoughts of her at bay all through aperitifs and dinner, but after the port, when he walked into the drawing room and saw her, laughing and smiling with the other ladies, all his hard-won efforts went straight to the wall. And a few minutes later, when she came over to him, Jack didn't know whether to be glad or bolt for the door.

Making a run for it was probably the wiser course, but he hadn't the will to act on it. The temptation to be near her was too strong to be gainsaid by thoughts of mere self-preservation.

"I saw Lady Trubridge pull you aside last night,"

she said, halting beside him. "Did she call you on the carpet for . . . for what happened?"

"A bit," he admitted, and took a sip of his port.

"I was afraid of that." She bit her lip. "I'm sorry."

"Don't be sorry," he said at once. "I'm not. I should be, of course," he added, "a fact Belinda put to me when she raked me over the coals. But I'm not sorry at all, Linnet."

She turned her head and met his gaze. "Neither am I."

Her smile hurt somehow, squeezing his chest, and longing flooded him. He looked away, trying not to think of all the ways he might get her alone, and felt almost relieved to see Hansborough coming their way.

"Hansborough," he greeted, pasting on his most genial smile. "Come to join the conversation, have you?"

"If I'm not intruding?" His answering smile made it clear he knew he was.

"Of course not," Jack lied, and gestured to the tray of decanters and glasses on top of the liquor cabinet beside him. "I was just about to offer to pour Miss Holland a drink."

The viscount's smile took on a subtle hint of disdain. "Playing footman, are you, Featherstone?"

"Why not?" he countered with a shrug, set down his port, and picked up a glass. "Linnet, what will you have?"

"I'd better not have anything. I adore sherry, but I've had one glass already." She gestured to her empty glass on the table by her mother. "And a girl isn't supposed to have more than one digestif in an evening. I fear if I had another, my mother would be very disappointed in me."

Hansborough gave her a beatific smile. "Your consideration and sweetness do you credit, Miss Holland."

"Sweetness?" Jack's sound of derision at that nauseating compliment was out of his mouth before he could stop it. "Linnet's not sweet at all," he said, and looked at her. "She's a lioness."

He was rewarded with a smile.

Hansborough didn't notice it, for he had transferred his attention to Jack. "Really, Featherstone, I can't think *Miss Holland* appreciates your comparison. A lioness is a wild, savage, predatory creature. Miss Holland is none of those."

"Still, he's right about one thing," Linnet said, bringing the viscount's attention back to her. "I'm not the least bit sweet."

Hansborough glanced down and back up, and Jack read his thoughts like a book. He moved, an involuntary, savage jerk forward, but then he checked himself and stayed where he was. Brawling in the drawing room, he feared, would be the last straw as far as Belinda was concerned.

"I can't agree, Miss Holland," Hansborough said at last. "I think you are very sweet. Sweet and golden . . . like honey."

It was Hansborough's turn to be rewarded with one of Linnet's radiant smiles, and Jack's hand closed around his glass so tightly he was surprised it didn't break. "So, Linnet," he said, desperately keeping jealousy in check, "are you certain I can't tempt you with another sherry?" He gestured to the decanters. "It is your favorite, after all."

"Miss Holland already refused you once, Featherstone," Hansborough said, biting inflection beneath the pleasant, well-bred voice. "Must you continue to press her?"

Embarrassment flamed in Linnet's face at this not-so-subtle reference to Newport, and Jack opened his mouth to return the viscount's insulting implication with a scathing rejoinder of his own, but Linnet spoke before he could. "On the contrary, Lord Hansborough. Lord Featherstone wasn't pressing me at all. He was just being courteous. If you gentlemen will pardon me, I must rejoin my mother."

Hansborough's mouth tipped politely. "Of course," he said with a little bow.

Jack bowed as well, and Linnet departed, leaving the two men alone. A moment later, she was cornered by Lord Tufton. "Well done, Hansborough," he said. "Now she's deprived us both of her company and left the field wide open for Lord Tufton. Well done."

He turned away, returning his attention to the decanters, but if he thought the other man would move to another part of the room and leave him in peace, he was mistaken. Hansborough remained where he was, much to Jack's aggravation.

He started to reach for the port, thinking to refill his glass, but then he changed his mind. If he couldn't have Linnet, he decided, he could at least have a taste of her. He shoved aside his glass, reached for a fresh one, and picked up the bottle of sherry instead.

"Sherry?" The viscount gave a laugh that to Jack's admittedly biased ears sounded condescending as hell. "Drinking her favorite cordial to impress her when she's not even here? You have got it badly, Featherstone."

Jack smiled, wondering what the viscount would think if he knew the true reason for his choice. "You seem amused, Hansborough," he said as he set aside the decanter. "Do you have something against Miss Holland's favorite drink?"

"It's understandable for her to enjoy sherry. After all, it's what the ladies drink. But it's not a fitting drink . . ." He paused a fraction of a second. "For a man."

Jack gave a laugh at that clumsy attempt to goad him, and he turned with his drink to lean back against the cabinet. "Oh, I don't know," he told the viscount, and cast a pointed glance across the room to Linnet, "I developed quite a taste for sherry in Newport."

Hansborough turned toward him as if pulled by a string. "Let's take off the gloves, Featherstone."

"If you like." Jack straightened and turned as well. "Speak your mind, Hansborough."

"After your despicable actions, do you think you've any chance with her at all?"

Jack swirled the contents of his glass, giving the other man his best amused glance. "Worried, old chap?"

The viscount's answering look was equally amused. "About you? Hardly. A man who does what you did isn't fit to be the husband of any lady, much less a glorious creature like Miss Holland. Though I confess, when I learned the gossip of your barbaric conduct in Newport, I was a bit surprised. The Featherstone men are usually much more skilled at seducing wealthy young ladies than that. You're letting your family name down . . . *old chap.*"

He walked away before Jack could respond, which was just as well. If the other man had said one more thing, there might have been a brawl in Belinda's drawing room after all, they'd both be sent packing, and Carrington could very well win by default.

No, better to let Hansborough have the last word and think he'd won a victory tonight. As for tomorrow, the viscount had insisted the gloves come off, and Jack decided it was time to show him how painful bare-knuckle fighting could be.

He toasted that decision, swallowed the contents of his glass, and grimaced in aggravation. Sherry tasted so much more luscious on Linnet's mouth than it did from a glass.

Chapter 14

Linnet felt a desperate need to get away. "Yes, I'm sure," she murmured, leaning as far back from Tufton's cigar-laced breath as she could manage without being rude. "And I'm glad your hunting was so enjoyable today, my lord." She cast a furtive glance around and caught the Duke of Carrington's eye.

Something pleading in her face must have told him to rescue her, for he responded at once, crossing the room to join them.

"Your Grace," she greeted with grateful fervor. "Was your grouse hunting successful, too?"

"Indeed it was, Miss Holland. Seventeen birds."

"Marvelous." She cast about for a subject that would drive Tufton away. "Tell me more about the latest plans for Irish Home Rule. Do you believe it will come to Ireland or not?"

"To my mind, it's inevitable. It might even be a good thing for Ireland in the long run." He smiled, an amiable smile that crinkled up the crow's-feet at the edges of his eyes. "Don't tell anyone I've said it, Miss Holland, for I should be *persona non grata* among my fellow Tories if they knew I'd breathed such heresy." He paused and leaned a bit closer. "It shall have to be our secret."

She smiled back at him. "I shan't tell on you, I promise. Still, the Unionists will fight it all the way, it seems to me. Could they ever be brought to accept it, do you think?"

"That is the sticky wicket," he agreed, and the two of them began an in-depth discussion on the ramifications of Home Rule for Ireland. Within fifteen minutes, Tufton wandered off, unable to keep up.

"Thank you," she said when the marquess was out of earshot. "I owe you a debt for that."

"You owe me nothing, my dear. I'm happy to drive him away and have you all to myself. But . . ." He paused and tilted his head, studying her, smiling a little. "Your knowledge of British politics has improved markedly in the past few days, I must say."

"Has it?" She tried to dissemble. "It must be that your lectures have enlightened me—" She broke off as he shook his head, his smile widening.

"My dear child, this pretense of ignorance on your part won't do. This afternoon, your mother was kind enough to inform me of your three governesses and four years of finishing school. And I understand you studied British politics extensively?"

"I've been caught, I see. It's just that you've been so

pleased to explain things to me, and I haven't had the heart to undeceive you."

"You mean I've been rambling on, and you haven't been able to get a word in," he said with a show of humor she hadn't seen from him before. "You're a very tactful young lady."

She wrinkled up her nose. "Not always," she told him. "You haven't seen my temper."

They both laughed, and Linnet was reminded again what a nice man he was. That reminder did not make things easier. He still admired her, she knew, and at the end of the house party, he might offer for her a second time, and if she accepted him, her life would be agreeable, filled with purpose, and so pleasantly dull.

She looked past his shoulder and caught sight of Hansborough. He was talking to Lord Trubridge, but he was watching her, and all of a sudden, Linnet felt smothered, hemmed in, trapped by a choice she didn't trust herself to make. "Thank you again for saving me, Your Grace," she murmured, "but now, I must return to my mother. If you will excuse me?"

"Of course." He bowed, and she moved to where her mother stood by the fireplace, talking with Lady Trubridge.

"Mother," she said, feeling desperate, "I'm going out on the terrace. It's so hot in here, and I want some air."

She didn't miss the two women's exchange of glances, and then Lady Trubridge looked past her to where Jack was standing on the other side of the room. "Quite understandable, my dear. And since you've left the duke on his own, Miss Holland, I believe I shall go and keep him company."

Linnet knew the marchioness's reason had little to do with solicitude and a great deal to do with the fact that talking with Carrington gave her a view of the open doorway onto the terrace over the duke's shoulder. That didn't bother her, since she had no intention of letting Jack dare her into anything naughty again. She went outside, straight to the railing, where she could look over the moonlit gardens while remaining fully under Lady Trubridge's protective eye.

What was she going to do? She breathed in, deep, measured breaths. She ought to pick Carrington. He was the sensible choice. Hansborough might offer for her, if she indicated she would welcome such an offer. He was a darker horse than Carrington, more attractive, and yet—

Footsteps behind her had Linnet glancing over her shoulder, and when she saw Jack approaching, she groaned and looked away.

He heard that sound and paused a few feet away. "Do you want me to go?"

She gave him a wry look. "Since you never listen to me anyway, does it matter?"

"I'll go back in," he said, "if that's what you want."

She sighed. "You make things so much harder when you're being nice to me."

That made him grin, and he came to stand beside her, a fully respectable three feet away. "I can be nicer."

A warm, tingling glow started in her midsection and radiated outward. She ought to tell him to go back in. "It doesn't matter," she said. "Stay, and have your port out here if you like. But know that Lady Trubridge is watching us like a hawk, and I'm not moving from this spot."

"Fair enough." He took a sip from his glass. "But I'm not drinking port, Linnet. I'm drinking sherry."

The warmth in her deepened and spread, and when he lowered his gaze to her mouth, her lips began to tingle, and she remembered with vivid clarity what had happened last night two dozen feet from where they now stood. Her toes curled in her slippers, and she looked back out at the garden, reminding herself of her priorities. "I'm thinking of all the reasons why marrying Carrington would be a splendid decision."

"Again?"

Out of the corner of her eye, she watched him lean one hip against the stone railing and take a sip from the glass in his hand. "Weren't you doing this night before last as well?" he asked.

"I'm thinking what an excellent political hostess I'd be. At the center of everything in London, and in the world, too, really."

"Is that what you want?"

"It would be exciting. I like excitement. I could be like Jennie Jerome."

"Yes, I daresay Lord Randolph's resignation and the ruin of his political career proved very exciting for her after all the years she'd spent building it. A myriad of hopes and years of work crushed in a single day."

"And then there's Hansborough." She knew she was treading on dangerous ground with that, but Jack's comments were flustering her enough that she wanted to needle him in retaliation. "He loves fishing. He even offered to teach me."

"Well, given your love of excitement, that should prove a most enjoyable outing."

She felt another pang of uncertainty and scowled at him.

He smiled in response. "Do you really believe going over all the practical considerations again and again will help you decide whom to marry?"

She looked away again. "Isn't that what people do when making decisions? Go over the considerations?"

"Of course. Because people insist on thinking it will help. But it never does. Practical considerations always prove meaningless in affairs like this."

She felt a sickening little lurch of dismay in her stomach. If he was right, she was doomed, and she felt impelled to argue the point. "I don't see how a careful weighing of pros and cons can ever be unhelpful."

"Because it's never reassuring, that's why. It just stirs up self-doubt. You have to go by what you feel is right. If you don't, you'll never be happy with the decision you've made. Doubt will always linger in the back of your mind. When you do what you're sure is right, you can't ever go wrong."

"I used to believe that, but it isn't true." She turned toward him. "I was absolutely sure I loved Conrath, and I was just as sure that he loved me. I had no doubts, no fears at all. And I was so, so wrong."

He shrugged, took a sip from his glass, and set it down, then he straightened away from the rail. "You made a mistake. It happens to us all."

"More than one mistake. I was so sure I wanted an American husband because I was convinced all the British ones were just after my dowry. Then came Frederick. Again, I was sure I knew what I was doing. I didn't love him, but I was positive he loved me, that I could trust him, and that I'd come to love him and our future would be happy. Again, look how wrong I was. And," she added with a little laugh, "if all that's not enough to shake a girl's confidence in her own judgment, there's what I found out about my father."

He stiffened. "What about your father?"

"All my life I've adored my father. I never had a doubt he loved me and wanted what was best for me. After Conrath, I had no desire to make a transatlantic marriage, but my mother insisted we do a London season anyway. The longer we were here, the more sure I was that my future was back home in New York."

"And your mother disagreed."

"Oh, yes. We fought like cats and dogs. But Daddy backed me up, assuring me he was on my side and that I was right to hold out for what I wanted. That night in Newport, I found out it wasn't my happiness he was thinking of at all. The whole time he was pretending to support me and what I wanted, he was making his own plans with Franklin MacKay for me to marry Davis when we came home. It was never about me or my happiness, it was about him wanting to use me to make a business deal."

"Hell." Jack let out his breath, tilting his head back. "Holy hell."

She couldn't help a wry smile at his reaction. "Yes, that's rather how I felt."

He lowered his head, looking at the ground, and sighed again. "Linnet, I think your father loves you—"

"Oh, yes," she cut in, the words bitter on her tongue. "Using me to make a profit. That's love, no doubt about it."

Jack looked up again, into her face. "Things aren't always black and white, Linnet. There might be—" He broke off circumstances. "Hell," he said again. "I'm sorry."

She waved a hand, for she didn't want to talk about Daddy. "It doesn't matter. The point is, I no longer trust my feelings to guide me. A sensible decision based on facts is wiser."

"Why? You're just as likely to make a mistake over a decision based on facts as you are one made based on your instincts."

"Mistakes happen, is that what you mean?"

"Yes, and it's not always a bad thing when they do." He moved closer, glanced at the doorway, gave a sigh that told her Lady Trubridge was still watching them, and stopped. "Some of my biggest mistakes have led to some of the best things in my life. Kissing you being a prime example."

Uncertainty twisted her heart with a painful pang. "You don't know that kissing me was one of the best things of your life," she said in a fierce whisper. "You can't possibly know that."

"But I do know. I know it because I feel it."

"So I should just trust to my feelings no matter what?" She shook her head. "That's a very convenient philosophy for you to offer me now, given that just last night I confessed no other man makes me feel the way you do."

He chuckled suddenly.

"What's so amusing?"

"You and convenience coupled together. It's a bit like oil and water, or matches and dynamite." He must have sensed she still didn't find that humorous, for he sobered at once. "Do you regret kissing me last night?"

"It's not that simple. This isn't just about the glorious feeling you get when someone kisses you."

"Was it glorious?"

She didn't answer, and he took another step closer, then glanced at the doorway and stopped again. But he didn't give up the question. "I know how I felt, and I think you felt it, too. But then, I thought the same thing in Newport, before you cut me down to size, and I'm not taking anything for granted. So answer my question. Last night . . . was it glorious?"

She looked at him, feeling wretched, doubts and desires clawing at her. "You know it was," she whispered.

"Well, then . . ." He lifted his hands and let them fall with a sound of exasperation. "Then why won't you marry me? Why are you being so stubborn?"

The word flicked her on the raw. "Is that what I'm being? Stubborn? So it's stubborn of me, is it, to want to make a considered choice about whom to spend my life with?"

"I don't know. But I do know this is the second time you've stood in my hearing and tried to reason yourself into picking Carrington or Hansborough over me, and it's getting a bit wearing."

"Well, pardon me for wearing on you," she shot back, working to keep her voice low even as she felt her temper giving way. "Pardon me for not being willing to commit my entire future to you based on two kisses and a blueberry muffin."

"It's a better basis for making a decision than trying to talk yourself into it. Especially considering that last night you wrapped your arms around my neck and kissed me of your own free will."

"Sshhh," she admonished, casting a frantic look at the doorway.

He didn't seem to care, for he took another step closer, but when he spoke, his voice was a murmur. "A kiss you just admitted was glorious."

"I'm also saying there's more to making a decision of whom to marry than a man's kissing ability." She took a step closer, too, for she had to make it clear that she wouldn't be railroaded into a decision when her life and her future hung in the balance. "My future is at stake, and I have a much better idea of what sort of future I'd have with the duke or Hansborough than with you."

"I'm not sure I want to hear how you come to that conclusion."

"Well, not because I've kissed them, that's for sure. Though maybe I should, since you seem to think it's such an important part of the decision."

His expression grew grim at the prospect. "The fact that you think it isn't important is what baffles me."

She took a deep breath, working to keep her temper in check. "I know the duke has proved himself to be a good husband and father already. His first marriage was a happy one, and his two daughters think the world of him. Lady Trubridge tells me Hansborough has four sisters, and all of them adore him—"

"I'm sorry I don't have sisters or daughters who adore

me or a previous happy marriage to my credit so that I might prove my worth as a husband and father. But I couldn't afford to marry a poor girl, for I'd have had no way to support her, and I couldn't bear to marry a rich girl and have everyone think me a fortune hunter. So what do you want from me, Linnet? How do I prove myself?"

"I don't know, Jack." She lifted her hands helplessly. "Demonstrate to me what kind of husband you would be, what kind of father you would be, what kind of life we would have. How you prove those things is up to you, but until you can show me what kind of life I would have with you, until you've demonstrated that I can trust you, I can't agree to marry you."

"So last night counts for nothing?"

"It wasn't nothing, but it wasn't everything either. Marriage is a long business. I'm trying to make a careful and considered choice."

"The longer you take to make that choice, the more likely it becomes that your reputation will be damaged beyond repair."

"Don't you think I know that? Believe me, I don't want to spend my life in ruin and disgrace, shamed and pitied and ostracized by society. But I also need time to decide which man is my best choice, not just for the sake of my reputation but also for the sake of my future."

"But damn it all, Linnet, I am that man. I know it."

"How?" she cried, then bit her lip, glancing through the doorway to find Lady Trubridge still watching them from the drawing room. "How do you know?"

"I just do." He pressed his fingers to his chest, not

to his heart, but to a point just below it. "I know it here."

"What are you saying? That you're in love with me?"

He blinked at the question, taken aback. "I am," he said after a moment, then he laughed as if confounded by a wholly unexpected discovery. "By God, I really am."

She stared back at him, dismayed. She'd asked the question fully expecting either an ardent and eloquent declaration of love meant to lull her into a decision, or a light, witty equivocation that meant nothing at all. But he'd given her neither. When he spoke of love, he sounded . . . damn it all, he sounded sincere.

Pleasure kindled inside her at the realization, pleasure that warmed her heart and aroused her senses, until she remembered that she wasn't a good judge of any man's sincerity.

In their first meeting, he'd given her every reason to mistrust him and his motives. Less than three weeks had passed since then, hardly time for him to assuage her doubts, but she didn't have the luxury of waiting until he redeemed himself. On the other hand, how could she fall in love with a man she'd didn't trust? How could she trust a man she didn't know? How could she ever learn to believe in him when she couldn't even believe in herself? Her whole future hung on her decision, a decision that once made, was irrevocable. What if she made the wrong one?

All her doubts and fears rose, stifling pleasure, bringing panic, and she groaned. "Being around you is like being on a roller coaster. Every second a new twist or turn or drop off a cliff."

He grinned, seeming to enjoy the comparison. "Don't you like roller coasters?"

"No, I don't. I rode the Switchback Railway at Coney Island when I was sixteen. When it was over, I stepped out of the carriage onto the platform, doubled over, and threw up all over my shoes. It was one of the most humiliating experiences of my life." She scowled at him. "A bit like the kiss in Newport, when I think about it."

His grin faltered, and he gave her a doubtful look. "You didn't go home after the ball and throw up, did you?"

"No, but—"

"Then we'll be all right," he said, his grin coming back, all his cocksure confidence seeming to return with it. "I just have to make you love me, too."

"This is the same battle we keep fighting. I can't be *made* to love you any more than I can be *made* to marry you."

"You want me, though. I know you do. And I think you could love me if you let yourself."

"How do you know?" she demanded, hating how sure he was of everything when she was a muddled mess of doubts and fears. "Because of a kiss?"

She stepped back before he could reply, shaking her head in denial, panic pressing up against her chest and making it hard to breathe. "A kiss isn't everything, Jack."

He sobered at once. "It was for me, Linnet," he said simply, and it was his turn to take a step back. He opened his arms, spreading them wide. "It was for me."

His arms fell to his sides, and he turned and walked

away, down the steps and into the shadows beyond the terrace.

"But that's the difference between us, Jack," she whispered into the darkness. "I don't trust my feelings. Not anymore."

THE DISCOVERY THAT he was in love with Linnet wasn't any great surprise when he thought about it. She'd owned his body and soul since Newport; why not his heart as well?

It had settled into him like a fact of life the moment he'd admitted it. Not that the admission had done him much good, for she'd seemed dismayed by it rather than glad, relieved, or reassured. He didn't blame her for her reaction, he supposed, given everything that had happened. She didn't trust him, and why should she? The Van Hausen business, he appreciated with chagrin, still hung between them, and it probably always would, a secret he'd never be able to tell her. She wanted him to prove she could trust him with her future, but was that even possible?

Conrath had broken her heart, Van Hausen had shamefully attempted to use her. The men who had betrayed her in the past made his efforts to gain her trust even harder.

Even my own father . . .

Jack frowned, staring up at the ceiling of his room as he lay in bed late that night, her words from earlier echoing back to him.

It was never about me or my happiness, it was about him wanting to use me to make a business deal.

There was no mistaking the bitterness in her voice, and he couldn't blame her. This was why Ephraim hadn't wanted him to tell her about the deal they'd made in New York. The other man had been sure Linnet would never agree to marry him if she knew of it. Jack feared he might be right.

Still, there was no reason to bring up the issue of the African investment company until she had agreed to marry him. Then, perhaps, he could soften her stance toward business deals with her father if he put it to her the right way. Once they were engaged, once Ephraim came and they were negotiating the marriage settlement, then he'd explain to her why he wanted it, why investments like this were a good way to secure the future of their estates and their children, and that through those investments, he could earn his living, hopefully she'd understand. In any case, explanations of the business deal could wait.

Right now, winning her was a much greater priority. Without that, the dowry meant nothing anyway. And despite his declaration of love, it was clear that winning Linnet's hand in marriage was by no means a certainty. The question was how on earth was he to persuade her? It wasn't as if he could use seduction. Belinda had taken that strategy off the table. What other courses were open to him?

Demonstrate to me what kind of husband you would be, what kind of father you would be, what kind of life I would have with you.

Jack sat up in bed, struck by a sudden idea. He could show her at least part of what she wanted to see. It wouldn't be all that difficult either, he realized, thinking it out. Tomorrow afternoon over tea, he decided, would be the perfect time for just the sort of demonstration she demanded. And, he realized, it would serve a secondary purpose, too, one that would give him a great deal of satisfaction.

He grinned, savoring it, and fell back into the pillows. Five minutes later, he fell asleep, the grin still on his face.

THERE WERE SOME moments in a man's life when luck was everything. But luck, Jack knew, could often be helped along if a man employed a bit of forethought and put in some effort. The morning following his declaration of love to Linnet, Jack applied both, and by teatime, his arrangements were made.

Everyone was gathered on the south lawn for tea and croquet, and though he was involved in a keen and competitive game of the latter with Nick, Belinda, and several members of the local gentry, he was also keeping an eye on the flagstone path beside the croquet green, for he expected to see a certain party come strolling by at any moment, and he had no intention of missing them.

His eyes, however, proved unnecessary in that regard, for his ears detected the arrival of little Colin and his nanny long before the pair came round the rhododendrons and into view, and the moment he heard Colin's angry wails, Jack knew that he not only had forethought and effort going for him today, he also had luck. Very good luck indeed, he amended as he glanced at the tea table and saw that Linnet and Hansborough were sitting side by side, a little apart from the others.

Any other time, that fact might have been aggravating as hell. But not today. Today, it made him grin. This was going to be fun.

"Nanny Brown," he called with what he hoped was a convincing amount of surprise, and as she brought the pram to a halt, he set down his mallet, ignoring the protests of the other players, who were waiting for him to take his shot.

"It's time for a spot of tea, I think," he explained. "Let's stop for a bit. Besides, I want to see Colin."

"I can't think why," Nick said wryly. "He's having the devil of a tantrum, in case you hadn't noticed."

"All the better for me, my friend," he said, and laughed at his friend's perplexed frown. "All the better for me."

"You're mad, Jack," Nick declared, setting down his mallet. "Mad as Carroll's Hatter."

"And that surprises you?" Jack shook his head as he walked away. "All these years you've known me," he added over his shoulder. "I should think by now you'd have stopped being surprised by the things I do."

He turned his attention to the stout lady standing on the path. "Good afternoon, Nanny," he greeted her, and peered into the pram. "Colin, my boy, whatever's the matter?"

"He's in a righteous fury at the moment, my lord," she told him, raising her voice to be heard above the din.

"Yes, so I noticed."

"I brought him along as you asked, though I doubt you'll be wanting to see him now."

"Nonsense," he replied, earning himself a look that said Nick wasn't the only one who thought him off his onion. "I'll have him anyway. Perhaps I can soothe him down."

"You've a bee in your bonnet about babies today, my lord," she said, laughing. "I've never seen the like. But if you're sure, you're welcome to him. Though you'll have your hands full, with him in this state, let me tell you."

"I don't believe it," Jack said, and lifted the baby out of the pram. "He's just a bit cranky, that's all."

Colin did not seem pacified by being held. He wailed even louder.

"Now, now, young man, none of that," he murmured. Pulling Colin up against his chest, he rested the baby's bottom on his forearm and flattened his free hand against his back, just as Nanny had shown him this morning. "Let's go see your mother and father and have some tea, shall we?" He looked up, meeting Nanny's amused gaze over the baby's dark head. "Any advice on what I could do to make him stop crying?"

"You might try a bit of shortbread. Not too much, or he'll not have a proper feeding later."

"Right." Jack drew a breath, feeling a bit nervous now that he was about to be left on his own. "Anything else?"

"Distract him. Bright or noisy things sometimes work. Or you might try swinging him up high. Do you want me to follow along?"

"Not a bit. I'll bring him up to the nursery in a short while, or her ladyship will do."

"Very well, my lord. If you're sure?"

When he nodded, she whirled the pram around, and, shaking her head in bemusement, she started back toward the house as he made his way to the tea table, and he could only hope Colin didn't decide to stop crying before he got there.

His luck held, though, and by the time he approached the tea table, he could tell from one quick glance that Colin's tantrum was grating on Hansborough's nerves. This plan was succeeding beyond all his expectations.

"Hullo, everyone," he said, pausing by the tea table, bobbing the baby on his arm gently up and down as he dipped at the knees and reached for a couple of shortbread biscuits.

"Really, Jack," Belinda said, laughing up at him, "you are a brave man to take on Colin at a time like this."

"Stuff," he scoffed, and moved toward the empty chair across from Linnet, but he kept his attention on the baby. "What's the problem, little chap, hmm?" he asked as he sat down. "Giving Nanny no end of trouble again today, I see. You shall be quite the hellion when you grow up."

Red-faced, his round cheeks streaked with tears, Colin wailed even louder in response and batted Jack's shoulder angrily with a chubby fist.

"Yes, yes, you've every right to be upset," Jack murmured, twirling the shortbread in his fingers in front of the baby's eyes. "Nannies are no fun at all. They shove you around in a pram where you can't see anything, then they make you have tea alone in the nursery afterward. What fun is that?"

"Isn't that where babies are supposed to be when they

cry?" Hansborough asked, raising his voice a bit to be heard above the din.

"What's wrong, Hansborough?" Jack asked, transferring his gaze to the viscount, smiling a little. "You look terribly grim. Don't you like babies?"

"I like them well enough," Hansborough answered, staring back at Jack. "When they're not mimicking Irish banshees."

His voice was even, but despite Colin's wails, Jack heard the peeved tone of his voice.

Linnet heard it, too, he noted, watching as she turned her head to give the viscount a thoughtful, considering glance, and after last night's events, that was something Jack was quite gratified to see.

"Babies cry, Hansborough," he said with a shrug, and returned his attention to Colin. He pressed the biscuit to the baby's quavering lower lip, making soothing noises.

Colin, however, would not be soothed. He stopped crying just long enough to mouth the biscuit for two seconds, then with another wail, he grabbed the shortbread and hurled it past Jack's shoulder across the grass.

"You don't seem to be having much luck calming him down," Hansborough commented, acid in his voice.

"That's all right." Jack twirled another piece of shortbread in front of the baby. "We're just beginning, aren't we, Colin?"

Hansborough's reply was tight. "Lovely."

"Unless . . ." Jack paused, smiling faintly at the other man. "Unless you'd care to have a go?"

"God, no." The viscount sounded appalled. "Crying

babies belong in the nursery with the nanny, not out and about, irritating the guests."

Linnet was still watching Hansborough as he spoke, and Jack felt positively gleeful when her thoughtful frown deepened. The viscount must have sensed her gaze on him, for he turned, giving her what Jack could only think was a pathetic attempt at a smile. "Crying babies need a nanny's comfort."

"Of course," she murmured, her frown vanishing. She smiled politely back at him, but Jack felt a surge of triumph, for he knew the damage was done.

Hansborough knew it, too. He studied her face for a moment, then with a stiff movement, he took up his gloves and stick from the grass beside his chair and stood up. "If you will pardon me, Miss Holland," he said, bowed to her, then he turned in Jack's direction to go back toward the house. As he passed Jack's chair, he muttered something under his breath. It sounded like, "Bastard."

Jack laughed, turning to look over his shoulder as the viscount walked away. "Don't forget your gloves."

If the viscount made a reply to that wicked parting shot, Jack didn't hear it over Colin's crying. Still grinning, he turned back around in his chair to find Linnet watching him, and something in her face caused his grin to falter and his satisfaction to evaporate, and he wondered if what he'd just done had been an utter waste of time.

Chapter 15

"What did you mean about gloves?" Linnet asked, and she couldn't help noticing that he wasn't looking quite so pleased with himself as he had a moment ago. "Hansborough had his gloves in his hand," she added, frowning in puzzlement. "So what did you mean?"

He gave a shrug. "Last night after you left us, Hansborough suggested we both take off the gloves. That's boxing cant. It means—"

Colin interrupted this explanation by striking him again in the chest and wailing even more loudly. Jack held up the shortbread, but again, Colin remained unimpressed. Since most of her friends were married by now, Linnet was quite accustomed to babies and could have offered him some advice, but she refrained, deciding after his mischievous teasing of Hansborough, a very angry baby was no more than he deserved.

As it turned out, however, Jack proved more adept with babies than she'd have thought. After studying Colin's furious face for a moment, he shifted the child a little and reached down, working to free the T-bar of his watch fob from the buttonhole of his waistcoat. With the pocket watch free, he held it up by the chain, dangling it and the winding key in front of Colin. Startled by the sudden appearance of this shiny new object, the baby stopped crying.

"Deuce take you," Jack said, laughing as if he was as surprised as the baby.

Linnet sniffed. "It would have served you right if he wailed all afternoon, and Nanny refused to take him back."

He looked up, and his grin was back in place as he rolled the chain in his fingers, twirling the watch and key before the baby's eyes. "That wouldn't matter," he said. "I'd never abandon Colin to Nanny. That would be deserting a friend in need."

He returned his attention to the baby. Lifting the watch higher, he began to swing it back and forth, and Colin tilted his head back, following the movement as if entranced. Suddenly, he reached up, grabbed the watch, and yanked it out of Jack's hand. With a gurgle that sounded decidedly possessive, the baby gripped the watch in both hands and jammed it partway into his mouth, sucking on the smooth brass edge.

Linnet burst out laughing, and Jack laughed with her, shaking his head at the baby. "Really, now, old chap. I gave you some delicious shortbread, and what you want to suck on is my watch?"

It seemed so, for Colin mouthed the watch with obvious contentment.

"Most people don't know what to do with crying babies," she said, watching him. "They feel helpless and uncomfortable."

"Are you making excuses for Hansborough's boorish behavior?" Jack leaned back in his chair, watching her as he leaned back in his chair and settled Colin on his lap. "Or perhaps you agree with him that babies ought to be shut up in the nursery when they cry?"

"Neither. But he was right that a crying baby irritates some people."

"Colin ruffled his feathers, certainly."

"Not just him. When you brought the baby over, nearly everyone started edging away from you as if you'd caught the plague."

He studied her over the baby's head. "You didn't."

She smiled a little. "Yes, well, I like babies, even when they cry."

"I like babies, too, Linnet."

With those words, her smile vanished, her throat went dry, and she had a sudden, strange notion that she was looking into the future. That picture tilted the whole world a little off its axis. "Is that what this was about, then?" she whispered. "Bringing Colin over to impress me with your talent for babies to make you seem a better marriage prospect?"

"Well, yes, that's part of the reason." He grinned, holding up one hand, fingers crossed. "Did it work?"

She very much feared it had, but she sniffed, striving to seem unimpressed. "You're holding a baby, not performing a miracle," she said. "Any man might hold a baby."

"Any man but Hansborough."

She laughed, all her efforts to be unaffected going to the wall. He laughed with her, but after several moments, their laughter faded, floating away on the warm afternoon air, and in the silence, she watched him with the baby, and her heart constricted, making it hard to breathe.

She forced herself to say something. "You were terrible to tease Hansborough. When you saw how annoyed he was, you should have taken the baby away."

"And miss showing you how much he dislikes babies? Not a chance."

She stared at him, frowning. "How do you know Hansborough doesn't like babies? How could you possibly know something like that?"

"Nanny Brown brought Colin in when we were having port the first evening because Nick had just arrived home from America and wanted to see his son. Colin started to cry, and I noticed Hansborough's reaction. He was quite put out about having the port interrupted by a crying baby."

She felt a pang of dismay. "So it wasn't just to impress me with your abilities. It was also to show him up?"

"Oh, he deserved it, Linnet. After his obnoxious reference last night to what happened in Newport, he needed to be taken down a notch."

"Why? Because he pointed out that your behavior on that occasion was less than exemplary?"

"You think that's what bothered me?" He made a

sound of derision. "I couldn't care two straws what he thinks of me. But that reference to Newport embarrassed *you,* and that bothered me enormously."

Pleasure welled up within her, but she worked to tamp it down, reminding herself of his keen ability to take advantage of any situation. "So when the nanny was strolling by with Colin today, you decided it was a perfect opportunity to exploit his dislike of babies? Or perhaps you even arranged for Nanny to come by?"

He hesitated and shifted in his chair, looking a bit guilty, confirming her guess, and more visions of the future flashed into her mind, a future of sons who would look just like that after being caught red-handed with a stolen batch of strawberry tarts. Black-haired, dark-eyed sons with knowing smiles and a talent for playing her like a violin. "You did," she whispered, and shoved visions of a future with him aside. "You staged the whole thing."

He was saved from replying by the approach of Lady Trubridge. "I see someone has stolen your watch, Jack," she said, pausing beside his chair, smiling at her son as she held out her hands.

"Oh, yes, now you want him," Jack complained as he stood up. "After I've got him nicely settled for you."

"Well, of course," she agreed at once. "You don't think I wanted him when he was screaming loud enough to wake the dead, do you?"

Linnet watched as Jack pressed a kiss to the baby's head, and her heart constricted in her breast. What he'd done had been a ploy, a calculated move to manipulate her, she knew that, and yet, even now, she felt as if her heart were hovering on the brink, ready to fall into his hands as inevitably as a ripe plum fell from a tree.

As he handed the baby to his sister-in-law, Linnet jerked to her feet and turned her back on him and the rosy picture of the future he'd been attempting to paint for her.

She heard him call her name, but she pretended she hadn't. She kept walking toward the house, but, of course, he didn't let her get away. She'd barely reached the flagstone walk that led to the terrace before he fell in step beside her.

"Yes, I staged it," he admitted. "Well, not the crying part. That was pure good luck."

"Good luck?" She shook her head, amazed at how he defined things. "Exploiting a crying baby to do another man down is good luck?"

"Given the fact that it got you to see what sort of father Hansborough would be, I'd say it was damned good luck, yes."

"Why is it that every man who isn't you is somehow a bad choice for me?"

"Linnet, I'm only doing what you wanted me to do."

She stopped, so abruptly that he'd gone three steps farther before he stopped as well. "What I wanted you to do?" she echoed as he turned to face her, not quite able to believe she'd heard him right. "It's a ploy, a calculated move. It's not real. How could you ever think something so artificial would be something I'd want?"

"It's not artificial if it's the truth. I like babies. Hansborough doesn't. Those are facts."

"Convenient facts that show you in a good light and

him in a bad one, so that I'll deem you a better choice as a husband than he."

"Of course, but so what? Everyone in the world does that sort of thing every day. We all present ourselves in the best light we can to impress others. I'm doing it, yes, but Hansborough is free to do it, too. We all do it, even you."

She started to deny that, but he interrupted her. "I've seen you in an evening dress, Linnet. Those low-cut necklines of yours are a form of manipulation, too, at least by your definition of it."

"Oh, that's absurd. It's not the same thing at all."

"No?" He folded his arms. "How is it different?"

"Well, for one thing, it's much more innocuous."

"But still the same thing: an obvious ploy to elicit a very specific result."

"And the result you hoped for was that I'd think you a good candidate for fatherhood merely because you can pacify a baby with your pocket watch?"

"It's not as if we have time for a long, drawn-out courtship where you have plenty of opportunity to determine my winning ways with children. You wanted to know what sort of father I'd be, so I decided to show you the only way I could think of in the limited time we have. You say it's artificial, but these are artificial circumstances. It doesn't make what I did any less genuine or what I showed you any less true."

"Still, a demonstration at Hansborough's expense was hardly necessary. You could have explained those things to me."

"I could have. But my words and explanations don't seem to impress you. Like my words about how that kiss in Newport was for me, or the fact that I'm in love with you."

"Jack." She glanced around, but thankfully, no one milling around the lawn was within earshot of where they stood, though several people, including Lady Trubridge and her mother, were watching them.

"Those declarations didn't do much convincing, as I recall. My words seem to bounce off you like arrows off stone walls."

"That's not true," she protested. "I—"

"I could have sworn up and down hill and dale how much I adore babies, and that, unlike Hansborough, I'd never have the nanny take the baby away just because he's crying in front of the guests at our latest party, but would it have made any difference?"

He didn't give her a chance to answer. "I could have explained that unlike my father, I don't believe in keeping the children scuttled away in some dark, depressing part of the house with only Nanny for company. I could have said that sending them off to boarding school before they're ten years old is not acceptable to me, and that seeing them only once or twice during the summer holidays isn't good enough, and that a good thrashing with a riding crop isn't the solution to every disciplinary problem."

"Good God." Linnet stared at him, her chest tight as his words sank in. "Is that what your childhood was like?"

He looked away, staring out over the grass. "I could have told you that if my son were a champion footballer, I'd actually attend the festivities on Prize-Giving Day," he went on, and she had the answer to her question.

"And if my son ever got into trouble at school, it would occur to me that his wild behavior might be a bid for my attention, not a demonstration of his worthlessness. And I'd never ridicule him, or belittle him for being merely the second son, and I wouldn't withhold his allowance on a whim just because I could."

She made a wordless sound, appalled, appreciating the connotation.

"Yes," he added, returning his gaze to her face, his dark eyes glinting with defiance, "now you know why I would insist on an income being spelled out in our marriage settlement. My father, and my brother after him, loved holding my quarterly allowance over my head. They knew it was my only source of funds, and they found it vastly amusing to keep me in a perpetual state of suspense."

Linnet stared into his resentful face. "I never dreamed you were refusing it for that reason."

"It doesn't matter."

"But it does." She swallowed, pain on his behalf making her throat tight. "You should have told me, explained—"

"Again, would you have believed me? I doubt it," he added before she could answer. "You asked me what sort of husband and father I'd be, but how is a man supposed to define those things in words?"

"You seem to be doing fine with words right now," she murmured.

"Nonetheless, I decided a demonstration of my fondness for babies was a simple, expedient, and far more effective way to show you what sort of father I'd be than to tell tales of my rotten family and tragic childhood."

He didn't give her a chance to reply. Instead, he turned, and this time, he was the one who walked away.

DURING THE TWO days that followed, Jack was a perfect gentleman.

In the mornings, as she rode the park with Carrington, he hoped the duke was explaining the latest political maneuverings of Cecil's cabinet and boring her to tears, but he didn't try to encourage the duke in that regard, as tempting as it might be.

Tufton's efforts to capture her attention, he was happy to see, went nowhere. Whenever she was with the marquess, Jack could observe her leaning back or edging away, and though he did feel a bit sorry for the chap, he was of no mind, in the name of fair play, to advise Tufton to gargle eau de cologne or chew a bit of parsley.

And though Jack had demonstrated Hansborough's abysmal lack of paternal capability, Linnet seemed of no mind to forgo his company. And though every time Hansborough danced with her or laughed with her or admired those low necklines of hers, Jack's ever inventive brain conjured up plenty of other ways to show up the viscount to his own advantage, he didn't act on them.

No, though it was the hardest thing he'd ever done, Jack behaved himself. He made polite conversation with her and her mother over tea, and he tried not to dwell on all the devious ways he could have maneuvered Helen into leaving them alone. If there was dancing in the evening and he was lucky enough to have a waltz with her, he kept their bodies the perfect, proper distance apart and made polite, proper conversation. And if he happened to encounter her during a rare moment when she was alone, he bowed, said a few innocuous words, and moved on, just as a gentleman should.

His impeccable conduct didn't gain him any favor, but he didn't really expect it to do so. His main reason for maintaining his distance wasn't for her benefit at all. No, his reason was much more selfish than that. Keeping his distance was the only way to keep his sanity.

As strict as his control over his actions was, he couldn't seem to control his wayward thoughts. His memory reverted to that kiss in the boxwoods time and again, and the touch of her lips, the taste of her tongue, and the hot burn of her body seemed almost as vivid in his imagination as they'd been in reality. The part he treasured most was the astonished pleasure in her face after they'd pulled apart, because it reminded him that he'd succeeded in one goal, at least: banishing forever the unwillingness that had tainted her view of their first kiss. But in the days that followed, that was cold comfort, because he yearned to kiss her again, and he could not do it.

Kissing, of course, was just a delightful prelude to much more carnal imaginings which, at this rate, were never going to become reality. His mind came up with a myriad of ways to pleasure her, ways that matchmakers and chaperones could never approve, ways that slid into his thoughts during the day and invaded his dreams at night, ways that to his way of thinking would be far more effective at wooing and winning Linnet than polite conversation over sherry in the drawing room.

Nonetheless, he remained stalwart, adhering to all the rules though it baffled him how he could ever coax her into loving him back by talking about the weather and turning pages for her at the piano. By the last day of the house party, he despaired of ever finding a way to bring her closer without breaking the rules, and when he heard she'd gone for the afternoon, he decided that practicing golf shots by himself on the other side of the park was his wisest course.

His reprieve from civilized courtship lasted a mere two hours before the sound of hoofbeats interrupted him, and when he glanced over his shoulder and saw her riding in his direction, he knew fate had at last decided to reward him—or annihilate him—for being on such good behavior.

Desperate, he returned his attention to his ball, adjusted the grip on his midmashie, and swung. The ball sliced hard left and went into the woods. Grateful, he went after it at once, hoping she'd ride on and leave him in peace.

She didn't, of course. Why would anything about Linnet ever be easy?

The hoofbeats came closer, slowed, then stopped. His mashie in one hand, he crouched down amid the shrubbery, pretending vast interest in locating his ball.

"Jack?"

He closed his eyes for a moment, gathering what restraint he had, which was precious little, and looked up. The sun slid between the leaves overhead, illuminating her with dappled light as she dismounted and tied off her horse. Despite her black broadcloth riding habit, when she turned toward him, he was reminded of those wood nymphs of folklore that lured men into all sorts of temptation.

Christ have mercy, he thought, and dove back into the shrubbery as she came toward him.

She paused by his side. "Looking for your golf ball?"

"Yes." His answer was clipped, not the least bit welcoming, but he was in no frame of mind for civilized courtship. Not today.

She stepped even closer. "I can help you look."

"It's not important. I have others." His fingers tightened around the mashie in his hand, and he stood up. As he did, his gaze traveled up the luscious curves he'd been dreaming about, along the slender neck he'd been kissing in his dreams for days, and into her face, but he couldn't quite meet her eyes. That would do him in. He stopped at her chin. "Good afternoon. I'd best carry on."

He bowed and started to step around her, but her voice stopped him.

"Jack?"

He stopped, prayed for fortitude, stared at her chin. "Yes?"

"Did—" She stopped and bit her lip. "Don't we have a truce?"

"Of course we have a truce." He strove to seem amiably puzzled. "Why do you ask?"

She licked her lips as if she was nervous. "Things haven't been the same since that afternoon with baby Colin. You've become so distant. We haven't played twenty questions for several days, and you haven't cornered me on the terrace even once." She laughed a little, but it sounded forced. "You haven't given Lady Trubridge any reason to watch us like a hawk."

"No, I suppose not."

He fell silent again, and he knew he wasn't helping her, but what did she want from him?

"I fear it's because we quarreled. That's why I came to find you." She paused, faltering, then went on, "I wanted to patch things up."

"That's not necessary. There's nothing to patch up."

"I think there is." She paused. "I just wish I knew what it was. If I knew what was causing this breach between us, maybe I could fix it. We're friends, you said. Can't friends talk about things? I know you feel that talking doesn't accomplish anything, but I can't agree with you."

Despite the situation, he couldn't help a smile. "You not agree with me about something? What a surprise."

She smiled back, and he felt desire flicker dangerously inside him. He stirred, glancing around. "We shouldn't be out here alone, Linnet," he said. "Belinda will have my head on a plate if she finds out."

"I know, but the house party is ending tomorrow, and I wasn't sure I'd have another chance to speak with you. Everyone's going tomorrow. Are you going, too?"

Just now, he wished he could. "Not tomorrow, no."

Something came into her face; it might have been relief, perhaps even pleasure, but he knew that could just be wishful thinking on his part. When it came to Linnet, his perceptions could not be trusted. "I can't go until I've seen Stuart—the Duke of Margrave. He and his duchess are arriving the day after tomorrow, and I must meet with him about a business matter."

"And after that?"

Desperate, he sought excuses to go. "I ought to go home to Featherstone Gate for a bit. I haven't been there since I was home in May. And I should have a look at the other estates, too, while I'm in the north."

"Could you stay longer? We could have a bit more time that way, and—"

"I can't," he cut her off, his voice brusque even to his own ears. "I can't do it. I know I'm supposed to be conducting a proper courtship, but it's becoming rather a rough go for me. You see . . ."

He paused, but hell, what was the point of prevaricating? "All I want, all I think about is kissing you and touching you, and I can't because I don't have the right, and that's driving me a bit mad. I need to get clear of you for a bit."

"Oh." Her face was crimson, her eyes wide. "Of course." She pressed a gloved hand to her mouth, looking stricken. "I'm leading you on," she choked. Her hand fell, and she ducked her head. "I'm so sorry. I didn't realize. I'll go."

She turned as if to depart, and even though he knew it was best if he let her, suddenly, he couldn't. Even though he'd been the one avoiding her for days, even though just being here alone with her was breaking every rule in the etiquette books, even though he just told her he had to resist her, he couldn't do it. He dropped the mashie, reached out, and caught her by the arms before she could escape. "You're not leading me on. It's not that at all."

She stilled. Her chin lifted to that proud angle he recognized, but her voice, when she spoke, was tentative, uncertain. "I thought perhaps after our quarrel, you had come to regret what you said the other night, and that's why you were avoiding me. I thought . . ." She faltered, her chin lowered, and she stared down at the hat in her hand. "I thought you might want to take it back," she whispered.

"I don't want to take it back. I'll never take it back."

His hands tightened on her arms. He knew that if anyone saw them, he would be regarded as even more of a cad than ever, for not only was he detaining her when she was unaccompanied, but holding her this way when it was clear she was walking away could not be excused.

Let her go, he thought. But even as he gave himself that command, he glanced around to be sure the woods around them were thick enough to hide them from the view, and then, he pulled her closer. When he bent his head, the scent of heliotrope came to his nostrils, and the effect on his body was instantaneous. Desire came over him in a thick, hot wave.

"When I'm sitting across from you in the drawing room," he murmured by her ear, "all I'm thinking about is what you look like without your clothes, and I'm imagining how it would feel to caress your naked skin."

A tremor ran through her, and he pushed his advantage, for this was a form of courtship he knew and understood. "When I'm in bed at night, I imagine what it would be like if you were lying there with me, your body under mine, and your hair, loose and golden, spread across my pillows."

His gaze skimmed her flushed cheeks, the long,

graceful line of her neck, moving down past the pristine high collar of her riding coat and shirt, to the generous curve of her breasts. Her breathing was quick and shallow. He could see it and hear it.

He let go of one of her arms and slid his hand up along her rib cage to cup her breast, and even through the stiff layers of her clothing, the shape of it seemed a perfect fit to his hand, proving—not that he needed any convincing—that Linnet was his woman, that she was made for him. He shaped it, squeezing gently, and she gasped, her knees caving.

He slid his other arm around her. "I think about making love to you," he said, his voice harsh to his own ears, a rasp of raw lust in the turgid summer air. He dipped his knees, nestling his erection against her bum. "I think about bedding you, and taking your virtue, and making you totally mine."

She gasped, wriggling in his hold, sending teasing pulses of pleasure through his body. His arm tightened around her, keeping her in place as he pressed his erection even more deeply between her buttocks, and when he flexed his hips, the sensation was so exquisite, it almost sent him to the ground. He groaned, a primitive sound low in his throat, and he stifled it in a kiss against her hair.

This was beyond pleasure now. It was becoming pain. He was shaking with the effort of holding back, and he knew he was a prize idiot for ever thinking he could behave himself when she was in reach. When thoughts of shoving her riding skirt aside and opening the breeches beneath started going through his mind, he knew he had to stop.

Desperate, he dredged up a speck of will and lifted his head. "But I can't do any of that," he said. "Because you are not mine."

"If I were," she whispered, "would you kiss me again?"

She tried to turn around, but he grabbed her arms, knowing he couldn't let her. One taste of her would shred any scrap of willpower he still possessed, and he'd take her virtue right here. In the shrubbery, for God's sake.

His hands tightened on her arms, and this time, instead of bringing her closer, he pushed her away, and when she turned around, he said, "I'm not going to engage in hypotheticals, Linnet, and I won't let you toy with me while you make up your mind. Yes," he added, as she started to protest. "You're toying with me, whether you realize it or not, because you don't trust me."

"Trust takes time."

"I realize that, but we don't have the luxury of a long, drawn-out courtship here. And even if we had all the time in the world, trust is what this is really about."

"Trust is a lot to ask for, Jack."

"Is it?" He considered, then acknowledged that with a nod. "Yes, I suppose it is, but I won't take less. So it comes down to one thing: Will you choose to trust me with your future, or won't you? It may not be an easy choice, Linnet, but it's a choice you'll have to make."

"Is it a choice?"

"Trust is always a choice. But here's the rub: Like all choices, you won't know if it's the right one until after you've made it."

He took a deep breath and took another step back. "I'll be away all day tomorrow, because as I said, I need to be away from you for a bit. While I'm gone, I want you to make that choice. I want you to send all those other chaps packing and make it clear you won't be seeing them again. If you do that, then I'll stay as long as it takes, and we'll proceed at whatever pace you like. I'll even give up the dowry," he added wildly, desperate for an end to this torture. "But I won't be alone with you. I won't touch you, or kiss you, or make love to you, as much as I might want to do so. I won't even hold your hand under the table, because just that could prove too much temptation for me. All that's off the table until you agree to marry me."

He stepped around her, picked up his club, then paused, unable to resist saying one last thing. "Just don't make me wait too long, Linnet, for I don't know how much more of this I can take."

He walked away, and this time, he didn't look back. He caught up his golf bag and started down the long stretch of turf, but he abandoned any notion of golf. His body was on fire, and he decided what he needed was a swim though he suspected that even a good dunking in cool water wouldn't be enough to restore his equilibrium.

As for restoring his sanity, well, walking away from Linnet when he was in this state proved it was already too late for that.

LINNET WATCHED HIM go. She couldn't have followed him, even if she'd wanted to, for she couldn't seem to move. His words of a moment ago were reverberating through her mind like rifle shots, their impact every bit as powerful, hitting her square in the chest.

It wasn't his erotic confessions that held her riveted in place, as gratifying as those had been to hear. And it wasn't his assurance that he intended to continue this newfound resolve to behave like a gentleman, for truth be told, that particular promise left her feeling rather let down. No, none of those were what paralyzed her and left her feeling as stunned as a bird that had just hit a window.

Trust is always a choice . . . but you won't know if it's the right one until after you've made it.

Yesterday, making that choice had seemed impossible, and yet now, standing here, she realized she'd already made it. Having her horse brought round instead of paying calls with the other ladies, riding the park in search of him, following him into the woods, hinting for him to kiss her . . . all of those things had been part of making her choice, part of handing over her trust, her heart, her life, and her future to him.

Now, standing here in the aftermath, she felt none of the agony or doubt that had been plaguing her since their very first meeting. She felt sure, with every fiber of her being, that her choice had been the right one. Because she loved him.

Galvanized by this discovery, she moved to follow him, to tell him, but then, she stopped, remembering that he didn't want to be near her, not right now. He wanted distance, and she had to give it to him. Slowly, she walked to her horse, untied the reins, and mounted. By the time she led her mare out of the woods and onto the long stretch of turf, he had disappeared.

He didn't come down to dinner that night either. He stayed in his room, pleading a slew of business correspondence that required his attention, but Linnet knew that wasn't what kept him away, and she hugged that knowledge to herself, a secret that made it easy to smile and laugh with the other guests. Jack's torrid words kept running through her head, and every time they did, she felt exhilarated, dazed, and happier than she'd ever felt in her life.

If she'd told anyone else what she was feeling and why, they'd call her crazy. Girlfriends would be shocked that a man's confession of illicit, wicked imaginings would evoke more joy in her heart than his declaration of love had done, and the idea that his kisses had thrilled her more than his marriage proposals was one they'd find unfathomable. As for shamelessly following him into the woods and flinging herself at him, they'd be horrified.

Linnet grinned every time she thought of it.

He wasn't at breakfast the next morning either. Just as he'd told her he would be, he was gone all day. But that gave her time to comply with his wishes. She said farewells to other house-party guests and stood with Lady Trubridge and her mother waving good-bye as each carriage departed for the train station.

Carrington, Tufton, and even Hansborough all made polite inquiries about seeing her again, but as tactfully as she was able, she made it clear that wasn't going to be possible, and each time she made the point, it only seemed to hammer home the certainty she felt about her decision.

None of her suitors seemed surprised to be put aside,

and she could only conclude that everyone else had seen long before she had just which way the wind was blowing. But she didn't mind being a foregone conclusion, not this time, not even when her mother made a delicate inquiry about Jack's intentions and murmured the names of possible dressmakers for wedding gowns. She didn't respond, for she had no intention of telling her mother anything until she'd seen Jack.

Jack, however, continued to elude her all day, and all evening. By bedtime, he still hadn't returned, and she began to appreciate with a vengeance just what it had been like for him during the past few days.

That didn't matter, though, for she knew her course was set, her choice was made, and there was no going back. Still, when everyone else was in bed, she sat by her window in the dark, looking out over the moonlit drive, hoping he'd come back, waiting for the moment when she saw his horse come up the lane. She wanted to tell him now, tonight, how she felt, what she'd decided, and how right he'd been.

You have to go by what you feel is right. When you do what's right, you can't ever go wrong.

Jack's words of the other night echoed back, and she appreciated for the first time just how true that was. Even her past mistakes weren't really mistakes because they'd led her here, to this man and this moment, and she didn't have a single scrap of regret. She'd throw her reputation away a thousand times over and do it happily, and she wanted to tell him that as soon as possible.

She grinned, contemplating it. The look on his face was going to be worth every shock he'd ever given her, that was for sure. And when she told him she loved him, too, well, he'd better throw his newfound sense of propriety out the window and start acting on some of those torrid thoughts he'd been having about her. Otherwise, she'd have to ravish him. She still didn't quite know what ravishment was, but her grin widened, and her anticipation grew as she attempted to imagine it, for she knew whatever it entailed, ravishing Jack Featherstone was going to be fun.

Chapter 16

It was late by the time Jack returned to the house, but, fortunately, the moon was full, lighting his way as he rode home from the village. He was tired though he knew it wasn't the lateness of the hour or his day of aimlessly wandering around Maidstone that had done him in. Love, when it hit a chap, was an exhausting business, and his pledge to her in the park made it obvious that many more strenuous days lay ahead.

He handed the horse back over to the stableboy waiting up to receive it, and paused below stairs long enough to inquire of the hall boy—the only other servant still about—if the other house-party guests had gone. Much to his relief, they had, though he couldn't be quite sure Linnet had told them all good-bye. He doubted he'd ever be sure of anything when it came to that woman. That, he supposed, was part of her charm.

Obtaining an oil lamp from the boy, he went upstairs

to his room. There, he found one letter and one telegram awaiting him on the writing desk near the bed.
He opened the letter first. It was from his agents in
Paris, confirming they'd found a tenant to sublet his
town house for the remainder of his lease. The telegram was from Ephraim Holland, informing him of his
arrival from New York in one week's time, expressing the hope that news of Jack's engagement to Linnet
would be forthcoming upon his arrival. If so, his share
of the capital for their venture with Margrave could be
made over to him at once.

He didn't want to think about what might happen if,
despite all his efforts, Linnet refused to marry him.
Facing her father would be difficult, and her reputation would be more damaged than ever. And then there
was his heart, which would be shredded utterly if she
refused him.

He didn't want to think about any of that. Contemplating failure was pointless. He tossed the correspondence back onto the writing desk and moved to the
washstand. What he wanted right now was a bath and
a shave, for he smelled of road dust, horses, sweat, pub
food, and other gentlemen's cigar smoke, and his face
was as rough as sandpaper. He hated slipping between
sheets in this sort of condition. Besides, he wasn't the
least bit sleepy, and lying in the dark, unable to sleep,
would lead to thoughts of Linnet, and what man needed
that sort of agony?

He moved to the washstand, hopeful. Sure enough,
Maguire had laid out a towel, his razor, and his shaving
soap and brush for him before seeking his own bed.

Relieved and grateful his valet knew him so well,

Jack pulled a clean pair of trousers from the armoire, grabbed one of the towels and the water basin, and left his room. He traversed the length of the bachelor's corridor to the bathroom that serviced this wing of the house, glad his sister-in-law was an American and had an American's passion for cleanliness, modern plumbing, and hot-water boilers. He turned the taps, filled the slipper bath half-full, and opened one of the jars of soap that had been placed by the bathtub for guests. He washed all traces of the day from his skin and hair, then dried off, filled the basin he'd brought with fresh, hot water, slipped on the clean trousers, scooped up his dirty clothes, and returned to his room.

He dropped the clothes into the closest corner of the room, took the basin to the washstand, and prepared to shave, glad to have a task that required his full concentration. But after he'd shaved, after he'd rinsed the blade one last time, dried it, and flipped it back into its ivory sheath, he began to feel a bit desperate. Keeping thoughts of Linnet at bay had proved harder and harder as the day wore on, and now, because he was still wide-awake, going to bed would only bring back memories of the torrid things he'd said to her the day before.

Even as that thought passed through his mind, his body began to ache, and arousal began stirring.

I think about bedding you, and taking your virtue, and making you totally mine.

He set his jaw, fighting all the erotic images dancing through his mind, and leaned closer to the mirror to dab the last vestiges of shaving soap from his chin with the towel. He would not think of her again. Not tonight.

That resolve had barely passed through his mind when he heard the click of the latch, and when he turned his head, he saw the door open to reveal the very object of his thoughts standing in the doorway, her loosened hair tousled and tawny and hanging down around her shoulders.

"Linnet? What are you doing down here?" He dropped the ends of the towel, and they fell to his chest as he strode to the door. "Are you mad? You can't be in this wing of the house. This is the bachelor's corridor."

"But you're the only bachelor here now. Other than you, this part of the house is empty."

"Yes, but still—" His gaze slid down her body, over a frothy white nightgown and pale pink silk robe, all the way down to the floor, to where her bare toes peeped out from beneath pristine white lace.

Fire curled in his loins.

"You are killing me," he muttered as he grabbed her arm, hauled her in from the corridor, and shut the door behind her. "Killing me by inches."

"I've been thinking about the things you said," she whispered. "Ever since you said them, I've been thinking about them."

Just now, he couldn't remember what he'd said even though he knew in the vague recesses of his addled masculine brain that he'd been thinking about those very things just half a minute ago. All the more reason why she shouldn't be in his room. Her virtue wasn't safe with him, not in his present state, and if they were caught, her reputation wouldn't just be tainted, it would be ruined, and even all Belinda's hints and delicate inferences wouldn't save her if he didn't marry her. He had to get her out of here, send her back to her own room. He should tell her that.

He didn't speak.

He ought to grab her, shove her pretty little bum out into the corridor, and lock the door behind her.

He didn't move.

Instead, he made the mistake of looking down again, and he saw those pretty toes curl, vanishing under that absurd, frilly hem. Desperate, he forced his gaze back to her face and strove to find order amid the chaos inside him.

"Linnet, for God's sake, I don't remember what I said in the woods, but I'm sure it was all terribly naughty and not worthy of discussion at one o'clock in the morning, especially not in my bedroom. You are going back to your own room right now."

He put his hand on her arm and reached for the doorknob, but she—stubborn, strong-willed woman that she was—didn't seem any more inclined to follow his orders than she had three weeks ago.

"You said we'd proceed at the pace I'd like." She pulled her arm away and smiled, shaking back her hair as she looked up at him. "This is the pace I've decided to set."

He shook his head. "You don't have a clue what you're saying."

"Yes, I do. Jack. You said you'd be a perfect gentleman until I agreed to marry you. That's why I came." She spread her hands, opened her arms. "I'm saying yes. I'll marry you."

He stilled, staring into her upturned, smiling face. "You will?"

"Yes." Her smile widened. "You proved what I asked you to prove. I watched you holding baby Colin and playing with him, and I fell in love with you right there on the spot."

"You did?"

She nodded, and he plunked his hands on his hips and let out his breath in a huff of frustration. "Well, you might have told me that at the time, Linnet," he said, feeling quite nettled. "I've been through three days of agony, while you flounced around with Carrington and Hansborough and near drove me mad."

"You deserved it," she told him, and eased closer to him, smiling a little. "Using an innocent little baby to soften me up. It was a shameful, blatant ploy on your part."

He refused to smile back. "And what about Carrington and Hansborough, and Tufton? You made it clear to them today they haven't a prayer, I hope?"

"Yes, Jack." She sounded so meek, so sweet, and very unlike the Linnet he knew, but then she gave him a wicked smile. "After all the shocking things you said to me yesterday, I'm afraid their skill at conversation pales by comparison."

He didn't move. He remained rigid as she pressed herself closer to him. "And near as I can recall, Linnet, one of the things I said was about taking your virtue. And if we do what you're so prettily asking for by coming here, your virtue's gone. Do you know what that means?"

"Yes. At least . . ." She bit her lip. "I think so."

He suspected she didn't have a clue. He doubted virgins ever did. And anyway, this was the girl who thought a man's fingertip caressing her palm was the pinnacle of carnality.

The problem was that right now he just didn't have the fortitude to call a halt and explain that cabbage patches and storks were fiction. He settled for something simple and unequivocal. "If we do this, there's no going back. Do you understand? You'll have to marry me."

"Is that a proposal?" she asked, smiling. "Or an order?"

"Given your complete inability to follow any order if I'm the one issuing it," he muttered, "this has to be a proposal, doesn't it?"

She laughed. "I accept."

She looked so incredibly beautiful when she smiled and laughed. His own radiant, golden lioness. And she was his now, she had, at last, agreed to marry him. He bent his head to seal the engagement with a kiss, but just as his lips touched hers, his brain insisted on remembering certain inconvenient little difficulties. Like other deals, deals with her father.

He jerked back. "Linnet, there are things we have to talk about if you're going to marry me."

"I don't want to talk now." She lifted her arms, entwining them around his neck, and when the tips of her breasts brushed his naked chest, he felt his resolve slip another notch.

"You did a lot of talking in the woods about what you wanted to do to me, Jack Featherstone," she went on, molding her body against him, rising on her toes. "It's time to back up all that talk with some decisive action. Kiss me. Make love to me. Just like you said you wanted to."

His wits were slipping more with every word she spoke. He made one last valiant attempt to keep his head. "I thought you wanted me to be a perfect gentleman."

"You thought wrong." Her hands raked through his hair, and she rose on her toes and kissed him. "Perfect gentlemen," she said against his mouth, "are overrated."

He groaned in capitulation, good intentions went straight south where they were always wont to go, and any notions of discussing deals and dowries went right out of his head. He caught her up, wrapping his arms tight around her, and he bent his head, capturing her mouth with his.

As he held her tight and kissed her, Linnet's mind went dreamily back to that night in Newport. This was similar in so many ways. His embrace was just as strong and powerful, and his kiss every bit as hot and demanding. But this kiss wasn't quite the same. She wasn't the same shocked, outraged woman she'd been a few weeks ago, offended by the possessive kiss of a perfect stranger.

And this man wasn't a stranger anymore. This was Jack, the infuriating, outrageous man who said things to her no man ever dared to say, who did things to her no man had ever dared to do, who called her bluff and took up her dare and never backed down, no matter what challenge she threw at him.

So now, instead of fighting what he'd made her feel in Newport, this time, she savored it. She relished the scorching intimacy of his full, open-mouth kiss, tasted him as deeply as he tasted her. This was part of what she'd come for. To feel his powerful, shocking, tumultuous kiss. Her arms tightened around his neck.

Without warning, he broke the contact with her lips and pulled back, panting. "You're sure about this?" he muttered, cupping her face, pressing kisses to her forehead, her nose, her cheeks. "You'll marry me?"

Even before she nodded, he was reaching for the satin sash of her robe. "We'll have to be quiet," he told her. "No noise. Even if this wing is empty, we can't take any chances. I don't want you going down the aisle double shamed."

She assumed he was going to do to her all those wicked things he'd told her yesterday, and she didn't quite see why those things would be noisy, but she didn't want to ask and show how naïve she really was. "I understand."

He pulled at the edges of her robe, and when she lowered her arms, the garment came apart, and he slid it from her shoulders. As it fell to the floor behind her, he lifted his hands to her collar and started slipping buttons free. Down, down, until by the time he reached her navel, she was quivering inside, and when he caught up handfuls of her nainsook nightgown in his fists and dragged it off her shoulders, down her arms, and over her hips, the garment pooled around her ankles, and the cool air on her skin made her shiver, not with cold, but with intense, aching heat.

Suddenly, he stopped. With his hands on her arms, he took a step back, and when she saw his gaze skim downward, she realized with a jolt of alarm that she was bare to his gaze, and he was seeing what until now he'd only seen in his imagination. If she'd had time to think about it, she might have felt shame at standing here before him naked as a jaybird, but he spoke before there was time for shame.

"My God," he muttered, and laughed a little. "You're even lovelier than I imagined. You're perfect."

He lifted his hand and cupped her breast in his palm, another shock, and she gasped. And then he took her nipple between his thumb and forefinger and toyed with it, played with it.

Sharp sensation pierced her, and her knees gave out. His arm was back around her in an instant, and as he held her tight, her body pressed to his, and the hard part of him that had pressed against her back yesterday now pressed against her tummy. As his hand shaped and played with her breast, she shivered in his hold. She heard her breathing quickening and her pulses racing. "Jack," she gasped. "Oh, Jack."

He kissed her bare shoulder, holding her tight, but after a moment, he had to have another look at her, and he eased back again. Taking her hands in his, he spread her arms apart, and his throat went tight at the sight of her full, round breasts, so pink and white, at the slim indent of her waist, and the graceful outward curve of her hips. Her skin was pale and luminous in the lamplight, and when his gaze came to rest on the gold curls at the apex of her thighs, a fierce, hot wave of love and lust and protectiveness rose up in him, making him feel primal, almost savage, in a way no woman had ever made him feel, and he was more certain than ever before that Linnet was his woman, to protect and defend and care for as long as he lived upon this earth.

He wanted her so badly, he could feel his insides

shaking, but he knew he had to bank his own desire, for he was determined that her first time making love with him was going to be beautiful and right, no matter what it took.

He kissed her mouth once more, then he took her hand and led her toward the bed. "Come and lie with me."

"That's part of what you said you wanted," she murmured, following him.

"I seem to have said a lot of things in those woods." He took her by the shoulders and guided her down onto the bed. "Lie down," he ordered, and she complied, but as she stretched out on the pale green counterpane of his bed, he realized the implications of what they were about to do. Servants, he reminded himself, had sharp eyes.

He glanced around and spied the towel on the floor, the one he'd shaved with earlier—a towel, he decided, that was going to go missing sometime in the night and never be seen again. He started across the room.

"Jack?"

He picked up the towel from where it had fallen from his shoulders earlier and came back to the bed. "Lift your hips," he told her.

She complied. "What is that for?" she asked, as he folded the towel and tucked it beneath her.

"I'll explain later."

He reached for the top button of his trousers, but then he glanced over her magnificent, glorious, naked body, and decided he'd better keep his trousers on for now. There was only so much temptation a man could endure, and he needed all the restraint he could get right now. With his trousers on, he stretched out beside her. Resting his weight on his forearm, he spread his hand over her stomach and caressed her, stroking, his hand moving up and down her torso.

She responded at once, a low moan in her throat as her body stirred. He smiled, looking up, seeing her parted lips and closed eyes. He moved closer, but when his erection pressed against her thigh, she shied a bit, opening her eyes.

"Jack?" She looked at him, her pretty eyes wide with alarm.

He'd never made love to a virgin, but he knew fear when he heard it. He took a profound, shaky breath and cupped her chin. "It's all right, Lioness," he promised. "Trust me."

He leaned over her and kissed her again, making love to her mouth while he waited for the fear in her body to ease. When she relaxed again in his hold, he pulled back to look into her face and put his hand again to her breast. He relished the weight of it, full and round, and the velvety softness of her areola, and the turgid hardness of her nipple. He smiled, as he watched her eyes close and her lips part, and her breathing came faster.

He moved down a bit, and took her nipple into his mouth. She lifted her arm, moaning softly against her wrist, instinctively following his caution to keep quiet.

His hand moved to her other breast, shaping it as he suckled her, relishing the way she shivered as his tongue gently drew the tip of her breast against his teeth again and again.

Her hips were moving now, stirring, brushing against the tip of his erection through his trousers, but this time, she didn't shy away. Wanting to see her face again, he lifted his head as his palm slid over her body, from her breast, down over her ribs and her stomach and even farther down, until his fingertips grazed the soft triangle of golden curls at the apex of her thighs. He eased his hand between her legs, and she gave a shuddering gasp. Her legs squeezed convulsively around his hand, as her eyes opened in shock. "Jack," she whispered, and her hand closed over his wrist, trying to shove him away.

"Don't stop me," he said, moving his fingers, pushing deeper between her thighs. "I've been dreaming of this," he told her. "Let me touch you here."

"All right." The whisper was so low, he almost didn't hear it, but her hand fell away, and her legs opened a fraction, letting him ease his finger into the crease of her sex.

She was wet, slick, and inviting, but he knew she wasn't ready for what was to come, so he stroked her, gliding his finger back and forth along the seam of her sex, watching her face as her eyes closed, her breathing quickened, and her hips began to move against his caress. Words aroused her, he knew that now, and he used them.

"Do you like this?" he murmured. "Do you?"

Linnet heard his question, but she was too overwhelmed to reply. When he said he'd imagined touching her, she never thought he meant this. Her mind had never conceived any touching like this.

"Do you like this? I want to please you. Does this please you?" When she still didn't answer, he started to withdraw his hand.

"No," she protested, her hips arching up, her body following his withdrawal. "No, Jack."

"No?" he murmured, laughing under his breath, teasing her. "No, you don't like it?"

"I do like it." She was panting now, a helpless victim to this tender teasing. "I do. I do."

Her hips were jerking now, her body moving against his hand of its own volition, the tip of his finger was sliding back and forth over her most intimate place, and each tiny move sent another throb of pleasure through her body. As he stroked her, the pace seemed to quicken until she was moving in frantic, helpless little jerks. The pleasure thickened within her, deepened, and she moaned. At once, his other hand came up to touch her face, his finger pressing her lips, and at last she understood what he'd meant about making noise.

"Hush, love," he said, even as his stroking fingers moved faster. "Hush."

She bit her lip, for the tension of keeping silent only seemed to heighten the anticipation building inside her, higher, hotter, and more intense with each stroke of his fingers. She felt as if her body needed something more than this, but she didn't know what, and as the pleasure built within her, it became so acute she began to whimper, soft little sounds stifled by her teeth pressing against her lip.

"That's it, my love," he murmured. "You're nearly there. Come for me. Come."

She didn't know what he meant, but somehow her body knew, for the low, thick coaxing of his voice seemed to enhance the pleasure of his touch, and suddenly, she felt a burst of sensation like she'd never felt before, an explosive rush of pleasure that arched her hips upward and tore a startled cry from her lips. He kissed her, catching the sound of her cry even as she made it, as her thighs clenched around his hand and ecstasy flowed through her again and again. His fingers continued to pleasure her, even as she collapsed, panting, against the mattress.

"Linnet, it's time." His voice sounded harsher, more urgent than before. "I can't wait much longer, so you have to listen to me."

He withdrew his hand and moved onto his back. She turned her head, and when she saw him unbuttoning his trousers, pulling them down, she remembered that part of him hard against her bottom yesterday, and the groan of his pleasure that had echoed through the woods, and she realized in sudden shocked insight what was going to happen.

"Jack?" Her voice was a panicked squeak. "Jack?"

The trousers went flying, then he was on top of her, and she squeezed her eyes shut, feeling another jolt of panic at the weight of him, solid and heavy on top of her, and the hard, burning part of him that pressed between her legs.

He stilled, and she felt his hands caressing her face. "Linnet, look at me."

She forced herself to open her eyes. His black eyes seemed to bore into hers, and she saw the desire there, burning for her. "Listen to me, Linnet," he said, and his voice was strained now. "This will hurt. There's no way to avoid it, but I promise . . ." He paused to kiss her. "I promise it won't ever hurt like this again. Trust me?"

She nodded, and sucked in a breath. "Yes."

"It'll be all right," he promised, kissing her. She felt his hand ease between their bodies, to caress her stomach, then move lower, over her hip and across her thigh. "Open your legs, love. Open for me. It'll be all right."

His voice shook, and she realized the strain was from holding back for her sake, until she was ready. "Come to me," she whispered, guided by instinct and love as she spread her legs wider apart, wanting to give him the same thing he'd already given her. "Come to me, Jack."

He moved his hips, and she felt the tip of his hardness brushing her opening. It was delicious, and she felt that excitement rising again as she had when his fingers had caressed her. "Take me in your hand," he told her, and he was guiding her hand to wrap around his shaft. He was scorching hot, and it startled her. She'd have drawn back, but his hand was holding hers around him. "I want you to bring me inside you."

He showed her how, guiding her, but she felt terribly awkward, and when she felt him pushing deeper into her, she drew her hands out of the way, and wrapped her arms around his shoulders.

"Oh, God," he groaned against her neck. And then, his hips surged, and he came fully into her.

She gasped, her body arching, the pain like a cruel pinch deep inside. He kissed her mouth as his body stilled.

"Are you all right?" His voice was a harsh whisper. "God, Linnet, are you all right?"

She nodded. "Yes, I . . . I think so." She wriggled her hips, and grimaced, for it still hurt a little.

But then, he began to move within her, and as he did, the pain seemed to ease a little more with each stroke, and she became aware of the pleasure, too, for there was pleasure in this—the hard, thick fullness of him inside her, the way he moved, like a caress from the inside. His pace began to quicken, and he thrust a little harder each time, a little deeper. She began to move with him, and the pleasure increased even more, and, without warning, those ecstatic waves came over her again, even more intense this time with him inside her, and she wrapped her legs around him, clenching tighter, then tighter still.

He made a rough sound against her mouth, then his arms were sliding beneath her back, seeming to want her even closer than she already was. Holding her in this tight embrace, he thrust into her again, then again, and yet again. At last, a shudder rocked him, and it was his turn to cry out, a full-throated groan buried against her neck. He thrust twice more, his body shuddering with what she knew to be similar sensations to those she had felt. At last, his body sank down on hers, his arms wrapped tight around her, his breathing warm and labored against her hair.

Linnet stared up at the ceiling in wonder, her palms stroking the smooth, hard muscles of his back and shoulders. This strange and wondrous coupling, she now knew, was what brought the giggles and knowing smiles to the faces of her married friends when they talked about married life and sleeping with their husbands. This was what Jack had imagined with his talk of caressing her naked skin and lying with her and bedding her. This was making love.

Linnet felt dazed and awed. The pain she'd felt earlier seemed inconsequential now; she hardly felt it at all.

Instead, with his strong body heavy and solid on top of hers, his masculine invasion still within her, and his strong arms tight around her, all she felt was a sweet, aching joy and an overwhelming tenderness. She loved him, and she wanted to marry him, and when she did, she knew there would be many sweet, tender moments like this.

He stirred on top of her. "Still all right?" he asked, pressing a kiss to her hair before he lifted his head to look into her face. "Does it . . ." He paused, grimacing. "Does it still hurt?"

She shook her head. "No. Not anymore."

"I'm sorry about that." He kissed her mouth. "It won't hurt like that again."

She was rather relieved about that. "I love you."

That pleased him. A smile creased the edges of his eyes and the corners of his mouth. "Well, I should hope so, after the merry hell you've been putting me through."

She made a face. "You poor, poor man," she replied with mock sympathy. "You've suffered so much."

His smile became a grin. "It was worth it." He kissed her, and his hand slid between their bodies to cup her breast. "Worth every torturous moment."

She could feel heat flooding her, quick as that, a blush that spread through her body.

He saw it, too, the wretched man. "I'd like to," he murmured, palming and shaping her breast in his hand, playing with her nipple as he'd done before, stirring arousal in her just like before. "But we can't." His hand slid away and he kissed her nose. "Not until the wedding."

"Oh, you are such a tease, Jack Featherstone!" She pressed a hand to his shoulder and gave him a push.

"You think this is a tease?" His grin became downright wicked. "Just wait until I'm sneaking kisses from you behind the rose arbor. Then you'll know what teasing is, Miss Holland."

He stirred again, as if to roll off her, but she tightened her legs around him, reluctant to move. She felt blissful, lethargic, and all she wanted was to sink into sleep. He seemed to realize it, for he lifted his head and smiled, and took her mouth in a soft and tender kiss.

"As much as I'd love to lie here with you all night and all day, too," he murmured, "we can't. You have to go back to your own room now, while it's still pitch-black. Scullery maids will be up to build the fires in a couple of hours, and we can't risk anyone's seeing you."

She nodded, knowing he was right. Her legs relaxed, opened, and he lifted his hips, slipping free of her. She grimaced, feeling a hint of soreness and what seemed an abundant amount of moisture between her legs.

"We'll discuss wedding plans after breakfast," he told her, then he kissed her one more time, rolled off the bed, and stood up, holding out his hands to her.

She rose, and as she did, he held her hands in his. Smiling, he looked at her, his gaze drifting down over her naked body. No one but her maid and her mother had ever seen her unclothed before, and she felt shy and flustered, and yet, rather wonderful, too, standing naked before his heated gaze.

"You're so lovely," he muttered, reaching up to tuck a tendril of her loosened hair behind her ear. "So, so lovely."

She couldn't quite enjoy the compliment at this moment. "I'd feel lovelier if I could wash a bit before I go," she said with a grimace.

"You can. We have a bit of time. I'll fetch you some fresh water."

He bent to reach for his discarded trousers, and as he slipped them on, she took a peek at his body, at the part of him that had been so intimately joined with her moments ago. It was only the barest glimpse, for he was buttoning the trousers before she could manage a better look, but what she saw was enough to surprise her. That part of him seemed to have been tamed by their coupling.

What extraordinary creatures men were, she thought, smiling a little.

His hands stilled at his waistband, and she looked up to find he was smiling, too. "After the wedding," he told her firmly.

With that, he turned away and walked to the washstand, where he picked up the basin. He left the bedroom to get water for her spit bath, but she didn't like the sticky residue on her legs, and she turned, remembering the towel he'd laid on the bed earlier. But her hand stilled as she reached for it, seeing the red smears that marked the white cotton. She'd bled? Another surprise in a night full of surprises.

She picked up the towel, folded it again, and used it to wipe the wetness from her legs. As she straightened, her attention was caught by the slip of paper on the desk beside the bed where she stood. A telegram, she realized, and thought at once of bad news.

It wasn't her business, though, and she started to

turn away, but not before she saw the initials at the bottom.

ERH.

She froze, and the floor seemed to rock beneath her feet. Without even taking time to think, she lifted her gaze to the top of the missive, ignored any inconvenient pricks of her conscience, and read every word.

ARRIVING SEPT 26 STOP HOPE ENGAGE-MENT YOU AND LINNET CONFIRMED STOP WILL GIVE YOUR SHARE OF FUNDS FOR OUR INVESTMENT WITH MARGRAVE RIGHT AFTER WEDDING STOP EXPECT OUR DEAL WILL MAKE US MILLIONS STOP ERH

She stared at the words, dumbfounded, numb, and disbelieving.

Deal? What deal? Jack and her father. A business deal made over her.

You have to marry me now.

Of course she did. She and his father had a deal. Lots of money to be made. Of course.

Pain shimmered through her, the pain of betrayal, a pain with which she was becoming quite familiar. Tears stung her eyes. With every man in her life, it always came down to the money.

His footstep sounded, a soft creak on ancient floor-boards, and she jerked, moving away from the desk and back toward the bed just as he reentered the room. She tried to hide her shock, her pain, but some of it must have shown in her face, for he frowned as he kicked the door gently closed behind him.

"Linnet?" He came toward her, the basin of water and a fresh towel in his hand. "What's wrong?"

She wanted to confront him, throw the telegram and his deals with her father in his face, but she couldn't, not now, not when she still had the result of their plea-sure between her legs, and shock, rage, and pain were erupting inside her, and her pride and her innocence were as ruined as her reputation. She tried to paste on a smile. "Nothing."

She must not have sounded convincing, for the frown on his face deepened. But the towel in his hand re-minded her of the one in hers, and she seized on it as an excuse.

"Now I see what this was for," she murmured, look-ing down, her face puckering as the stains of her lost virtue blurred before her eyes, and she fought to keep tears back.

He set the basin on the floor, dropped the fresh towel beside it, and pulled the stained one from her grasp. "Don't worry," he said. "I'll wash it myself in the bath. The servants won't know."

She nodded, and when he cupped her cheek, she endured it. When he guided her to sit on the bed, she complied, and when he dipped the fresh towel in the water and washed the traces of what they'd done away from her thighs, she gritted her teeth and stared at the ceiling in order to bear the tender, solicitous sham of it.

You liar, she wanted to shout, her heart breaking. *You manipulative, fortune-hunting bastard.*

"Are you certain you're all right?" he asked.

The tenderness in his voice was almost her undoing, and she wondered how a man could be so tender and also be such a scoundrel.

You and my father made a business deal over me. A business deal.

Linnet curled her fingers into the rumpled sheets on either side of her hips, steeled herself, and lifted her head, but she couldn't quite meet his eyes. "Of course. I'm tired, and . . ." She had to pause for a deep breath. "It's been quite an evening."

"Yes." He leaned forward to kiss her, but she jerked back, unable to bear it.

"Jack, I have to go."

"Of course." He sat back on his heels as she rose, and though she saw there was still a tiny frown between his brows, she knew she wasn't a good enough actress to stay here any longer and keep pretending everything was fine. All she wanted was to get away and go back to her own room before she debased herself further.

He set the towel in the basin, then stood up, stepping back so she could move past him. She walked to where her nightgown and robe lay on the floor, picked up the former, and slipped into it, and forced away recollections of how tenderly he'd removed it from her body such a short time ago. She started to do up the buttons, but she couldn't, for her hands were shaking.

"I'll do it," he said, coming to help her.

"No." Once again, she jerked away. "It doesn't matter. I'll just put my robe over it anyway."

He scooped the robe up from the floor and held it open for her so that she could slip it on.

"Can you find your way alone in the dark?" he asked, following her to the door.

"Of course," she whispered, opening it before he could. "I got here that way, didn't I?"

Without waiting for an answer, she started down the dark corridor and didn't look back. Instead, she navigated her way through the silent house, blinking to keep tears at bay until she could get to her room. Once there, she'd let the tears fall. She'd cry all night, until every bit of the pain she felt at his betrayal was out of her. The rage, though, was different. She intended to hang on to that, because tomorrow, she was going to kill him. And when her father arrived, she'd kill him, too.

Chapter 17

Jack frowned as he watched Linnet's white-sheathed form slip away down the dark corridor like a ghost, shimmers of disquiet rippling through him. Something was very wrong.

She'd seemed well enough until she saw the stained towel, and he prayed she wasn't feeling regret. The consequences of what they'd done were enormous, of course. Even now, he wasn't certain she understood just what the result of tonight could be. But as he'd told her, there was no undoing it now.

The white glimmers of her nightdress vanished as she rounded the corner and disappeared, and he stepped back into his room to fetch the basin.

He took the blue delft bowl and the stained towel to the bathroom and poured the used water down the sink drain, then he scooped soap out of the jar, added fresh water to the sink, and scrubbed the soiled towel until every trace of Linnet's blood was gone. He draped the wet towel over the bar on the side of the washstand and returned with the basin to his own room, where he put it back on his own washstand. He nestled the matching pitcher inside it, returned his shaving equipment to his dressing case, and walked to the side of the bed.

Perhaps she was just tired, he thought as he unbuttoned his trousers. Tired and overwrought. Any girl would be, he supposed. One's first sexual experience was always quite shattering.

Almost, but not quite satisfied by that explanation, Jack stripped off his trousers and tossed them aside. He started to reach for the counterpane to pull it back, then his gaze caught on the writing desk nearby and the slip of paper that lay unfolded on top of it. Holland's telegram.

He swore.

I was just another business deal.

He rubbed his hands over his face and swore again.

JACK DIDN'T SLEEP a wink. He spent the remainder of the night in bed, but as he'd been wont to do many nights of late, he didn't sleep. Instead, he pictured Linnet stretched out naked beside him, with her golden hair loose and tumbled across his pillows. The agony of it was harder to bear this time than it had ever been before, for it wasn't a picture borne of his imagination now; it was a picture formed from reality.

Hot, sweet thoughts of touching her beautiful skin, of hearing her passionate cries, of her face as he'd brought her to the first climax of her life—these were memories that haunted him, and tortured him, and made him more certain than ever about his chosen course.

Winning Linnet had never been a choice, not from the moment he'd kissed her. Now, however, he began to fear that his certainty and his determination might not be enough. He didn't have her trust, and now, he didn't know if he'd ever have it.

There was just one option open to him. His original intention had been to wait until they were engaged before telling her about the deal with her father. In hindsight, of course, he appreciated that sort of reticence had been a serious mistake on his part, but there was nothing he could do about that now. And it was no longer an option. The thing to do was discuss the deal with her openly and completely, and hope he could find the words to keep her.

Such a discussion, however, could only take place if she were in the same room with him, and that, he soon discovered, wasn't going to be an easy thing to arrange. She didn't come down for breakfast or lunch, but instead stayed in her room, pleading a headache, and short of breaking down her bedroom door, an act that would put him forever beyond the pale in Belinda's estimation and probably Linnet's as well, there were very few options open to him. In a hasty consult with her mother after luncheon, he confirmed that he and Linnet had quarreled, and she confirmed that Linnet did intend to come down for dinner, and he seized on that as his only possibility. If Helen could somehow persuade her to a walk in the gardens half an hour before the dinner gong—perhaps with a suggestion that it would help her headache—and if Helen would then allow him a private consultation with her, he intended to ask her again to marry him. He felt sure, he told Helen with a confidence he didn't feel in the least, that they would mend their quarrel, and he would at last obtain her consent to marry him.

It was with that assurance that Helen agreed to allow him the privacy with her that he needed.

Stuart and his duchess arrived on the afternoon train, and Jack took his friend aside the moment he arrived, for even though Holland wasn't due in Kent for a week, he wanted to make the final preparations for their meeting with the American now, before he talked to Linnet in the garden.

Stuart, as he'd had no doubt his friend would do, agreed to all his plans for the venture and promised to have the appropriate documents drawn up by his attorneys. He also had several promising investment possibilities to present to Holland. Jack grinned at that. "Baiting the hook well, I hope?"

Stuart grinned back. "Damned straight. He'll bite, trust me."

At half past six, when the others were gathering for aperitifs in the drawing room, Jack went to the gardens, and found that Helen had done her part, for she and Linnet were walking the herbaceous border.

He waited until they had wandered into the rose garden to find some late roses before approaching them. Helen, who had been watching for his approach, saw him coming and managed to lead Linnet through an arbor and into a part of the garden where she had very few ways to escape. He paused beneath the arbor behind her.

"Out and about at last, I see," he said. When she whirled around, her eyes seemed so vividly blue in the twilight that he caught his breath, but the appalled expression on her face was a painful indication of just how much persuasion he'd have to do in the next half hour. He took a deep breath. "Headache gone, I hope?"

"It just came back." She tried to come through the arbor so that she could escape, but he moved forward, blocking her path.

"We have to talk, and you're not going anywhere until we do," he told her. "Helen?" he added to the woman behind her without taking his eyes from hers, "I fear Linnet still has a headache. Would you be so kind as to find a housemaid to fetch her a Beecham's Powder? She and I will follow you shortly to the house."

"Of course." She moved at once toward the only other path of escape, and Linnet gave a huff of vexation as she turned her head and watched her go.

"Traitor," she called after her parent. "This is conspiring with the enemy."

Helen didn't reply but waved a hand in dismissal of that accusation as she walked away.

Linnet's gaze returned to him. "I can think of nothing you and I need to discuss," she said, and since he was blocking the arbor where she stood, she turned to follow her parent down the only other available path.

He fell in step beside her. "We have plenty to discuss. That telegram, for one thing. What it means, and everything it represents, and every doubt and every fear it planted in your head."

Her steps did not slow. "What telegram? I don't know what you're talking about."

"Liar. I know you read it, so don't pretend you didn't."

That stopped her in her tracks, bringing him to a halt as well. "Oh, so pretending is wrong, is it?" she asked, turning to face him, and the glint of battle in her eyes told him the fight was on. "You seem to have quite a hypocritical set of ethics. Pretending seems a perfectly acceptable thing when you do it. Lying, too," she added before he could respond. "And fortune-hunting . . . well, we know you think that's wrong when other people do it—your brother, for instance—but when you do it, it's just dandy. And then, there's betrayal . . ." She stopped, swallowed hard, and resumed walking away, as quickly as she could in her evening gown of shimmering green silk.

He followed her, his long strides enabling him to be beside her in just a few seconds. "I didn't betray you. I didn't lie. I admit I did withhold certain facts from you—"

"You didn't lie? So, that afternoon in the woods when you declared you'd give up the dowry, that was the truth?"

Had he said that? He frowned, vaguely remembering something desperate like that coming out of his mouth. "Damn."

She stopped, causing him to stop as well. "Yes," she said. "Damn. Shall we go on to the part about pretending?"

"Let's discuss the lie first, shall we? I said I'd give up the dowry, yes. And yes, that was a lie. I have no intention of giving it up." He sighed, raking a hand through his hair as he thought of that afternoon, knowing there was nothing to do but admit it. He looked into her eyes.

"I have no excuses or explanations to offer. All I have is my reason for lying."

That, understandably, made her laugh. "What makes you think I care two bits for your reason?"

He ignored that question. "Your father offered me half a million dollars as a personal settlement if I married you. He wants to do investments in Africa and use my connection to the Duke of Margrave to make money there. That's the venture the telegram is talking about."

Her lips parted in astonishment. Her face went pale. "Did you do what you did in the pagoda at his behest?"

"No, no," he hastened to assure her. "No, this was afterward. You were already on your way to England. But he decided I'd be a better bet than the other chaps you had in mind because of Margrave. But he also felt that you wouldn't marry me if I accepted a settlement, so when he made his offer, he suggested we keep it a secret from you until after we were married. His idea was that you'd never marry me if I took a personal settlement, so I was supposed to make the noble gesture and assure you I didn't want anything for myself. As you know, I didn't do that."

"Until that afternoon in the woods."

"Yes. You see . . ." He paused, taking a deep breath. "I was, as you may appreciate, in the throes of almost uncontainable lust. Not that's any sort of excuse, mind you, but because I was in that rather vulnerable condition, I was trying to avoid you that afternoon. I was trying to keep a proper gentleman's distance, and it was killing me. I wanted you, more than I've ever wanted anything or anyone in my life, and when you were standing there in front of me, I succumbed to your father's idea and pretended to make the grand gesture."

"Knowing all the while you had no intention of giving up the money."

"Yes." He swallowed hard. "I very much fear I'd have said anything, done anything, crawled on my knees to Lucifer in that moment, in order to make you mine."

She pressed her lips together and looked away. "But it was still a lie, Jack. How can I marry a man who lies to me? Who betrays me? Who makes deals behind my back? No."

She started to walk around him, but he stepped in front of her, blocking her way. When she stepped the other way, he blocked that, too, and she stilled, scowling up at him. "Honestly, what part of 'no' continues to elude you? It's a simple word, really, one most people comprehend without much difficulty."

"I'm extraordinarily obtuse about that word, at least when it comes to you. But Linnet, I'm going to make you listen to me, even if I have to chase you all over the grounds to do it. Because I love you."

"More words. More explanations. But as you demonstrated so eloquently the other day, deeds are much more effective."

He ignored that. "I also think you still love me."

He got the look, narrowed eyes and uplifted chin. "So when deeds and explanations fail to impress, words of love are the next tactic? My answer is still no."

He was getting desperate. Continuing to refuse to

marry him was simply not an option now, and he didn't think she quite understood that.

"It's not a matter of persuasion at this point. It's a matter of necessity. Linnet—" He broke off, grabbing her shoulders as she started to step around him again. He leaned closer, casting a quick glance around the garden to make doubly sure Helen had gone, and they were completely alone. "You might be carrying my child."

She went still, dawning awareness and horror in her face. "Oh, God," she whispered, her voice faint. "Oh, dear God."

He watched her shake her head as if in denial, and he added, "What happened last night makes babies." He winced at how late in the day it was to point that out. "You don't go and find them under cabbage leaves."

She scowled and jerked out of his hold. "I know that! My married friends explained all that business to me ages ago. But last night, I didn't think it mattered. I thought . . ." Her voice faltered, fear sprang up in her eyes. "I was sure we were getting married."

"So we are."

She shook her head again, and he watched her take a step back. "Why should I marry you?" she cried. "How can I, when I still can't trust you? You knew my father plotted behind my back for me to marry Davis MacKay as a business deal. You knew how that hurt me, how betrayed I felt, and yet you . . ." She stopped, her face twisting with pain. "You were prepared to do the exact same thing."

"When I agreed to your father's proposition, I didn't

know about the business deal with MacKay. I only found out about that when you told me."

If he thought that was going to cut any ice with Linnet, he was mistaken. "And when I told you what he'd done, about how he plotted and worked on me all those months, and how much it hurt me to find out it was so he could marry me off to Davis MacKay and make a profit from it, I don't suppose you could have mentioned your own little deal with him then?"

Guilt nudged him. "I could have done," he admitted. "But I thought it better to wait."

"Wait?" she echoed in disbelief. "Wait for what? Until you'd done what Daddy suggested, and we were safely hitched?"

He could see her expression hardening even more, and he shook his head in violent denial. "No, I told your father I was going to wait just until we were engaged. That way, when you did find out—"

"I'd be sufficiently softened up. After you sweet-talked me with blueberry muffins, and talk of truces and friendship. After you'd aroused me with your kisses and seduced me with your torrid words. After I fell straight into your arms and gave you my heart and came to your bed like a naïve little fool. Yes, after all that, you were going to tell me. Well, you waited too long."

"Before we leave the subject of last night, can I at least remind you that you came to me? I didn't come to you. I tried to say at the time it would be a mistake—"

"The worst mistake I've ever made. And one I can assure you I don't intend to make again." She ducked around him and kept on walking as if the matter were settled, but it wasn't settled, not by a long way, for as he'd already told her, he'd chase her around the entire garden until she stopped running and listened.

"Either way, it's done, Linnet," he reminded her, striding along beside her as she exited the rose garden and turned down a path lined with tall boxwoods that led to the cherub grotto. "As I said last night, it can't be undone."

"And yet, after I agreed to marry you last night, you still had every opportunity to mention the scheme you and my father had cooked up. Yet, even then, you didn't breathe a word."

Guilt nudged him again, harder this time. "I intended to tell you right then. I did," he insisted at her sound of disbelief. "I started to, but then, you started kissing me . . . and I knew you were naked under that nightdress, and my wits started slipping . . . and I just . . ." He sighed and raked his hands through his hair. "I forgot."

"You forgot?" She stopped on the path, so abruptly he'd gone two strides past her before stopping also. "What you mean," she choked, glaring at him as he turned to face her, "is that you knew if you told me about the deal at that point, I wouldn't bed you."

He grimaced at this more brutal, and perhaps more accurate, version of what had been going on in his head last night.

"After all," she went on, "if you waited until after you'd bedded me to tell me the truth, it would be so much better, wouldn't it? Just a little insurance, you know, in case I kicked up a fuss."

"Wait." He stepped in front of her as she moved

around him. "You think I didn't tell you last night as a calculated move? You think I wanted to be able to force your hand if you changed your mind about marrying me once you learned what your father and I were doing? That I would use the possibility of a baby as leverage?"

"Isn't that what you're doing right now?" She looked up, tears in her eyes. They glinted like steel blades, driving into his heart. "As you said not five minutes ago, if there's a baby, I'll have to marry you or I'll be ruined beyond amendment. If that's not forcing my hand, what is?"

Her face puckered, she ducked around him and kept walking.

He was shocked that she could think so little of him, and for a moment, he stood there, fixed to the spot like a sundial. By the time he turned, she had reached the grotto. He followed, his long strides catching up to her as she reached the fountain.

"That is not why I didn't tell you." At the end of his tether, he caught her from behind, wrapping both his arms around her, pulling her back against his chest, holding tight as she struggled to free herself. "That is not why. Good God, Linnet," he murmured against her hair, "what sort of man do you think I am?"

"That's just it," she cried. "I don't know."

"Yes, you do." He pressed a kiss to her hair. "You do know if you would just listen to yourself."

She froze in his hold. "Let go of me."

He hesitated, knowing she would flee the second he released her. "Give me your word you won't run until I've had my say, and I'll let go."

She writhed in his hold. "I don't want to hear any more of what you have to say."

"Very well, then," he said, holding her fast, "I'll just stand here while you exhaust yourself."

"Using brute force, as usual, I see." She struggled in vain for a bit longer, then stopped, panting. "All right, all right. I give you my word, I won't run."

Linnet might be strong-willed, stubborn, and angry as hell with him right now, but she'd given her word, and he chose to accept it. Trust had to work both ways. Besides, he could outrun her any day of the week. He released her.

She turned, facing him. "You ask what sort of man I think you are. My question is: How can I know, given the secrets you keep? You won't explain the true reason you interfered in my life in the first place and why you did what you did to ruin Van Hausen—"

"And as I already told you, I cannot explain my reasons for that. I am honor-bound to keep silent."

"You said we're friends. Do friends keep secrets?"

"Sometimes, yes, they do. If you told me a secret, I would take it to my grave. I would never tell anyone."

"Nonetheless, I have to wonder just how many people's secrets you're keeping, Jack. One I could accept, perhaps, but how many more are there, lurking in the shadows?"

"There aren't any others."

"That's what you *say*. But how can I be sure?"

"You will have to trust me."

She stared at him as if he was deranged, a look he'd become quite familiar with during the past month. "You've just admitted you lied to me, manipulated me, and kept more than one secret from me. You've demonstrated yet again that I have no reason whatsoever to trust you, and yet you expect me to do so anyway? Why on earth would I ever give you my trust again?"

"Because I love you," he said simply. "I realized it the other day when I said it to you, but I think I've really loved you from the moment I kissed you. And you love me. And we are getting married. I didn't bed you to force your hand, but I also refuse to allow any child of ours to be born a bastard."

"We don't know if there will be a baby," she whispered.

"And we can't wait long enough to find out. You and I will be married, Linnet Holland. Even," he added over her attempt to interrupt, "if I have to carry you to the altar."

"An act that would be perfectly in keeping with your uncivilized character."

"Be that as it may, we will marry. And you'll be my countess, and you'll take charge of the estates, while—"

"I will?" That took her back, and she eyed him askance. "You'd hand the running of the estates over to me?"

"Well, someone has to run them, and it shan't be me. I shall have my hands full with the African investments company. Yes, I'm still doing it," he went on before she could even open her mouth to object, "and yes, your father is staking my share as my personal settlement for the dowry, and no, I'm not backing out of the deal, even if you don't like that I'm in partnership with your father."

"But you never asked me why I don't like it."

"I haven't asked because it's obvious. You hate his interference in your life."

But she was shaking her head before he'd even finished. "That's not why. You don't know what you are getting into, Jack, when you make deals with my father. He's using you to make a profit."

"So what? I'm doing the same to him. Do you have something against profits? I thought Americans were all about earning one's way."

"He's buying you, Jack. He's making it so that you owe him, that you feel obligated to him. He's manipulating you."

"No, he's not."

"Yes, he is, and you don't even see it. I know my father, I know what he's like."

"My darling Linnet, do you think I don't know what sort of man your father is? I grew up with two of the most manipulative men in England. Compared to my father and brother, your father is child's play." He studied her baffled face for a moment, then sighed. "I can see I shall have to elucidate matters further. The agreement your father and I made was to share out thirds."

"And because of that, you think you're going into this evenly, with a fair deal on the table, but—"

"On the contrary, it won't be fair at all. I stipulated that the percentages be thirty-three percent to me, thirty-three to him, and thirty-four to Stuart. Your father agreed, because without Stuart's knowledge of Africa and his connections there, we wouldn't have a prayer of making sound investments. In other words, Stuart has the controlling interest."

"Jack, I know you trust your friend, but—"

"Will you let me finish? Honestly, Linnet, you ask me for explanations, and when I try to give them, you immediately start interrupting."

She bit her lip. "Go on."

"I cabled Stuart and asked if he was willing to do this, and he agreed, and we decided to work out the details when he arrived, which was about two hours ago. While you, my love, were sulking in your room—"

"I was not sulking."

"Sulking," he went on firmly, "and cursing my name and wishing my soul to perdition, I have no doubt—while you were doing all that, Stuart and I have been making our plans. When your father arrives to negotiate the final deal, he'll find that Stuart is demanding a change in the terms. He will insist that I have thirty-four percent and he thirty-three. He won't do the deal otherwise."

"Daddy will never agree to let his son-in-law be in charge."

"Yes, he will, because if he balks, Stuart won't do it. Your father isn't going to let you be ruined, so he won't risk antagonizing me. And he won't want to antagonize Stuart, either, for that might queer the deal altogether. He might try to bluff, but I'll call him on it."

"So you and my father are going to play metaphorical poker with my reputation and my future?"

"No, we're playing poker over the dowry. Your reputation is already saved, my darling, and your future is set. Because you are going to marry me. And, besides," he added before she could point out that she hadn't accepted him yet, "there's no risk from our side. Your father may be a manipulative bastard, but he's panting, absolutely panting, for connections into Africa. He has been for years. I know that because your mother told me so. He won't balk. He'll agree to the terms, I will have the controlling interest, and Stuart will back anything I want to do with his share. You father won't control anything. The bylaws will be written so that his one-third share allows him no say in how the company is run or where we invest the funds. He'll have no power over me at all. So you see? Your father isn't moving me around like a chess piece. I'm moving him. He won't like it, mind you, but he'll do it."

"But why not just insist on a personal settlement? Why go into partnership with him at all?"

"Because there's a great deal your father can teach me about business and investing. Between him and Stuart, I shall learn a great deal. I don't want him to just give me money for marrying you. This is a chance to earn my way, to have some useful knowledge, to have a purpose in the world. I can build something, make something of my life, and this deal with your father gives me the chance to do all that. When he offered it, I jumped at it. Of course I did."

He put his hands on her arms. "All my life, I've had nothing, Linnet. I've been nothing. I was always the second son, the afterthought. When I told you the other day about the sort of father I wouldn't be, I think you got a pretty fair idea of what my father was like and what my childhood was like. I'd given up hope of ever having anything of my own before I was ten years old. When my brother died, and I became the earl, I inherited the estates, yes, but it was still worth nothing because between them, he and my father managed to mortgage everything we had."

"I hope it's all right with you if I stop you long enough to say I think your father was a horrid man, and your brother was every bit as bad."

"I completely agree with your assessment of my family, but please believe that I am not like them. If you believe nothing else I say, for God's sake, believe that."

"I do believe that. But you've got a long way to go, Jack Featherstone, before you'll convince me why I should marry you."

"I'm glad you've decided to stop running long enough to give me the chance to try."

She gave him that deceptively sweet smile of hers. "I believe in giving a man plenty of rope. Carry on."

He took a breath, taking a moment to gather his thoughts, knowing this was the most important speech he'd ever make. "When we met, you thought I was a fortune hunter, and you've no idea how ironic that is. Before I was twenty years old, I had resigned myself to the idea I'd never marry because I didn't think I'd ever have the means to support a wife and a family, and I'd always been adamant that the one thing I'd never do was marry for money. And then you walked into that ballroom. I looked at you, and I thought you had the most beautiful eyes I'd ever seen in my life. And then, later, when we were standing there in the pagoda, and your mother and Mrs. Dewey were coming, I just . . ."

He paused, lifted his hands, and let them fall. "I just lost my head. All I'd intended to do was stop Van Hausen. I didn't go to the pagoda with any devious plan to propose to you myself, or kiss you, or ruin you, but I've never been the sort of man who plans things out. I'm very much a man of impulses. You'll just have to accept that about me when you marry me, by the way, because it isn't going to change."

She sniffed, and he didn't know if she was the least bit impressed by his little speech. "Yes, I believe I said you were like a roller coaster."

He grinned. "Which means your life will never be dull."

She tilted her head, looking at him, and he fancied he might not have to carry her up the aisle after all. "You're never going to tell me about the Van Hausen business, are you?"

"No."

She bit her lip, considering. "But you're willing to hand over the running of your estates to me?"

"Yes." He took her hands in his, and this time, she let him. "As I said, I shall be quite busy with duties of my own. Besides, I trust you. And since it's your dowry that's saving the estates anyway, it's only right you be in charge of them."

"I don't know anything about running an English estate."

He smiled. "I'll be helping you every step of the way. But I don't think you'll need much help. You're such an army general, you'll have my stewards quaking in their boots within a week. And I've no doubt you'll manage to turn Featherstone Gate—which is a fusty old mausoleum of a house, by the way—into a home. We'll have half a dozen children, at least, all of whom will no doubt be as stubborn and hardheaded as their mother—"

"I'm hardheaded?" She snorted. "Pot, meet kettle."

She pulled her hands out of his, and he was sure that despite all his efforts, she was going to turn him down again, but then, her arms slid up around his neck. "You are the most hardheaded man who has ever lived, Jack Featherstone, and if our sons prove to be anything like you, it'll be a good thing indeed that I'm an army general."

With those words, joy welled up in his chest, pressing against his heart, but with all the will he had, Jack kept his expression as implacable as possible. "Those sons are damn well going to be legitimate sons, so you'd better marry me."

"You're so romantic when you propose marriage," she murmured. Keeping one arm around his neck, she slid her other hand down to toy with his jacket lapel. "You aren't really going to carry me up the aisle of the church if I refuse you, are you?"

"Damned right I am. In my best Petruchio fashion."

Those stunning eyes narrowed a fraction. "Are you calling me a shrew?"

"Not at all," he said without blinking. "I'm likening our situation to the play, darling. So . . ." He paused, and his arms slid around her. He pulled her close. "Now that I've explained everything, declared my love, and proved that I've got the means to support you, even if it is through your bastard of a father—are you going to agree to marry me?"

She laughed. "You mean you're actually going to allow me to decide something for a change?"

"I always let you decide. If you decide wrong, I work to change your mind."

"Your self-delusion knows no bounds, Jack. And it's a pretty safe bet if I marry you, our life is going to be full of fights just like this one."

"Oh, you love fighting with me, and you know it."

"That's not true." She paused and grinned at him. "I like the making-up part much more than the fighting part."

He laughed. "I believe we're in complete agreement for once. So now that we've mended our quarrel, your consent to my suit had better be forthcoming. Otherwise, I shall drag you behind the rosebushes and employ much naughtier means of persuasion."

"Oh, very well," she said, heaving a sigh of long suffering he wasn't quite sure was exaggerated. "I suppose I must marry you. If I don't, there's no telling what outrageous thing you'll do next."

"Quite so," he agreed. "So kiss me, damn it all, for I really don't want to use force."

She laughed. "I believe that's the first time you've given me an order I'm willing to obey." She kissed him then, and quite lusciously, too, but before Jack could contemplate the possibility of a sweet, compliant Linnet, any such notions were dashed.

"Speaking of obeying," she said, pulling back, "I know marriage vows are written so that the wife promises to obey, but I must warn you, I'm not going to be very good at keeping that part of my vows."

"Good, because the day you ever start obeying me, Linnet, I shall keel over from the shock," he said, then hauled her against him, and kissed her before she could reply. Sometimes, a man just had to have the last word.

*Next month, don't miss these exciting
new love stories only from
Avon Books*

Diary of an Accidental Wallflower
by Jennifer McQuiston
When pretty and popular Miss Clare Westmore
twists her ankle on the eve of the Season's most
touted event, she is relegated to the confines of her
drawing room. Dr. Daniel Merial is tempted to de-
liver more than a diagnosis to London's most unlikely
wallflower, but he doesn't have time for distractions.
So why can't he stop thinking about her?

At Wolf Ranch by Jennifer Ryan
After years on the rodeo circuit, Gabe Bowden is
ready to settle down. And when he finds a woman
on the deserted, snowy road leading to Wolf Ranch,
the half-frozen beauty changes everything. Ella
Wolf is headed for her family's abandoned Montana
ranch to uncover a secret that led to her twin sister's
murder. The last thing she expects is to be rescued
by a man who almost makes her forget how dangerous love can be . . .

I Loved a Rogue by Katharine Ashe
Eleanor Caulfield is the perfect vicar's daughter.
Yet there was a time when she'd risked everything
for a black-eyed gypsy who left her brokenhearted.
Eleven years later, Taliesin has returned to Eleanor, promising her a passion she's so long denied
herself. But he's utterly unprepared for what will
happen when Eleanor decides to abandon conven-
tion—and truly live.

REL 0215

Available wherever books are sold or please call 1-800-331-3761 to order.

#1 *NEW YORK TIMES*
AND *USA TODAY* BESTSELLER

TEN THINGS I LOVE ABOUT YOU
978-0-06-149189-4

If the elderly Earl of Newbury dies without an heir, his
detested nephew Sebastian inherits everything. Newbury
decides that Annabel Winslow is the answer to his problems.
But the thought of marrying the earl makes Annabel's skin
crawl, even though the union would save her family from ruin.
Perhaps the earl's machinations will leave him out in the cold
and spur a love match instead?

JUST LIKE HEAVEN
978-0-06-149190-0

Marcus Holroyd has promised his best friend, David Smythe-
Smith, that he'll look out for David's sister, Honoria. Not an
easy task when Honoria sets off for Cambridge determined
to marry by the end of the season. When her advances are
spurned can Marcus swoop in and steal her heart?

A NIGHT LIKE THIS
978-0-06-207290-0

Daniel Smythe-Smith vows to pursue the mysterious young
governess Anne Wynter, even if that means spending his days
with a ten-year-old who thinks she's a unicorn. And after years
of dodging unwanted advances, the oh-so-dashing Earl of
Winstead is the first man to truly tempt Anne.

Visit www.AuthorTracker.com for exclusive
information on your favorite HarperCollins authors.

JQ3 0113

Available wherever books are sold or please call 1-800-331-3761 to order.

USA TODAY BESTSELLING AUTHOR

Laura Lee Guhrke

Wedding of the Season
978-0-06-196315-5

When Lady Beatrix Danbury made William Mallory choose
between her and his lifelong dream, Will chose the latter . . . and left
two weeks before their wedding. Now the duke has returned, and
although he has no illusions that Beatrix will welcome him back with
open arms, six years did not dim his love or desire for her.

Scandal of the Year
978-0-06-196316-2

Aidan, Duke of Trathern, is supposed to be looking for a bride, yet
his scandalous liaison with Julia is all he can think about. What is it
about this brazen seductress that he finds so hard to resist? And how
can he stop himself from falling into her bed a second time?

Trouble at the Wedding
978-0-06-196317-9

The last thing Miss Annabel Wheaton wants is true love and the
heartache it brings. That's why she agreed to marry an earl who
needs her money. He's got a pedigree and a country estate, and
he won't ever break her heart. The only problem is Christian
Du Quesne isn't about to let her marry that pompous prig.

Visit www.AuthorTracker.com for exclusive
information on your favorite HarperCollins authors.

GUH1 0112

Available wherever books are sold or please call 1-800-331-3761 to order.

New York Times Bestselling Author
LISA KLEYPAS

Somewhere I'll Find You
978-0-380-78143-0
Julia Wentworth guards a devastating secret:
a mystery husband whom she does not know,
dares not mention . . . and cannot love.

Prince of Dreams
978-0-380-77355-8
Nikolas burns to possess Emma Stokehurst, but the proud,
headstrong beauty is promised to another.

Midnight Angel
978-0-380-77353-4
Enchanted by her gentle grace and regal beauty, widower
Lord Lucas Stokehurst impetuously offers "Miss Karen
Billings" a position as governess to his young daughter.

Dreaming of You
978-0-380-77352-7
Curiosity is luring Sara Fielding from the shelter
of her country cottage into the dangerous
and exciting world of Derek Craven.

Then Came You
978-0-380-77013-7
Lily Lawson is determined to rescue her sister from an
unwanted impending marriage to the notorious Lord Raiford.

Only With Your Love
978-0-380-76151-7
Abducted by a man who has paid a king's ransom for her,
Celia despairs for her safety.

Visit www.AuthorTracker.com for exclusive
information on your favorite HarperCollins authors.   LK3 0809

Available wherever books are sold or please call 1-800-331-3761 to order.

At Avon Books, we know your passion for romance—once you finish one of our novels, you find yourself wanting more.

May we tempt you with . . .

- **Excerpts** from our upcoming releases.

- Entertaining **extras**, including authors' personal photo albums and book lists.

- Behind-the-scenes **scoop** on your favorite characters and series.

- **Sweepstakes** for the chance to win free books, romantic getaways, and other fun prizes.

- Writing **tips** from our authors and editors.

- **Blog** with our authors and find out why they love to write romance.

- **Exclusive content** that's not contained within the pages of our novels.

Join us at
www.avonbooks.com

A V O N *An Imprint of HarperCollinsPublishers*
www.avonromance.com

Available wherever books are sold or please call 1-800-331-3761 to order.

FTH 1013

Give in to your Impulses!

These unforgettable stories only take a second to buy and give you hours of reading pleasure!

Go to *www.AvonImpulse.com* and see what we have to offer.

Available wherever e-books are sold.

AVONIMPULSE

IMP 0811